To my w
friend Jean.
Your support and
eloquent appreciation
of my writing has
been so heart-warming
I love you Jean —
we'll be friends always

Gill
x

About the Author

Gill Gascoigne has always had a keen interest in people, history and writing and these passions come together in her first book *A Memorable Man*, fulfilling a lifelong ambition to be a published writer.

Gill is married with a son and daughter and a grandson who shares her passion for storytelling!

Dedication

For my family: past, present and future

Gill Gascoigne

A MEMORABLE MAN

AUSTIN MACAULEY
PUBLISHERS LTD.

A CIP catalogue record for this title is available from the British
Library.

ISBN 9781784552695 (Paperback)
ISBN 9781784552718 (Hardback)

www.austinmacauley.com

First Published (2015)
Austin Macauley Publishers Ltd.
25 Canada Square
Canary Wharf
London
E14 5LB

Printed and bound in Great Britain

Acknowledgments

I would like to thank the few special people who:
Inspired, encouraged, read, listened to, kindly criticised, appreciated and praised my writing during the creation of this book.
You know who you are, and I love you all.

Author's note

I have felt an irresistible pull to the past for as long as I can remember. Always too been fascinated by people and the way they live together and weave relationships with each other in their lifetimes.

When my own Mother died some years ago, I found comfort in looking back into my family's past. How I wished I could have gone back in time, met some of the people I found, and come to know them.

Some of those long dead family members and their stories, mixed with some long buried memories of my own unearthed whilst searching, inspired my writing.

Some of the events and the places still in existence in the age and the village in which my story is set, inspired this book.

Essentially though, it is a story of people and the way they live and die, bound by the intangible, unbreakable bonds of love, friendship and family.

In the end, for me, these are the things that define a life. No matter how many years or centuries pass us by, love and family will always be the ties that bind.

This book is for my family, for the ones that came before me and made a place for me.

For my own family, those I live among, gave life to and love so very much.

And lastly, it is for those who will come after me and know me through the words and emotions that fill these pages.

Gill Gascoigne 16th March 2013

A Memorable Man

Prologue

It is autumn 1650 and England stands on the brink of historic change. For the past eight years the country has been torn apart by cruel civil war as Englishmen have chosen sides to fight for or against the rule of a King. Many thousands have died, the bloody madness culminating in the execution of King Charles I a year earlier. Only one campaign now remains to be fought as the dead King's son, the would-be Charles II, returns from exile to claim his birthright...if he fails, England will enter into an unprecedented age of civil governance.

In a small village in rural east Lancashire, the momentous events that play out on the national stage mean more to some than others. Some have seen their families destroyed, suffering the loss of loved ones, fortune and status. Others have prospered from the shifting social sands of this revolutionary conflict, gaining personal wealth, power and influence. Most of the poor and ordinary folk in the small community have been merely witnesses to history, the pressures of living in a country at war with itself only adding to the already heavy burden they carry through life and their daily battle against poverty and hunger.

For Thurston Hey, the young man at the centre of our story, the events of the past eight years have seemed so insignificant that they have created hardly a ripple on the surface of his life. But change, like an unstoppable tide, is coming...

1.All Hallows Eve 1650

Thurston Hey might have had a memorable name but he was not on first acquaintance a memorable man.

"Ne' mind lad…" his mother used to say when he stumbled into the little cottage, his face dirty and tear-stained from the bully boys "…tha'sl 'ave last laugh!"

Thurston missed his other. He couldn't ever remember the softness of an embrace but her unquestioned faith in him always gave him comfort…comfort that he had missed in the two years since her death.

The little cottage, built with his ather's own hand before he was born, was quiet now when he entered it. No bully boys chased him home in tears these days, no stoic words of comfort welcomed him in. Home was his only comfort now; his short leg didn't matter in the little cottage. He was master in this house, in this little world.

He was lucky he knew. After all he had bread to eat, a roof over his head, and a fire to warm him to bed. It was a hard life for some outside the little cottage and he was grateful for its comforts.

It was the eve of All Hallows. "Mischief night" his Mother used to call it. He and his Father and mother would sit in his long ago childhood years, waiting for the rattle on the door, the mud at the window. The same chill, stomach-churning fear that was such a part of his young life reached through time and made him shiver again. He had no fear of ghosts or witches abroad this night. As always, the ever present dread was of his fellow man, even though those years had long since passed.

Thurston looked out to see the lane outside brightly lit by the moon, "the parish lantern" his mother would call it… and its light soothed him a little. He settled back into the old wooden chair that had always stood by the fire, exhausted now at the end of his day of labour. The comfort of his home washed gently over him as he relaxed, bathed in the warm yellow glow of the crackling fire, his belly full as he nodded. Pictures of a dark haired boy running, running and hopping on his short lame leg flickered in the flames of the fire as his eyelids closed.

The cottage stood on the edge of the hamlet of Appley Cross, a smattering of little dwellings that had sprung up in a ramshackle way about a quarter of a mile from a crossroads. To the South and North lay the growing cities of Manchester and Liverpool. To the West, a larger village built around its namesake, a pretty, willow-fringed square of grass, Appley Green. To the east of the little hamlet lay miles and miles of flat, black peat moss as far as the eye could see. Drained a hundred years before, it now provided good growing land in times of plenty and some sustenance even for those who hadn't a farthing and lived on what they could gather from the earth. Peat fires in the winter, wheat and grain when summer reigned and turnips…always turnips.

The night was still and quiet, bright in the glow of the autumn moon, the first frost of the coming winter settling on tiptoe at the edge of dawn. The little cottage seemed almost to breathe softly as the girl approached. She had walked from the crossroads, down through the little hamlet, her heart heavy with despair as she looked at the empty darkness ahead and realised she had taken the wrong road. The dim, yellow glow in the window of the little cottage drew her troubled mind like a moth to a flame. She stood, lit by the moon and looked back through the hamlet. She thought the houses looked like they too had ended up there by mistake, as if they also were lost as she was and were too tired to go on. She pulled her heavy woollen shawl around her, silently thanking her mother and tears came at the thought of the loving fingers that had made it. The memory wearied her heart and her courage.

The little cottage had a porch, stacked with dried rushes, rolls of peat and bundles of wood and before she really even thought to huddle there, she was nestled in covered by her shawl, sheltered from the wind that blew out of the inky blackness. As she drifted into uneasy sleep, the frost settled like silver dust on her eyelashes.

And so the night passed, both our characters sharing the chill dark hours within feet of each other, both oblivious to the physical discomforts which threatened to disturb their fitful sleep. So exhausted were they from the exertions of their different days, they passed the night without waking, unaware of the intertwining of their lives to come.

Thurston awoke with a start as the fire fell and the early morning cold pinched. His back ached from his few hours' sleep in the single wooden chair and as he stretched, the pale stone dust from his working clothes danced in the shaft of milky light which pierced the thick glass of the single window. He felt the loneliness most in the early morning. For as long as he had lived until she went, he had awakened to the sounds of his mother moving and clattering between fire and table. Warmth and wood smoke would drift up the open hole in the ceiling of the cottage to the little room that was just big enough for his hay-stuffed mattress. So many nights in the last few months, he had been too weary to climb the wooden ladder up to his bed and had awakened in the bed he had been born in twenty-four years before. It was the same bed that his mother had died in and which had stood all his life in the corner of the small downstairs room which served for sitting, cooking and sleeping.

He stood, arching his back in a delicious stretch and opening his mouth wide in a loud yawn. He bent to stir the embers of the fire and to his delight there was still a faint glow and he knew that a minute spent now would save him a chilly hour when he returned home. He went to the door to fetch wood and peat to bank up the fire so that it would still be smouldering at the end of his working day.

The door was bolted, they had always kept it so, always afraid of what was outside and the bolt slid noisily, the wooden door swollen in the damp air. Half asleep still and settling into the calmness that always accompanied the return of the day, Thurston cried out loudly at the sight and sounds emanating from the bundle at his feet, the ever-present memories making him instantly a child again. He was darting back inside preparing to bolt the door against his fear when he saw her face appear from beneath the blanket, eyes wide and clearly as afraid as he was. He was shaking as he calmed himself and he bent down to take her hand, babbling with relief:

"Eeh! Tha gi' me a freet! 'Ow longs tha bin theer? Weer's tha cum from? Tha mun cum in an' warm thisen up!"

The girl stood shakily, unsure of her welcome. The only words she had understood were "Cum in" and the fear and uncertainty showed in her face.

"Nay, tha's safe wi' me lass...cum in, cum in."

Within half a dozen steps, she was in the wooden chair as Thurston busied himself putting wood on the fire and rummaging in a wooden box for blankets which he laid around her shoulders most carefully. The girl began to thaw inside and out as moments later she sipped a bowl of warm milk and bread 'pobs', and suddenly in the face of such kindness she began to cry.

"Nay lass, thi mun buck up, tha's safe, th'all be 'reet."

She was pretty he thought, with the flames of the fire flushing her cheeks and the tears sparkling like dew on her dark lashes. Her mouth was set in a firm pink line as she struggled to hold back the clearly unwelcome tears.

'Proud too' he thought. Not that Thurston was any judge of the prettiness of women. The last female he had looked on appreciatively was Lizzie Pendle and she had boxed his ears for his trouble. He had been ten at the time. In his experience girls hit just as hard as boys and he had avoided women ever since. When the girl eventually spoke her voice was like the sound of leaves in autumn, crackly and whispery and inexplicably pleasurable as if it held every memory he ever had of kicking through the lanes on his way home.

"You are kind," she said. "I should have knocked on your door last night, I almost did but I was too afraid."

Her mouth softened and dimples appeared at its corners as its shape changed into a smile.

"My name is Elspet...Elspet Sydall, and I am most obliged to you for your kindness in my trouble."

"I am Thurston..." he answered, entranced "...Thurston Hey."

"A memorable name," she said.

****

Thurston was mesmerised by every move she made as they walked together an hour later towards the crossroads. He was fascinated by the youthful bounce of her step and the occasional glimpse of her slim, tiny pointed boots. He was entranced by the shining black hair that swung like a curtain when she turned to look at him mid-sentence and the little white teeth that lit up her face when she laughed which she did often as she spoke.

How had he ever thought Lizzie Pendle pretty! People came out of their houses and commented to each other:

"By 'eck its Thurston 'ey wi' a lass!"

For the first time he could remember on stepping outside the safety of his home, Thurston felt the same safe feeling that he only ever felt inside the little cottage.

Elspet talked easily, a sweet and sparkling flow of words which swiftly swept him into the little runnels of her life. She had come from Manchester on a wagon-load of bricks she said, but she had come to Manchester from Derbyshire on her Father's cart. She was very tired but always had a lot of energy and could manage very well on little sleep she said. She was bound for her Aunt and Uncle in Appley Green, where she would stay for some months ... her face seemed troubled as she recounted this detail but her smile soon recovered.

"Who is tha uncle?" Thurston had asked, and he was answered:

"Nathaniel Speakman...Aye ...," she said at Thurston's look of surprise "...restorer of the Church at Appley Green. I am to keep house for them, my Aunt is very ill."

"Well ...Ah'm sorry for that," he said, struggling to make a suitably mournful face when he felt happier than he ever had in his life.

A pause in the chatter followed and then she asked,

"What's amiss with thy leg, Thurston?"

It was as if he had been thumped. He fell, crushed from the dizzy heights of his happiness, down, down into the frightening spaces of his past when all he wanted to do was to duck past the boys and flee with his hopping gait to the safety of the little cottage. His face betrayed nothing of his feelings however... always as a child he had only ever cried when he could see the sanctuary of the little cottage. He still limped alongside her though the sudden heaviness of his heart made it harder to walk.

Somehow she knew. She stopped and faced him.

"Forgive my question. It matters not," she said. "You are a kind, good man. Come with me and meet my Aunt and Uncle. I would introduce you to them as my friend and my guardian angel!"

He looked down. She had clasped his hands and he could feel her warmth flowing into him.

"Ah was born with one leg shorter than t'other," he said.

"Well...what is missing from your leg has made your heart bigger Thurston. Will you come?"

He nodded, unable to speak for a moment. At length he replied "...Aye...Ah will."

****

Eliza Speakman was hot though the morning was chill and no fire burned in the room in which she lay, alone in her bed.

She knew this was her last illness, that her time would come soon. That she would leave this world and everything she loved in it. Of course, none knew that she knew this; it was a secret she kept from them and that they kept from her. A sore too painful to acknowledge, better to keep it covered with a veil of secrecy and shed her tears when she was alone.

How it cheered her dear Nathaniel when she smiled and so she did, even through her pain because she loved him so. He had been out since daybreak over at the site of the Church. The reason she was lying so late in her bed, she told herself, was that she would have enough strength to rise and meet her half-sister Margaret's girl when she arrived which she surely would today. All through the day before they had expected her on the wagon-load of bricks from Manchester. By the time word came that they had arrived many hours late, a dark wintry night had fallen. Nathaniel had gone down to the crossroads with a lantern but there had been no sight of Elspet or the driver, only a wagon-load of bricks without horses. He had hardly slept for worry.

Eliza had woken from her sleep as daylight filled the room, instinctively reaching out to the empty space beside her to feel only the still warm imprint of her husband's body. Poor Nathaniel, he would be at the site of the Church doing his duty, guiltily aware of his Eliza at home when he should be with her, as was his duty. Now he would be worried that he had failed in yet another duty, to safeguard his niece. Nathaniel had always been a worrier, what would happen to him when she was gone? There would be no-one to stroke his hand by the fire in the evening and tell him what a wonderful man he was. She hoped the girl was of a good sort and she hoped with all her heart that she would like it here and stay long after…well, she hoped she would stay.

As her memory wandered, Eliza drew again in her mind the picture she had created of Elspet Sydall. The features she imagined were drawn from long ago memories of her own half-sister, dark eyed and beautiful and her brother-in-law, wiry and ever-busy with no time for conversation. She included however his slight build and energy as estimable characteristics in the picture she drew of his daughter. And finally, to that picture she added the ever-present memories of her own long-dead little girl ... soft pink cheeks and long dark hair completing her imagined face of Elspet.

The letter announcing the birth of her niece had arrived just a week after she had put her own daughter in the ground. How hard Eliza had fought to put aside her terrible feelings of jealousy towards her half-sister Meg! But the ever-rolling sea of life had in time calmed her turbulent emotions and now all Eliza hoped for was to see some living reminder of her long-dead daughter in the grown-up face of her niece. As Eliza felt the familiar waves of tiredness wash over her again, she allowed her memory to take her little Susannah in her arms and stroke her soft, pink cheek as they drifted into sleep together.

****

Nathaniel Speakman was indeed a worrier. He stood at the building site of St Stephens Church and worried about the lack of speed with which its walls were rising. Once November was in, the hard frost would crack the mortar as it hardened. He needed more hands. He needed more time... time was not his friend. He could just see the black and white walls of his cottage through the trees, as if looking every few minutes was any help to his dear Eliza who lay so weak and helpless within its walls. But she would get better, she must. The nimble feet of his running mind stayed well away from the dark pit of the possibility of life without her and ran on to the problem of his niece.

He turned and scanned the road which led up to the crossroads but there was no sign of the wagon-load of bricks or his niece who should have been on it last night. What if the driver had made off with her? Shall he go back down to the crossroads? How was he to build without his bricks? And so the wheel of his mind whirred and worried.

Thurston and Elspet left the little hamlet and approached the cross roads, laughing at the swaying walk of a man Elspet soon recognised as the driver of the brick wagon.

"'e must've stopped in t'Grapes," said Thurston. Elspet looked puzzled. Thurston continued "Th'inn ower t'road."

"I've come a distance from Derbyshire of fifty miles Thurston but I feel like I am in another land. I do not understand a half of what you say!"

"Then it's a good job Ah don't talk much," he retorted.

She stood stock still, a puzzled, questioning expression on her face, waiting for translation.

He sighed:

"He must have stopped the neet- pardon- the night, at the Grapes..." She shrugged, he clarified "...the inn, over the road."

She laughed at his attempt to speak, as her Mother would say, 'the King's English'.

"Of-course...I see. They serve good ale there then?"

"Aye...an''e looks like 'e's 'ad plenty!"

The tinkling sound of her laughter again.

By the time they reached the crossroads, the driver was in a state about his horses:

"Dirty, theivin' beggars, they've pinched my 'osses!"

Thurston stood tugging his cap:

"Beg pardon Sir but there's not much call for pinchin' round 'ere. Nowt to pinch dost see? Is them thine osses in t'field yonder?"

Mumbling and holding his head, the driver crossed the dirt road to reclaim his horses.

"The bricks are going to Appley Green. Shall we wait for a ride?" asked Elspet.

"Nay...," said Thurston, thinking the longer he could spend with her the better "...let's walk ....if tha'rt not too tired?"

She shook her head, and they walked over the crossroads in the direction she should have walked the night before, towards Appley Green.

****

Nathaniel had returned home to see Eliza. The Speakman's house fronted the dirt road at the spot where it petered out at the end of the village. He had built it with his own hands thirty years earlier and he was proud of his work. He had built many of the houses in the village since, as it grew and stretched its way down to the crossroads. His reputation had also grown over the years, his commissioning to restore the ruinous Church the pinnacle of his career.

He entered his house by the low front door and climbed the staircase to where she lay. She was sleeping still, she slept more and more these days. Her tiny hand rested against her pale cheek and although she looked ill, her face seemed peaceful, even happy. A sudden rush of love, fear, sadness and gratitude for all she was came into his throat and he struggled to stifle the silent sob, so as not to wake her. Calm again he covered her shoulders and walked quietly away, suddenly aware that every prospect of happiness in his life lay in that room. He descended the staircase, the dark spectre of life without her edging for the first time into his consciousness.

He stepped outside into the watery sunlight and looked across at the Church he was restoring. He hoped she would see it finished. For the second time that morning, he mused that time was not his friend.

****

The brick wagon passed Thurston and Elspet on its way to Appley Green.

"My Aunt and Uncle shall think I have fallen off," she said and laughed. Thurston felt he could spend every waking moment listening to that sound and never tire of it.

"You do not talk much at all, Thurston. I feel I have rambled on all morning"

He shrugged his shoulders. "Ah like to listen to thee…anyroad tha can't understand me as Ah'm forrin aren't ah?"

He smiled at her and she laughed but remained silent, sensing he would speak again.

"Truth be told," he said "Ah don't talk t'anyone much, Ah'm a solitary man, allus av bin."

Distant but ever present memories danced in his head of cruel words and vicious blows received in silence, always in silence.

"Well Thurston Hey, I will bless the day I met you! I have enjoyed our talk and hope for more of it. I will need a friend in my time here...please say you will seek me out again."

He looked down as she clasped his hands once more. All the peat on the Moss could never warm him like this! He nodded.

"My Uncle approaches," she said, gesturing to Nathaniel Speakman who walked quickly toward them, waving.

****

"Lass, lass..." a gentle voice, a soft rubbing of her hand "...wake up, she's 'ere, she's 'ere!"

Slowly Eliza Speakman struggled awake, the low autumn sun piercing the window with a shard of light that hurt her head. She raised a hand to shield her eyes and as sleep slowly receded, Elspet came into view. Though very like the picture she had imagined, in reality the girl was much prettier. Slightly built like her father, small of stature like her mother and as Eliza beckoned her with an outstretched hand she saw with a gladdening and gratified heart, the shining dark hair and pink cheeks of her dreams. Only Elspet's eyes surprised her, being the deep beautiful, shining green of leaves after rain.

2.

Thurston took unusual care with his appearance as he dressed two days later. As he did so, he could hear the voice of his mother chiding "Cleanliness is next to Godliness!"

He remembered her licking her fingers and smoothing down his hair before he left for Church, inspecting his face when he had washed it and saying: "Ah said 'av a wash, norra cat-lick!."

Thurston had hardly washed his clothes since his mother had died and only ever washed his body when it itched. When he had returned from Appley Green the day he had taken Elspet to her Uncle, he had boiled water in the big copper pot and soaked his shirt and breeches just as he had seen his Mother do so many times. He had stood and washed his body and his hair by the fire, then he had sat wrapped in a blanket while the steam rose from his drying clothes.

He had not had much chance to say farewell to Elspet so keen had been her Uncle to take her upstairs to meet her Aunt Eliza. He had waited outside for some minutes and had almost made his mind up to leave when Nathaniel had re-appeared.

"Thank 'e lad for bringin' t'wench 'ome. Ah were so worried."

Nathaniel had asked him many questions about his life and his family.

"So, art tha William 'eys lad then? Well! Ah knew thi Father...and thi Mother."

Nathaniel recalled working alongside William Hey when he had first brought his new wife to settle in Appley Green thirty years before. He told Thurston tales of working on the farms, on the moss, building pens and maintaining farm buildings with William Hey in the early days of his career.

"That's worr ah do still" said Thurston "It's 'ow ah make my livin'!

"Is it now?" said Nathaniel. "An' is it a good living?"

"Ah manage well enough Sir," answered Thurston.

Nathaniel had taken in the dirty, worn clothes and bony frame of the lad then rubbed his sparsely bearded chin.

"Tell thi what lad, cum back Thursday dinner... we'll 'ave another talk."

Thurston set off for Appley Green on Thursday as requested, taking a short cut through the fields. He had taken Elspet the long way round the day he had met her so as to enjoy her company the longer. Now he walked through the farmland that belonged to Abbots Hall and the Bagshawe family, the largest landowners in the area. It was good, green undulating land rising up from the edge of the peat moss and stretching for miles. In the distance he could see the rambling old, ivy-clad house of Abbots Hall, built, his Father had said, by the hands of the Hey's ancestors over two hundred years before.

Thurston's few memories of his long dead Father were all the same. Stories of how the rich trod down the poor...how he had been trodden down all his life. Bitter, blame-filled words that always made Thurston feel guilty for his lameness, as if it were the final straw in the back-breaking load William Hey was forced to carry through life.

It was late in the bright, clear morning and an early winter mist still swirled inches above the ground making Abbots Hall appear to float on the horizon. The light frost still lingered and the ground crunched softly beneath his feet as he walked, breathing in the chill air and feeling a tingling that was nothing to do with the cold as he anticipated seeing Elspet again.

As he continued his walk he began to use the enticing prospect of Elspet's many charms as a talisman to ward off the memories that always assailed him when he walked alone anywhere, but especially now as he approached the very spot. Why had he walked this way, today of all days?

Suddenly he was there...at the well-remembered place where the ground dipped suddenly into a shallow bowl and brambles grew twisted and malformed as if something turgid and evil disrupted and poisoned the ground beneath. In this place had been the worst of days.

His mind whirled with the intercut sounds and images of past and present; the crack of stone on bone, the sting of brambles... Elspet's laugh. He felt the remembered pain, fear and panic...and pictured Elspet's long, smooth, black hair. He heard the shouts, the swishing sound of willow sticks, remembered the taste of his own blood and the hated face of his tormentor... and as his pace quickened involuntarily into his hopping, running gait...he saw Elspet's beautiful green eyes.

Breathing heavily he approached the stile that led to the end of the lane where the back of the Speakman's black and white walled house came into view. His eyes were stinging with unshed tears. Strange, he thought, he had only ever cried when he had seen his sanctuary.

She was waiting at the door smiling, even lovelier than he remembered her.

"I saw you running from the window upstairs. Are you so keen to see me Thurston?"

She laughed but then again she sensed his feelings and touched his face to look into it.

"What is it? What ails thee?" she asked, seeing his reddened eyes.

Thurston drew back from her touch. A touch he struggled to understand. Was it pity? He did not want pity, not from her. She laid her hand on his arm again and gently pulled him in through the door.

"Come you in Thurston, my Uncle will be home soon. Come in and be warm, I am happy to see you again."

Her words and manner comforted him like a warm blanket and for the first time in his life he wondered how it would feel to be enveloped in another's arms. For the first time in his life he craved it and the craving was a new, confusing feeling.

"My Aunt asks that you forgive her not coming down...," said Elspet as she motioned him to sit down in one of the curve-backed wooden chairs by a roaring fire.

"She's been meaning to get up since I've come but...well, she is very ill."

Thurston looked about him. He had never been in any place indoors so clean and bright and pleasant. The walls were white and smooth, the gleaming floor reflecting the light from two small windows beneath which a beautiful polished table stood with two chairs set opposite each other - so the occupants could sit and talk while they ate, he assumed. To one side of the stone fireplace were shelves filled with bright, gleaming pewter plates and jugs which seemed molten in the dancing orange light of the flames. Another chair identical to the one he sat in faced him, each flanking the fire, and a wooden settle stood along the wall opposite, on its seat blankets folded neatly to be used against the draughts on chilly winter nights. In front of the fire on the polished floor lay a beautiful rectangle of coloured fabric, the like of which he had never seen.

"'t is lovely is it not...," said Elspet "....the rug?"

"Rug?" replied Thurston.

"Aye, the rug," she said, pointing to the floor.

"Ah've never seen such an object...," said Thurston "...but it is beautiful, aye."

"My Aunt made it herself from scraps of all the cloth she ever had since coming to this house as a bride. There..." she pointed to a pale pink ruched piece of fabric "...from her wedding dress. And there, that's my uncle's wedding shirt. There a piece from her baby's shawl and that, a piece of cloth from a pretty blue shift she made and sent to me when I was a child. I remember it coming..."

"She must be a clever woman," said Thurston.

"Aye and kind, the kindest woman I ever met. My uncle says she calls it her 'memory rug'. Sometimes at night when she was well, he said, they used to sit together and talk and laugh and sometimes shed a tear over the memories it holds.

He says there's more than two thousand pieces of cloth in it, all bound together by love."

Thurston nodded "Aye ah can see that. Ah can feel it an all...this room... it 'as a nice feelin'...like it looks after folk."

Elspet smiled. "Thurston, what a nice nature you have."

He flushed. "Warm in 'ere i'nt it?" he said.

****

Nathaniel Speakman stood in what would be the newly refurbished Nave of the old Church of St. Stephen. For the first time when looking up he could not see the top of the building line. That wagonload of bricks had made a difference in the two days since they had arrived. The feeling of a good job well done had come at a cost however. He cast his eyes about at his lads sitting about eating their dinners, hands all wrapped up with bits of scrap cloth. He looked down at his own upturned palms, calloused skin raw from building. They had worked so hard these last few days. By the end of the week when the bricks had all gone, they would be a bit nearer the target set for him by Sir William Bagshawe. He needed to meet that target, the lads needed money for what looked like might be a hard winter, and he needed it too with another mouth to feed and his Eliza needing warmth and the best of care his living could provide. Poor lads, they had worked like ten men.

"Get off now lads," said Nathaniel. "Get over t'Bulls 'ead for a warm... but don't 'av too much ale!" he called after them. "And tha must come back for two of the clock...' reet?"

His workmen nodded and cheered in jovial approval.

"Aw reet Mr Speakman" shouted Arthur White his foreman, "Ah'll mek sure they be'ave." And off they walked to the ancient inn that nobody in the village could remember being built or their Fathers before them, so long had it stood.

Nathaniel followed them as they walked to the edge of the building site through the graveyard of the old Church. He stopped as he did every day, at the moss-covered stone beneath which his little Susannah lay, together with her two sisters, neither of which had drawn a breath in this life. It was a pretty spot for his beloved child to spend eternity in peaceful rest. A little brook ran tinkling softly a few yards away under the old pack horse bridge which brought the road into the village. Always it brought to his mind a picture of his little girl shaking her favourite toy of jingling bells, a bright smile on her sweet little face.

He looked up and saw the lads enter the Bulls Head Inn on the other side of the brook and turned to look across again at his house for the hundredth time that morning. At least Eliza wasn't alone now, he knew she was safe with Elspet. What a blessing the girl was going to be in the months ahead.

"Ee little lass," he said aloud as he looked down again and silently read by heart the inscription on the stone:

Susannah,
Beloved daughter of Nathaniel and Eliza Speakman.
Departed this life on the 30th September 1630, aged 6 years.
"Safe in the arms of the Lord."

He tried not to think the thought but it slipped nimbly through the narrow crack of his conscience.

"Tha'll be safe in the arms of thi mother soon."

With a heavy heart he turned and walked towards his home and his midday meal.

The painful disappointment he always felt when entering his house without the sight of his wife coming to greet him was today mixed with surprise at the sound of a male voice. For a second his heart leapt "Josiah!" Then realisation…William Hey's lad was coming to eat dinner. Nathaniel strode into the room.

"Ah lad, Ah'm pleased to see thee. Our little Elspet makes thee comfortable I see."

"Aye sir, she does that" replied Thurston, standing with his pot of broth steaming.

"Aye she's a good girl, she is," said Nathaniel as he grasped Thurston's hand and gently stroked Elspet's cheek.

"Pardon me lad, Ah must go upstairs to see my dear wife. Ah'll be down in a few minutes." Thurston nodded as Nathaniel left the room to climb the narrow staircase.

Eliza was awake, her hair newly brushed and colour in her cheeks and the sight of her gladdened his heart.

"Eeh, lass...tha looks bonny!"

He took her in his arms, unaware of the pain in her bones as he squeezed her, her eyes betraying it momentarily and even that swiftly hidden as he laid her back onto her pillows to look on her again.

"Does tha feel well today, my love?"

"I feel better than I have for many a day" she answered truthfully.

Elspet had been a Godsend, literally. The past two days had seemed as if God had sent an angel into her life. The guilty thought that had grown from a little seed in her mind, the thought that somehow some part of her Susannah had filtered into the soul of Elspet Sydall, was now a firmly rooted belief. It was as if she had always known her, as if her child had come home after many long years away.

"The lad's downstairs," said Nathaniel, "and for the life o' me Ah cannot think of 'is name!"

"How can ye forget a name such as his? T'is Thurston" she answered. "Ye must be kind to him Nathaniel..." chided his wife "...Elspet says the lad a'nt 'ad much kindness in 'is life."

"Me? Not be kind?" he exclaimed, affronted. "When am I ever not kind?"

She smiled. "Th'art always kind to me my love"

"Indeed so...," he said, mollified "...for no wife was ever loved more."

He kissed her again, gently, and smoothed the greying hair at her temples.

"Ee, tha looks bonny!"

She pushed him gently, playfully, feeling again the gnawing pain.

"Get thee downstairs and eat...," she said dismissing him gently "...and remember thy promise about the lad."

"Aye Ah will lass, an' Ah'll be up again to see thee afore Ah go."

"Send Elspet up," she called after him, the sweat starting to break on her brow as he left the room.

Nathaniel motioned to Elspet as he re-entered the room downstairs and she dutifully rose to go up to her Aunt. As soon as she vacated her seat by the fire, he sat down in it opposite Thurston.

"Ne'then lad, so tha's plenty o work on then?"

Thurston nodded "Ah 'av some Sir... Ah'm busy on most days."

"Doin' what, labourin'?" asked Nathaniel.

"Nay Sir," replied Thurston "Ah'm mi own boss...Ah toil in the craft mi Father taught me as a lad, Sir."

"Buildin'?"

"Aye Sir," said Thurston "...well...nothin' so fine as tha does Sir, but Ah can build and mend Sir."

"Good, good..." nodded Nathaniel, taking in the lad. "Well, 'urry up and eat tha broth an' I sh'll tek thee over to t'Church in a bit... show thee some proper buildin'!"

Nathaniel had a twinkle in his eye and Thurston smiled, taking the comment with the good humour with which it was intended, shovelling in the broth.

He ate, Nathaniel thought, like it was the first proper cooked meal he'd had in months...which of course it was.

3.

Thurston sat on a cold winter night in his own little cottage, in front of his own fire in his wooden chair and marvelled at his change of fortune in the last four weeks. In essence, he was much the same man he had been. He was Thurston Hey, twenty-four years old, living alone in the cottage he had been born in, grateful for the small mercies in his insignificant existence. But the appearance of an angel on his doorstep in the early morning had changed his life in ways he could never have imagined.

The day he had visited the Speakman's house, Nathaniel had taken him over to view the building site and before he had left for home, he had accepted the job he was offered...to work alongside Nathaniel restoring the beloved old St. Stephen's Church.

He ate supper most nights at the Speakman's house after work before walking home to the place which, unbelievably for Thurston, was no longer the place he most liked to be.

The Speakman's house was the most welcoming home. Elspet had seamlessly stitched herself into the fabric of their family, bringing new life into a home that had begun to take on an air of sadness and a sense of mourning for the happiest of times now past.

Thurston could see the difference in Nathaniel in the three weeks he had known him and although he didn't realise it, everyone had noticed the change in Thurston. Despite his limp, he seemed to walk with a heightened air of confidence. He was putting on weight, that very night he had left Elspet sewing him a new pair of breeches and had returned home with a pile of shirts Nathaniel had grown out of. And it was all due to

Elspet, dearest Elspet! How he had grown to adore her! She was the dearest thing in his life.

Life without her was unimaginable. He could never face going back to the lonely existence he had before she came. In fact the reality of the life he had lived up to the point where he had found her on his doorstep like a parcel from heaven, only now seemed sad, lonely and bereft of happiness. All that he had come to know in the last three weeks had shone a light on a part of life he may never have known. Without knowing her, he would have continued on the lonely path of his existence, oblivious and content. Now it was as if he had lived in another land and he knew he could never go back to the place he had come from.

He knew he loved her and feeling love for another human being had lifted his spirit. She accepted him for who he was. She sought out his company. She was kind to him in a way he had never known. She was a friend to him when no other in the world had been his friend. He knew she would never love him in the way that he loved her...how could she? But just to have her as his friend was enough and he hoped with all his heart that he could have some little happiness with her until someone took her to wife, which they surely would.

At first her kindness had been difficult to understand. He had confused it with pity although he had never experienced either reaction from another human being, save his mother in her tight-lipped, arms folded, touch-me-not way. He struggled also at first with Nathaniel's interest in him although that became resolved in Thurston's mind when Nathaniel arranged to pay him for his labour... that at least was a motive he understood. But Elspet's attention to him had been a puzzle he could not solve. She came to look for him, to ask him how he was, to bring his dinner. After several days he had accepted that she really wanted to be his friend and that was the moment he had begun to find his self-worth.

He felt as he sat in his old chair that at last all his sore places were healing over. This was the eve of what would be a special day. For the first time since her arrival, Elspet would have no work to do. Nathaniel had insisted that she took a

Sunday away from the house to amuse herself and she had chosen Thurston to spend it with. He was to call for her at the hour of eleven and until church at three, he would spend what he felt would be the happiest hours of his life!

When he looked into the flickering flames of the fire that night, he no longer saw the crying, hopping boy in the sparking flames but the amber flecks in Elspet's green eyes.

*****

The cart loaded with barrels bounced and lurched over the ruts in the road and the driver seemed oblivious to the sickening, rolling, jolting movement. The young man who rode by his side began to think that walking the five miles the cart was taking him nearer to his destination, would be preferable to the ride. As he ducked the swinging iron lantern that shone a light on the road ahead for the hundredth time that night, he opened his mouth to speak to the driver but before he could say a word, the man shouted a loud "whoaaa!" and the giant cart horses slowed to a halt. The driver spoke the only words he had spoken during the journey:

"Ah'm stoppin' 'ere…too dark, too cold. If tha's no money that can sleep in t'cart, if tha 'as tha can join me yonder."

The young passenger looked toward the inn the driver pointed at.

"Aye, I have money," he said.

The young man's money bought him a hard, narrow bed in a room full of hard, narrow beds, a meal of stew made from unidentifiable meat of indeterminate age and with the aid of a lice- ridden, threadbare blanket, a little more warmth than the cart. Sleep came quickly however, his long journey from the North having wearied him more than he had realised.

As he drifted into sleep, the face of his Mother swam before him and as always the deep love he bore her was tinged with the bitter feelings of rejection and resentment. Feelings never voiced but a part of his conscience since he was a child, too young to understand them. They had been inextricably woven into his being and into their relationship, much as his mother fastened thread and fabric together before the fire in the long ago evenings of his childhood.

The letter had found him many weeks after it had been sent, put into his hand late one autumn night as he sat with his comrades round the campfire. He had left the warmth, created as much by the company and easy acceptance of the men with whom he shared his life as by the blaze and returned to the solitude of his tent. By the light of a candle he read the letter and knew that as soon as he could, he must return and make an end to the deep and lifelong conflict within him. A conflict that would not be settled by means of sword and musket but with words, understanding and, he hoped and prayed, forgiveness.

4.

Thurston arrived for his afternoon with Elspet at the appointed hour. In truth he had been sat in the old churchyard for quite a time having set off early, unable to sit for the evermore frequent lurching of his stomach and swellings in the parts of his body his Mother had so often threatened to cut off in the years he had been growing into a man.

The Churchyard seemed the most appropriate place to go and wait, vainly hoping that thoughts of God would calm the problematic stirrings of what he knew was the sin of lust.

Having sat in the Churchyard for a while, he got up and wandered over to the grave he had seen Nathaniel visit at some point of every day. Thurston could not read and although he felt no shame in this, he did feel frustration. There were carved pictures of flowers on the stone. It was a female then? Was it Nathaniel's Mother perhaps? Thurston knew his numbers, he used them often in his building. He saw the number six. Could it be a child of six? Or six people? Six feet under was all he really knew:

"No matter how high folk rise, they must all end six feet under!" …Another of his Mother's sayings. Well, whoever lay there, the visits always saw Nathaniel return in a thoughtful mood.

Through the still, silent morning he heard the sliding bolt of the Bull's Head Inn as the Landlord, old Jack, opened its doors for the day. Eleven o-clock. Thurston got up from his knees and walked over to the Speakman's house. Elspet answered the door the second he knocked.

"Come in!" she said excitedly. "There is a sight to behold!"

She pulled him by his hand into the lovely welcoming room. Lying on the settle, propped up with pillows lay the woman he knew was Aunt Eliza.

"Is it not wondrous Thurston? 'it is the first time she has been out of bed in many weeks. Aunt Eliza....," she said pulling him over to the settle "...this is Thurston Hey!"

She looked like how Elspet might look, years hence. Although fading, the remains of her beauty were plain to see. Her eyes were the same amber as those flecks in Elspet's eyes which only became visible in the brightest light and although they swam with the milky cloudiness of age and illness, they were beautiful still. She took his hand.

"Thurston, my dear, how much I have heard of you. Will you sit?"

Nathaniel, who Thurston had not yet seen, stepped from behind the door.

"Nay, nay lass! Th'art tired by all the exertions of the mornin'. Let the young one's be off an' we shall sit and 'ave this time to sit side by side a while."

He looked to Thurston and Elspet with a pleading in his eyes. Elspet of course understood. A bit of normality was all he craved, the chance to have his wife to himself in their home for a little time while she was well.

"Yes," she said "Come Thurston, I have made a basket of good things for our dinner. What a good day we will have!"

She kissed her Aunt and pulled at Thurston's hand.

"Ah'm glad to see thee improved Mistress Speakman. Ah wish thee Good-Mornin'. Thurston tugged his forelock as he was pulled from the room.

"Church at three Elspet!" called Nathaniel just as he heard the door bang shut.

"Ne'then lass," he said, as he pulled a blanket on to the floor and settled down with his head on her lap. Eliza stroked his once golden, now course, greying hair lovingly.

"Nathaniel..." she whispered "... th'art like a little lad sometimes."

He snuggled his face into the softness of her covers to hide the longing and pain of unsaid words upon it.

****

Thurston, filled with excitement, first led Elspet to the Churchyard. She was unimpressed.

"But I've been here," she said "every day for nigh on four weeks. I bring my Uncle's dinner…I bring thine too!"

"Aye lass ah know…but Ah need thee to 'elp me…can tha read?

"Why, what do you want me to do….read thee a story?" she asked, coquettishly.

Something in her manner stirred the longing again in Thurston.

"Tha'rt daft tha'rt!" he laughed, his blush betraying his discomfort for a fleeting moment. He pulled her to the grave. "Can tha read me that?" he said.

"Oh…" murmured Elspet, sinking to the ground "…so this is she."

"Who…who is it Elspet?" Thurston knelt beside her, his leg burning where it had touched her arm.

"My Aunt and Uncle's child… Susannah. She died a few months before I was born of a terrible fever my Mother said. My mother said Aunt Eliza never got over it, even when…OH!!"

A dove flapped out of the tree above their heads, showering them with the last of the leaves that had been clinging to its branches and they laughed, relieved they had not been visited by the ghosts they had imagined. For a second too long they looked at each other when their laughter subsided, and in that split second Thurston was mesmerised by the small white teeth that grasped and chewed her bottom lip.

"Come," she said "we waste our day among the dead."

All thoughts of death forgotten, Thurston led Elspet round the high stone wall that stood opposite the Church site.

"What's behind this wall?" she asked.

"Moreton House," answered Thurston "Tha can't see beyond this wall at all apart from one place, an' that's weer ah'm tekkin thee!"

She laughed. "I like adventures," she said.

On the way to the promised revelation as they followed the seemingly endless high wall, he showed her all the places that held the few good memories of his childhood. Places that had been his salvation when he needed to be alone. Leaving the little cottage had always been dangerous for him as a child, it had been important to have places where he could find solace…and solitude. At length they came to the promised breach in the wall, hidden from view by carefully placed branches laid by Thurston himself. Moving the branches aside, he led her through, over the ivy-covered fallen stones until they emerged into a beautiful expanse of grass and wild garden.

They walked slowly, the prospect of discovery adding an almost unbearable thrill to the proceedings for Elspet.

"Who lives here Thurston?" she whispered. Theatrically, he put his finger to his lips, sensing her excitement and he pointed to a clump of trees a short distance into the garden. They moved toward the trees and as they approached, Elspet could see glimpses of water. In a moment they were moving through evergreen fronds that fringed a small, beautifully tranquil moat and Elspet gasped with pleasure at her first view of Moreton House reflected in the still, green water. The house was a vision, a beautiful miniature of the great houses she had seen in her native Derbyshire.

"Who lives here?" she asked again.

"The Moreton family…" replied Thurston "…for over 'undred years."

"Do you know them? What manner of family are they?"

"Course Ah don't know them as such," whispered Thurston "There's Master Nicholas Moreton, 'e's very old, 'is wife's dead. They 'ad two sons but they died years ago, in the war."

"Oh, so the poor man is all alone in this lovely place, none to share it with… how sad."

Thurston watched her face as she looked at the lovely old house with a heartfelt sadness in her eyes.

Silently he said to himself: "Elspet Sydall...that is why Ah love thee!"

Almost as if she had heard him speak his thoughts aloud, she turned to look into his eyes, their faces only inches apart. The leafy green gloom added an ethereal glow to her beauty, her eyes darker and even more beautiful as they reflected the green water beneath a winter sky. He struggled to break the maenad spell she cast over him.

"Come on," he said, breaking away and pulling her hand "Ah'll tek thee somewhere nice to 'ave our dinner."

The soft rustling of dead, damp leaves muffled the sound of her sigh as he pulled her away, the moment lost.

As the morning passed, they rounded the grounds of Moreton House. Crossing the stepping stones over the brook and within sight of her Aunt and Uncle's house, Thurston led her down by the side of the Bulls Head Inn, following the path of the little brook as it bubbled and splashed its way towards the fertile farmland in the distance.

"It's pretty here," she said as they stopped a little further on by a grassy bank.

"It's cold," he replied. "Shall we put the blanket on the ground to sit on?"

Elspet thought for a moment.

"Why do we not sit on these rocks, then we can sit together and pull the blanket around us so we will be warm"

"Aye," he agreed, and that was what they did.

He ate hungrily, happy as always to sit silently and watch her pick pieces from her food and feed herself like a little bird.

"You do look at me a lot Thurston!"

He was shaken from his dreamy enjoyment, embarrassed.

"Forgive me. Ah'm sorry...'course... Ah will stop."

She laughed her sweet tinkling laugh and he squirmed further in his embarrassment.

"Thurston, I jest with thee!" She grabbed his hand, sensing his discomfort.

"I jest with thee!" she said again. "What woman would not want a man to look at her?"

Her eyelids fluttered, showing to best advantage her long, dark lashes. She confused him so! If he were not Thurston Hey, he would think she wanted him to look at her as a man looks at a woman!

"Shall we walk again?" he said, rising, leaving her alone wrapped in the blanket, suddenly much colder.

"Aye," she muttered to his back as he walked on with the basket "Where to next?" she asked with another sigh, this time loud enough for any to hear except , frustratingly, Thurston who strode on ahead.

Irresistibly wrapped in each other's company, despite Elspet's frustrations, they soon fell again into comfortable step as he pointed out in his lovely soft, affable voice, the local landmarks. They followed the brook until it turned sharply north following the road to Liverpool.

"Take me to thy cottage Thurston, I would like to see it again," said Elspet.

Thurston panicked at the thought of Elspet seeing the inside of the little cottage. Since he had begun working with Nathaniel, he had hardly touched his home and it wasn't too clean at the best of times.

"Nay it's too far. Ah'll tek thee another day. Besides, it wouldn't do for folk to see thee goin' in a place wi' a man? They might think we were up to summat improper."

"Of course," she said "How thoughtful of you Thurston."

He fancied he heard an edge to her voice as she walked on without him, a little faster than before. He shook his head, she was in a funny mood today. Women were a puzzle.

"Wait on," he said as he ran to catch her up.

Again she warmed and they fell easily once more into each other's company as they had from the first. The day was cold but bright and the route he chose was pleasant. As they turned south in the direction of Appley Green once more to be home in time for Church, Elspet noticed Abbots Hall in the distance.

"Oh, Thurston what a fine place that is. Whose place is that?"

Thurston recounted the tale of the building of Abbot's Hall, the history of the family that had lived there and his knowledge of the family currently residing within its walls.

"Can we go there one day Thurston? Will we be able to see it like we did Moreton House think you?"

"Aye," he laughed, enchanted by her girlish excitement "Per'aps tha will. Sir William Bagshawe is thy Uncle's boss d'ye see? He is in charge o' the building o' t'new church. May'ap tha'll even get an invite for dinner!"

"Thurston are you teasing me? "She playfully punched his arm and ran, looking over her shoulder, an invitation in her eyes.

"Ah'll not catch thee," he laughed "Ah'm no runner!"

For the first time that day Elspet was aware of his leg, she never seemed to notice it. She waited for him.

"Worry not Thurston… I'll not run too fast, I will always make sure you can catch me."

There was that look again, those lashes, the small white teeth between parted lips.

"We must get back." he turned suddenly and headed back to the road.

"Wait!" she cried. "Thurston wait!" He stopped.

"Can we not go that way?" She pointed in the direction of Abbots Hall.

"That must be the way I've seen you come to my Uncle's house, from the window upstairs… can we not go that way?"

He stood silent, unable to explain or show his fear to her. He could not bear to lose the esteem she seemed to have for him, it must at best be fragile.

"Aye," he said "'course we can go that way."

He was silent as they walked the dreaded path. He could feel the butterfly of panic fluttering in his chest as they approached the place. He was aware of his quickening breath, fear leaden in his stomach. Why did it not stop? It was years ago, he was a man now! But it was no use, the child in all of us was never far from the surface for Thurston and there was no protection from memory.

"Thurston, what is it?" She could hear his ragged breathing. "What's wrong? Is it thy leg? Are you ill?"

She saw the fear in his eyes as he turned to her, shivering. She pulled the blanket from the basket and threw it around his shoulders, soothing him with her voice:

"'t is the cold, we have been out too long…we shall go home now and get thee before the fire!"

Frantically, she rubbed his arms to warm him but he was lost to her, fear glazing his eyes. "Thurston, what is it? Thurston...?"

The rising panic in her voice brought him back to the present and reality.

"Can tha 'old me?" he asked, his face white. She didn't understand.

"In thy arms…," he said "…'old me in thy arms."

Gladly Elspet flung her arms about him and held him tight. She stood on her tiptoes and as she did so his head came to nestle so naturally in the pretty hollow where her neck met her shoulder. His senses reeled from the feel of her. His breathing had become silent, subdued sobs which racked his frame and she held him ever tighter. He felt the soft mounds of her breast's pressing into his chest and he knew that though the feel of her was wondrous, he must withdraw from her embrace.

"It's alright….Ah'm alright now...Ah'm alright."

Although she could see that whatever had affected him was passing, she held on to his hand and glad he was that they were connected still.

"What is it?" she whispered "What troubles you so?"

He sat down on the blanket, momentarily exhausted by the experience and she knelt down beside him, grasping his hand again.

"Speak Thurston… tell me my dear!"

He looked into her eyes. I am her 'dear' he thought...she cares for me. Someone in the world cares for me. And then slowly he began to speak, to tell her the story of his early life. Of his cold Father, his mother, who though good to her son in her own way, had never seemed able to touch or put her arms about him. But these were the least important things, things not past bearing. Little by little, he told her the story of the cruel beatings which had marred his early life physically and, all his life since mentally.

He told for the first time in his life how he had suffered at the hands of his peers. In the beginning it had been young children beating a weaker child, then how as they grew into big strapping lads, they had beaten him still. He told her of the taunting, the whipping, the humiliation that had been an almost accepted part of his life and she quietly listened, sensing his feelings of shame as he told her of the last attack…the last beating that had almost become a murder, here in this place.

When he finished, he turned his back to her and pulled up his shirt. His back was criss-crossed like lattice work with deep thick red scars. Elspet's hand flew to her mouth as she felt the burning rise of vomit.

"They left me 'ere for dead. Mi Mother come to find me or Ah would be dead. Ah lay on me bed for weeks an' Ah didn't leave the little cottage for months after. That was the last time… it never 'appened again."

There were tears like smooth beads of glass in Elspet's eyes and as he turned back to look at her, he saw them spill over her lovely lashes and run down her cheeks.

"Who did this to thee Thurston?"

He shook his head. "Ah never knew, they always covered their 'eads wi' cloth's, even as children. Only one Ah ever saw, when Ah was set upon in this place. Ah reached up under 'is coverin' an' Ah scratched 'is face wi all mi strength. Ah must 'ave nearly ripped out 'is eye. 'e pulled off 'is cloth an' Ah saw 'is face covered in blood. They whipped me then till Ah passed out. But Ah will know 'im again, by God, Ah will know 'im again!"

She put her arms about him once more but he did not respond. Please God, he thought, let her not pity me, not her. She knelt before him and sat back on her heels.

"Cowards!" she spat. "All of them cowards! My brave, brave Thurston! You are a man a thousand times their worth!"

She held his face in her hands and kissed him softly on his cheek, his forehead and then his other cheek.

"Come…" she whispered, her fingers tracing the line of his jaw with the gentlest touch "… let us go home and get you warm."

She pulled at his hand and he held it as they walked. With the other, he felt the places where her lips had touched him, the moisture from her mouth still warm in the growing chill of the afternoon.

They were still hand in hand when they reached the Speakman's house. Nathaniel opened the door, his face filled with happiness and emotion.

"My dears" he exclaimed "Oh my dears! Come and see what the good Lord has done for us!"

Before the fire they saw the figure of a man, his back toward them.

"My son is returned to us Elspet, thy cousin Josiah!"

The man stood and turned to face them.

"How do you do cousin?" he said. Elspet turned as Thurston gasped loudly, grasping the lintels of the door to steady himself, his breathing ragged again as he looked after so many years into the hated face of his tormentor. He looked into Elspet's face and she knew, could see again that same fear in his eyes.

"Thurston, wait…" she cried. But he was gone, running and hopping down the road toward the crossroads.

"Thurston… Thurston!" she shouted again and again but he ran, on and on, without looking back.

Josiah Speakman sighed and turned to sit again by the fire, fingering the long scar at the corner of his left eye as he looked into the flames.

5.

Nathaniel sat holding his wife's hand. They sat in companionable silence as they often did in the evening, the fire burning in her room, the windows curtained against the cold. But there was a difference in the silence tonight, an almost tangible hanging of unsaid words in the air which both of them tried with much discomfort to ignore. The emotional force of the subject that threatened to suck the very air from the room in its struggle to be recognised, finally forced Nathaniel to speak.

"Tis good to see him after all this time, is it not my dear?"

She withdrew her hand from him and his face, as she looked into it, had that hurt little boy look which often melted her heart. Yet sometimes, as now, when the guilt and memories cut her too deep, it made her uncharacteristically angry. She spat her anger out in words to wound him.

"Why did you write to him? Why did you bring him back?"

Nathaniel could not hide his shock at the coldness with which she spoke and the words she had said.

"Why would tha not want to see him Eliza? Thou art his mother. Ah 'ad to tell him tha were so ill. He would never have forgiven me if anythin'…."

"It would be better for me not to see him!" she spoke the harsh words through gritted teeth, shaking with emotion.

"My Dear, please calm thi'self. What is it lass?"

Even as he spoke, Nathaniel realised that the time for hiding the truth between them was past, the time for talk was at last here and, painful though it was, he knew the matter that had twisted both their hearts for so long needed to be brought out into the open.

"Tha must talk to me, lass. Tha must tell me what has troubled thee all these years?"

Tears rolled slowly down her face as she struggled to finally give voice to the feelings that had been for so many years like an anchor, dragging unseen and unwanted along the sea bed of her life, down in the deep place where lurked all of her long-buried hurts. Slowly, falteringly, they came to the surface and she felt the first stirrings of a storm of emotion she had known must come. She feared it and the fear shook in her voice.

"It is easier.....it is easier to love him when he is not here!" She was weeping now.

"I cannot love him when he is here!" Her voice was a whisper.

Nathaniel shook his head, confused, unable to believe what he had heard. He spoke without thinking, he spoke from his heart in a way he had not done through all the years he had been silently aware of the emotional struggle between mother and son. His voice was louder than she had ever heard it raised and she knew the storm was rising in him too.

"Not love 'im? Not love our son? Ah don't understand...Ah don't understand lass..."

Then, slowly dragging to the surface all the resentment he had held in check for so long, he spoke the words that would unleash all his pent up feelings.

"...Ah never did understand."

He tried to be calm but all the love he felt for his son and all the heartache he had silently witnessed in the boy would not be suppressed. It was time to mend this if it was not too late. That was why he had sent for Josiah, he knew that now. He was calmer, quieter, knowing what he must say, over the fear at last.

"Ah don't want to 'urt thee lass. Ah would die first. But Ah beg thee do not spoil his homecoming for me."

Eliza opened her eyes and looked into his face as he continued:

"All 'is life Ah've loved that lad, and watched 'im suffer so as he begged for some show of love from thee. Ah lost 'im too young because tha could not give it. Ah beg thee lass, Ah beg thee mend things with 'im now! Do it for my sake if tha will but it should be for his. Much as Ah love thee Eliza, Ah must say…'tis time you did right by the lad."

For a moment, she thought his piece was spoken and Nathaniel began to weep as he looked at her, the pain in her face plain to see. But the words he had wanted to speak for so many years began to spill again from his mouth like a flow that would not be dammed.

"It was not 'is fault Eliza! It was not 'is fault our little lass died! He was but an infant 'imself, a little child who needed 'is Mother! Tha should'na blamed 'im…it was wrong of thee! An' worst of all…Ah should'na let thee!"

Nathaniel's sobs overcame him and he could no longer speak but as he looked at his wife's stricken face he could see that the pain he had carried for years like a sheathed knife, had at long last been uncovered and cut deep into her heart. She lay still, eyes closed and with a deathly pale face. Her breathing was so shallow as she struggled to contain the emotion churning in her chest that Nathaniel feared he had hastened her end and he clutched her hand to his lips sobbing again. After a moment when he again fell silent, she turned her head away from him. Her voice was but a cracked whisper as she began to speak.

"You are right Nathaniel. I did blame him. I knew it was wrong but I could not help it. It **was** my fault! I was nursing Josiah when she died… she died alone, she died alone!"

The final word became a long wail so pitiful, held in for so long, Nathaniel feared she would lose her mind. He lay on the bed and held her.

"Shush, shush lass, come now… 't is out, 't is out, there was no fault… shush now, shush."

He soothed her with his gentle voice and the deep love he had always shown her. At length her breathing slowed and as her sobs subsided, he gently dried the tears from her anguished face. They were exhausted and lay side by side for long moments not trusting themselves to speak unless the weeping began afresh. Eliza breathed deeply for a long time before she spoke again.

"It is easier to love him when he is not here… no Nathaniel…" she shook off his hand from her mouth "No, it is time to speak, please, I want to!"

He held her hand and presently, breathing deeply, she began again.

"When he is here he reminds me of the guilt I bear. Oh, not just the guilt of leaving Susannah to die alone but for leaving my little son to live alone and to grow up without the love he deserved to have. I didn't just leave my child in the grave that terrible day Nathaniel, I think I left my right mind there too. I told myself that if I did not love my boy the way I had loved her, I could never be so broken hearted again. For a long time there was some madness in me and I was wrong, so wrong. I have known it for many years. But surely Nathaniel, it is too late! How can I make amends to the boy now? So many years, so much hurt!"

Tears flowed once more.

"Sshssh, nay, come now lass. Tha knows better than most, there is always room in the human heart for forgiveness. He knows tha loves 'im, he just needs to hear thee tell 'im so an' even now things can be mended… even now."

He stroked her cheek, soothing away the fresh tears. She heard him breathe a long deep sigh as his lips rested on her temple and although she could not see his face, she sensed, through all the many years she had known and loved him that he meant to speak again. She knew too from years of being comforted and strengthened by his wise, compassionate reflections, that these would be important words.

His breath warmed her cheek as at last he found the words and spoke slowly and quietly…

"Tha'rt both of thee set on a path that may not see thee together again in this life, lass. This is the time, my love. This is the time."

She nodded, holding him tighter for long moments as the horror and fear and pain and regret ebbed away to the corners of the room until she could no longer feel them.

"I am ready," she said "Send him to me."

Josiah still sat in the chair by the fire, habitually fingering the scar. For the last hour, he and Elspet had sat in silence opposite each other, listening to the rise and fall of muffled voices above, both of them aware that the arrival of Josiah Speakman had created some discord within the household.

Josiah watched her as she sewed by candle and firelight. He thought her very pretty, her face reminding him of someone he had known long ago but he could not place who it was. He took in all her womanly charms, the soft curve of her cheek and the stubborn little point of her chin. Long dark lashes curling onto soft white translucent skin as with downcast eyes she stitched the minutes away. He lingered only lightly on the black hair, swung over one shoulder, its lustrous sheen reflecting the firelight as her small, high bosom rose and fell with her breathing.

'Steady lad!' he said to himself as he put his thoughts swiftly away.

She had stirred in him a momentary longing for the feel of a soft, lovely woman. For too long he had taken comfort with the harsh women who lived on the fringes of the life of a Soldier at arms.

At last he broke the silence.

"You remind me of my Mother, always endless sewing. Making this..." pointing at the rug "... always making and mending. What are you sewing?"

She looked up "You do not talk like your Father and Th.....the others in the village."

He smiled "No. I have been away for some years. Dialect must be quickly lost when giving orders."

"You lead men?" she asked in a sharp voice.

He was shocked at the incredulity in her voice. Did she dislike him so? He nodded in answer to her question.

"I am making a pair of breeches...," she said. Her conversation was diverse indeed he thought. Did she ever pursue one subject? "....for Thurston Hey," she ended.

Elspet watched as he digested the name.

"Aye Thurston Hey, you recognised him earlier did you not?"

She was surprised at his reaction, expecting not to see the reddening flush of shame spread across his cheeks. He was silent for what seemed long moments, and part of her enjoyed the visible squirming signs of the turmoil within him that her words had created.

"I did," he said at length. "It was good to see him looking so well."

"Indeed," she spat, knowing without doubt now by his reaction that his was the face that Thurston had seen on that day.

"He must have looked much better than when you saw him last!"

Then at the sound of Nathaniel's footsteps on the stairs she whispered, with palpable contempt:

"Brave soldier...fight ye not in my name!"

He stood up sharply to leave, to remove himself from her despising eyes but Nathaniel came into the room.

"Go and see thi mother, lad. She wants to talk to thee."

Nathaniel patted his son on the shoulder. Josiah turned to look at Elspet, the silent plea on his face was clear: "Please do not tell my Father."

****

Nathaniel sat staring into the fire. He looked older tonight, Elspet thought. It was clear he had been weeping. Elspet already had great affection for her Uncle, having spoken and laughed with him more in the last month than she had in her whole nineteen years with her own Father. She reached across and laid her hand over his and in turn he covered her's with his own, smiling with watery eyes. At length he spoke as she knew he would. He took a deep breath and sighed before he began.

"When our little girl died Elspet, somethin' died in Eliza too. My poor lad, all 'e ever wanted was her love. 'e 'as spent all 'is life up to now thinkin' 'e did not 'ave it. Because of that lass, 'e was lost to us too soon d'y'see?" Elspet nodded, silently. "Goin' off to war, that damned war! Pardon me lass. 'e were sixteen...sixteen! Fightin' all these terrible years for our King, even tho' they've took 'is 'ead off. Our Josiah's still fightin'!."..only, Ah don't think 'is fightin' ever 'ad anything' to do with the war. D'y'see lass?"

Elspet, wise beyond her years did see... she did. She patted her uncle's hand and they continued to sit in companionable silence, as he had for years of evenings with his dear Eliza. Nathaniel forgave his wife... would forgive her anything because he loved her so. If there was one he could not forgive it was God, though he would never speak it aloud or even admit it to himself. He would make his peace with his maker one day but not yet. He looked over to Elspet, so young, so innocent yet so much older than her years in many ways. If God had allowed his little Susannah to grow on Earth he would have liked to see her like Elspet. He hoped with all his heart that her life would be long and happy and that nothing would spoil her sweetness.

"Th'art a good lass Elspet," he said "Ah do not know what Ah would've done without thee these last weeks."

They both looked up as Josiah came down the stairs and passed the open door, silently walking through to the scullery.

"Stay by the fire and rest Uncle," she said "I will go to him."

Nathaniel lay his head back gratefully, exhausted by the emotion of the day and let her go.

At the back of the house was a kitchen garden which Eliza told her smelled wondrous in the summer when the sweet smelling herbs grew. Josiah stood just outside the open door, his back to Eliza, his broad shoulders hunched, his dark head bent. She sensed the sadness emanating from him and for a moment hesitated, wondering whether she should leave him to his sadness, sometimes it was best. Slowly his head turned towards her and she saw him really for the first time. The fine profile of his face, the strong chin, straight nose, the dark shading of a growing beard around his gaunt cheeks and as he looked at her, his almost black eyes.

53

"Don't go," he said, catching her just at the point when her body moved before her mind had finished the thought, turning to leave.

"Please," he said "… talking is not a thing I do much but I think it would help me now….please, stay a moment."

She walked towards him, choosing her words.

"Your mother tells me this garden smells beautiful in the summer. I suppose you remember that in your childhood?"

He nodded vigorously "One of the few happy memories I have of being a child. Were you happy as a child cousin?" he asked.

His voice trembled with emotion. The kindness and sweetness that were such a part of Elspet's character compelled her to relent and comfort Josiah. She must put for these few moments her feelings about Thurston away and help this man who stood before her. She could no more hurt him when he was so clearly in pain than she could give up breathing. She moved closer and answered his question.

"I think it was," she said. "There was never any time to be unhappy. With six brothers and sisters and a farm to run, my Mother had no time. We all got our love and affection from each other..."

Before she even finished the sentence, Elspet realised she had broken Nathaniel's confidence in speaking of love and affection and Josiah saw her discomfort.

"Do not worry," he said. "I think my Mother and I have spoken properly for the first time in my life tonight. If I died tomorrow I would die with a lighter heart and so I think would she."

Elspet sighed and opened her mouth to speak but there were no words to be said. Even though she could chatter like a bird, she knew when to be silent. Silence hung between them for a few moments until Josiah took a deep breath and broke it.

"Thurston Hey," he said.

Silence still. Elspet did not trust herself to speak. Wait…she told herself, as she watched him choose his words before speaking. When he was ready, he continued.

"I torture myself every day for the part I played in his suffering. It is another thing I would like to set aright before I die Elspet."

She struggled to find the words to reply, feelings of revulsion and anger surging within her again. She hurt so for what had happened to Thurston, for the damage done to his body and mind and to the man himself for whom her affection she knew was growing daily.

"Why do you talk of dying so much?" she asked at length, diffusing her feelings.

Josiah laughed, strong white teeth flashing in the darkness.

"I am a soldier Elspet!"

She smiled back "Of course, it must be indeed a constant hazard....and fear."

He looked at her, waiting for her words.

"Thurston is in fear of you," she said. "He must conquer that fear before he can go on with his life."

Josiah looked at her for just long enough to make her cast down her eyes. He lifted her chin with the crook of his finger.

"Little Elspet, you are wise. You are fond of him, Thurston Hey?"

She nodded, blushing pushing his hand away. "He is a good man," she said.

"He is a lucky one," Josiah smiled. "I leave again for my company tomorrow so I have no opportunity to set things right. But, I hope, I will come back again and I will do right by him, I promise you little cousin."

Elspet's eyes filled with tears and for a moment she struggled to speak.

Nodding, struggling to keep her quivering chin firm, she replied.

"Then I will tell him. I will tell him of your regret for the part you played in that terrible day. I will tell him that you owe him a great debt and of your promise to pay it. I thank you for your words, Cousin Josiah...I know your own heart is full."

She touched his hand "I must go now and settle your Mother."

He bowed slightly to her and then she left him there in the garden, knowing that tears of regret for many things would come when he was alone.

Eliza was asleep and Elspet covered her up to her chin and made safe the fire. Before leaving the room she looked out onto the cold December night. The moon sat low in the dark winter sky, a misty halo around it casting an eerie glow on the churchyard. The black crooked fingers of the leafless trees silhouetted against the white disc of the moon made her shiver with an inexplicable feeling of dread. As she pulled her shawl tightly about her, she prayed as she often did that God would remove all fear and suffering from the world but more than that she prayed that he would heal the heart of just one person. She wished herself for a chance to heal it. Closing the curtains again, Elspet hoped Thurston was warm in the little cottage. Her final wish was one she wished with all her heart... that she could go and let on his doorstep tonight and bring him the comfort she knew she could give him.

6.

Josiah and his Father left the house before dawn and walked down to the Smithy at the crossroads where Nathaniel had secured a horse for his son. It was bitterly cold and Josiah had a long ride ahead but at least his journey would be swift with the roads hardened by frost and in the darkness he could move through the country lanes unseen.

"Why dost tha 'av to go lad? Stop 'ere with us weer tha's safe. The war is over...why can it not be over for thee?"

Josiah sighed. "Father, please understand. My companions await me, my cause depends on me! The war will not be over until we have a King on the throne again and justice is done! I will fight for that if it takes all my life."

"Aye..." Nathaniel could not help himself "...all tha life might be just a few weeks or a few days! Fightin' for the royal cause is more dangerous than before lad. People do not give up power easily. Per'aps best to bide thi time, stay...live 'ere amongst us...if only for a short while."

Impatience gnawed at Josiah, though he held it in check, unwilling to marr their parting with harsh words. Did his Father think he would not like to live warm and comfortable and sleep safe in his bed?

"Father you cannot expect me to turn coat? To live my life bowing to the will of the parliamentarian's after years of risking my life and watching good men die? I cannot desert them and make their sacrifice wasted!"

Josiah at that moment grasped his Father's arm as he lost his footing on the ice. The incident diffused their emotions and Josiah spoke again, calmer now.

"Do not worry Father. There will be no real fighting for a while yet. A few skirmishes perhaps but nothing to trouble me."

"Men do not die in skirmishes then?" asked Nathaniel.

Josiah laughed "Not this one Father. I have soldiered for many years…I must be good at it. I am still here!"

They both laughed despite the gravity of the conversation. Their breath fogged in the cold night air as they walked, the heaviness of their coming parting settling heavier on their shoulders at every step. Nathaniel broke the silence.

"Ah'm proud of thee son. Proud of the way tha 'as stuck to thy task, though Ah would give anythin' to 'ave thee at 'ome."

Josiah thought quietly for a moment before speaking.

"I Thank you Father…it was all I ever wanted, to make you proud and be a dutiful son."

For a second they both remembered in silence the epitaph on the stone in the Churchyard and the cruel taking of a young life that had so altered the lives of those around her. In a flash of realisation he remembered where he had seen Elspet's features before. He had seen them in the face of his older sister and that of his Mother as a young woman… before life robbed her of her happiness. Features locked in a corner of his memory since he was a little child, before his life too changed forever. He gave voice to his memories without meaning to.

"I remember Mother holding me now. I remember the smell of her and the softness of her lips on my cheek. I had forgotten for so long…now I remember."

Nathaniel sighed "Ee lad, Ah 'ope tha can forgive 'er. She's a good woman and she loves thee well."

Josiah nodded, unable to respond for a moment.

"All is well between us Father, all is well. I am so glad I came home and God willing, I will come home again."

They had reached the crossroads. The lantern was burning in the Smithy window and Tom the Blacksmith was already leading the horse toward them. Nathaniel took a folded paper from his pocket.

"She wrote this for thee lad. Ah know not what it says. She said it will be a comfort for thee."

Josiah took the paper and kissed it before putting it away safely in his dark clothing.

"Give my love to her.... and to Elspet, she is a sweet girl."

Before climbing on to the horse he turned back "Father, will you do something for me?"

"Aye, lad... what is it?"

"Thurston Hey... I owe him a great debt. It is a thing from our boyhood, and I pray you... never tell him. But I ask you to watch over him for me until I can repay him as I should. Please Father, promise me this."

Nathaniel, though puzzled, agreed.

"Aye lad Ah will, an' Ah will be silent...worry not."

Impulsively Josiah threw his arms about his Father.

"I shall see thee again, I shall see thee again!"

Then he was mounted and away. Nathaniel watched his dark clothed figure speeding onward in the bright moonlight until he was swallowed up by the darkness of the night and the horrors of what his father could only imagine he was going back to.

7

Elspet rose earlier than usual the following morning, entering her Aunt's bedroom as soon as she heard Nathaniel leave for his work. Thurston was always on site before anyone else...if he wasn't there, she didn't know how she would get through the day for worrying. She opened the curtains just a little, not wanting to disturb her Aunt who still snored softly.

She watched Nathaniel walking across the Green to an empty Churchyard and her heart began to sink. Then suddenly his dark head appeared from behind the building, he was walking toward Nathaniel, respectfully tugging his cap. Relief washed over her! He was alright. He had carried on with his day despite the shock he had suffered. How brave he was! Her heart swelled in that strange way it always did when she saw him. She could hardly wait till dinnertime when she could take him his food and spend a few precious minutes in his company.

The time dragged so as Aunt Eliza slept the morning away, and Elspet had the dinners packed and ready long before it was time to take the food. She had to fight with her feet to stop them running to the building site.

As soon as she saw him, she knew he was well. She sat with him for a while as he ate and he smiled at her, thanking her for the bread and cheese. He asked as he always did about Eliza, about her morning. They talked of the weather, would it snow did she think? She suddenly realised what that would mean, work would stop...she would not see him!

The night before, lying in her bed, worrying about his peace of mind had been hard...she had been so desperate to know he wasn't suffering. She knew she must break his silence on the subject:

"Josiah...he is gone...," she said.

He looked embarrassed.

"Aye, Ah know...Master Speakman told me. Ah said Ah was sorry for runnin' away...but 'e seemed not to notice. 'e just asked me not to tell a soul 'e 'ad bin 'ere....'e said it would be bad for 'im...And so Ah shall not...just for Master Speakman's sake."

Elspet nodded, choosing her words carefully.

"Well I'm sure my Uncle will be most obliged to you Thurston...but how do you feel...seeing him?"

He shrugged his shoulders, his face blank.

"Ah don't know...Ah can't believe Ah'm sayin' that but...'t is true...Ah think Ah shall let it lie awhile."

He looked into her eyes, lost for a moment in their beautiful green.

"There are better things to think on..." he murmured quietly. "Ah would rather think of the days to come than days long past."

There was that look again, that locking of souls, just for a split second. She felt herself flushing as she took the empty cup from his hand and as he uncurled his fingers from the handle, he stroked her palm.

"Shall Ah see thee if it snows?" he asked.

She nodded. "We must make a plan...if it snows on the morrow come to the house if you can get through. We shall see each other one way or another."

Her eyes never left his face as she slid the cup away, her fingers gently tracing the back of his hand to his fingertips. She left him there, feeling a new courage in him. She had worried that looking his enemy in the face would have pulled him down but instead she sensed that he was stronger...bolder.

As she walked back to the house, she thought strangely of her own childhood fears, remembering so clearly lying as a child in the darkness, seeing figures and faces in the clothes hanging on the back of the door. In the morning she had seen them for what they were and the fear was gone. The trouble was, when the darkness returned again so did the same stomach-churning fear. She hoped it would not be so for Thurston...she wanted happiness for him now.

The snow indeed began to fall over the next few days and Thurston made his way every day to the Speakman's house. Nathaniel was happy to welcome the lad, sensing that the young people each needed company and ever mindful of his promise to Josiah. Every day, he ate dinner before setting off home to the little cottage. They talked while they ate together, she telling him stories of her life on their farm growing up, he teasing her and making her laugh. She sensed that his playfulness covered a life-long loneliness which he was not yet ready to speak of. He never mentioned Josiah again but Elspet knew, by things he said and by dark circles that sometimes showed under his eyes, that his nights were plagued by hanging shadows of the past.

7. The Turn of the Year

Christmas came and despite the trials the family were living through, it was a merry time. There had been no news from the expected battle in the North so Josiah was assumed safe. Eliza seemed brighter since his visit and was lifted down to spend a few mornings on the settle before the fire, much to Nathaniel's delight. Thurston had quickly shaken off the spectres of his past life, wearing an air of jollity and happiness that seemed to warm him like a new coat and, in the early hours of 1651 Elspet and Thurston shared their first kiss.

He had stayed on the eve of the New Year, having had too much beer to safely walk home to the little cottage after the heavy snowfall that day. Elspet made him a bed of blankets on the rug before the fire and once Eliza and Nathaniel were asleep, she sneaked downstairs to take him an extra blanket and put another log on the fire. He touched her fingertips as her hand moved inches above his head and the touch sent a lightning flash through them both and it happened before they knew it. She knelt swiftly, smoothing his naked shoulder and placed her lips on his. She thought kisses were swift and fleeting things, but not this! This went on, from the first touch of their lips to a sweet lingering tasting of each other...like eating ripe, summer strawberries, Elspet thought idly as her senses reeled from the thrill of it. Eventually, he held her face in his hands and gently lifted her lips away. She was sure of the longing she had awakened and the love in his eyes. "Good night sweet Thurston" she whispered, and then left the room. He could hear her footsteps far away above and could imagine her preparing for bed. How he longed to follow her up the stairs! His Mother had often talked about the stairway to heaven, but he doubted she had ever meant this! He lay, warm in his longing and thought: "I love Elspet Sydall...I love Elspet Sydall...I love Elspet Sydall!"

****

Eliza took a turn for the worse as the hard snows of December began to recede. Nathaniel, some weeks before, had asked a carpenter from the town of Leighton Fold three miles along the road to Manchester, to make a bed small enough to fit beneath the window in the downstairs room. He had asked the man to keep it until such time as it was needed. On the morning of the fourth of January he sent word to arrange for its delivery.

By four o-clock that afternoon, Eliza was settled downstairs and though all three of them knew that she would never sleep within the walls of her bedchamber again, no word on the subject was spoken. To the people of the village however it was an occasion for much sadness, being an accepted fact that for someone to have their bed brought downstairs was an indication that their life thereafter would be short.

"'ast 'eard? They've brought t'bed down for Mistress Speakman."

Sad faces at the news for Eliza was much respected in the small community.

"Poor lady, I 'ope she will not suffer...poor Nathaniel too."

During the course of the afternoon, small gifts and tokens began to arrive at the Speakman's house. Lavender, tied and hung in the summer, dried and sweet-smelling now, an antidote to the smells of sickness. Herbs were brought to infuse and make soothing, pain relieving drinks and from the poorer of their neighbours, offers of help to cook for or sit with the invalid. So many callers had been in the afternoon that when yet another knock was heard at the door as the daylight began to fade, Nathaniel urged Elspet not to answer it.

"I must Uncle" she remonstrated. "They know we are in, it would be unkind!" With a teasing smile, he waved his hand.

"Go on then...if tha must," he said.

The face at the door was one Elspet had not seen before. He had an air of importance about him and Elspet saw that he had come on a fine -looking horse now tied to the iron railings that encircled the Speakman's small cobbled front entrance.

"I have a message for Master Speakman," said the man.

Nathaniel had heard the man's deep voice and came into the hall.

"Come you in Sir out of the cold" invited Nathaniel.

"Nay, I thank you Sir, I am damp from the ride. I only bring thee this." He handed Nathaniel a letter.

"Sir William asks only that you send a reply back with me tonight Sir."

Nathaniel took the letter and read it. After some moments he looked up

"Please tell Sir William that I am happy to accept the invitation. However my dear wife is very ill. Would Sir William mind, think you, if I brought my neice 'ere with me?"

Elspet looked surprised

"What about Aunt?" she asked. Nathaniel patted her arm "Worry not," he said.

The man looked at them both before he spoke again.

"I know my master would be pleased to receive thy neice Sir, indeed he knows of your wife's illness and bade me give you his best wishes for her present comfort."

Nathaniel thanked the man. "Then please tell your master we shall look forward to his hospitality."

"I shall Sir...the carriage will be sent for you tomorrow at seven of the clock...if that is agreeable to you Sir?"

"Well, that is most kind...please give Sir William my thanks."

With that the man mounted his horse and the door was closed on the darkening night.

"Well, little Mistress," said Nathaniel "... we are to dine at Abbot's hall tomorrow. What think you of that eh?"

Elspet was excited at the prospect of accompanying her Uncle on his visit to Abbots Hall, and to think Thurston had joked with her about that very prospect! As she turned to smile at her Uncle, she was aware of the look of regret in his eyes. Once again Elspet's compassion compelled her to speak.

"It should be Aunt Eliza who goes with you. I know this is a special occasion for you. I will do my best Uncle to be a dutiful niece you can be proud of."

Nathaniel picked up her hand and kissed it.

"Th'art a dutiful niece always lass, an' I shall be very proud to 'ave thee with me."

Glancing through the door he could see the foot of the little bed in which his wife lay in their front room.

"Why doesn't tha go next door an' see if Mistress Thomas will sit with Eliza tomorrow for an hour or two at six o the clock. Then tha must 'ave a bit o' time to thyself lass. I shall sit wi' 'er."

Elspet sensed that her Uncle wanted to be alone with his wife. He seemed to need it more and more, only requiring Elspet to sit with her while he worked or rested or to perform those tasks for her that it would not be seemly for a husband to do. She didn't mind, she understood and it was in her nature to contribute to other's happiness in any way she could. But since Christmas, she had begun to feel a sense of loneliness creeping up on her, longing a little for her home, family, and friends of her own age with whom she had grown up. The only person she had come to know was Thurston and of course Josiah, who Nathaniel and Eliza rarely mentioned but who she could tell was on their mind most of the time.

Dining at Abbots Hall was certainly something to look forward to. Thurston would laugh on the other side of his face when he found his joke about her being entertained there had come true! How she longed to tell him. She had not seen him since New Year's Day and then he had seemed quiet. Elspet had expected some change after the kiss but not that.

Impulsively she popped her head round the door. Nathaniel sat holding Eliza's hand even though she was sleeping.

"Uncle…" she whispered "…when I have seen Mistress Thomas, would it be alright if I nipped to see Thurston, just for a bit?"

Nathaniel looked out of the window, and thought for only seconds.

"Nay, lass... 't is too dark and too far to go alone. How would I face thi Father if anythin' 'appened to thee?"

Elspet opened her mouth to plead but stopped herself, knowing it would be to no avail, and being unwilling to press her Uncle. As she turned to close the door she heard Aunt Eliza's quiet voice.

"Elspet."

"Lass... Ah thought tha were asleep," said Nathaniel.

"Just restin' me eyes," Eliza said. "I heard all. Elspet, dear, why don't you ask Mistress Thomas if you can see what she keeps in her upstairs room? She's a seamstress, may'ap there'll be summat nice for thee to wear tomorrow. We can treat her can we not Nathaniel? She's earned it, lass 'as."

"Aye," said her Uncle "she 'as that. Go on with'ee lass. If tha'rt goin t'take the place o' this lady, thas'll 'ave to look beautiful indeed!"

***

The next morning after breakfast had been eaten and her duties done, Elspet danced round and round her tiny bedroom holding the pretty green fabric to her body. She could not remember the last time she had had new clothes.

"Elspet"...her uncle called from downstairs "...tha's getten a visitor!"

She lay the gown down carefully on her bed and left the room. Descending the stairs, she saw no-one at first.

"Ah caught 'im skulkin'outside," said Nathaniel.

"Thurston, I am happy to see thee."

His head had hung sheepishly but at the sound of her voice and the pleasure in it, he looked up. He saw the way her eyes sparkled at the sight of him and she saw, without doubt, the love he had for her shining in his. He opened his mouth to speak but struggled to get out his words.

"Ah just ...wanted to pay my respects to Mistress Speakman... well not just ... Ah wanted to see thee an'all. Ah mean ...not to see thee but, well aye, but..."

Nathaniel rescued him. "Eliza's sleepin' lad. I'll let 'er know tha called. Why doesn't tha make Thurston 'ere summat warm Elspet...'e looks frozen t'lad does."

Elspet led Thurston through to the kitchen.

"Sit down here by the fire. Will ye have some stew Thurston? It is early in the day I know but it'll warm thee up."

He nodded hungrily and sat down on the only chair, an old rocker, and took in his surroundings. The kitchen was almost as big as the Speakmans' front room, and as warmly welcoming. A huge brick fireplace dominated it in which burned a blazing fire. The stew hung on a hook a foot above the flames and Elspet ladled out a bowlful for him, tearing a chunk of bread from the crock on the large wooden table.

"Lovely," he said, smelling the bread but looking at her.

Elspet sat down by the hearth on a tiny stool she kept there for stirring the food and stoking the fire.

"This is where I have spent most of the last two days now Aunt Eliza's downstairs. My Uncle seems to want to be alone with her. I understand but...well, 'tis nice to have someone to talk to today."

Thurston ate slowly, saying nothing and she watched him while he ate. At length, struggling to eat, he lowered the spoon and stopped chewing.

"Eat up," she said brightly. "There's plenty more."

"Elspet." He held up his hand as she rose to fetch his bowl. Suddenly she knew what he was going to speak of and she sat down, remaining silent, knowing his heart would be beating so fast it was almost leaving his chest. She knew, because hers was too.

"T'other night," he said. She was silent still. "Ah...Ah know tha did not mean to do...well...what tha did. Ah just wanted to say ...it's alright. Ah just 'ope tha still will want to be mi friend. Ah'll allus want to be thi friend Elspet."

She chose her words carefully, so aware of his fragile heart.

"Not always Thurston… I do not hope to always be thy friend…"

"Elspet… Elspet"! Nathaniel called suddenly from the other room. "Can tha come?"

Thurston's face was a mask of despair though he was trying so hard to hide it. It was what she loved about him so much! He had no artful ways, just a heart of pure gold. She grabbed his hand as she walked by his chair.

"Thurston Hey you are the sweetest man! What I mean is, I will always want to be your friend…but in time I hope, much, much more than that!"

She placed a gentle kiss on his forehead and left to go to her Uncle's aid.

Thurston took up the spoon again but found he could not touch the food. Had she said what he thought she had said? Could it be true? Could he have the unimaginable happiness that surely would come with the love of a woman like Elspet? It was a dream, an impossible dream. Thurston was unsure what to do. For the last three days he had stayed away, worried that he had overreached himself, convinced she would dread seeing him after the kiss, certain that she must have had too much wine and made a terrible mistake. He had busied himself in the little cottage, cleaning and repairing it, inspired by the comforting home of the Speakmans. He had spent his evenings as he always had, in solitude, within the safety of its walls, warm and well fed thanks to the generosity of Nathaniel's wages. But since that kiss…since that first inter-twining of his being with hers, he was without that inner warmth that he used to feel when he settled down before his fire in the evening. That feeling had left the little cottage for ever and taken up residence wherever Elspet was. She was his hearth and home, his comfort and security, she was everything he would ever need in this life to bring him happiness. That was why he had come today. That was why he had risked all the dreams because he had to know if there was any chance of them becoming reality, and now his prayers had been answered.

He could hear the sounds from the room in which Eliza lay, could hear Elspet's sweet and gentle voice as she comforted the sick woman and Nathaniel's low murmuring as he gently lifted the body of his ailing wife this way and that. This was no place for him at this moment. He stood and scraped his remaining stew into the pot, she would be upset if she knew he had left it. There were some cheery, evergreen berried boughs in water on the window-sill. Thurston took two of them and pulling a hanging thread from his shirt, he tied them together. He placed the red and green posy by his empty bowl and left by the back door.

He didn't notice the cold on his way home. He could feel the years of hiding, fear and inability to believe he was worth loving, dropping away at every step. His heart soared with the tingling realisation that the source of all his happiness could in time be his. He resolved that he would return the next day to declare his love for her, beginning to believe at last that the irresistible future he had hardly dared dream of was now within his reach!

8.

Later that day as evening fell miles away, Josiah sat by a campfire as the wintry darkness began to close around him like a heavy cloak. He hated this time of year. The cold seemed to bite into his bones and for the first time since he had left his home so many winter's ago, he realised that the life he had lived this last eight years had aged him well before his time. Since he had visited his home and set things alright with his mother in the best way he could, he had begun to question in these, his quiet moments, why he had lived the life he had. He knew deep down in his soul that he had been running from a pain that was so hard to bear that the constant witness and threat of death had been preferable to the twisting, gut-piercing knife of the lack of maternal love which had marred his youth. He knew also now that when this job was finally done, he would return home, and please God if she were still alive, bring some peace to both their lives.

He carried the letter she had written always close to his heart and he touched it now, feeling as he always did, a rush of love and regret. If only those words had been spoken to him as he grew into a man, how different his life might have been. But there was nothing to be gained by these thoughts. She had put her love into words at last and his life was the better for it in so many ways. He hoped her heart was lighter too.

This was his favourite time of day, these evenings with his companions at arms and their easy company. This time and in the morning before the mist cleared and the day still held some promise. Everything else that lay between in this nomadic lifestyle of marching, camping and fighting in meaningless skirmishes, he had long since ceased to see the reason for. Nonetheless he was committed. Committed to restoring the murdered King's son to his rightful duty and of serving his own leaders, those men who had recognised his qualities and who had given him the self-esteem that had so eluded him in his early life.

The horrors of war had shocked and numbed him at first. He had been only sixteen when he had fought his first battle and the young friend he had made in the days leading up to the bloody encounter, had been killed by his side. The sight of the lad's spurting blood and his gurgling cries had made Josiah want to run. But he had stayed by his comrade's side and performed for the first time, the duties to the dying that he had performed whenever he could ever since. It was then that he had realised that he was a good man and from that moment his confidence had begun to grow. It grew from the foul, churning slime of guilt in which he remembered the wrongs done in search of acceptance by his peers. On that day he had ceased to be a follower and the seeds had been sown that would see him grow to be a leader of men.

Ever since those early awakenings of his true self, he had been atoning for the part he had played in the torturing of that helpless young man in his youth and the high esteem he was held in now by his men was testament to the qualities he had discovered within himself these last years. He prayed that he would have the opportunity to set right the wrong he had done to Thurston Hey in his lifetime.

He thought often of little Elspet, his barely known cousin. What a sweet breath of air she was in a dark and ugly life. He prayed and suspected that she would be a salve to the wounds cruelly inflicted on Thurston Hey. He hoped he would live to see them bound together by love.

He was lost in his reverie, a feeling of being a tossed and wingless bird on a dark and angry sea washed over him at times like these. His fate was in the hands of others...and God, wherever he was.

"Josiah! I have been calling you these five minutes past!"

Josiah stood quickly. "Forgive me Sir, I was lost in thought."

Colonel John Stafford laughed and clapped his favourite officer on the shoulder.

"Always thinking eh? Well, lad here's a thought for thee."

Josiah was alert, knowing what was coming.

"We march at dawn with a new King! Ready the men!" Stafford shook his hand, and with the other, clasped Josiah's shoulder.

"May fortune bless us all, Speakman."

Josiah nodded "Aye Sir. Indeed Sir."

His evening was at an end. The next, perhaps the last chapter of his life, would begin on the morrow. He turned from the fire and drew in a deep breath of cold air before shouting his orders to his men.

9.

Eliza was quiet and dozing when Nathaniel and Elspet left her in the care of Mistress Thomas and climbed into the carriage Sir William Bagshawe had sent for them. Elspet was excited for so many reasons. She was wearing and feeling wonderful in the first new gown she had had in years and she had sat before the old, tarnished tiny mirror in her room and put up her dark hair in the manner of the great ladies whose portraits she had seen, winding little wispy tendrils of hair round and round her finger into spiralling curls that framed her pretty face. The green fabric and delicate white lace collar set off her glowing skin and beautiful eyes and she was most pleased with her reflection.

She pictured what Abbots Hall would be like and had been practising her curtsey all afternoon. She vowed she would try not to be her usual chatty self and would remain quiet and sophisticated like well brought up young women must be.

The thought that excited her most, however and which warmed her despite the cold of the winter evening, was the little evergreen posy she had found on the table that afternoon. She knew what he meant by it and at last Thurston would know what he meant to her. Elspet could not wait to see him again now that things were clear between them.

As the carriage bumped along the rutted road through the slush, she closed her eyes and remembered again the feeling of that kiss, savouring the sweet promise of more kisses to come.

The beautiful mellow stone facade of Abbots Hall was lit by glowing lanterns and the old house looked magical in the pale reflected light of a white moon. Remnants of glittering snow garlanded its arched windows and the branches of the ancient yews which flanked the path to the front entrance. The big double doors opened as the carriage drew up and a flood of warm yellow light poured out on to the path to welcome them. Elspet, for some reason, felt suddenly afraid and grabbed Nathaniel's arm as he climbed out of the carriage to stand beside her. He patted her hand.

"Worry not, lass, worry not," he said, and then he calmly and carefully led her down the path toward the open door. The same man who had come to their house greeted them as they entered, taking their cloaks and Nathaniel's fine felt hat.

The wide hallway was covered from floor to ceiling in dark wood, and the smell of centuries of beeswax mingled with an aroma drifting from rooms away, of roasting beef. The man led them through a door to their left and they came into a large room lit by many candle sconces and a bright fire. The flickering light cast shadows on walls covered by old, heavy tapestries revealing tantalising shapes and obscure images of Biblical characters. Elspet looked at the windows which were the full height of the room. How she would have loved to see them with the light pouring through but they were heavily curtained against the cold night. The dimness of the room felt oppressive and even with the bright flames, thick tapestries and covered windows, Elspet shivered.

"My dear Master Speakman, Good Evening to you Sir."

Sir William Bagshawe walked toward them, hand outstretched.

"It is a murderous cold night. I hope your wife is keeping fair?"

Nathaniel grasped the proffered hand.

"'t is cold indeed Sir but welcoming within these wall's. Ah thank thee Sir, my wife is comfortable but we will not overstay our welcome ...we will need to get back to her before too long."

***

Sir William was all affability and understanding. Nathaniel turned to Elspet.

75

"Sir William, may Ah present to thee my niece, Miss Elspet Sydall from Derbyshire."

Sir William took her hand, and she noticed his was cold.

"Welcome, my dear young lady," he said.

Something in Sir William's manner unnerved her and she thought fleetingly that he must be a stern master. Elspet executed her well-practised curtsey, looking up into his white whiskered face as she rose, aiming to catch a glimpse of his eyes before he turned away. Eyes to Elspet were indeed the windows of the soul. She believed one could see much more within them than could be learned in any conversation but Elspet was too late, her host turned away as she completed her curtsey.

"May I present my son, Edwin, to you."

A tall young man with a head of long, pale straw-coloured hair stepped forward from the shadowy corners of the room. He took her hand and placed dry lips fleetingly on to the back of it.

"Hah...Court manners!" Sir William scoffed.

Elspet looked into Edwin's eyes as he raised them to look into her face and she saw two frozen pools of pale blue ice.

Dinner was eaten with only the most formal conversation taking place across the table. Sir William was complimentary about Nathaniel's work on the repairs to the Church but was clearly impatient to see its completion. Nathaniel fell into a long and apologetic explanation about the weather, his wife's illness, his shortage of men but Sir William cut him short. "Come, come Speakman, finish your dinner. All these things will be better discussed on a full stomach eh?"

Elspet could see the worry lines on Uncle Nathaniel's face beneath the strong light of the silver candelabra on the table. What a time he was having and such a good kind hearted soul he was. Why did God see such men as Sir William Bagshawe raised up and such men as her dear Uncle and her dear Thurston obliged to them?

Life and all its trials were very much a mystery to her still, covered as they were by the veil of her youth and inexperience and the innocent sweetness of the nature she had been blessed with. Yet for all her innocence she knew as her Uncle did not, that he was dealing with a dangerous man. For all her Uncle's looks at her and his silent pleadings to her across the table not to worry, for all his agreement with Sir William that business was not a subject for ladies to bother their heads with…she could see a side to this man that he could not. As Sir William washed down his beef with goblet after goblet of wine, the conversation turned to a subject which clearly discomforted Nathaniel even more than the suggestions that the speed of his building programme was less than satisfactory.

His eyes, which Elspet had by now had time to judge, twinkled slyly as Sir William spoke:

"What think you of this business of the King's son returning to our Northern shores eh Speakman? Shall we have a King again think you? Shall we have another war?"

Nathaniel put down his fine, crystal wineglass, his hand shaking.

"I hope we will not Sir. The war caused so much suffering and strife among our people."

"Of course!" agreed Sir William loudly "Are not we all men of peace? Yet there are some who would make a King again. Some men are bent on war, I say."

Elspet shivered at the ominous silence which followed his remark. Sir William spoke again.

"What news of your son, Master Speakman? I hear tell he too is in the north. Working is he?"

The tension in Nathaniel's voice was tangible.

"Aye Sir, he is workin' in the North."

"Shall he see our 'King' think you?" Sir William's words hung in the air unanswered for a long moment and Elspet sensed the danger. The tension was broken by Sir William's hearty laughter at his own joke and they all joined in as befitted respectful guests,

"I do not think Master Speakman" Sir William continued "that we shall have another King in this land. So determined am I to repel this pretender and his supporters, I have bought my son a commission in the company of Colonel Stafford to ensure it!"

He laughed loudly again, taking another gulp of wine. For the first time during the evening, Edwin spoke. His voice was soft and strangely hesitant, with a tinge of fear fortified by wine.

"Forgive me Father, I think you refer to Colonel Milburne's Company. Colonel Stafford is a well-known Royalist Sir."

The look on Sir William's face confirmed all Elspet's fears. His face grew red as he vainly struggled to hide his anger at his son. His voice was steady and frighteningly quiet as he began to speak.

"You dare correct me Sir before company? You dare to correct your Lord Father?"

His voice rose steadily. "Colonel Milburne is fortunate indeed to have such a clever Officer in his ranks, is he not Miss Sydall? A young, stupid chit of a lad who thinks he knows better than his own Father!"

The room was deathly silent, the final shouted words hanging in the air. Edwin was pale and quiet though beneath Elspet could sense his seething rage and burning embarrassment. She saw his cheeks slowly begin to redden.

Sir William suddenly seemed to become aware of his outburst and the shocked faces of his guests. The speed at which his expression changed frightened Elspet and when her Uncle met her eyes she could see that he too was disturbed by the incident.

Sir William again was all affability.

"Come Master Speakman, we must discuss the business which you came to discuss, Sir. You will be wanting to return home soon I am sure." Then to Edwin:

"Boy, take Miss Sydall to the stables. Show her the fine mount your Father bought you to ride like a hero to our Protector's defence!"

Elspet, though she was certain she did not want to go, could think of no words to say nor any way that she could get out of the situation she found herself in. A look at Uncle Nathaniel's face told her that he thought it was a good way to expedite their early departure from what had proved to be a less than enjoyable visit. She had to agree that the sooner business was concluded and they could take their leave, the better.

Consequently, moments later, she found herself speedily cloaked and being led, almost dragged, by a still seething Edwin, so fast that her feet were slipping in the melting snow. His fine, almost white hair was blown back from his face by the biting chill wind and the speed at which he walked. Edwin's rage was palpable, and as they became more and more distanced from the house, she knew she did not want to be alone with him. She did not like the way he held her wrist a little too tightly and she sensed, as she often did in a way beyond her years, that she must diffuse his anger lest it was turned on her. She searched her mind for the right words.

"Sir William is a powerful man about here is he not?" It was not the best opening to conversation she had ever made.

"My Father is a black-hearted son of a whore!" he stopped momentarily and turned to her, tightening his grip on her wrist and repeating the words into her face.

"He is a black-hearted son of a whore!"

They continued to walk apace. Frightened by him now, Elspet wanted to return to the house. "Please do not feel obliged to show me this new mount Sir, if it does not suit. I am indeed no lover of horses."

He laughed mirthlessly. "Indeed I must Miss Sydall. My Father has asked me to show you my horse and as a dutiful son I will show you my horse!!"

The stables were large, clean, dry and warm though dimly lit. Edwin unhooked a lantern and held it up to shine on a beautifully groomed tall, black stallion.

"Well...here he is Miss Sydall, my handsome mount. What think you Miss Elspet?"

Ignoring the familiarity, she reached slowly up to touch the beautiful creature's shining neck. Bagshawe stopped her hand with the tip of a riding crop she had not seen him pick up.

"Be careful...he bites."

His face in the gloom unnerved her. She sensed hatred and cruelty running in his veins.

"Boy!" he shouted loudly "Boy!!" Then again seconds later with his first shouts still ringing in Elspet's ears:

"Get here now you lazy, good for nothing boy!!!"

The sound of running and ragged breathing and a boy of about fourteen appeared, shivering with fright and cold.

"Bring the chestnut mare." The boy tugged his cap "Aye Sir," he replied and left.

Bagshawe had thankfully dropped her hand although the crop remained held against her forearm. He hung the lantern on a hook above the stall so that the light shone on the beautiful animal and she sensed its fear of him.

The boy re-appeared leading the mare and the stallion immediately began to kick in its stall. Bagshawe took the rein of the mare and dismissed the boy. Skilfully he turned the mare by tickling her hind quarters with the crop until her rear faced directly into the stallion's head. She watched fascinated by the stallion's reaction as Bagshawe raised the mare's tail with the crop.

"Now then Miss Elspet, that is a stallion eh? What think you eh?"

The stallion's phallus was long and thick as a man's forearm and the animal reared up, crazed in his efforts to get to the mare.

Elspet felt herself reddening, and suddenly she felt unsafe.

"Well, well little Elspet, for a young lady who does not like horses you seem truly interested." He reached up to casually pat the horse's neck but the animal, wildly in the grip of his instinctive behaviour, sank his teeth into Bagshawe's arm. He pulled away, enraged but holding his anger in check, he led the mare away and tied her up before returning to bring his crop down heavily on the stallion's neck. He swung the whip...one, two, three...harder and harder onto the animals flesh, red welts springing up on its black skin as it screamed in terror and pain.

"No! Stop! Stop!" she cried, a sudden flashing picture in her mind of a boy whipped and bleeding.

"Stop it you cruel bully!!!"

Elspet was thumping and thumping his arm and suddenly he stopped, holding the crop at her neck as he breathed sharply, looking into her eyes. She could feel the heat of the horse's blood on her neck. She knew she was in danger and as she ran for the door, his hand caught her roughly on her left breast. He was strong, as madmen are strong, so she had heard.

"Well Miss Sydall, I find myself in the same state as my horse."

Before she could fathom what was happening, he grabbed her upper arms with great strength and pushed her back yards and yards past all the stalls until she lost her footing and fell, with him on top of her.

His hand was so hard pressed on her mouth and nose that she struggled to breathe or fight as her vision blurred and she feared she would die for lack of air. Her struggle for breath and fear of death dulled her conscience, only dimly aware of what was happening until she felt the cruel thrust of him inside her, tearing the undiscovered parts of her womanhood. It was over quickly and she lay shocked and helpless, dimly aware of his ragged breathing as she drifted into unconsciousness.

As Bagshawe watched her eyeballs roll slowly up into her head, he released his fingers from her nose and immediately he saw her come back to life and greedily begin to take in air through her tiny nostrils, enjoying the fear in her eyes and the feeling of power it gave him. As she came quickly back from the brink and some clarity of mind returned, she saw the look in his eyes and she knew as a certainty he had done this before, so practised was he at holding her down and covering her mouth in such a way that she lived or died by his control. She knew at that moment that his mind was flawed.

He lay on her still, breathing heavily for what seemed long moments. She was helpless, fragile and broken, used like the mare. As his breathing subsided he began to speak.

"You will say nothing of this, my little filly" his voice was a whisper.

"If you do, your Uncle will not get his money. I will see to it. Your Aunt will die in poverty and your Uncle's career will be finished. And as for you little Elspet, if you speak of it....well perhaps I shall marry you and we can do this every night. How doth that sound? 't is a tradition in my family, after all, to marry whores. But by God, thou art pretty! Truth be told, I think I could manage again. What think you Miss Sydall...once more for the King, eh?"

She lay still and prayed for it to be over and to be alive at the end of it. The sight of his red face and bulging eyes through strands of pale yellow hair would reside in the dark corners of her memory down the years in her lifetime to come.

***

Time was a concept lost to her. She could not tell how many minutes or hours had elapsed since she went into that stable but in truth it was less than half an hour later when she followed him meekly out and into the cold night once more. She felt as though she were in another place, an unreal place. She heard him shout "Boy!" but the sound was muffled, as if he were miles away, yet she was aware of his hated figure by her side.

She saw the boy appear again and take the mare. As he turned away, he looked into her face and she thought she saw a look of pity and understanding in his eyes. The short walk back to the house was dreamlike. Everything seemed like it was happening somewhere else, somewhere far removed from her. Even the sound of her footsteps was muffled, as if her head was in water. Yes! Water! It was the same sensation she had had when she dipped her whole head in a basin when washing her hair as a child. All her brother's and sister's voices had seemed faraway and unclear and in search of peace from their relentless demands, she had dipped her head back in the bowl again and again. She dipped her head into the imaginary bowl now as she walked, struggling to control her overwhelming need to scream, dimly aware of Edwin Bagshawe's threats repeating over and over in her head.

She raised her head out of her watery sanctuary only at the sound of her Uncle's distant voice. The welcome sight of his round, kind face prompted a sudden, short return to reality as she said "I think I have caught a chill." Then back she had drifted into her safe place under the water. Wrapped in her cloak, unable to feel the touch of Sir William Bagshawe's hand as he bid her Goodnight, turning her back on the cruel face of Edwin and covering her mouth as if to cough, feeling the sting of vomit rising in her throat, she left that evil place.

Her uncle led her carefully to their transport and as their journey home began, the lurch of the carriage and sounds of the horses revived her like an icy blast.

The house was ugly and menacing as she looked back at it from the carriage and mercifully the building fell slowly out of view, hidden by darkness and stark winter trees which seemed to reach for the brightness of the moon with skeletal fingers. At last, as the shock finally took possession of her, she began to shake uncontrollably.

"My Dear, my Dear, what is it? What ails thee?"

Nathaniel put his arm about her and unable to speak for fear of what may come out, she silently lay her head on her Uncle's shoulder.

"There, there lass...Tha'll be awreet. Soon be 'ome. Tha must get straight into bed. Tha'll be as right as rain in the mornin'!"

But Elspet knew with a certainty that she would never be right again.

10. The coming of spring

Just before dawn on the twenty-eighth of March Eliza Speakman drew her last breath.

She had suffered long, agonizing weeks but through her last night and all the day before she had been sleeping deeply, in a kind of half death, Elspet had thought.

Elspet stood alone at the little kitchen window moments after Eliza had slipped away. She watched as the light of a new day diluted the darkness, slowly revealing pretty little spring blossoms she had been too busy to see before. Death itself could not hold back the promise of new life she thought…the promise of new life.

Eliza's condition had begun to decline the day after their visit to Abbot's Hall. Elspet had taken to her bed for three days in a kind of madness on her return home. Half sleep, flashes of memory, constantly retching into a bowl Nathaniel had left by her bed. She had wanted to die. Once in the morning she had woken up and thought: It was all a dream! It was just an awful nightmare! But her relief was short-lived, reality cruelly confirmed as she rose up to see the green gown hanging on the back of her door and as she came fully awake, the desolation crushed her once more.

She had lain upstairs on that first day and heard Thurston's knock upon the front door and his sweet voice as he asked to see her. She could picture his face as Nathaniel told him of her illness. She imagined him walking away, sorrowful, back to the little cottage. She wept and wept at the realisation that her dreams of happiness with Thurston were clearly over now. She knew she could never face him again.

Nathaniel had come to her room on the third night.

"Lass!" he knocked and called softly from outside her door. "Lass, Ah must return to my work tomorrow, building begins again. Will you be up to see to Eliza? She does not do well"

Elspet roused herself and opened the door. Nathaniel was shocked at the sight of her. Her eyes were red and swollen, she had lost weight. No wonder, for every meal Mistress Thomas had taken up for her had been left uneaten.

"Yes Uncle, I will see to her. I will watch with her tonight. I am so sorry to have let you down."

"Nay, nay lass, tha's not let me down at all. But are ye sure? Are ye well? Tha looks poorly lass."

"I am much better Uncle," she re-assured him "I shall watch with Aunt Eliza tonight."

"Well, if tha'rt sure my dear...Ah could do with the rest, Ah must say."

Nathaniel did look exhausted. His usually bright eyes were dull and darkly shadowed and Elspet felt a sudden stab of guilt for lying abed in the midst of all their troubles. Yet even in that fleeting moment, she realised the enormity of what had happened to her and the terrible damage that would result if she did not keep it locked within her own heart.

"Get you to bed now Uncle. I shall go down and see to my Aunt."

Nathaniel had kissed her gently on the forehead and gone to his lonely bed.

Elspet had closed her door and resolved to pull herself out of the terrible, oppressive black pit she had fallen into. Once Eliza was settled and Nathaniel was snoring upstairs, she had taken the green gown into the garden and buried it. Even as she was stabbing at the frozen earth, she feared she had lost her mind but as she covered every trace of the green fabric with soil and stones, she knew it was a symbolic act. With it, she buried the terrible memory of the night she had worn it, the happiness she had enjoyed before it came into her life and the secret fantasy she had had of wearing it for her beloved Thurston one day. All hope of the future she had so briefly dreamed of, she buried too.

Aunt Eliza had continued to worsen over the next few weeks and the sheer, all-consuming work that came with looking after her had taken every minute of Elspet's day. She hardly had time to think between cooking, cleaning, fetching and carrying for, soothing, feeding and washing the invalid in her sole care. By the end of each day, she had fallen exhausted into the little pallet bed Nathaniel had set up for her in the room where Eliza lay. Even in the night, she was up at the slightest murmur her Aunt made. In those last terrible weeks Eliza knew not if it was day or night, so deranged with pain was she.

Elspet had never seen anyone endure such suffering and it drained her watching Eliza writhe in her agony. It sickened her to bathe and clean the terrible, suppurating sore that was eating the poor woman's spine away and the relief that came with Eliza's sleep was overwhelming. Guiltily, at times, Elspet prayed that her Aunt would not waken but she did, she lingered on. Crisis after crisis, Nathaniel and Elspet had watched through together, sitting, praying, kneeling at Eliza's bedside. So often they paced the floor, Nathaniel unable to sleep, distraught with grief at the agonies his dear wife endured.

Then, as suddenly as it began, it would end. She would fall into a deep and death-like sleep but still she breathed, a white, waxy sheen upon her face. And then they would wait for the agony to begin all over again.

Mistress Thomas had called one morning towards the end of February. The rain had been falling all morning, lashing the window and obscuring Elspet's view of Thurston, toiling alongside Nathaniel and his men, raising at last the roof of the Church. Nathaniel had taken to coming home at dinner, leaving Thurston to eat with the men but she saw him every day from the window. Even though the sight of him pierced her sore heart like a needle, she had to look.

She had opened the door to their neighbour and let the old woman in to see the invalid who thankfully slept. Terrified of waking her, so desperate was she for some respite however short, Elspet had led Mistress Thomas into the scullery.

"Ee lass, tha looks tired! 'as Mistress 'ad a bad night then?"

Elspet nodded. Mistress Thomas had sat on the wooden rocking chair with a folded rag on her knee.

"Ah've brought thee summat lass...," she said. "...Well 'tis for Mistress Speakman, but it will 'elp ye all."

She opened the cloth and revealed a flattened pile of what appeared to be dead leaves.

"These are the best thing there is for pain...," said Mistress Thomas "...grind the leaves as you need 'em...'tis best you leave 'em 'ole till they are to be used. Mix with a bit of 'oney if ye 'ave it...?" Elspet nodded "...and a bit o' boilin' water. It'll ease 'er pain....an' thine lass."

Elspet had touched the dead leaves as if they were some miraculous relic. She was afraid. "Will they harm her?" she asked the old woman.

Rebecca Thomas smiled "Tha'rt a good lass Elspet. Nay, nay, they will do no 'arm, just ease 'er pain an' 'elp 'er sleep. That is what she needs to do now, lass. Fightin' illness is an exhaustin' thing. Ah've nussed many a one like Mistress Speakman in mi time."

For a few seconds her pale, milky eyes swam with emotion.

"Come to me lass, whenever tha needs this, an' at the end, Ah've other things that can 'elp. Be not afraid, let 'er not suffer because tha fears to give 'er this. Promise me now."

Elspet had promised and thanked her. Mistress Thomas rose painfully to leave but as she reached the kitchen door she had turned to look into Elspet's face. The look seemed to reach right into her heart.

"Art tha well lass? Tha looks troubled, tha'rt pale. Is all well with thee?"

Elspet had cast down her eyes, unable to meet the old lady's gaze. Mistress Thomas took her hand, and with the other, she gently touched Elspet's abdomen.

"Whatever ail's thee lass... an' women's troubles are many...Ah can 'elp thee. Come an' see me, when tha needs to. Ah'll see myself out."

And off she went, limping down the stone corridor to the front door.

Elspet roused herself and followed her. Standing at the open door, she had watched Thurston through the slanting rain until he seemed to feel her gaze. He turned, watched for a moment and then raised his hand to her. It was hopeless to dream anymore, he would never want her now. She had put her hand to her mouth to force down the sob which threatened to engulf her. She dare not cry... she could not have stopped. Slowly she had closed the door.

****

During the last weeks of Eliza's life there were periods when she was incredibly lucid and eager to talk. She talked in a way Elspet had not heard her talk before. The calm exterior Eliza had maintained since Elspet had come to know her had fallen away, and all her emotions were revealed in the words she spoke and the manner in which she spoke them. Elspet knew not if she spoke like this with her Uncle. As she had sat by the fire night after long, lonely night in the kitchen, she had heard no murmurings of conversation. It seemed to be in the mornings when Eliza had the clarity of mind and the need and energy to speak.

Consequently, as her Aunt lay dying, Elspet came to know her in a way that no-one else had.

Eliza talked about her girlhood, running in the hills of Derbyshire in the place Elspet herself had grown up. She talked of her younger half-sister, Elspet's mother Meg. Though her Mother's second child had been her favourite, Eliza had felt no jealousy. She knew that her mother had held no love for Eliza's own dead Father and had found happiness with her second husband whose child she had adored. All who knew Meg loved her sunny nature and Eliza had cared for and safeguarded her sister as she ran, gambolling through life, unaware of danger or duty. Still much the same, Elspet reflected, though a grown woman, wife, and mother of a large family.

She talked about Nathaniel…of her first sight of him on a fine horse in the town on Market day. He had come to Derbyshire to study the fine country houses of Hardwick and Haddon and she had ridden with him through the beautiful estate of Chatsworth. She talked as if it had all happened yesterday… but so it is with the ever-spinning wheel of life, turning with such irresistible speed and promise that time like distance, slips away almost unnoticed.

One morning at the beginning of March, Nathaniel had just left the house, and Elspet stood by the bed, watching her Uncle walk to the Church. She waited for her first glimpse of Thurston. Suddenly, she had become aware of a change in her Aunt's breathing, a sound to which she had become so finely attuned. She looked down to see Eliza's milky eyes blinking in the morning light.

"Does the light bother you Aunt? Shall I close the curtains?"

Eliza moved her head from side to side on the pillow.

"Nay, nay lass…each new day is my friend."

Her voice was growing weaker every day and at times Elspet had to put her ear close to her mouth to hear all she said. The words she had said next caught Elspet unaware.

"Thou art un'appy my dear, I know it. What 'as 'appened to thee?"

Elspet had always been, inside her head, older than her years. She had always known it for she had always been treated as such. Even as a child she could never remember a time when she was not responsible for herself, her siblings, and at times even her Mother. She had never resented the responsibility laid on her shoulder's…that was just how it had always been. Even when she had been innocent, she was grown up. Now she was no longer innocent…now the vista of human cruelty had been revealed to her and her silent suffering had stripped away every vestige of her youthful character. She knew that the bright young girl she had been only a few weeks before, had gone forever. She had started to cry for the first time since that terrible night and Aunt Eliza held her hand until the tears had subsided. When she was calm again Eliza asked:

"Is it me, my dear?"

Elspet shook her head, tears brimming again.

"No Aunt. It is hard to see you suffer but no, it is not you."

"Is it Thurston then?" Elspet could not speak for fear her weeping would return but her Aunt's question was clearly answered.

Eliza stroked her hand. "Sit with me Elspet."

Elspet perched on the little pallet bed by her side.

"Listen to me, my dear…whatever 'as come between thee and Thurston, let it not harden thy heart to him." She had paused then as if in preparation for a momentous revelation.

"When my little lass died so many years ago, it was as if the pool of my heart froze. Oh I lived, I went on. I was a wife, I was a Mother. I loved my Nathaniel, I loved my Josiah, but my love for them was…. behind a veil. It felt like summer in my heart, but when I tried to show it…it was as if it was …chilled by a frost! Nathaniel was alright, he knew, he was alright. We still had those times between husband and wife that thaws all frost's…But my son… he was lost to me for so many years. So much damage done by my hardened heart, I can never, ever fix it. It took my life more than death will do my dear. It wasted my happiness."

Eliza squeezed her hand as hard as her frailty would allow.

"Whatever it is that 'as caused this sadness to come to pass, promise me, promise me, as I have grown to love thee these last months lass, do not let it waste thee! Do not let it spoil thy life for there is no going back. Face it! Fight it! And fix it!"

Eliza was exhausted and lay back on her pillows, her eyes filled with tears, her breathing laboured. Her words, spoken with such passion, had moved Elspet to fresh tears and raked over all the pain she had struggled to cover for so many weeks. Yet, so accustomed was she becoming to her new found sadness, her heart was already growing chill. She heard the words but in her agony they drifted, unheeded, down into a dark corner of her mind where they lay forgotten beneath the turmoil of unresolved feelings. And there they would remain until uncovered, months into the future.

Eliza spoke her last words in the morning on the day before she died, before she sank into the mercifully deep sleep in which she remained. She slept, undisturbed, even though the sound of her breathing could be heard wherever they went in the house. She had opened her eyes and blinked as the morning light slanted through the window. She was awake and lucid for only a moment and Nathaniel had held her hand whilst Elspet stood behind him.

"Kiss my son for me..."she said, and then as Nathaniel bowed his head onto her chest, her eyes met Elspet's for a moment. In them, in spite of the pain, Elspet saw all the love in Eliza's heart. Silently, her lips formed the word "Susannah" before her eyes closed again in that final, death-like sleep.

Twenty-four long hours later, moments after her Aunt had finally just stopped breathing and her life had ended as suddenly as a draught blows out a candle, Elspet stood alone in the kitchen. As the breaking day slowly filled the room with pale light, she could hear the sound of her Uncle's muffled sobs in the room next door and the tears which had begun to fall onto her own cheeks, sparkled in the first rays of the early spring sun.

11.

Scotland was a dreary country, Josiah mused. Even the excitement of the march and the events of the past few weeks were dulled by the interminable rain and cold. Spring didn't feel the same so far north. He couldn't smell the new grass or breathe in the clear, dew-filled mornings. The longing for his home had grown over the last few months into a heartache and he found himself day-dreaming about it in quiet moments... of which this last month, there had been many.

The irony of his situation was not lost on Josiah. For seven years he had chased his cause. He had fought for his King, deprived himself of every comfort, content to be in the company of men who looked up to him. And now, after the terrible events of these last years, the cruel battles and the suffering of his countrymen, now at last he had seen the murdered King's son crowned in Scotland. On the morrow, he was preparing to march with the new Charles to England, to fight by his side as he regained his Father's crown. At last justice would be done and wrongs set right. Yet all he could think about was his own land, his own family, his Mother and his own lost years.

Although Thurston Hey had made a physical appearance in his life once again, the memory of him had been an ever-present spectre in the mind of Josiah Speakman. The day of the beating had been Josiah's last day in his home. On that May day as a lad of sixteen, he had joined once again the gang in the sport of tormenting Thurston Hey just as he had many times in his childhood. His place in that gang was demanded and driven by one who had claimed him as a follower along with other boys in the village. He would never forget that cruel face and had questioned ever since that day why he had been lead so easily into that cruel pastime. Although the terrible guilt still ran deep, he now knew that the anger and hurt that had become such a part of his childhood had found release in that bullying. More than ever these days, the shame of it burned him.

Even as a youth he had felt the shame of wrongdoing but then he had been able to bury it deep within his own pre-pubescent chaotic mass of negative feelings. Acceptance was all for him then. He stood by or joined in because he could not bear to be rejected by their leader, the one who sought Josiah out to be his friend and whose influence caused others to seek his favour. Acceptance and status were a heady mix for a troubled adolescent, and worth anything…until that day.

The day of the beating had been the most significant day of his first sixteen years. It was that day which had set him on the path that had brought him to this point. He had left the scene of that terrible beating, sickened by the sight of a degradation he could not bear to witness. The frenzy and crazed excitement of the other boys had meant he was able to slip away unseen from the horror and even as he ran he knew what he must do. He almost vomited with fear and the realisation of what he had been part of but he had banged hard again and again on Mistress Heys door and begged her to go and save her son.

That was the moment he knew he must cease to follow the boy who had become his cruel mentor. He knew also that the only way he could escape him was by physical distance. The plan had formed so swiftly and clearly in his mind as he ran home that day. He packed his bag silently in the night and stole away to the site of the battle he knew was destined to be fought some miles away. And so began the battle which he had fought within himself from that day on, the fight to regain his own sense of honour.

Josiah had reached the outskirts of the town of Bolton at the beginning of June 1644, a month before his seventeenth birthday. By July he had aged ten years. In less than a month, he had played his part in the sacking of a town and the capture of a city and was marching into another County in the army of Prince Rupert. In those few weeks he had seen more cruelty and murder than he could ever have imagined in his worst nightmares of hell. All his boyhood fantasies of war games became dreadful reality as his sword and musket slashed and pierced flesh and none of his opponents rose and laughed and lived to fight another day.

He saw cruel treatment of women and children and the abominable savagery turned his stomach and felt wrong deep in his gut. He had run away to find something in life which he thought would be honourable and just, something to give his life meaning and fill the deep emptiness he had carried within him for as long as he could remember. Instead he found disillusionment, a feeling that carved an even deeper hole in his heart. Not only was there no love in his life, he doubted whether there was any real love in the world.

As he sat cradling the head of his young comrade who had fallen by his side in that first terrible battle, he told the boy the thing he knew he himself would most need to hear if his own last moments should come soon.

"Mother," cried the boy "Mother!"

"She's coming Will, she's coming," said Josiah.

"Is she..." the dying boy had begged "...is she?"

"Aye, aye..."Josiah had sobbed, tears running down his face. "...she is comin' Will, save thi strength. She shall be 'ere when tha wakes."

"D'ye promise...promise?" He was bleeding badly then, his face grey as stone, his eyes flickering.

"Ah promise thee Will, she shall be with thee soon. Sleep...Sleep now."

His friend lay quiet while his life's blood drained into the mud and Josiah knew that his Mother's face was the last thing the boy had seen. He laid his friend down and wanted to run, run for home. Any life was better than this carnage.

It was then that he looked up into the face of a man, a man of about thirty, he guessed. It was a strong face, humanity still shone in his eyes.

"Cover him lad," said the man "and come with me."

Robert Staveley was a Captain in Sir Thomas Tytherton's Regiment of Foot.

"Thou art a brave soldier to see to thy comrade so lad. Many would have run from it. The fight is here is over, there is madness now in this place. Come with me."

Captain Staveley took him back to his camp, gave him a warm meal and saw that he received care and attention over the next three days in the aftermath of the battle and the shock of the events he had witnessed. In return, Robert Staveley received Josiah's unswerving loyalty and respect in the ensuing years as they fought side by side.

Through those first years, Josiah came to look on Robert Staveley as another Father. Though he loved Nathaniel and missed him sorely when he left his home, he soon realised that he had always, in a way, missed his Father. Nathaniel was devoted to his wife and always Josiah had known that she held dominion over his Father's love. Father and son's time together was hidden and secret, tinged with a feeling that Nathaniel was always looking over his shoulder. Josiah had thought no less of his Father for this... he had always felt secure in his Father's affection. He thanked God for it for that was the only thing that had preserved some semblance of honour in him. That honour had been recognised and nurtured by Robert Staveley until he had died, three years ago, in an unimportant skirmish in an unremembered place.

"Oh yes Father," thought Josiah "Men do indeed die in skirmishes and good one's too......but not this one, not this one!"

12.

On the morning of Eliza Speakman's funeral, Thurston stood and looked at his reflection in the window of the little cottage, the only means he had of guaging his appearance. It was not something he had ever been used to doing. He did not think he had known as a child what he looked like at all. In fact, it was only when, in the days of trying to fathom why Elspet had looked on him favourably, that his curiosity about his own looks had been awakened. In truth, Thurston had a fine, darkly handsome face with a chiselled nose and a full, soft, almost feminine mouth. He touched his cheek where Elspet had last kissed it. It all seemed so long ago now, he almost wondered if it had happened at all…

He had awoken early that day in January…the day after the posy. He had dressed hurriedly but with some care then he had paced for two hours before he felt the time was right to go to her. He had made up his mind what he would do. He would talk to her, tell her how he loved her and if she said she loved him back, he would ask could he speak to her Uncle with regard to their marriage! He almost had to punch himself that morning to be sure he wasn't dreaming!

"Me!" he thought "Is this really happening to me?!"

The feeling that had welled up in him, unrecognised, was confidence. He had felt he could take on the world because she loved him. So sure was he that he had won her love. There was no doubt in him and it was a new, intoxicating feeling, this absolute certainty of the man he could be! He couldn't eat for the excitement which churned his stomach, he couldn't sit for lack of concentration. He walked around the confines of his little home and counted the minutes until he could go to her.

She would be excited too, full of tinkling laughter and chatter about her visit to Abbots Hall and as he walked to where she was, his boots ankle deep in greying snow, he had wondered when he would choose his moment. He had imagined her face, that look he had seen in her eyes so often. This time when he saw it, he would take her in his arms and kiss her as he had wanted to do ever since that first moment he had seen her huddled in his doorway.

He had walked through the fields that January day, past the places he had avoided for so long. Those places held no fear for him now, the memories buried deep under the snows of his old life. The pleasures to come would spring like snowdrops as the snows of his past melted away forever. He hadn't noticed the cold biting into his skinny frame or nipping at his toes as he walked that day. The promise of her warmed him like a cosy fire that he carried within him and would carry for all his life to come. His heart lurched as he saw the back of the house and he skirted around the little lane to approach the Speakman's front door. Shivering with anticipation, he knocked and again after a moment, impatient to see her pretty, smiling face.

It was Nathaniel who had opened the door. His face was grey and he had clearly not slept well.

"Ah've come to visit Elspet," Thurston said, his heart sinking a little.

"Aye lad, Ah'm sorry but she's poorly…she 'as a chill," said Nathaniel. "Ah cannot ask thee in lad. Ah'm seein'to Eliza an' seein' to Elspet. Ah'm sorry. Shall ah sithee on t'site on Tuesday? All shall be back to rights then, Ah'm sure."

Thurston was crestfallen.

"Of course," he said "Aye, of course…..give Elspet my best wishes then… an' Mistress Speakman too. Right then…Tuesday then…"

"Aye lad…" Nathaniel had said, hurriedly closing the door "…Tuesday."

Every day since he had hoped to see Elspet but he had not seen her, not these twelve weeks past…except on one morning as she stood at the door of the Speakman's house. He had known somehow that she was there. He could feel the pull of the invisible cord that he knew would always bind him to her. He had turned to look. She stood and watched him, making no movement or sign to him. Although he could not see her face clearly enough to judge her expression, he could feel her terrible sadness. He had raised his hand and if she had beckoned to him, he would have run to her as fast as his leg would allow him. But she lowered her head and closed the door and Thurston had felt his heart would break.

Now Eliza Speakman was dead and she would be buried this day. Satisfied with his appearance and certain his attire was sober and respectful, he prepared to leave the little cottage for the walk to Appley Green. Smart in his new felt hat and the clothes he had bought for the occasion, he set off to pay his respects for a good life which had ended, hoping that from this day his own life might begin again.

He walked along the roads, for although he made the journey every day, he no longer took the short cut through the fields. The snows had indeed melted but only to reveal his past fears again. The memories which had begun to recede when he basked in the warmth of his feelings for Elspet had returned quickly once his new found happiness had begun to crumble. The memories which had returned were more detailed with flashes of images he had not recalled before. He had seen, for the first time, incidents which had scarred him. Heard again and remembered anew, voices, names, hurts. And always through these new and dreadful recollections, an unseen menace lurked somewhere in his mind. Something he knew he did not want to remember...something hidden from him by the psychology of unbearable suffering. Something he feared to uncover.

Though the spring day was warm, Thurston shivered. What he would not give now for the warmth of Elspet's company. He knew he would see her today. He also knew that all the reasons Nathaniel had given to placate him were at an end. Elspet no longer needed to spend her days a nurse. She no longer would struggle to leave the house. Thurston knew that today he would have an answer but feared that the answer may not bring him the happiness he craved.

A dozen people walked from the hamlet of Appley Cross to Appley Green to see Eliza buried. By the time they reached the makeshift wooden chapel which had served for worship whilst the old Church was restored, no space was left on the wooden benches in the little building. Thurston stood along the back wall, craning his neck to see Elspet who sat, head bonneted and bent, close to her Uncle as the Minister spoke his words over Eliza's remains like ancient magic spells. When it was over, he followed as the coffin was carried into the Churchyard, hiding himself behind the many mourners, not trusting himself to look into Elspet's eyes.

Eliza was laid to rest in the grave in which her daughter lay, re-united at last in heaven.

Thurston hoped with all his heart that it was so.

He stood some distance away and watched the mourners leave until only Nathaniel and Elspet were left at the graveside. Only the gravediggers stood at a respectful distance, hunched over their shovels, waiting like scavengers to remove all trace of Eliza Speakman's mortal remains. After some moments, Nathaniel kissed his niece and walked towards his home leaving Elspet alone in her grief.

Once Elspet thought she was alone, she began to weep. Her shoulders shook so hard and Thurston felt again the tug of the invisible cord pulling him to her, unable to stop himself. Even before he had even really decided to approach her, she seemed to sense he was there and turned to face him.

"Elspet," he said, his voice cracking. She bent her head at the sound of his voice and he quickly moved to her side, grabbing her hand to comfort her. She continued to cry as she looked up at him, unsure who she was weeping for.

"Ah know tha must've suffered," he said "but Ah've missed thee, Elspet...so much."

She slowly composed herself, saying nothing, looking down at their joined hands. After a moment she spoke.

"I have missed you too Thurston. I see you are well."

He nodded. "Ah'm all the better for seein' thee again. Ah'm sorry to see the passin' of Mistress Speakman, she was a good woman."

Elspet nodded. They stood for a few moments and then slowly Elspet withdrew her hand from his.

"I must return to my Uncle, he needs me now."

"Ah need thee Elspet...," he said as she turned away. The words were out before he could think to speak them. "...Ah need thee."

She set her mouth in a way he had never seen her do and she seemed for a moment, a person he did not recognise.

"Things are changed with me Thurston," she said. "I need time, I need to think. I must go... and you must let me go."

She turned away and began to walk.

"Shall Ah call on thee Elspet? Shall Ah see thee soon?"

His words remained unheeded as she continued to walk with her head bent, unable to see where she put her feet her eyes were so full of tears.

Thurston watched her go as a shower of spring rain began to fall. He knew that the answer he had most dreaded had at last been given to him and it was the worst hurt he had ever felt in his life. Worse than any beating, worse than the grief for his mother, it sucked the very breath out of him and drained him of all hope. Unable to control his legs, he fell on his knees and began to weep, his tears mingling with the rain and falling onto the freshly turned earth.

****

Nathaniel sat at the table and stared into the dying embers of the fire. The room grew colder as the fire's glow dimmed, just like his heart now that the flame that was his Eliza had flickered and gone out forever.

He was at a crossroads in his life, he knew that. His spirit was struggling. He woke up in the mornings no longer wanting to face the day, and the thought of a month or year passing by and increasing the distance between him and the person he had loved most in the world was unbearable. If only his son was here, at least he would have something to hold on to and live for. But he had let Josiah go a long time past…when the fear of losing him had turned into a half-acceptance of his loss. His letting go was the armour he had worn against the hurt to come.

Elspet had gone to her bed weeping again. He feared for her sanity as much as his own. Surely she must leave now and go back to her own county? Life would be better for her there and her own family must miss her so much. Of course he dreaded the words she would surely speak to him one day soon. He would hate the loneliness that he knew would descend on him. He had never been good at being alone. He had hoped that something would come of Elspet and Thurston and that would hold her here but it was clear that all hope was lost there now. Nathaniel knew he should talk to the girl but his own heart was so heavy, he would not be able to find the words without weeping. And so they existed, silently within their own misery, side by side in the sad house.

He looked down again at the paper on the table and the pen in his hand. At last he began to write, the words he had waited for over an hour to come were freed at last and spilled onto the page.

"My Dear Son,

It is with a heavy heart that I write to tell thee that thy dear Mother was buried this day. She suffered long but died in God's love and lies now with thy dear sister and I pray they are together in Heaven.

Her last words on this earth were for thee my boy. I would give all to see thy face and welcome thee home tho'I know that may not be possible for some time.

I send all assurance to thee of the deepness of my love Josiah and send all comfort to thee in thy sorrow which I know will be grievous.

Written this day, 2nd April 1651, with sincere affection by the hand of thy Father,

Nathaniel Speakman."

13.

Elspet first felt the child move on the morning of the 28th day of April. She had just risen from her bed and was moving to the window to open the curtains on another wearisome day when it happened. She stood still for a moment, unsure of what the feeling had been. At the second she dismissed it as imagination, it happened again. Like a little fish, swimming in her stomach.

A picture suddenly flashed into her mind of her Mother, years before, sitting back down on her chair, holding her stomach. "The child has quickened!" she had said.

Quickening...the first movement, the first real confirmation of a child growing, the first sure stirrings of a life to come.

Elspet never got to the window...as her mother, years before, she had fallen back in shock, holding her stomach. It was real. It was happening. There would be a child, made on her by the very devil himself and she had no choice but to bear it.

She had known it of course when her bleeding stopped. She had been so aware of the 'doing's' of a woman's body from such a young age, she was well acquainted with the signs. She thought she had known from the first day after that terrible night, all through the retching's of February and March, she had known it. But she had hoped, with the irrational, self-denial of women who dread conception, that she was wrong. That it was all imagined. She had even gone to Mistress Thomas in the days following Eliza's death, going so far as to knock, rehearsing over and over the words she would say to ask for the help the old lady had so subtly, yet so clearly offered on the day she brought the leaves.

"Could you.....could I....please ask to borrow a cup of flour?" she had said when the door was opened.

Well...it was too late now. That morning at that moment, it became real, undeniable truth. Every fibre of her being wanted to be rid of the burden she carried but every well taught religious value, every moral sense of right and wrong, told her that she could not harm this child or she would damn her soul for all eternity.

She sat, perched on the edge of her narrow bed and looked toward the sunlight which always fell first on the back of the house, dappling the walls of her room with little leaded diamonds. All those little nuances of life in which her old, innocent self had found so much pleasure, had gone forever now.

Her tears and longing for what had gone before must be put away. She knew she must face her future the best way she could. She stood, covering her face with her hands for a moment, breathing deeply. Then she strode forward to open her curtains and begin a different life from the one she had planned.

14.May-time

At last the repairs to the Church of Appley Green were finished and what a handsome sight it was! Plain Lancashire brick and plain puritan style, but a stark beauty shone from its plainness. It's newly-built, tall, square tower rose up fifty feet to a beautifully crafted, crenelated top which would house a new bell, already on order from the finest foundry in Manchester.

Storing up his treasures in heaven, Sir William Bagshawe was overjoyed with the restored building and had rewarded Nathaniel handsomely. Nathaniel with his kind and generous spirit had, in turn, rewarded his workers well. In that alone he felt satisfaction with the building he had created. God was in a hidden place for Nathaniel these days. He had indeed, secretly ceased to feel His presence for many years and since his dear Eliza had fallen ill and died, he found comfort in few things, religion least of all.

The building of the Church had become a burden these last months. If it had not been for Thurston, he doubted whether it would have been finished. But finished it was and from the Speakman's house, it made a pretty view. The daisy covered Village Green was flanked by the old moss-covered wall of Moreton House on one side and the pretty, willow-fringed stream on the other. Fronted by a circle of black and white houses and with the new Church rising behind the trees, it was a view Eliza would have found so much pride and pleasure in.

He missed her sorely, every day that dawned. He had no other plans for building, indeed he had no other plans for life. He was tired. Only one more thing was required of him and that was to make the building ready for the end of June when the new Reverend would arrive in the village. He would take up residence in the old Vicarage which was just visible from Nathaniel's window, beyond the wall which skirted Moreton House.

All wondered what manner of man he would be, an Anglican for certain. Religion to Nathaniel was a confusing and complicated thing. Always, despite his success, a simple man, he had thought that men either worshipped God or they did not. Such suffering had been caused these last years in the name of religion. Men unable to follow their conscience in the way they worshipped their God...churches destroyed, homes, lives and families too...his own among them. What kind of God allowed good people to suffer and be in strife with one another? These were dangerous thoughts in a dangerous time and Nathaniel thought it best that he live a quiet life whilst these turbulent emotions battled within him.

He had been offered the work of making ready the Vicarage for the new incumbent, but had respectfully declined, recommending instead that Thurston manage the work. And so it came to pass that on a morning in early May, Thurston walked his daily walk to Appley Green to direct a team of men who would now look to him as their Master.

Elspet was making Nathaniel's bed as her uncle breakfasted downstairs and, as she had planned, she saw Thurston arrive at the Church. He stole a forlorn look at the house as he passed and she hid in the shadows when he raised a hand to Nathaniel who sat by the window eating. Her heart ached as she glimpsed for a second the smile she so loved. He seemed taller these days, not so bowed down to the world as he had been when she met him.

"For all the hurt I have given him," she thought "...at least I have given him that."

Halfway through the morning, Thurston left the men sweeping and cleaning the stone floors, sanding and waxing the sweet smelling new cherry-wood pews and generally beautifying God's residence. Crossing the old cart road that led up to the town of Tytherton, he followed the wall of Moreton House to its end where stood the old Vicarage, set back off the road in a bramble-covered, once pretty garden.

He looked at the house, turning the old, black iron key in his pocket. It was a fine old place though sadly in need of his ministrations having stood empty for the last three years. The last occupant had been hounded out of the village when Sir William Bagshawe had had his 'epiphany' and allied himself with the religious beliefs of Cromwell as many astute men of wealth had done.

Thurston thought briefly of the man who had lived here. He had seemed a good man although Thurston and his family were never Churchgoers. Only at harvest time and to celebrate Christ's birth and death had they ever made the journey to worship. It seemed harsh that one man should lose his home and livelihood on the whim of another. He wished the new man good fortune in whichever way he worshipped his God or extolled others to do so. Prayer had been an inconsistent thing in Thurston's life and in his experience never seemed to work...except for only one time, when he had prayed not to die. Few things made him think of Heaven: a bright sunlit morning, frost on a spider's web... beautiful green eyes.

As he stood, turning the key over and over in his pocket, he thought back to a moment early that morning. He had been alone in the Church, always first to arrive at his work. He was standing in the Nave when the sun shone through the big mullioned window suddenly illuminating the very spot where the new altar would stand. He had shivered, involuntarily, wondering if he had felt the presence of God and without thinking, he had bowed his head. The latch of the heavy oak door had clicked loudly as Arthur White entered the Church to begin his day's work.

"Beg pardon" he had said, tugging his forelock "Ah didn't mean to disturb thee."

Thurston walked towards him.

"Tha didn't Arthur. But why did tha do that?"

Arthur was puzzled "What?" he asked, confused.

Thurston mimicked his gesture, tugging the dark curl that fell onto his brow and inclining his head to Arthur.

"That," he said.

Arthur laughed "Why Thurston, th'art mah master now! Ah'm showin' mah respect to thee!"

Thurston had felt himself redden, unprepared for what he had heard.

"Nay, nay Arthur…" he had said, stammering "…Ah…Ah look on thee as a friend…a…an 'elpmate. Tha's been so good to me these last months. Nay, nay… Ah'm 'appy to 'ave thi respect, as Ah respect thee, but as a friend."

Thurston swallowed hard, composing himself before speaking again.

"Ah was not born to be no man's master, Arthur, least of all thine. Do we 'ave an understandin?"

Thurston had stood, holding out his hand. Arthur White had had many masters in his fifty-five years… old, rich, good-natured and cruel. He had sold his labour all his life and in return snatched a meagre living for his family now grown. Unbeknown to Thurston, he felt something for this lad akin to the pride he might have had in a son, if he'd ever had one. Arthur had grasped Thurston's hand firmly.

"Aye, lad," he had said. "We do."

Thurston walked up to the door of the Vicarage as he reflected on the morning and his new status in life. So many new emotions had been awakened in him in the past few months, he felt as if he had been sleeping, living half a life for twenty-four years. No childhood happiness, the only pleasant memories he had for comfort were of places, not people. His life had been barren of beauty and those moments of inner warmth that others took for granted. In these last months, he had come to know so much about his own heart. The feeling of loving someone…and being loved in return as he was so sure he had. The pain of losing that love, so deep that he thought he would die from it and the bravery with which he had picked himself up from that and so many other beatings, to find a life again. He had come to recognise in himself ambition, a determination to live a full life and now, at this moment, he felt pride. Pride that a man like Nathaniel had trusted him with his reputation and pride that a man like Arthur White respected him.

He thought of his own Father's miserable disdain for the world and everything in it and he thanked God for the awakening that had come from that fateful meeting with Elspet. For all that had taken place and would take place in the future, he vowed to seek out that unknown barrier to his happiness and win Elspet's love one day. Even after all, he still had hope, and even if that hope never became a reality, he knew he was set on a path to a life very different from the one he could have travelled his whole lifetime on. For all the hurt, what a gift she had given him.

His spirits lifted, he turned the key and opened the door to a new challenge.

15.

There were no defined start and finish times for the working day under Thurston's leadership. The day's labour was led by the light and the needs of men's stomachs. Thurston had always risen at dawn or soon after, breakfasted and walked to his work, wherever that may have been. Dinner was eaten when the sun was at its height and the day's work ended when the light failed or worker's stomachs rumbled then home -all would go to whatever food was waiting for them.

And so it happened some days after he had first opened the door of the Vicarage, that Thurston was walking wearily home to the little cottage, his stomach rumbling, wondering what he would eat that night. He remembered those first days when he had been welcomed into the Speakman's house. Good food, the feeling of a full belly...the feeling of being cared for. The loneliness bit hard now. That loneliness too was part of Thurston's awakening... he had never recognised his solitude as loneliness before.

As he approached the little cottage, he began to wish he didn't have to go in, make a fire and prepare a meal to eat alone. Thurston took his key from his pocket and looked over his shoulder before opening the door. Sometimes he thought that he would spend the rest of his life looking over his shoulder. But, he was a man of some means now. He had been paid generously by Nathaniel these last months and spent little. All the coin was hidden in a box in the little cottage. Times were hard and people were desperate, the wars had taken their toll on simple folk. He feared robbers, he feared violence. He had meant to ask Nathaniel's advice on what to do with the money but it had never seemed the right time and so it sat in its box under the eaves in Thurston's old attic room.

The next minute, Thurston almost jumped out of his skin as he sensed someone behind him and he turned suddenly, ready to strike!

A little child of about two years old stood before him, moved to crying by Thurston's angry face and sudden movement. The child cried loudly, rubbing his eyes with dirty hands and Thurston was beside himself to have upset him so.

"Shush…shush," he said, kneeling. "Ah didn't mean to frighten thee…shush."

But the child wouldn't shush, he cried louder and louder.

"Weers thi mother?" asked Thurston kindly, gently pulling the child's hands from his face. The child sensed Thurston's kindness and stopped wailing, sobs punctuating his breathing as he stood looking into the stranger's face. Thurston was entranced by the boy. Though his face was dirty and streaked, its shape was exquisite with full childish cheeks and a pointed dimpled chin. His eyes were large and blue, he looked so beautiful and vulnerable that Thurston was almost moved to tears himself.

"Isaac… Isaac!!" The boy turned and ran to the woman who had called his name. She was walking from the moss covered in dirt and Thurston guessed that she had been working on one of the farms. She reached Thurston holding the child in her arms.

"He ran off," she said. "Ah 'ope 'ee's not bothered thee Thurston."

She clearly knew him and Thurston looked into her face, trawling his memory for some recollection of her. "Ginny," he said at last.

"Aye," she replied "Ginny Green...as was. Tha remembers me then?"

He nodded. "Aye…Ah do. Ah thought tha'd left the village."

Her breathing was slowing as she cuddled the child.

"Aye...Ah did…" she replied "…but…well… Ah married a man who were no good, so Ah've come back 'ere...nowhere else to go."

"Oh...right… tha'rt with thi Mother then?" asked Thurston.

She nodded.

"That must be 'ard...so many in that little place"

She nodded again, close to tears. "Aye," she said. "There's no room, no bed, not enough food, no money...an' Ah must work in the farms...."

She suddenly began to cry, clearly near the end of her tether. "Forgive me," she said "Ah'm tired, so's the child. Ah'll ger'im 'ome. It's nice to sithee again Thurston."

The child looked over his Mother's shoulder as she carried him away. He waved his little hand as they disappeared from view, down the lane to the misery of the dirty and dilapidated little hovel in which they lived.

After his lonely meal, Thurston sat in his old chair in the little cottage all evening, unable to get the picture of that little lad waving to him as they turned the corner. He couldn't help thinking that even after all the turmoil of the last months and the difficulties he had faced all his life, he could still count himself lucky...lucky to have a roof over his head, lucky to have food to eat, lucky to have work. And then the idea hit him. Why had he not thought of it before? Then he knew why... fate had been waiting for Ginny.

Thurston remembered her now very well..."Ginny Green - teeth." That was the name she was known by, the name she had been taunted with all her young life. Her teeth were not green nor ever had been green, it was a name invented by the cruelty of children, chanted louder and louder as they recognised her vulnerability. Her only crime was dirtiness and an air of neglect. As a child, like her brothers and sisters, she was uncared for by a mother who, if she had ever possessed any pride or vocation as a homemaker, had lost it in the relentless grinding poverty and chaos of her beleaguered life.

Thurston could imagine where they lay tonight, in fact the smell of the boy and Ginny had been the one thing that had jogged his memory and caused him to remember her. She had never been pretty, but was so changed by the trials of her young life. She deserved a better existence for herself and her bonny child. She had been a victim too in her life, lashed by cruel tongues and driven into the arms of a man who had surely beaten her.

Thurston had a better night's sleep that night than he had in weeks, thanks to the decision he made by the fireside. There was nothing like the prospect of easing another's suffering for easing one's own his Mother used to say.

16.

Elspet awoke from her restless sleep the next morning, uncannily aware of someone else in the house.

Nathaniel was still snoring, the light was beginning to filter into her little room and she could smell wood smoke from a freshly lit fire drifting up through the house.

She was not afraid. She simply rose, wrapped her shawl about her and crept down the stairs.

She could hear the fire crackling now, the hiss of boiling water spilling on to the flames and sounds of movement in the kitchen. A fleeting frisson of fear shivered through her body as she pushed open the door.

"Josiah!" He turned to smile at her, his face weary, his eyes sad.

"Elspet."

His smile faded as he continued to look at her, and she was suddenly aware of where his eyes had let. She pulled her shawl close about her.

"When did you come?" she asked, moving close to the fire. He was quiet for a moment before answering.

"Late...in the night...after you had retired. I can only risk travelling in the darkness Elspet. There are too many roundheads in these villages now."

She nodded "Of course."

Silence again whilst his eyes continued to burn into her. She felt herself reddening.

"And from whence do you come? Where do you go to? And how long will you stay?" she gabbled.

"Elspet...," he said quietly, moving towards her "...best you know not these things."

She nodded again, feeling foolish and embarrassed. "Of course," she said, followed then by another long moment of awkward silence.

"I am so sorry for the loss of your dear mother," she said at length "I loved her well."

Josiah nodded. "I received my Father's letter only a week ago. I know I can do nothing for my Mother now but at least I can be of some comfort to my Father ….and to you perhaps."

Elspet talked, as she always did when she felt nervous, or afraid…or ashamed.

"I have grown to love your parents Josiah, almost as much as my own these last months. Your Father does not do well… but at least the Church is finished and that I think relieves him. It is beautiful. Have you seen it yet…?

"Elspet!" He spoke firmly, silencing her abruptly. She waited silently for the question she sensed was coming.

"Whose child do you carry?"

Her eyes filled with tears as she shook her head. She withdrew her hand from his even though she was so desperate for some physical comfort she wanted to throw herself into his arms and weep. He could see it.

"Speak to me!" he said "Tell me!"

Just then the snoring upstairs ceased abruptly. "Not here" she whispered "Not here!"

"Then where?"

"I will dress," she answered. "Will you walk with me? Somewhere where no-one will see?"

He nodded. "Quickly…. before he is up."

Nathaniel entered the kitchen half an hour later to find a good fire and the thing he dreaded most… an empty house. He knew Josiah was with Elspet. He knew there were secrets. He fancied he knew there would be an outcome for Elspet that would keep her from returning to her family home in Derbyshire... and, God help him, Elspet staying was the only outcome he cared about. He settled down to his bread and milk by the fire, knowing that on their return, the future would be made clearer for them all.

Elspet had dressed hurriedly, and led Josiah across to the wall of Moreton House. The Speakman's house was the last in the village before the road forked. The right fork led up past the Vicarage and to the town of Tytherton and the left, a less well-used road, led to the town of Leighton Fold three miles away. Elspet and Josiah took the left fork and followed the wall until it stopped abruptly, turning to the right down the little track where Thurston had taken Elspet on that cold day in November. Josiah followed her silently until they came to the covered hole in the wall and he helped her move the branches to reveal the expanse of garden beyond. She put her finger to her lips and they slipped, tip-toeing across the grass to the willow-fringed moat.

"We are safe here," said Elspet. "No-one will find us...'t is a secret place." She sat down on the blanket she had brought with her.

"I cannot believe I never knew this place...in all my childhood, so close to my home!" said Josiah.

She sat silently for a moment watching his face before whispering in her crackly voice. "It is Thurston's place...the place he came to hide from his tormentors...from you."

Guilt flushed Josiah's face. His voice was low and halting when he spoke.

"One day Elspet, I will tell you of my part in Thurston's suffering ....but for now, it is thy suffering I need to know about. Talk to me, tell me Elspet. I take it this is Thurston's child you carry? Why are you not wed?"

Elspet's pent up tears spilled on to her cheeks as she shook her head. She was quiet and still and Josiah knew she would speak again but he was too impatient now to wait.

"Tell me!" he entreated.

"It is not Thurston's child!" At last the words were out. "He does not even know!"

Josiah was shocked, confused. He remained silent, unable to respond. Something in the way she spoke, some inflection in her voice made Josiah sense something sinister. She was not the same... something had been destroyed in her. The suspicion became a question and the question was asked before he could stop himself.

"Then who was it Elspet? Who did this?" And then the words he could not help but speak:

"Elspet…were you forced?"

She looked up at him and she knew the answer was written on her face. She must speak of it or she would go mad with the ever-present memory of it.

"It was Sir William Bagshawe's son."

Her voice was quiet and soft, still with its little crackle but she sounded so different. She felt so different. She realised in that moment that she was changed for ever. She was shaken from her moment of silent acceptance by the awareness of Josiah's heavy breathing and the sight of him stumbling to his feet. Covering his mouth he turned away from her and leaned for support against the twisted trunk of the old willow.

"Josiah!" She was shocked at his reaction and rose to aid him but he held out his palm to still her and keep her from looking into his face.

"A moment," he said and she waited, seated on the blanket as he composed himself. He sat down beside her at length, his face grave and asked:

"When did this attack happen cousin?"

She explained, telling as little of the story as possible. He listened, not speaking, his mind, she inexplicably felt…on other things.

"When will you bear the child?" asked Josiah, the anger within him palpable.

Her guess was September or October.

"Does anyone else know?"

She shook her head. For long moments there was silence between them before suddenly, as if the thought had just popped into his head, Josiah said:

"Marry me, Elspet!"

Despite her sadness she began to laugh, though a mirthless and unfamiliar sound it was to her.

"I mean it…..marry me!" He took her hand. She looked at him in the green gloom and for a bitter-sweet moment remembered that day with Thurston when their eyes had met in this place for a second too long and the magic had begun to weave its spell over them both.

"I cannot marry you, Josiah. Why do you say this?"

He held her hand tighter. "Why not...? I am not the bad man you think me. I can give your child a name. I can make sure you are well thought of and safe. None would ever know your secret Elspet...and, in some small way ...I can right the wrongs I have done."

She didn't understand. "How...? How and why must you right wrongs done to me? You have done me no wrong Josiah."

And as he looked into her eyes, he knew she was right. He should have done the right thing many years before. If he had, this wrong that had been done now would never have been. He realised that there was only one way to right all the wrongs and he knew what he needed to do. That must be at some other time and in some other place but it would be done if it was the last thing he ever did in this life.

"Josiah, listen to me!" Elspet's voice was calm and her mind was clear as she shook him from his deep thoughts.

"I am grateful for your sweet offer cousin. But I think you must know, I love Thurston Hey...and for him to see me marry you would hurt him all over again, as cruel a hurt as those that were inflicted on him in his youth. I would die rather than cause him such pain."

Josiah nodded, remaining silent, beginning to release her hand, helpless in his longing to ease both their burdens.

"There is something you can do for me though, cousin," she said. He looked up at her again, "Anything," he replied.

She smiled, touched by his kindness. "Tell your Father for me. Let him not think ill of me or Thurston and tell him not the truth of it. I kept it to myself because of threats Bagshawe made to do evil to your Father. I know he is devil enough to carry them out .Tell your Father in a way that means I can stay here, Josiah, for despite all I still hope to find happiness in this place."

Josiah nodded, he understood. How he admired her strength, he knew she was far, far stronger than he had ever been. He knew the action he must take.

"I will speak to my Father. I will tell him that I have asked you to marry me...." Already she was shaking her head.

"...It is the truth," he said emphatically. "He will assume I have fathered your child..."

"No. It would be a lie!"

Josiah was firm "Then how do you explain this? You say yourself you do not want him to know about that monster Bagshawe, or think ill of Thurston...?"

She was quiet, but still shook her head, despair returning. He took his chance, continuing to persuade her.

"Father will assume he has a grandchild coming. It will fortify him in the years ahead and it will make you safe Elspet!"

She almost was weary enough to give in but she made one last moral effort to resist the idea that she was beginning to see the sense of.

"It would be a lie!" she repeated, but without the same conviction.

"Better a lie that aids a life than a truth that destroys one Elspet."

He was right, she knew it and it was a solution that at least gave her some hope. He could see she was about to agree and he reached again for her hand. She was so touched by his kindness and his support yet confused by her conflicting feelings about him. His history with Thurston did not fit with the picture of the man drawn before her. She slowly nodded her acceptance.

"I am grateful cousin, you have helped me and I would be content if you would speak to your Father and set his mind at rest in whatever way you think fit. I thank you for your kindness in my trouble...I will thank you all my life."

He looked into her eyes again, and she knew he would say more.

"I am happy to help you Elspet. I owe you much for the way you have served and loved my parents these last months…but I want more than your thanks, sweet cousin. I want you to make me a promise."

She waited, looking into those dark and sorrowful eyes that had seen so much.

"If I come back from this war and you are still unmarried, I want your promise that you will think favourably on marriage with me. If I should be given the gift of a future then I can think of no sweeter woman that I would want to spend it with."

She blushed, so unbelievably touched by his words. One day she would ask him the truth about the events which had taken place between him and Thurston so long ago. One day, but not now…there was only one response she needed to make to him now.

"I promise," she said "I promise."

17.

Thurston had awakened early that morning, refreshed and excited about the new day for the first time in months. He watched by the window, determined not to set off for the Vicarage until he had seen her even if it meant being late for work.

He sat for so long he thought he must have missed her, that she had passed by before he was awake and his heart began to sink. Then he saw the boy skipping, his long light brown hair bouncing and shining in the sunlight. He saw Ginny, running to catch up with him, looking like she had hardly slept and facing another long day in the fields.

Thurston jumped from his chair and ran to the door. Oh why had he not unbarred it as soon as he was up? By the time he had opened the door and stepped outside, she had passed. Other folk too were walking toward the moss, desperate to pick up a day's work.

"Ginny!" he called. She carried on, not hearing. He began to walk after her, starting to run. "Ginny... Ginny !"

She stopped and turned. She knew that if she turned back to see what Thurston wanted, her day's work was lost. Thurston knew it too but somehow he needed her to make the decision to trust him. He stood and waited.

"Isaac!" she called to the boy "Come here Isaac!"

The child stopped and looked back to his Mother and beyond her to Thurston. It gladdened his heart to see the child run back. Smiling, he grabbed his Mother's hand and the pair walked back towards him.

"What is it Thurston? Does tha need 'elp?"

He was so touched by her, by the fact that she had given up her work, by the fact that she had put him above her own need.

"Nay," he said "tha does."

Half an hour later, Thurston and Ginny left the cottage together, Thurston setting off for the Vicarage, Ginny holding a basket in one hand and her child's hand in the other, facing the day with a new energy. They parted when Ginny crossed the cart road to set out on her task for the day and little Isaac waved his hand again to Thurston, laughing as he ran to keep up with his mother's purposeful pace.

"Well if Ah do nothin' else this day" thought Thurston "Ah've done a good days work theer!" He continued to look back as he walked until he could see them no more.

Ginny could hardly believe the turn her life had taken in the last hour. She had money in her pocket to buy all she would need for a good nutritious meal that she would prepare for herself, Isaac and Thurston on his return that evening. She was to spend the day cleaning and making the cottage a comfortable home for Thurston to return to at the end of his working day and in return for the work, Thurston would pay her four pennies and the same every day for three days out of every week! She could really scarcely believe her good fortune, it was more than she could hope to earn in a month picking turnips on the Moss. As she walked along to Ma Jenkin's cottage, she felt a lightness in her heart such as she couldn't remember feeling for many a year, if ever.

Ma Jenkins cottage stood close by the ginnel down which Ginny's family lived and consisted of one little room with one big table in the middle of the floor. Ma Jenkins was well known in the little community for her cleverness and her kindness. Her one great fortune in life was to have inherited her Fathers little cottage with its long thin strip of garden behind it, together with her mother's green fingers. Her kitchen garden was full of whatever vegetables were in season, fertilised by loads of manure transported by Old Man Jenkins in his ancient cart. Ma Jenkin's hard work and her husband's business head provided ready ingredients for those villagers who had money in their pocket and a good living for the old couple.

Ma Jenkins had seen hard times in the little hamlet and its surrounding villages in the last ten years. Whole companies of soldiers tramping through their little hamlet, taking what they wanted from the farms, leaving little for those poor souls who made their living off the land nor those who depended on them. Ma Jenkins had seen people close to starvation some winters. The last two years had been a little better, praise God.

"God save us from those who war…" she prayed every day, "…just bring us peace again no matter who rules over us."

As she prayed her silent daily prayer and arranged her bounty of food to tempt her neighbours, in through her door that morning walked a young waif of a girl with a sweet child in her arms. Ma Jenkins despite her business head, cared for all in her community and often gave away vegetables that were spoiling to her poorer neighbours but never before the end of the day.

"Come back love, just after t'workers come 'ome. Ah'll 'ave summat for thee then."

Ginny was puzzled for a moment then realised she was being offered charity.

"Nay, nay Mistress…," she said, setting Isaac down "…Ah've money! She held out her palm displaying the coins. "Ah'm to buy all that's needed for a good meal!"

Ma Jenkins often said after that she could swear Ginny grew an inch or two when she said "Ah'm to keep 'ouse for Master Thurston!"

"Well…art tha now…?" Ma Jenkins was interested "…'ow long's tha bin doin' that then?"

Ginny smiled. "Since this mornin'" she answered brightly. Then suddenly, a look fell across her face. It was as if a cold wind had blown out a light. Something about her countenance made Ma Jenkins recognise the daughter of her troubled neighbour.

"Ginny? It is Ginny i'nt it?

Ginny nodded. "Ah don't think we could've gone on much longer Mistress. Thurston's saved mi life 'e 'as."

She looked down at Isaac, who stood mesmerised by the piles of carrots, potatoes and rows of rabbits and pullets laid out on the table. Ma Jenkins took a jar down from the table and held it low so the boy could see into it.

"Go on little 'un," she said, handing him a spoon "tek thee a good spoonful!"

Isaac looked up at her with his beautiful eyes. When he was sure no slap would come such as he often got from his granny, he put the spoon into the jar and scooped the preserve into his mouth.

Ma Jenkins looked up at Ginny's face, she was smiling again.

"Good luck to thee lass. Seems to me tha deserves it, and Master Thurston too! Come on, Ah'll fill that basket fit to make ye all a feast!"

Ginny was surprised at the almost forgotten sound of her own laughter when she looked down at Isaac happily shovelling the sweet blackberry preserve into his mouth, the sticky, dark red juice running down his dimpled chin.

***

Thurston walked to his work giddy with the feeling that comes from the performance of a truly charitable act. Again he felt the power of the overcoming of his trials. The inner strength he was beginning to realise he had always had long before he met Elspet, was returning...like blossoms peeping through the snows of winter. He marvelled at the pleasure that the gratitude of a troubled soul and the prospect of a child's happiness had given him and found he had hope of new pleasures to come. Again he thought that it was time to put away the sadness of the past months and to be glad for the awakening to life which Elspet had brought him. He knew he would never again be that lonely soul, shutting himself up against his fears. He was out in the world now, part of the trials and turmoil of the lives of those he lived amongst. For the first time he felt that he was now a part of the community he had lived in all his life.

"ow do Thurston," said his long known neighbours as he passed. "Master Thurston" some said. He no longer walked with his head bowed low...instead his eyes met the world as an equal.

At length he passed, as he did every morning, the Speakman's house. For all his new found purpose, the thought of Elspet shut up inside in her self-imposed exclusion pierced his heart. For the first time he pitied her, for her loss, for whatever it was that had caused her to deny the feeling that could have brought her so much happiness.

"God bless thee, Elspet" he muttered as he passed by.

He had almost reached the gates of the Vicarage when something made him turn...just the way it had pulled at Elspet that day in the graveyard. In the same way, it had pulled at him that day she had stood in the doorway...the invisible cord.

He turned and saw the unmistakable figure of Josiah Speakman, his arm about the shoulders of the woman Thurston would love all his life as he ushered her into the house where he and Elspet had kissed and they had tasted the promise of a lifetime of love. A promise that was so clearly and so brutally broken now forever.

For the first time in his life, Thurston wanted to fight. The strange new feeling churned low in his stomach. As it rose to his chest his heart pounded, the blood pumping in his temples and roaring in his ears. Every muscle in his lithe body tightened as he involuntarily rose up onto his toes, preparing to run toward that hated man, his mouth opening to roar his name in a cry of war!

"Master Thurston!"... it was as if he was being shaken from a dream. He looked down, still poised to run, yet held by a strange little woman with her hand on his sleeve.

"Master Thurston!" He breathed again, a long drawn out expulsion of all the emotions that had suddenly risen in those few seconds. He looked back at the Speakman's house. The door was firmly shut.

"Master Thurston. Are t'ill? Tha mun come wi' me. T'Master wants to sithee!"

He could hardly speak. "Who...who is thy master?" he croaked.

The woman was exasperated "Why Master Nicholas Moreton of course! Tha mun come...now Master Thurston!"

He followed her as if in a dream, through the gates of Moreton House and on through the trees up a wide, winding path until the house came into view. He stopped and looked at the old place, his emotions still tangled in the scene he had witnessed moments before .Slowly, he pulled free and began to try and process what was happening now.

Thurston was used to seeing the house from a distance, its tree framed façade romantically reflected in the lake. Up close the house looked neglected and broken, still beautiful but its beauty faded and ravaged by age. He began to come round, looking down again at the woman who still clung to his arm. He doubted she'd ever had any beauty for age to ravage.

"ast tha bin drinkin?" she asked, clearly frustrated at Thurston's lack of urgency in helping her accomplish the task she had been set.

"Ah've bin after thee this last hour," she said. "Tha'll be gerrin me sacked! Tha mun 'urry up Master! Come...quick now!"

She let go of his arm at last and scurried round the side of the house. Thurston, still not fully in command of his thoughts, mused that he must not be grand enough to use the front entrance of a gentleman's house. The old woman seemed to have read his mind.

"We don't use t'front door no more," she said. "We've not bin able t'open it for many a year now."

Thurston tentatively attempted to speak, testing his voice to see if it had regained its full strength:

"'ast tha bin 'ere a long time then Mistress?" he asked.

"Oh Aye..." panted the old woman as she continued to walk briskly "...my mother was the old Master's cook. Ah was born 'ere. Guess 'ow many years?" she winked.

A hundred, thought Thurston. "Forty!" he said. The old woman laughed displaying her four remaining teeth.

"By 'eck tha'rt a rum un!" she said, still laughing as they entered the house through a side door.

The inside of the house was gloomy after the bright June sunshine and it smelled of old lavender and the musty odour of ancient damp wood. For the first time in the last ten minutes, he paused to draw breath and wonder why he was here. What had happened before that, he tried to shut from his mind as firmly as the Speakman's door had been shut.

"Wait 'ere," said the old woman disappearing through a tall, oak door. Thurston waited. He was in a passageway lined with dark panelling and he fancied the smell was coming from whatever was behind the old wood. The place was grand nonetheless, and held for him already the promise he had always known would lie within its walls. He felt there had been happiness here though the times were long gone. There was a kindness here, and he warmed to it. The old woman appeared again. "Come In" she beckoned.

He followed her into a room of such beauty it made him gasp. Light poured in through beautiful high, wide windows such as he had never seen even in Church. The light was behind the man who rose to greet him, masking his face until Thurston became accustomed to the brightness. The man held out his hand and as Thurston clasped it he looked into a good face...it was the face of the man whose character filled this house.

"I am happy to meet thee at last Thurston Hey. I have heard many good things of thee and I am led to believe thou canst help me young man."

18

Many hours later as the night hurtled across the sky towards its end, Nathaniel sat in his chair by the tiny window of his bedchamber, looking out at the blackness of the hour before dawn. He waited, longing for the first light and the dilution of the dread the night had brought for him. He had sat here on many a night in his life, his mind whirring with worry as it often did, but it was different now. Now no outstretched hand or loving word beckoned him back to bed, no soft comfort waited there to soothe away his troubles with a gentle touch. He was alone, his mind fliting this way and that between fervent hope for his son's life and fear of his death. It was always so when Josiah left, the dread that he had seen that beloved face for the last time. Yet again, in this there was a difference in the whirring of his mind tonight...Elspet.

He realised that he had known there was a child coming. He had buried the thought, not hard to do beneath the heavy weight of grief that had engulfed him these last months. He knew it could not be Thurston, had never suspected the boy. Nathaniel could read people, it was a gift he had. He had read Thurston like a book and had seen his good soul. He had wondered if Elspet had come to them with child. He had almost asked her but his tongue was too tied with grief and the fear that she would leave him and he knew for sure he could not have borne that. But the news today had shocked him to the core. That she carried a child fathered by his own son? The son he so loved...of whom he was so proud...to use her so? He could not understand it. Perhaps Josiah had lived for so long on the edge of society he had ceased to know its proper ways? But Nathaniel could not see it, he had read his own son's character too and knew he had a good, though troubled heart. Whichever way he looked at it, it made no sense. At least Josiah had offered to marry the lass. At least he had lit a candle to brighten the future.

Nathaniel, though troubled for his niece and the shame she would live with, felt his dampened spirits rise at the prospect of a child in the house again. His son's child...his grandchild! He knew he would do his duty to the girl, to his son, to the memory of his dear Eliza and to the babe to come. He must.

He was suddenly roused from his thoughts by the sight of a flickering flame in the Churchyard. He breathed again...it was only the watchman, hired by Sir William to protect his new treasure. The sight prompted him to recall again as he had on many nights since his visit in January to Abbots Hall, an event he had witnessed on such a night as this...three years before.

He had seen the flicker of flame that night too late to help. By the time he had run outside in his night shirt and cap shouting the alarm, smoke was billowing from the Church Tower. The sound of centuries old beams cracking in the heat could be heard by all in the village. As Nathaniel had stood helpless, watching the burning, he had seen, silhouetted by the orange glow of fire and showers of sparks lighting the sky, the figure of a man running from that terrible scene.

He had seen that man again on the night they had supped at Abbots Hall, recognising his profile only when he shook out his damp hair by the fire on their return from the stables. So eager had Nathaniel been to get away from the man he thought must be descended from the very devil, he had not even let Elspet warm herself before dragging her out into that blizzard again.

He had thought on it many times since that night. Had Sir William set his son to burn the Church? His patronage of the building had raised his influence and enhanced his power. Had that evil boy burned the latest thing that took a greater place than he in his Father's affections? There was clearly no love lost between Father and son. In part it was this realisation of the bad blood within the family who had employed him that had caused Nathaniel to withdraw from the building...that and the loss of his dear wife and all interest in life that had gone with her.

He stood and walked back to his lonely bed, hoping for an hour of peaceful rest before the sun rose.

God help any child with that family's blood running in its veins thought Nathaniel as he closed his eyes and tried to remember the face of his dear Josiah as a newborn babe.

19. Midsummer

The Reverend Samson Kingsley arrived in the village of Appley Green on the Eve of Midsummer's Day in June 1651, amidst great ceremony and celebrations.

Sir William Bagshawe, his benefactor, was feared rather than respected for the power he had gathered through the forging of clever alliances during these last years of civil war. Nevertheless, the people who lived in the village and the surrounding little hamlets, were grateful to him for the restoration of their Church. And now that he had brought a new incumbent to minister to their spiritual needs… well, it was as if God himself had returned to reside in their community!

The Reverend Kingsley had rested at Abbots Hall the night before and was brought to the Church in Bagshawe's coach which had been festooned with flowers to welcome him. He walked across the village green surrounded by dozens of people who had come to wish him well, applauding, eager to see the man who would caretake their moral wellbeing in the years to come. They saw a kindly faced, grey-haired man with piercing blue eyes. The more discerning of the onlookers that day would also have noticed his almost imperceptible discomfort at the hand of Sir William Bagshawe, clapped firmly on his shoulder as he guided the Reverend toward the Church.

Nathaniel of course, had his part to play, as to a lesser extent did Thurston and his fellow labourers, as the men who were responsible for restoring the Reverend's places of work and rest to their former glory. Nathaniel bowed to Sir William, and warmly shook the hand of the new Reverend, clearly feeling an affinity with Samson Kingsley.

Elspet watched from her Uncle's bedchamber and saw the moment when Thurston was presented to the new Vicar of St. Stephen's parish. He was dressed in the new clothes he had worn for Eliza's funeral and her heart swelled with love and that need he always stirred in her, to care for him. He deserved to be loved more than any person she had ever known and how she wished she could be a part of this day...a day when he rose a little in their small society, as he so deserved to do.

She had refused to go out and join the celebrations despite Nathaniel's entreaties. She had no wish to have Thurston look on her as Josiah had done. No wish to witness the horror of realisation on his face. She struggled to hide her growing belly now, unable to lace her clothing until this last week when Nathaniel, at Josiah's insistence, had bought her new clothes. She lived as a nun, shut away in a convent, though her youth and vitality had not been given as a gift to God...rather robbed from her by the Devil.

Elspet watched the procession walk to Church and heard the soaring notes of the choir as they began to sing a joyous welcome. Unable to open the casement wide enough to hear, she ran downstairs and threw the front door open wide to listen. Some of the villager's looked over to her and Elspet became aware of their gossip as one head bent to another and another face looked over to where she stood. Instinctively she moved behind the door to hide herself and not even the beautiful sound of voices raised in song could lift her spirits again.

****

Thurston left the Church an hour later and was part of the procession which accompanied Reverend Kingsley to his new home. He walked beside Master Nicholas Moreton, at that gentleman's invitation, and they discussed again the subject that had thrilled Thurston since their first conversation some weeks before.

Thurston was keenly aware of the condescension shown to him by Master Nicholas and was as puzzled by it as many in the throng that day. Nicholas Moreton had been one of the most important men in the County, his family having an illustrious and proud history fighting for Kings for generations past. He had discussed openly with Thurston in their last few meetings, the way his fortunes and influence had changed since the wars had begun... an even greater change since the death of the King. Thurston had sensed in their recent conversations, the contempt in which the gentleman held Sir William Bagshawe although the two men had been affable enough in each other's company that afternoon, as polite society demanded.

Thurston had begun to realise these last few weeks how shut away he had been these last years...all his life really. He saw clearly now how unaware he was of the politics that had torn apart his country. He hadn't even really understood the concept of 'country'! His country, his world, had been the few miles between his little cottage on the edge of the moss and the villages nearby. He hadn't understood the war except for the destruction that it brought and the cruel side of men that it brought out. He, as his Father before him, had given allegiance to those who held over them the power of life or death, want or plenty. For generations, this power had never been questioned but he knew now that these years of war had caused men to question and to choose their sides. Men like he himself.

Nicholas Moreton had awakened the question in him and somehow Thurston knew that this man would feed his growing thirst for knowledge of the dealings between men of power and their impact on the lives of the simple people who lived beneath them. For now, however, the subject upon which they conversed, the one that at times beguiled Thurston so much that he could not sleep, was the gentleman's beautiful old house.

"Wilt thou come and share a cup of wine now with me Thurston?"

Thurston looked at Sir Nicholas, surprise tinged with humility showing in his face.

"Ah would be 'onoured Sir," he replied, bowing as he had seen so many fine gentlemen do that afternoon.

Just as Elspet's had done earlier, Nicholas Moreton's heart swelled with affection for the lad who stood before him. They left the Reverend at his newly refurbished Vicarage and fell into easy step and conversation again with each other on the walk to Moreton House.

"Thou art excited Thurston at the prospect of this work on my house I can see."

Thurston nodded, his spirit's rising as they entered the gate and began the walk up the shaded, tree-lined drive.

"Aye indeed Sir...Ah've loved this place all me life!"

"Love...?" Nicholas Moreton feigned surprise. "How couldst thou love it? Thou canst not have looked on it much?"

Thurston blushed, aware that he had almost unthinkingly given away the secret of his trespass over the years. He looked up to Nicholas Moreton in the gloom and to his amazement the old man was smiling.

"Worry not, my boy," he said. "I have watched thee for many a year, creeping to my moat. Thou seemest to need the place so...I could not bear to mend the hole in the wall and thus deprive thee of it!"

Thurston, to use his Mother's expression, was 'flummoxed'. He knew not what to say. Even if he did, he could not have said it, for he knew that if he opened his mouth he might cry like a child. Master Nicholas sensed that his remark had stirred an unexpected emotion in the lad. He placed a concerned hand on Thurston's shoulder.

"What is it, my boy? I only jest! It is of no matter that thou came here."

They had stopped walking just as the trees parted to reveal the front of the house in all its faded glory. They both looked at the place and it gave Thurston the moment he needed.

"Forgive me Sir," he said, hesitantly. Then quietly he continued, putting into words for the first time ever, the feelings that had led him to seek refuge in the garden.

"I did need this place...I believe it kept me goin' through...some dark times." He breathed deeply for a moment and Master Nicholas stood quietly waiting until Thurston's trickle of words ran their course. He did not have to wait long.

"I thank thee for thy forbearance Sir," said Thurston, unable to think on it more.

Nicholas Moreton knew that there was nothing to gain by pressing the lad. He knew he would speak when the time was right. He patted Thurston's shoulder comfortingly, sensing that the dark shadow of memory had cast a chill on his heart.

"It is of no matter, my boy," he said. "If thou hast needed this place in the past, then thou art welcome to whatever solace it hath given thee."

He laughed then. "Why! Now the tables are turned lad. This house hath need of thee!"

Thurston smiled back at Master Nicholas before he too began laughing, an endearing look of embarrassment on his face. Nicholas Moreton thought suddenly that he saw more and more promise in this young man every time they met. He placed his arm about Thurston's shoulder.

"Now then my boy," he said, waving his hand across the scene in an all-encompassing gesture. "Where dost thou think we should start?"

20.

Some hours after the celebrations had died away and the villagers had gone back to their homes, Elspet sat in the downstairs window overlooking the Green. The sun was disappearing behind the Church as evening approached, casting a beautiful orange glow into the room. Nathaniel sat by the hearth, reading. Soon it would be time to serve their supper and then begin the weary winding down of another wasted day. These evening hours were the hardest with no company but Nathaniel who more and more disappeared into his books. At least now the evenings were light, tomorrow would be the longest day and tonight bonfires would be lit to celebrate Midsummer's Eve. The village lads had built one on the Green that afternoon and Elspet was thankful that nightfall would bring her a little welcome entertainment.

She remembered the eve of Midsummer spent in her own village in Derbyshire. How the lads would leap through the flames of the bonfire for luck and to show off to the girls who sat nearby, weaving their garlands of St John's wort. They would squeal with delight at the boy's antics and giggle shyly, each one hoping that one of the lads would make her a husband one day...all except she...Elspet had always somehow known that her fate would play itself out in another way, in another place. Well, she thought, fate had indeed taken hold of her life and twisted it most cruelly. She looked again at the Green. There would be no such pagan activities around the bonfire this night. Strict religious practices had constricted such festivals these days. Tonight the people of Appley Green would simply celebrate the arrival of the new Vicar with a bonfire and games... and some might secretly make an offering in the flames to the forbidden, pagan gods of old.

She rose to prepare the evening meal and begin, while the light still held, the last tasks of the day. The boys and girls were just beginning to drift onto the Green as she left the room.

****

Ginny and Isaac walked through the fields towards Appley Green. Ginny had promised her boy that if he was good, she would take him to the bonfire in the evening and he had been an angel all afternoon.

How their lives had changed in the past three weeks! She wore the first new clothes she could ever remember wearing, Isaac too, after their trip to the market with Ma Jenkins. She was sure Isaac had put on weight and he was as bright and happy as she was. She thought back to that first night, so long ago now it seemed.

She had waited for Thurston in the little cottage for what seemed hours and he had eventually returned home much later than he had said he would. He had worn an air of sadness about him that night. She could feel it as soon as he entered but at the sight of her by the fire and the smell of food cooking, she had seen his spirits visibly rise for a moment. Little Isaac had fallen asleep and she had lain him in the bed in the corner of the room. Thurston had limped over and stood looking at the boy for some moments, and although he stood with his back to Ginny, she could sense his emotion as he watched the child sleeping without a care in the world, stroking his soft hair. She almost cried herself when Thurston turned, his eyes glassy, and said:

"Let 'im always know love Ginny…Ah think it must be more important than any other thing for a child."

She had nodded, silently affirming his words.

"Come an' eat," she had said.

In the next hour, enjoying her food and her bright company she had seen his sad mood fade away. She hadn't known what had caused his sadness that night but she knew that she had helped and in turn Thurston had lifted her spirits higher than

136

she had ever thought possible in her miserable life. And now, today, Ma Jenkins had asked her if she and Isaac wanted to board with her. She knew Thurston was behind it. She had seen him coming out of Ma Jenkins house the day before at the very moment Ginny had popped her head outside the little cottage door to see if he was coming home.

At last she could leave her Mother's house and bring her boy up in a proper home. She could pay her board and even give her Mother a little money now and then with the generous wage Thurston paid her. She had been finding it harder and harder to leave the little cottage on the days she spent there, so hard to return to her Mother's house with the filth and the smell and the want she had grown up with. She had begun to fantasise on those days that the cottage was her own home. She would wash Isaac in the wooden tub and then she would scrub herself, washing away the years of grime and neglect, cleansing herself like a baptism. It was as if she had found a new religion in which she celebrated her worth for the first time in her twenty years.

And now tonight, after the festivities, she would walk back with Thurston. He would bid the boy goodnight with his usual kisses then she and Isaac would go home to Ma Jenkins house and sleep a blissful night of comfortable sleep.

Ah yes, Ginny thought as she walked along with Isaac, she had much to thank Thurston Hey for. She swung Isaac's hand and began to skip, laughing as he jumped and skipped along beside her. As they drew nearer to the village, she could smell the smoke of the newly lit bonfire drifting through the still summer evening.

****

It was almost dark by the time Elspet and Nathaniel had eaten their meal and she knelt by the hearth to kindle the fire as the evening grew chill, lighting the first tallow candle from the flames. Struggling to rise, she returned to the table by the window where Nathaniel still sat and on the Green she saw the first flicker of flame as the bonfire was lit. Nathaniel walked across to the window and drew the curtain, shutting out the coming night and the only prospect of entertainment for Elspet. Wearily she left the room, taking the dishes to the kitchen. Having washed and dried the plates and tidied, she returned to the hall. Through the half open doorway she could see her Uncle now sat by the fire, lost in his book and his own mournful thoughts. She slipped past the doorway and began to sneak upstairs to her Uncle's bedchamber to watch the events on the Green. It was as she set her foot upon the first stair that the banging began on the front door.

****

As Ginny and Isaac approached the Green, the flames were already high and the child could sense the excitement.

"Turton!" he said.

Ginny laughed: "In a bit," she said "Thurston will be 'ere in a bit. Remember? Ah said 'e was busy. 'e'll be 'ere soon." She chucked Isaac under the chin.

Some of the men were playing penny whistles in a corner of the Green and young girls were stepping to the tunes of the old country dances as they had for generations past. Many wore the gaily coloured ribbons they had worn on May Day. Farmer Shuttleworth's son had brought his sister's favourite little pony and was giving children rides around the Green. Ginny joined the queue with Isaac in her arms.

"Ginny...Ginny!"

Her younger brother Joseph waved and ran towards them, his sandy hair flopping as he ran, the way that Ginny and Isaac's did. He lifted the child, swinging him high over his head and Isaac screamed with delight, flying like a bird as he rose and fell in his Uncle's arms.

"Joseph, tha'll make 'im sick!" Ginny chided.

The lad put Isaac down and they both laughed at his dizzy stumble.

"Ginny, tha looks well. Ah'm so 'appy for thi good fortune."

She touched his cheek. A big family, they had always got their affection from each other.

"Aye...life'll be a bit easier for us now, that's for sure." She grabbed his hand: "But Ah shall 'elp thee, little brother...all Ah can."

"Nay!" he said "Ah'm awreet! Come on...dance wi'me!"

He picked up the child in one arm and grabbed her waist with the other, whirling them both round and round to the tune of the penny whistles and the rhythm he had found in his cup of ale.

After a few moments of whirling, Ginny suddenly became aware of a commotion over by the bonfire. She heard the sound of shrieking girls and the sound struck a discordant note in her memory.

"Stop Joseph, stop!" she cried, craning her neck to see over the people who were moving across the Green, drawn to the scene of the shouting.

"Watch Isaac," she said to her brother and she ran, pulled by some instinctive compulsion to catch the moving crowd. She had a sickening feeling in her stomach as the sudden remembrance of the cries of bullying girls reached through time to taunt her. She pushed her way through to the front of the crowd and was appalled to see Master Speakman's niece, held by six or seven girls, her arms forcibly outstretched, her condition plain for all to see in the blaze of the fire.

Some women of the village approached, the mothers of those girls who held, poked and prodded Elspet. Nathaniel nearby, struggled to free himself from the grip of two strapping young men who restrained him. Something told Ginny to run...run for Thurston. She knew where he was. She knew as all did of his regard for Elspet Sydall. She had not run so fast for years, her threadbare boots hardly touching the ground as she ran, panting, up the drive of Moreton House. She hammered on the ancient front door so hard she thought her knuckles would break.

"Thurston! Thurston come quickly!'t is Mistress Elspet... she is in danger! Thurston please come!"

She shouted again and again at the door, wondering why no-one came. It seemed like hours before he appeared, from the side of the house running towards her.

"What is it? Is it Isaac?" he held her shoulders.

"Elspet," she breathed "...Elspet!"

He didn't wait to ask what, who or when... he just ran into the night as fast as his crippled leg could carry him. Master Nicholas took her arm, sensing her shock.

"Come, my dear," he said "let us walk together."

"Maggie!" he called to his old servant, who just now was hobbling round from the side of the house.

"Send young Billy to run for the Reverend Kingsley... hurry now!"

Thurston was demented as he ran towards the fire. Through his watering eyes, he began to make out the scene through the trees and the heat of the blaze. He saw her held there and something snapped within him, anger that he had held inside for so long was unleashed in that moment. Flashes of hidden faces and sticks and cries of pain swam in his head as he ran, headlong into the throng. With a strength and bravery he never knew he had, he pulled her away from her captors and held her behind him, his arm outstretched in a gesture which said: keep away... touch her not!!

He looked round at Nathaniel, held by the two young lads who should have known better.

"How dare you hold Master Speakman so! Let go of 'im you dogs! Let go now!"

He roared at the lads like a wild animal and they dropped their arms sheepishly, releasing their captor who ran to the side of his niece. Still Thurston held her behind him, guarding her like a lion.

Then the crowd parted as Nicholas Moreton walked through.

"What madness is this?" he demanded.

All were silent. Some bent their heads, some moved away suddenly ashamed.

"Well...? What occurs here I say?"

From the silent, murmuring crowd, a woman stepped forward. Mistress Sarah Eaton took hold of her daughter's hand as she spoke.

"'t is not these girls ye should rebuke Sir! 't is this young woman 'ere...," she said, pointing at Elspet "... 'er shame exposed for all to see. We are decent folk."

"Decent folk!" shouted Nicholas Moreton "decent folk? Is this how decent folk behave? Abusing a young, defenceless woman who has not even been given a chance to speak?"

Thurston's head was swimming. Shame...what was Elspet's shame? He was just beginning to take in the scene, to wonder what was happening here.

Master Nicholas turned to Nathaniel.

"Master Speakman ...I think it is time thou should'st take thy niece home."

But Mistress Eaton stepped forward another step, her face determined.

"Nay Sir, Nay! He must speak!" Turning to the crowd she cried: "What say all? Tha's all gossiped enough!"

Nathaniel stepped out to face the throng, preparing to speak. Thurston still held Elspet, his arm around her, slowly becoming aware of the feel of her body pressing into his back, realisation slowly dawning of the cause of Elspet's shame. He slowly turned letting her go, looking into her eyes for the first time in months. Her face was beautiful, her lovely, tear-filled green eyes sparkled in the firelight. He remembered suddenly, for a fleeting moment, that kiss on the eve of the New Year before the fire and all the promise it had held. As he looked down, he knew all was lost. He had never loved or hated anyone more. Nathaniel was speaking and Thurston could just about hear him over the thumping of his own heart.

"My niece is betrothed to my son, Josiah. They will marry on his return from the North."

Whispers rippled through the crowd and then for a moment there was silence before Sarah Eaton spoke again:

"And where is the proof of that, Master Speakman? And what difference does that make? She still bears a child out of wedlock and that is a sin before God! I say again she brings shame on us all!"

"I believe I speak for God here Mistress!"

The Reverend Samson Kingsley commandingly took his place on the stage as the drama continued to play out on that Midsummer's Eve.

"Thou hast before thee one of the most respected men in this village" he continued. "I doubt not that Master Speakman tells the truth and I am sure that this young woman here can confirm that truth."

The Reverend gestured to Elspet who knew that she could never confirm it though they tear her apart. She looked as though she would crumble to her knees at any moment.

Thurston put out his arm to steady her as he spoke, his voice shaking.

"We need not ask her. Ah know they are betrothed...Ah was a witness."

Everyone who was there that night would recall for a long time, the wave of sympathy that ran through the crowd. All had seen Thurston's love for Elspet Sydall and all felt that if he could forgive her, so could they. Even Mistress Eaton could no longer meet his eyes and bowed her head. The crowd slowly began to disperse, their entertainment over. The girls were ushered away by their mothers, contenting themselves with only a look of contempt at Elspet who stood, oblivious to them, her heart bleeding for Thurston, once again her Saviour.

Nathaniel thanked the Reverend and Master Nicholas and the three men moved to usher Elspet back into the Speakman's house. Suddenly Nathaniel turned and put his arms about Thurston.

"Ah shall never be able to thank thee lad! Th'art a fine man...a fine man indeed."

Master Nicholas too put his arm about him. "Come and see me tomorrow lad," he said.

Reverend Kingsley simply bowed to him, like one gentleman would bow to another but in that simple act, Thurston felt he had the stranger's respect.

Thurston stood after they had gone, numb, feeling lost like he had all his life before the morning he had set eyes on her. He felt suddenly an overwhelming urge to weep in a way he had not wept for years.

"Tur'ton!"

He turned to see Isaac on his mother's hip, holding out his arm's to him. He took the child from Ginny and held him close.

"'orsey!" said Isaac, pointing at the pony that was being led away. The evening was over before it had even begun.

"Aye, little 'un …'orsey! Come on, let's catch 'im up. Tha can 'ave a ride eh?"

He turned to Ginny and grasped her hand tightly.

"Let's go 'ome," he said.

And she followed as they chased after the pony, her heart going out to him.

Why does God always make the good one's suffer so? She thought.

21.

Josiah stood on the quayside. The smell of the incoming tide and the power with which it smashed against the harbour walls filled him with an energy he hadn't felt for many months.

He loved the sea. He loved the rough feel of it beneath his feet as he stood on deck when sailing over it. He loved the way it rocked him to sleep as he lay in his narrow bunk beneath its surface. Most of all he loved the moment when all land disappeared from view, when the last traces of the place he had left were swallowed up into the invisible distance and the place to which he sailed, was still confined to his imagination. In that short time, he felt a brief freedom and it was intoxicating to him.

He had been on this island for some weeks now, waiting for what he knew must come. He sensed an ending. He felt a coming change of fortune. He hoped that soon the servitude to which for the first time he felt unwillingly bound, would soon disappear into his past. He prayed that freedom of one sort or another would come.

He had followed this past seven years with unswerving loyalty, Sir Thomas and his company. The journey had led him across counties and countries and overseas and now at last to this island... this stepping-stone to England, this springboard to their ultimate goal, the restoration of the rule of a King.

He would see it through to whatever end was destined for him and if he was alive at the end of it, he hoped for a life that he had never thought possible, cursed as he was with his turbulent heart and mind. He longed for peace, he longed for a family. He hoped for the love of a woman and adventures of a kind which would never cause him to leave again the village to which he would soon, God willing, return.

Each day he waited here on the quayside, his eyes scanning the grey waters for the first sign of their discovery. They were hiding here, resting and preparing for the victory to come. All they need do now was remain in this safe haven given to them by the loyal Earl of Derby and wait for orders to set sail for the Lancashire coast.

He stood on the harbour wall, his long hair blowing in the vicious tidal wind. The high walls of the ancient castle which defended them rose heavenward from the outcrop of land which edged the harbour, its huge, stone-hewn presence sheltering the sprawling encampment that had sprung up in the wake of their arrival. It was a bustling community of soldiers, farriers, armourers, saddlers and brewers. There were cooks, stablelads, dress-makers, laundresses and those who provided one of the most important services of all…the women who met their most intimate needs.

Josiah had long since ceased his association with the whores who followed the camp, preferring instead to find a bedmate from the throng of women who made their living through more moral means. For some weeks now, he had found comfort in the arms of a young woman called Rachel who worked in the camp laundry. Rachel was pretty with long, smooth sand-coloured hair that flowed like silk over her naked shoulders when when they were alone in his tent at night. Her beauty was marred only by a missing front tooth and so she smiled rarely, covering her mouth when she did. It gave her an air of modesty and innocence and Josiah had taken her under his wing from the first. In return for his care and protection, he had taken pleasure in her body, feeling no disgrace in this knowing that if it were not he that claimed her it might be a far rougher man.

She stood on the edge of the camp, looking across at him, waiting to catch his eye. The unasked question was written on her face: "Why? Why do you not ask me to come to you this week past?"

He sighed as he looked at her. He didn't know why he hadn't wanted to see her these past few days and nights. Perhaps, deep down, it was fear? The fear he felt in the sure knowledge of an end in sight. He was not ashamed of this fear...fear is not the same as cowardice. Perhaps it was the hope that he would return home and settle down with Elspet, or if not her some other village girl who would demand nothing of him but his love? Perhaps it was the weariness with which he bowed to the demands of those mistresses he had chased for so many years...Patriotism, and Lust for Victory? But these passions he knew were in their death throes for him now, though he had no choice but to spend his final energy fighting for them in the deciding battles to come. Then, please God, this chapter in his life would end and a new one would begin.

He recalled, as he had so many times since that meeting with Thurston in his Father's house, the memory of that fateful day when he had left his home at sixteen. He recalled for the hundredth time the scene he had witnessed and the sickening events which had changed the course of his life. He needed to go home but he needed to go home having atoned for the wrongs he had done. He needed to right the wrong done to Thurston Hey and through that, release himself from the terrible guilt that still haunted him. This last week in the lonely darkness night after night, he had tossed and turned tormented by visions of him dealing out justice to the one man who had come to embody for Josiah, the enemy. He knew he must seek him out in that final battle and mete out the justice that would free them all... himself, Elspet and most of all Thurston Hey. Since that morning he had spent with his troubled young cousin, he had begun to see his destiny clearer than he had ever seen it and a determination had begun to grow in him. He recognised the taste of fear and the danger in that determination... the possible ending of his own story on the battlefield. No new chapter to be written with a wife and a child and a Father growing old, secure in his son's love.

He looked across again at Rachel, carrying a basket of linen in one arm, fending off the drunken advances of a rough infantryman with the other. Hers was a destiny he could shape. He would care for her now and leave her with some chance of a better life when he had gone.

"Rachel!" he called her. She looked over at him with relief and setting down her basket, ran from her tormentor who shuffled away with a grunt, hiding his anger beneath a grudging subservience. She reached Josiah's side and he held her in his arms. A jumble of thoughts, memories, long-forgotten feelings and new emotions had tied up his mind for weeks. These last few days, the threads had untangled, his decision was made and with it came the clarity of purpose that had been missing for years. He breathed in the sea air as he held her, filling his lungs with a surge of strength and energy. Then he allowed the long-practiced ability of the soldier to trust his destiny to a higher power, settle around him like a cloak. He would think only of this day and would live only for each day to come until his fate played itself out, like the winds that were quelled by the ebb of the tide.

He lifted her chin, her smooth pale cheek turning to receive his kiss. Breathing in the sweet softness of her hair he whispered: "Forgive my neglect my Rachel, will you come to me tonight?"

She nodded, her small, freckled hand covering the broken smile, the ocean reflecting in her blue-grey eyes.

22.

Thurston awoke with a jump, his eyes struggling to adjust to the blackness. Relief washed over him as he realised he was in his own bed in the little cottage and not in the dark pit that he saw in his nightmares. For the last two nights since Midsummer's Eve, the nightmare had plagued him, each time the same. A crowd of people gathered, shouting and screaming around their unseen victim. One by one they stepped aside as he pushed through the crowd and as he passed through he saw their faces...Nathaniel's...children from his past...Sarah Eaton...and the most hated of all, Josiah Speakman. Then suddenly the victim was revealed and he saw that it was he himself, face down on the ground, naked and bloody. For a brief moment, he felt the body of someone pushing him down into the ground and he fought, struggling to shake off his unseen attacker. The black earth filling his mouth suddenly became black hair and he coughed and spat it from his mouth, moving it aside to reveal Elspet's face, her green eyes open and dull as if dead. Then again the unseen body pressed down on him so hard the ground beneath him fell away and he plunged, falling helpless into a pit of blackness. It was then that he awoke, sweating and moaning.

His Mother always said that if you fall in a dream you must never reach the ground because there awaited your death. It had terrified him as a child and it terrified him now. Even though the night was warm, he shivered. Cocooning himself in his blankets he curled up in his bed, hoping to sleep again undisturbed. At least until the sun rose.

***

It was mid-morning and the warm sun was drying the dew-damp lawn as Nicholas sat by the moat in his garden at Moreton. He looked across at the old house and realised that Thurston was right, this was the most beautiful view of the place. From here the blemishes which marred her faded beauty were less discernible and like the rambling ancient old wisteria which framed her façade, hers was a beauty only the passing of time could create. The house had always been female to him. She had nurtured him as a child and she had welcomed his own dear wife who had loved the house as much as he had. The house had indulged his children in the same way a Grandmother might, allowing them to run and play with their balls and their toys in her grand rooms. She had kept them safe within her walls as they slept and watched with pride as they grew into young men. It was why he would never leave this place, the memories this house held for him were his greatest treasure, more valuable than any fortune.

One of his many regrets was that he had been unable to look after her the way he should in these last years and he hoped that his long departed ancestors would forgive him.

The house had been built in 1513 by James Moreton with the largesse he had received form King Henry VIII. James had been one of many northern men who had rallied at the request of Queen Katharine in her husband's absence to repel an invading Scottish army. He had been severely wounded at the Battle of Flodden losing his right arm and eye. For his sacrifice and considerable courage, he had received substantial financial reward and lands and he had used both gifts wisely to provide for his children and their children to come, by the building of two beautiful houses.

Anne Rushden had been proud to marry into the Moreton family in 1624, her marriage coinciding with that of King Charles and his Queen in that same year. Nicholas had been thrilled with his new wife...she had a kindness and goodness which infected all whose lives she touched and he had loved her with a devotion that even death had not extinguished. Everything he did now and planned to do was a tribute to the shining example she still was to him. He had sat by her bed as she died, six years earlier and told her she was still as beautiful as the day she had married him and the last sound she made on this earth was that brief, embarrassed little chuckle she always made when he complimented her.

She had never rebuked him for his terrible mistakes, had never blamed him even when she suffered the sharpest pain a mother could ever bear in the death of her children. He blamed himself totally but her quiet composure and concern for him had humbled him so much that all the arrogance he had grown up with had fallen away. All his inbred sense of duty and right, his unquestioned observance of old loyalties...all ceased to have meaning for him. Love was all in those last remaining months after the death of the boys...love was all.

They had been bound so closely together, Anne and he, that when she slipped away he had wanted to go too...for a long time. Then one day, he had been sitting in the silent shadows in the lovely room overlooking this garden, admiring the colours of the setting sun as it played on the water when he saw a boy creeping clumsily from the undergrowth by the wall. He watched as the boy limped across the exposed expanse of grass, looking around him cautiously as he went, fearful of detection. The house had been in darkness, no candles had yet been lit and Nicholas had seen the boy visibly relax as he sat by the moat, the last orange rays of the sun slanting through the leaves lighting his dark hair and handsome features.

Something about the lad reminded him of his own lost boys. His twin sons hadn't been much older when they had left, marching to their separate deaths in those first months of madness in this most dreadful of wars. The boy by the moat had an air of melancholy about him and Nicholas' own aching heart went out to him. Night had fallen, Maggie had come in to light the candles and the garden had been cloaked in darkness...but somehow the sight of the boy had kindled a light in the blackness that had shrouded Nicholas Moreton. He had for some reason awakened in him some interest in life again.

Nicholas watched for him and had seen him many times over the last few years and at last he had met him for the first time only a few weeks before. He had not seen Thurston since the events of Midsummer's Eve. He had not called at Moreton the next day as Nicholas had asked or the day after that. If he did not come today, Nicholas meant to go in search of Thurston Hey. He had waited to know him for such a long time, he could not bear to lose his acquaintance now…so much depended on it.

23.

No matter how warm the day outside, the room in which Sir William Bagshawe had entertained Nathaniel Speakman and his niece on that January night always felt as cold as the grave.

Sir William paced before the fire which always burned, whatever the season. No heat from the sun permeated the large room nor did light from the windows reach with any strength beyond the hearth by which he now stopped, turning the two letters over and over in his hands. He had read them both on their arrival from the village and the contents of one of them had set his heart beating a little faster. He read again the letter from his son, written in a halting, spidery hand, the uncertainty and fear of rejection felt by the writer permeating the very paper. His Father did not feel it, he read only the words:

"Sir,

I trust this letter finds thee in the good health that thou enjoyed at our last meeting.

I write to tell thee of my contentment here in the company of Colonel Milburne. We have stayed encamped here for some weeks now but I know we will receive orders to march soon to some unknown place.

I have received the commission of Officer and I hope that thou receive'st this news with a proud heart, as I ever sought to please thee Father.

Colonel Milburne has agreed that all the company may have visitors on the second Saturday in July and as the distance is not too great, I had hoped that thou would'st travel to visit with me Sir.

It would gladden my heart to have thee wish me well on my first sojourn into battle.

I know time presseth hard on thee Sir and if it cannot be then, I would ask that thou pray'st for my safekeeping in the heat of the battles that must come.

I keep thee in my prayers.

Written this day 23rd June Sixteen Hundred and Fifty one, with affection by the hand of thy son,

Edwin Bagshawe."

Sir William read again the second letter. It had been written by the hand of an old friend and business acquaintance in Lancaster, a man with whom he had made a great deal of money as the Royalists fell from grace. His letter brought Bagshawe news of a sale of property in the Lake country. A grand house owned by a man he knew well, a man who despised him and thought himself above him. Here in his hand was the opportunity to vanquish an old enemy by buying his property at a knock-down price. The seller would be all too aware as a Royalist that if he didn't sell his property now it would be taken from him one way or another when Parliament brought the old Kings's supporters to account. Then after this house, the prize he had always coveted could not be far behind and his old adversary would face ruination, his high moral standards crushed under the heel of the Bagshawe boot.

Sir William resolved to go to the auction on the second Saturday in July and so begin the final campaign to finish this feud forever. The thrill of the prospect filled him with new energy! He felt like riding hard and fast over his land as he had in his youth. Carelessly he tossed Edwin's letter into the fire, feeling only a momentary twinge of guilt… as fleeting as the rise and fall of the flames as they consumed the paper.

24.

Elspet lay in her narrow bed in the little room in the house which had become her prison. She knew the hour was late. She had watched the daylight seep from beneath the tight cover of darkness and through hours of sleeplessness, she had watched as the sun slowly coloured the walls with the warmth of a new day. But she could not rise, she stayed in her bed, leaden with the knowledge that something inside her had died. It was not the child, oh no…it moved and pummelled her from within its own little prison. She rubbed her stomach, feeling she was sure, a little heel against her hand.

She had heard Nathaniel rise an hour before, heard him clattering below, eager to wake her without having to knock on her door. She just could not find the strength within her to rise and face the day and so she lay, staring at the ceiling…so tired, so tired…

Since Midsummer's Eve she had begun to feel that her life was worthless. She had truly wished herself dead, sinful though she knew that was. The shame she felt was unbearable and though she had borne it for such a long time now, she knew from the morning she awoke after that terrible midsummer night, that her strength was finally broken.

She could count on the fingers of one hand since then the days she had risen and dressed and gone about her duties. She knew Nathaniel was in despair but neither of them could talk to the other. There were too many questions that could not be answered, too many unspoken judgements made. The chasm of misunderstanding had grown too wide to be bridged by conversation now. She was totally alone in the misery that had become her world. Strangely, her only solace was the coming child. She could not hate it despite its beginnings. As it grew within her, she nurtured it, she soothed it and she longed to hold it in her arms. Something good must come out of the injustice that had been done her ...it must!

All her life she had been good and godly...why was she punished so now? It was the injustice that twisted into her like a blunt blade. She had lost everything, even now that blessed characteristic of fortitude which had sustained her through all her life.

She knew Nathaniel loved her though he seemed tongue-tied, unable to give her the support she needed. What an insight his behaviour had given her into how Josiah must have felt in all those years when his Mother seemed to have rejected him...Josiah must have felt that he had no-one. Nathaniel seemed to find it so hard to talk, as if words would pick like clumsy fingers at a wound that should be left to heal over. He didn't understand that the wound would always be open, weeping into the mind, tainting the whole of life to come. That was how she felt now.

She supposed the reason he could not talk to her was shame...shame that his dear Josiah was responsible for her trouble. He must be confused as to why she had given herself so quickly. Perhaps he thought that his own son was guilty of the terrible crime that had been done to her by another? Then it overwhelmed her again, the shame also of the lie. All her life, she had been taught that lies could never make things better. What a mess it all was. For the thousandth time, she wondered why Josiah had pressed her to make that promise. How could that act diffuse his shame for his dealings with Thurston? She knew that Thurston's past had something to do with it –she sensed that somehow making things right for her was a salve for Josiah's gut-wrenching guilt, but why?

In the end, her head hurt so much she just gave herself up to fate and vowed that as soon as the child was born, she would return to her native Derbyshire and try to erase the memory of this fateful year... but again despair as she realised that she could never take that escape route for how could she return to her home unmarried and with a child? She was trapped indeed. What if Josiah should come back and she was forced to keep her promise? Would it be so bad? Fleetingly, she remembered his handsome face and his surprising gentleness towards her. Then in her mind, his features began to blur and change into those of the man she loved…and on his face was the look she had seen as he had turned to look at her in the glow of that bonfire, in that moment when he had felt the swell of her in the small of his back.

She could see still so clearly now, him turning to face her and she had seen the face of a man cruelly betrayed. His struggle to hold back tears had distorted his beautiful mouth and she would remember the pain in his eyes forever.

She closed her eyes once more against the sun. No tears came, only a complete acceptance of her fate. It washed over her as she pulled the sheet up over her head to shut out the day. Drifting at last into sleep, she didn't hear the click of the door as Nathaniel left the house.

****

An excited Thurston waited inside the little cottage, hiding behind the door on a little stool so Ginny would not see him as she entered. He chuckled softly to himself, picturing their faces when he sprang his surprise!

He had been so busy these last weeks he had hardly seen Ginny or little Isaac and had woken this morning feeling more at peace with the world than he had since the eve of midsummer. So many people had carried him through, so different it had been from the lonely years when he cried in his bed or hid with only the trees and water for company in the garden at Moreton. Ginny had been an angel and the company of Isaac had healed him like a soothing balm in those first days after that terrible night.

He had told Master Nicholas not to expect him today as he was spending the day with Ginny and her child and the gentleman had approved wholeheartedly.

"Where will you go?" he had asked.

"Oh!" replied Thurston "Ah don't know...for a walk o'er t'fields...a paddle in t'brook? Tek a little basket an' 'av us dinner in t'sunshine?"

Master Nicholas smiled. "It sounds like a perfect day my boy...if thou hast time, why not bring them here to visit me? The child could play and run in the garden, we could all eat together by the moat? But of course I understand if thou wouldst be alone...'t is only a suggestion."

"Nay, nay Sir...me an' Ginny...it's not like that. We are friends 't is all...good friends, only that."

"I see...," said Nicholas "...then wilt thou come?"

Thurston was delighted. "Aye, Sir...well, that would be grand! Ah cannot think of a better place to spend a day."

And so he waited now for Ginny to arrive and to see the surprise on their faces. As he sat in the still, quiet gloom of the cottage with its windows so small the sun could hardly squeeze in, he thought on the events of the last two weeks.

He had gone to see Master Nicholas on the third day after Midsummer's Eve, meeting him in the garden, begging his forgiveness for not going to see him as he had asked.

Nicholas had waved his apology away.

"Worry not my boy...I know what it is to have a heavy heart. My dear wife always told me I had a good ear...and it is thine Thurston, whenever thou hast need of it."

Thurston had nodded silently but his face told Nicholas that he did not have need of the listening ear he offered...not yet.

From that day, on Thurston had begun work on the outside of Moreton House, fixing the door and repairing the old mullioned windows, meeting the Master every day when he came out to the garden to talk to him.

"I am not in a position to pay other men to help thee Thurston, not just yet..." he had said one afternoon "...but I hope soon to be able to hire other men to work alongside thee."

Thurston, for a reason unknown to him, felt a little jealous. He had no wish to work with other men who did not love the place as he did. It was his...the care of the house was his.

Master Nicholas became aware of his silence. "Thurston…what is it?"

Thurston shifted uncomfortably, shaking off the feeling that had descended on him.

"Aye Sir, Aye…that would be grand…we could crack on then…Aye."

"But…?" asked Master Nicholas, silently willing Thurston to speak his mind.

Thurston fumbled for the right words, unwilling to upset his new Master. What right did he have to pick and choose who he worked alongside? He was lucky just to work there…in the house and the gardens he had always loved. He looked up at Master Nicholas and he could see he was waiting and suddenly without warning, the words tumbled out.

"Aye…well… truth be told Sir, if Ah may Sir… this 'ouse…well she's special…she needs men that care for 'er to…make 'er beautiful again."

Sir Nicholas was moved to hear Thurston speak of the house as female, the same way he himself always thought of her.

"Go on Thurston" he urged "say what thou wilt!"

Thurston swallowed hard, afraid of overstepping the mark, yet bound to speak now.

"Well Sir, Ah know some good men, men Ah've worked with…men who Ah trust. When tha gives me the word…Ah could ask them… if tha would approve Sir, Ah don't mean to …well…forgive me if…." He ran out of words…and courage as he finished "…Sir."

Master Nicholas was silent for a moment and Thurston's stomach began to churn. If he was sent away now he didn't know how he would find the strength to go on. In that moment as he waited for some response from this man he had come to almost idolise in these last few weeks, he realised he had pinned all his future to him…and his house.

"Two things I will say to thee Thurston Hey. Firstly…any man thou think'st a good man must be a good man. I shall be happy to be guided by thee and thou can'st hire whomever thou choosest when the time comes…Secondly, my name is

Nicholas...we are business partners thou and I...and I would be much more at ease with our arrangement if thou would'st call me so."

Thurston was overwhelmed with his response. If only his own Father could have been just a little bit like this man, how different his life might have been.

"What art thou thinking?" Nicholas had asked then.

Thurston replied very quietly. "Ah was thinkin' what a grand Father tha must've bin Sir."

It was as if a cloud had descended on the older man's face. All the light disappeared from his eyes and his cheeks, despite the warmth of the day, took on a grey pallor.

Thurston was beside himself. "Forgive me Sir...Ah did not mean to trouble thee!" He was so fearful of harming this new relationship that was giving him so much.

Nicholas, seeing the worry in the young man's face, recovered his composure and laid his hand on Thurston's shoulder.

"Worry not, dear boy...worry not. We shall talk one day. I will tell thee of all the mistakes I made as a Father, and the price I paid for them...the highest price a Father can pay. And on that day Thurston, thou wilt talk to me so that I may give thee my understanding and advice. These are the only benefits that come from grief and regret for things not done well"

He patted Thurston's shoulder. "I am tired, my boy. I shall see thee on the morrow?"

Thurston nodded "Aye Sir..."then smiled as the older man lifted his finger, warningly. "...N...Nicholas."

Thurston watched him walk slowly all the way back to the house, the weight of memory seeming to weigh down his shoulders a little.

They had indeed met again the next day and nothing more had been said on the matter. It was as if the conversation had never taken place. Thurston had begun work and they chatted easily as usual but Thurston sensed that their relationship had grown deeper through that short interaction. Both men had exposed a troubled heart and each had found the promise of healing in the other.

The last time Thurston had seen Ginny and Isaac to spend any proper time was on that same morning, three days after Midsummer's eve.

"We will walk to Moreton with thee...we shall be company for thee!" Ginny had declared, desperate with worry for Thurston, trying to hide it with her usual bright manner.

Isaac had trotted along excitedly, pretending to ride again the little horse.

"Let's tek 'im through t'fields shall we?" she suggested, aware, as Thurston was not, of the pitying looks of passers by.

Thurston had followed her, unthinking in the aftermath of that shocking midsummer night, his spirit lifted a little by the sound of Isaac's laughter and the sight of his bouncing, sandy brown hair as he ran. What a wonderful thing is a happy child he thought, realising for the first time how precious childhood was...how it moulded a life.

"Come 'ere 'orsey!" he cried, infected by the child's play. "Ah'll catch thee!"

He had started to run after Isaac who ran as fast as he could on his little legs, his bright laughing face glancing over his shoulder, squealing as Thurston drew nearer.

Then suddenly he was there...at the place. The place he had avoided for months, the place that held such an unshakeable grip on his memory. All about him had ceased to seem real as if he were in a dream. He could see Isaac running ahead and Ginny walking behind but there was no sound except a loud rushing of blood in his head and the cold, clutching hand of fear choking his breath.

"Thurston?" He was out of the dream, Ginny had broken it.

"What's to do??"

He forced himself to speak. "Nothin'," he said "...a pain in mi leg. It is gone now."

Ginny didn't look convinced.

"Isaac!" she called to the running child. "Isaac, come back!" Then to Thurston she said:

"Take thi time...stay 'ere... Ah'll come back to thee..." before running ahead to catch her little son.

She had come back to Thurston and taken his arm and they had walked in silence to the gates of Moreton where she left him, almost having to pull Isaac from his arms.

Thurston had not had the terrible falling nightmare again...but since that morning with Ginny, there had been the same picture, flashing at odd times into his head... like one of the little flames that burst and blaze briefly in a cinder fire. In the picture, his face was in the earth and though forced to the ground by the unseen presence, he raised his head to see the glimpse of a door. Then the picture would be gone. Whatever he feared to remember, he knew it lay behind that door and no matter how many times the image might play in his head...he knew he never wanted that door to open.

Something was happening to him...he could feel it. Some final resolution to the hidden horrors of his past was coming...mysteries that he knew now had always lurked in the dark corners of his memory. It felt as if something had been disturbed...like his mother would weild the broom under the heavy bed stirring up the cobwebs... never quite managing to sweep them out.

He shivered at the thought now as he sat waiting on the little stool, wishing that Ginny would hurry up and come.

***

Ginny set out from Ma Jenkins cottage with a spring in her step that morning. She had a secret and it was the first secret Ginny had kept to herself all her life. As she approached Thurston's cottage, Isaac running alongside, she felt a pang of guilt over the secret she kept. But that, she decided, was something she would have to live with...it would not serve anyone to share her secret yet. So she held it close to her and it warmed her heart. She would get on with her tasks quickly today she vowed so that she could be on time to keep an appointment she had made. She took Thurston's door key out of her pocket and began her usual fumbling with the lock as she did every time she entered. Why Thurston spent so much time fixing other's houses when his own needed repair was beyond her...but that was Thurston, she supposed, God bless 'im! Suddenly the door opened and Isaac tumbled in. "Turton!" he cried.

Ginny popped her head round the door to find Thurston sitting on a low stool behind it, a big smile on his face.

"Well... 'tis good to see thee smilin' a bit but worr art tha doin 'ere?"

"Ah live 'ere," he said.

Ginny laughed. He didn't make to rise. Something about his playful manner infected her and Isaac jumped up and down in his happiness at seeing Thurston.

"What's goin' on?" she asked, suspiciously.

Thurston stood up at last, lifting Isaac up into the air. As he put him down, he put his finger to his lips conspiratorially and Isaac copied him, touching his own lips with his podgy little finger.

Thurston coughed before speaking, a twinge of poignant remembrance creeping for a split second into his memory as he spoke "the King's English."

"Mistress Ginny Green, and Master Isaac Green, thou art invited by Master Nicholas Moreton, to sup with him this day at his beautiful house. Shall Ah tell 'im that tha will accept his kind invitation?"

Ginny squealed with delight. "Oh yes! Yes indeed kind Sir!" she exclaimed and curtsied quite admirably. Remembering her appointment she quickly added: "...but Ah must be back at Ma Jenkins for two of the clock. She 'as asked me t' run an errand."

She hoped the guilt of the lie didn't show on her face but she need not have worried. Thurston was busy throwing Isaac up in the air and the child was beginning to get thoroughly overexcited as he always did when Thurston was about.

***

Mistress Thomas was busy, up to her elbows in flour, kneading the dough that would make the weekly bread and that of her neighbour who sweated before the oven on the already warm July morning. Nathaniel welcomed the small cup of ale she pressed into his hand.

"Now then, 'ow doth she do this day, Master Speakman?"

Nathaniel shook his head, his expression so sad and Rebecca Thomas felt for him. She knew that he was not a man to explore his feelings in words but ever since she had come to know him, she thought his face mirrored so well the troubles of his heart.

"She lyeth in bed again..." he murmured "...as quiet as the grave she is. Ah 'ope our plan works, indeed Ah do. She must take comfort from someone or Ah fear she shall lose her mind."

Rebecca Thomas looked up as she heard the unfamiliar crack in her neighbour's voice. For a moment she thought he would weep and she quickly bent her head again, working the dough, saying nothing and allowing the man to compose himself.

"Ah worry about the child Becca."

She warmed to the familiarity, knowing that it conveyed trust and respect and the comfort of years of neighbourliness. They had shared difficult times over the years, she reflected silently. Not just the deaths of Susannah and the other two infants who they had never had chance to know...but the loss of Josiah, the son whom she knew Nathaniel loved so dearly. Since Eliza had gone, the deepest loss of all, she knew how much Nathaniel needed him now. Rebecca herself had lost all six of her children, the last to go being her son, taken by a fever three years before at age thirty. It was a hard thing to outlive one's children... an unnatural thing.

"The child will be alright..." soothed Rebecca "...she will. She is 'ealthy, she is strong and we will get 'er mind right again Ah promise thee!"

She laid a comforting hand on his arm and as she returned to her baking, he looked down at the white residue on his coat, smiling fondly. Becca Thomas was a good woman, and wise. Even though Rebecca secretly was not so sure of the parentage of Elspet's child, she spoke the words she knew would comfort him.

"And tha shall 'ave a beautiful grand-child Master Speakman! By 'eaven 'ow could it fail to be beautiful! There will be 'appy times 'ead for thee to be sure. Buck up now…tha must be strong for the lass, eh?"

He nodded, eyes glistening.

"Ah look forward to the day…" he sighed "…Ah really do. Ah just wish…Ah wish Ah could tell 'er. What a one am Ah? Ah can talk t'anybody about things that don't matter till t'cows come 'ome…but Ah can never say the words Ah feel deep down."

Rebecca sighed and pressed her floury hand over his.

"Ah know…," she said "…but tha must learn to, it is time. She needs thee to talk to 'er…she needs thee!" Back to her kneading she went, still talking and soothing. "Worry no more on it, my little friend will help us…mark my words!"

"She is coming still?" asked Nathaniel.

Mistress Thomas set her loaves to prove and wiping her hands on her apron, lifted her newly baked ones out of the oven.

"She is indeed. She shall be 'ere at two o-clock… and now Master Speakman, 'ow about a slice of fresh warm bread?"

***

As Nathaniel sat in Rebecca Thomas' kitchen eating the best bread he had ever tasted, Thurston, having carried little Isaac most of the way to Moreton, finally lifted him down from his shoulders.

"Sorry little lad, thine 'orse is tired an' a little bit lame. Can tha walk for a bit we're nearly there?

Though he couldn't see her face, he could feel Ginny's look of disapproval.

"Tha spoils 'im Thurston, look 'ow tha's worn thisen out!"

And then to Isaac, who hadn't even spoken. "No Isaac, no more 'orsey. Look…look poor Thurston's leg is tired!"

Isaac looked at Thurston's leg, saw no difference and then mounted his own imaginary horse. He broke into a trot, smacking his own little flank as he accelerated to a gallop.

Ginny slowed her pace to walk by Thurston, knowing Isaac was safe running round the Green. She noticed how he turned his eyes away from the Speakman's house almost as if it hurt to even look at the building. In the three weeks since Midsummer, he hadn't spoken of the incident, not once. Ginny screwed up her courage not sure what his response would be, sure only that she must speak of it. No good ever came of burying unspoken hurts, her own history had taught her that. All they did was lie there covered in dirt...you always knew they were still there. She had a feeling that Thurston had so many hurts buried he had hardly any clear ground in his head to put any more away.

"I think that ye must love Elspet Sydall very much Thurston... so worr art tha goin' to do?"

His cheek reddened as if she had slapped it.

"Do? Do?" He raised his voice. It was louder than she had ever heard it even Isaac pulled up his horsey and looked over. She fancied for a moment that Thurston's raised voice had awoken a buried memory for the child of his own Father shouting at his cowering mother. She saw Isaac pulling his lip in a gesture of fear and nervousness she had not seen for many a month now. Thurston composed himself.

"Ah'm sorry Ginny...," he said. They had stopped walking. "...She made 'er bed. Aye she did that...in more ways than one!

She flinched at the bitter, uncharacteristic sarcasm in his words. He had not finished.

"She ...she did that with the worst man...No! Ah cannot forgive it!"

He shook his head, his lips pursed tightly and breathing deeply before speaking what she knew would be his final words on the matter.

"But ...you are right...Ah love 'er. Ah sh'll love 'er all mi life...though it matters not now."

Those were the words she had waited to hear. The conversation was over.

"Forgive me Thurston," she said, threading her arm through his. "Ah would not upset thee, not for the 'ole world. Come on, we shall be late."

She left him and walked on ahead, eager to cuddle Isaac and calm his fear. Thurston limped behind, stealing a brief look at the quiet house as he passed.

***

The sun was high in the sky when Nathaniel finally knocked on Elspet's door. She started awake, unsure whether she had heard it or dreamed it. The way the shadows fell in her room told her that it was early in the afternoon, her sudden hunger reminding her that no matter how she felt, she must eat.

Another knock at the door followed by Nathaniel's quiet, halting voice.

"Lass, art' awake...can Ah come in Elspet?"

She sat up, taking a moment to reach for her shawl at the bottom of the bed. She pulled her dishevelled hair over one shoulder, twisting its tangled mess into some sort of order.

"Come in Uncle," she said quietly.

One look at Nathaniel's face told her that he would rather be anywhere else on earth than in this room at this moment. It was as if he could feel the hurt and pain emanating from her and was afraid to touch it. He came closer, risking the contagion. Pulling the old wicker chair that sat in the corner close to her bed, he sat down and to Elspet's surprise, took her hand in his.

"Forgive me lass," he said.

She did not weep though she was well aware that at his moment, it would be an appropriate response. It was as if she was …numb somehow.

"I forgive thee Uncle? Nay, it is I who should ask forgiveness for bringing thee such shame…and in the face of such goodness shown to me."

He shook his head, vehemently.

"Ask forgiveness for what...for loving my son? For giving him some affection after all he has suffered?"

A twinge of guilt passed through her but she swallowed it down. The deceit was bad but the truth, she knew, was so much worse. She cast down her eyes, afraid her inner turmoil would show in them. Nathaniel squeezed her hand.

"I tell thee, be not ashamed. It is I who should be ashamed, letting thee carry this burden alone. Eeh lass! If only Ah could say what Ah need to say! But that is my defect...all my talkin' is done in my 'ead." He tapped his temple. "And what use is that eh?"

She tried to smile but said nothing, just looked into his kind eyes ...and waited.

"Ah want thee to know, lass, that Ah..." he struggled for a moment to form the words. "...Ah'm so thankful to thee for sharin' my burdens so unselfishly these last months. Ah could not 'ave gone on 'ad it not been for thee. Ah've never thanked thee...or taken any weight from thy shoulders. Just as always Ah tied myself up in mi own words and worries." He shook his head again as if in disbelief at his own foolishness.

"Tha knows what Eliza would say? That Ah need purrin in a bag and shakin' up! Eh? Remember eh?"

He chuckled, glassy eyed at the memory of his wife and the way she was with him. They shared a moment, each silently thinking of her before he spoke again.

"Ah loved 'er so lass...but Eliza...she were like glass. Sometimes she could be so 'ard and cold...Ah couldn't get through it...And then at other times...well she were like glass when t'sun shines through it...warm, lightin' up everythin'...glorious!"

Elspet was moved by his words.

"She was a fortunate woman...having thy love, Uncle."

He smiled and stroked her hand before standing, brushing his coat as if shaking the dust of memories from his shoulders.

"Well..." he bent to kiss her head "...then tha must be lucky too, because tha 'as it lass. Ah vow that Ah shall look after thee an' t'little un for as long as tha needs me, an' Ah 'ope that'll be for a long, long time."

She bent her head, unable to look into his face lest he saw the lie she lived written there. He pulled up her chin gently.

"Ne' then, Elspet. Tha must rise and get thee dressed for we will 'ave visitors this afternoon...Nay do not fret, nothing is required of thee but to come down and be courteous to Mistress Thomas and her friend."

"But Uncle, I am not...able...I..." She could not make the words. How hard things had been for him these last weeks and he had asked nothing of her, nothing except this one thing. She nodded.

"I will rise and get ready ...as you ask, Uncle," she said.

***

In the gardens of Moreton House, Thurston sat and watched Ginny and Isaac running in and out of the trees giggling, playing hide and seek. Isaac's sweet little face peeped out of the un-pruned branches that swept the grass in the light summer breeze as he hid, hands over his eyes, in that endearing way of children who think they can't be seen if they themselves can't see.

Thurston looked over at the house. How lovely it was from here. He could never tire of looking at it. For the hundredth time he wondered why Nicholas had let it all become so neglected. He was beginning to understand, however, through conversations they often had late into the evening, a little about the reasons behind Nicholas' reduced circumstances. As they talked more and more about the Moreton family, Thurston had begun to remember things his Mother had said. He knew Nicholas' Father had built the Chapel of St. Stephen...named it after the first Saint. He knew he had seen it consecrated thirty years earlier. And yet here it was now in the hands of Sir William Bagshawe...how had that happened? Much of the story of Nicholas Moreton he knew was hidden from him and more and more Thurson felt sure that one day he would know.

He was sure also in a strange, inexplicable way that he himself would have some part to play somewhere along the line. He didn't know what it would be or why he felt that...he just had the feeling. Thurston, though a young, uneducated man who had lived a simple life, knew nonetheless that he had a knowledge of feelings far beyond his years...they were the only things he trusted.

Isaac laughed loudly again as his mother caught him and Nicholas laughed at the sound, his face lighting up. Had Nicholas's own boys played in this garden as children? Was he remembering times past? Thurston was sure so, sensing that much as the past was never far from the present for him so it was also with his benefactor.

Nicholas had been kindness itself to Ginny and Isaac. He had arranged for a table to be set in the garden by the moat, laden with good things to eat. He had welcomed them heartily and spent time talking to them. He had taken Isaac by the hand and led him down to the water to feed the ducks, pointing out their differences and giving them names, delighting in the child. He had sat by Thurston on the blanket and pointed out his worries and concerns about the back of the house. He had left them only briefly to eat his own dinner inside at his housekeepers insistence, determined as she was that her Master's status be preserved.

Old Maggie made no secret of the fact that she did not approve of his condescension to the lowly village lad. It was after all (she was of the view), all that mixing and meddling with the social classes that had led to the war in the first place. The war that had seen her Master brought so low. She saw it as her duty to remind Thurston of his place at every opportunity but, despite her best efforts, she could not dissuade her Master from returning to the garden after he had eaten. He stood out of sight for a few moments, surveying the happy scene...Ginny and Isaac sitting together and Thurston stretched out in the afternoon sun, watching them lazily, always that look of well-hidden unhappiness belying his ever-present smile. What a puzzle Thurston was to him yet the older man felt he was slowly solving the puzzle, piece by little piece.

Thurston was enjoying this day more than many he could remember. He had had little experience of happiness...the only times he had been happy were the times he had shared with his mother by the fire when they were alone in that strange companionship they had, when he knew he had felt her love.

Also the times he had spent alone here in this place, watching the sun go down over the water. He had realised in those few short months with Elspet what happiness really was. That feeling that bubbled up into your chest so fast that it just had to come out in a smile or a laugh or a note. Nothing could ever again in his life he was sure, make him feel that feeling again. But today, with Isaac who he loved and sweet Ginny who looked up to him and treated him with such kindness...and Nicholas who was guiding him into something he was sure would enrich his life... at this moment, on this day for the first time since January, he felt a sense of moving forward. Perhaps he should just marry Ginny, he thought idly as he watched them playing happily together...what a happy childhood that would make for the boy.

As if she knew he was thinking about her she looked up, straight at him. She rose from her knees, smoothing down her skirts.

" t'is time Ah was off," she said. "Ah must go an' make my farewells to Master Moreton."

"Where does tha go again?" asked Thurston.

Ginny looked away. "Ah'm t'elp Ma Jenkins... wi' an errand...Ah know not what, but t'is proper important ...aye."

Thurston looked at her a little too long, sensing all was not as it seemed.

"Mmmm...," he said "...well tha best get thi bonnet on...tha's lookin' a bit pink."

Ginny bustled about collecting her things, getting Isaac ready, never looking at Thurston's face till he was safely in conversation with Nicholas who had come outside again. This secret mullarky i'nt all it's cracked up to be, she thought.

Ten minutes later, Ginny pulled on Isaac's hand as he trailed behind her, turning to wave at Thurston, who stood at the top of the carriage drive watching them go.

"Come-on, Isaac! We sh'll be late...'urry up."

Thank goodness Thurston had decided to stay at the house. She thought for a minute there that he was going to suggest walking with her! It had been a lovely afternoon though and how much more she understood now his pull to the old place.

Not just to the place either, she had seen the regard in which Master Moreton held him. To call him Nicholas and he such an important man! Ginny, like Master Moreton however, also held Thurston in high esteem so to her eyes it held no real mystery, it merely made her judge the gentleman to be an intelligent and good man. Thurston deserved to be held in high esteem by all who knew him. He deserved regard, praise, happiness and love. That was her mission today, the first step toward securing for Thurston the happy life he so deserved.

"Isaac come-on!" she chided again…still he dragged his little feet. Then, inspired by Thurston once again, she urged her son with the sing-song voice he always used when he spoke to the child and which Isaac always responded to:

"Come-on, jump on thine 'orsy and we'll gallop there! An' if we get there in time 'orsy, tha'll get a little treat!"

Isaac's face lit up with a smile and in a flash he was mounted on his imaginary horse and galloping away down the drive, Ginny sweating in the heat as she ran to keep up with him.

***

After Ginny and Isaac were out of sight, Thurston returned to the garden to find Maggie clearing up the remains of their meal. He could feel in the burning look she shot at him what she was thinking, could almost hear her voice: Not enough the Master invites this unworthy lad into his house, feed's 'im and gives 'im work. Now Ah'm expected t'clear up after 'is 'angers on. Ah'll be playing nussmaid t'all parish poor next!

Thurston sat by Nicholas who raised his eyes heavenward at the exaggerated clatter with which she cleared away.

"Ah don't think she thinks much o'me Nicholas." Thurston said as she returned to the house. Nicholas, though smiling, seemed thoughtful.

"'t is not that she thinks little of thee, Thurston…but that she thinks so much of me. She worries about my wellbeing, about my future and sometimes it causes her to have…opinions on things she should not. I overlook it because of the loyalty and devotion she has shown to me and my family over the years. She means no harm."

Thurston thought on his words for a moment then nodded, understanding. He too worried about Nicholas, seeing once again the man's kindness, wondering how he could survive in such an unkind world as the one he surely he moved in.

"Is she right to worry about thi future?" Thurston asked, immediately feeling he had overstepped the mark. This man was so easy to talk to that he sometimes forgot his place, as Maggie so clearly feared.

Thurston immediately apologised. "Forgive me…Ah spoke out of turn."

Nicholas clapped him on the shoulder.

"Nay, nay, do not be afraid to ask questions of me. If I do not want to answer, I shall not and if I do, it means that I am willing to share more of myself with thee. It is how relationships are built my boy!"

Nicholas grew quiet then for a moment. Thurston had come to know this silence, knew that it often preceded the kind of words that he found difficult to know how to respond to and in the next moment, sure enough they came:

"I like honesty in my relationships Thurston. It is why I enjoy spending time with thee. I want to share some of my business with thee and I hope in return that thou wilt share yours with me."

Thurston was confused, as he had feared, he found himself not knowing how to respond and as he so often did in conversation with this man, he remained silent, waiting for the next words.

"To answer thy question…" Nicholas continued "… my future is not safe. That of my family…well they are safe in the arms of the Lord and past any trouble this Earth can hold for them. But what of the future for my faithful staff, for those I support? What of the poor of this parish…the young, the sick? Their future is not secure…and what of thy future Thurston, and Ginny and Isaac?"

Thurstons thoughts were set running by Nicholas' words, realising that over these last weeks, he had become ever more aware of the falling away of his ignorance of the wider world...ignorance that had allowed his mind to wind a cocoon around itself. Thurston knew he was changing, for the first time in a long time he too worried about people who meant something to him...Ginny, Isaac...Elspet. A feeling that he had not felt for a long time settled on his stomach like a bad meal...a feeling of dread. Nicholas must have seen it in his eyes for he grabbed his wrist.

"Nay Thurston, do not disturb thyself. They will all be alright! All will be well. I have a plan in my head, my boy, which will secure the future of all those we care about."

Thurston was even more confused, finally wanting to ask questions but Nicholas went on:

"On Saturday next wilt thou make a journey with me? We shall be away for one night. On that journey I will share my plan with thee, a plan I have thought on for many a year. I will share with thee Thurston and thou...thou wilt share with me. I have come to know thy character but I would like to hear from thine own lips what hath made thee so forbearing...so brave in the face of adversity!"

Thurston almost laughed, shaking his head vigorously he protested:

"Nicholas you mistake me...I am not brave...I have never in my life done a brave thing..." Then he fell silent...thinking of the night of Midsummer and back long, long into his past.

"Aye, Thurston...thou seest now? Thou art brave indeed, and thou hast so many qualities which I recognise in myself, but without the arrogance I had at thy young age. That is why I ask thee Thurston and no other to come on this journey with me. All shall be made clear I promise thee...wilt thou come?

Thurston's mind was racing, full of questions, disbelief and gratitude that this man thought so highly of him. Above all, he knew with an overwhelming certainty that this thing Nicholas was asking him to do, would quicken the growth of the seed of change that already had taken root inside of him. He did not ask where, who or why, so absolutely confident was he in this man, he simply gave his answer.

"Aye, Sir...Aye indeed, I shall go on this journey with thee."

25.

Edwin Bagshawe awoke in his narrow cot, the ever-present smell of woodsmoke and cooking food turning his stomach. A cruel and unforgiving shard of light pierced the canvas that was his roof as it flapped in the incessant wind that always blew across the camp, stabbing his already aching head.

He wanted the comforts he was used to. A comfortable bed, his meal on a proper plate, good wine...well perhaps not the wine, just yet. His stomach churned as he sat up, a casualty of the excesses of the previous night... not that he could remember much of it.

"Watkin!!" he bellowed, his mouth dry, his throat hoarse. He rubbed his throat, his hand ached. Looking at it in the half-light, he saw the familiar purple spread of bruising and knew he had hit something...or someone. He rubbed his face and moved his jaw...no injury, nothing a shave wouldn't cure. Where was that boy?

"Watkin, get in here now boy or by God I'll kill you!"

He struggled to his feet, throwing over the small table by his cot, bellowing as best he could the boy's name, relishing the punishment he would give him for causing his master to wait...another opportunity to vent the latent anger that was within Edwin at every waking moment. The effort was too much for him and he flopped back onto his cot. Silence as he closed his eyes, waiting for the nausea to ebb away, the throbbing in his head to stop.

Eyes still closed he heard his servant enter but still lay quietly, letting the boy tremble and anticipate the punishment to come. Lazily Edwin stretched and slowly opened his eyes to see a giant of an infantryman he knew only as Shepherd, his great black shape filling the doorway.

Edwin sat up suddenly, feeling for a split second a frisson of fear.

"What the hell are you doing here? Where's that bastard Watkin? Go away and send him to me!"

Shepherd remained, standing still and silent in the doorway and for the first time Edwin really took in the sheer size of the man and the air of menace about him. The cowardice that was never far from the surface and which all his life Edwin Bagshawe had hidden with cruelty, bubbled up into his throat raising the tone of his voice an octave. Only he recognized it.

"Again I say what are you here for you smelly man? Where is Watkin?" Silence still.

"Answer me you ignorant soldier or else...!"

The man stepped forward, just one step. It was enough to make Edwin visibly recoil.

Shepherd had seen much of the cruelty of men. He had seen enough of this war in the five years he had fought in it to know that there were moral men on both sides. He knew that the real sadness of this war was that good English men were forced to kill each other while bad men, like the one before him, remained in the world.

He would like to take this man out and pummel him to within an inch of his life for what he had done and for a moment, he allowed himself to imagine doing that. The thought was enough to calm him and he was able to swallow down his disgust of the creature before him enough to speak.

"The boy is dead...Sir. He did not survive the...injuries he suffered at your hands last night ...Sir."

Edwin was silent. Forever after the infantryman would remember the coldness he witnessed in those eyes as Bagshawe composed and cloaked himself in that air of superiority and arrogance which had forged his dreadful character. For all the battles he would yet fight, Shepherd would look back to this encounter and it would fuel the hatred needed to kill another man. The hatred of Edwin Bagshawe would see him safely through this and other wars... but he did not know that yet. All he knew was blind, vicious hatred and the urge to make the 'man' before him suffer for what he had done to that young boy.

Edwin's transformation from cowardly wreck to the son of a rich man was complete.

"And did anyone of note witness this beating...or do we have only a common soldier's testimony?" he said, his voice trembling only a little.

Shepherd breathed deeply for a moment before crossing to the cot in a single step. Grabbing Edwin by the throat with one massive hand, he pulled him up so that he scrabbled in panic to get his feet onto the cot for support.

The soldier held him there and Edwin struggled for breath as the big man spoke in quiet tones, his mouth inches from his face.

"Sir...even men as fine as you can be punished for such cruelty. I have been sent by your Commanding Officer to tell you that because of who you are there will be no justice done here. He was only a poor boy after all, nothing compared to a grand man like you......but I saw what you did to that boy though his body is buried along with the truth."

Edwin's face was covered in spittle, his head was beginning to throb from lack of air but he heard the words clearly and the threat behind them.

"Watch your back...Sir. Your Commanding Officer would be upset to have you fall victim to an 'accident' one dark night but he would understand that these things happen. I have been assigned to 'look after' you 'Sir', to tend to your every need. I am known for my attentiveness...I will remain as close to you as the mother that bore you for the rest of this war, closer than any living soul I will be. Of this you can be sure...Sir."

Shepherd suddenly let his captive go with a rough push and Edwin fell back onto his cot, coughing and gasping for breath.

"I shall be back in a few minutes with your breakfast," said Shepherd before leaving the tent as quietly as he had entered it. He would see justice done in some form here.

"By God I will!" he vowed.

Once Edwin was alone, the anger which had begun to contort his features turned in a moment to anguish. His pale face grotesquely twisted as he struggled to hold back the tears he knew would come in a flood of self-pity and self-loathing. They were not tears of regret for the boy who had died at his hands nor were they for any of the dreadful things he had done in his past. They were the tears of the six year old boy who had cried in the night for his mother after she had gone. They were tears at the memory of pain inflicted on him by his red-faced Father as he spat out his shame at his boys' weakness with every stroke of the whip. They were tears of bitterness toward that cruel man who for years had taken out his anger on his helpless son because he could not punish the woman who had escaped his cruelty. But most of all, they were for the ever-present hurt that she had abandoned him to that same cruelty without ever having sight again of the boy who had so adored her.

26.

Elspet had washed, dressed and breakfasted and was now sitting by the kitchen window, hands resting lightly on her swelling stomach. Somehow, miraculously, that desire she had felt to just sleep, forget and shut out the prospect of her future life, had faded away. In its place was a new feeling...not happiness, it could never be that. More that an adjustment had been made somewhere in her mind that made life seem worth living again.

She knew that the change had taken place that first afternoon she had spent with Ginny and her boy when Mistress Thomas had brought her to visit. There was something about the girl's sunny nature, despite all her trials which Mistress Thomas had confided to Elspet afterwards. Her affection for her lovely boy and the bond that clearly lay between mother and child had somehow given Elspet a glimmer of hope that there may be something to hold on to...that she might find friendship and that in her child, she might finally have another human being who would love her completely. The glimmer of hope she saw that day had helped her turn a corner and see the future as more bearable.

She waited now for Ginny and Isaac to come as she had ever since that day when Nathaniel had engaged Ginny to come and help in their house. Isaac was the first to arrive, rushing in through the back door like a spinning jenny, whirling and whirling around!

"Isaac!" cried Elspet. "You shall hurt yourself you noggin!"

Reaching out she grabbed his flailing arms and pulled him to her, tickling his tummy, kissing his soft, silky head as he laughed. What a joy he was!

In her misery these last months, she had forgotten the joy of children and being with Isaac the last few weeks had made her think of her family fondly, yet without the burden of loneliness that before had weighed her down when she thought of them.

And now, here came Ginny, thin and nimble, running as always.

"Ah've bin runnin' all mi life" she would say. She came into the kitchen bringing the August sunshine with her.

"Ee this lad o' mine's got some energy! Mornin' Miss Elspet, how art'a this fine day...did tha sleep well...'ast 'ad thi breakfast?"

All the same chatter and questions, none of which needed an answer nor was any answer heeded if given as Ginny launched into her work with such cheer as always.

"I am very well, Ginny" replied Elspet. And she was.

They settled down into the morning routine that had established itself since the day after that first vist when Nathaniel had engaged Ginny to come and help Elspet. Ginny would busy herself with all the tasks Elspet no longer had to do whilst Elspet played with Isaac and enjoyed their light-hearted chatter.

Elspet had begun to realise since Ginny had come into her life how lonely she had been for so long. She hadn't set foot outside the house since Midsummer and had no intention of doing so, so fearful was she of those outside who would hurt and revile her. Ginny had brought life back into the house and already they had formed a strong bond. It didn't even occur to Elspet how poor Ginny had been or how far removed Ginny's upbringing had been from her own....she had a companion who she knew would be kind to her always.

They had never talked of Midsummer's Eve but Elspet knew that it was Ginny who had run for Thurston. She knew from Mistress Thomas that Ginny was keeping house for him and she had felt nothing but thankfulness that someone was looking after the dearest person she had ever known.

They had never talked of Thurston in these last weeks until yesterday, when Ginny had finished her tasks and they were sitting together as they always did at the end of the morning, Isaac nodding off on his Mother's knee.

"Is Thurston well?" Elspet had asked, haltingly, as if touching a sore place.

Ginny had known that Elspet would ask the question one day and she had been ready.

"Aye…" she answered "…'e is well in body. 'E eats well, Ah see to that, and 'e rests in a clean bed. 'E is well in 'is mind… Ah think.'e is well thought of by Master Moreton and that 'as lifted 'im…but rightly so 'e should be well thought of for 'e works 'ard in that old place! But then 'e loves it so that 'ouse, a body would think 'e'd grown up in it 'imself!"

She laughed and Elspet smiled, grateful that he had found comfort in something. Then Ginny grew thoughtful and after a moment spoke again.

"Aye, Ah think 'e is well in every way…except 'is 'eart. It seems so heavy some days Ah think 'e must struggle to drag 'imself out o' bed Miss Elspet."

At these last words, Elspet who had been sitting with her head bent, looked up, her green eyes shining.

"Oh I know that heaviness Ginny. Indeed I do…oh, my poor Thurston!"

Ginny then had screwed up her courage, it was what she had been waiting for…she knew it was time to speak.

"Is 'e thine miss Elspet? Is Thurston thine? 'e loves thee so, even after all!"

It was too much. Elspet had stood and left the room, her hand to her mouth, stifling her tears.

Ginny had gently roused Isaac, fearing she had lost her chance by saying too much.

Isaac was noisily guzzling the cup of buttermilk he was given every day as a reward for being a good boy in Master Speakman's house when Elspet came back into the kitchen. She picked up Ginny's hand.

"Thank-you," she said, to Ginny's surprise. "Those were good words to hear. Perhaps tomorrow we can talk more."

Ginny squeezed Elspet's little hand gently.

"Aye of-course, Miss Elspet…as much or as little as tha wants."

Things had been just the same between them this morning, chatting happily as Isaac played and Ginny cooked. As Isaac began to rub his eyes at dinner time, the two women settled down together, sitting quietly as Isaac drifted off into a child's easy sleep.

"Tell me about Thurston" whispered Elspet.

Then they began to talk and as they did, they weaved between them the closeness that grows between women, creating that safe place where secrets can be shared in the knowledge that when talk was done, they could be locked away in the secure vaults of deep friendship.

27.

Thurston sat as he had so often over the years, by the moat in Moreton House, hidden by the trailing green willow fronds, deep in thought's that could only be made sense of here, in this place, alone.

It had been two weeks since he had journeyed North with Nicholas and instead of questions being answered as he had been promised, the journey had only confused him more.

They had set off in the early evening of the Friday and travelled on horseback to the inn where they would spend the night. To be up and ready in good time for the day to come, Nicholas had said.

Thurston had found conversation on horseback difficult, for the pain he was in had filled his mind completely. His foot didn't reach down to the stirrup which caused him to use muscles he didn't know he had, to cling on to the beast. As a consequence, the poor horse had been mightily confused about direction due to Thurston's strange leg movements and the whole ride had been a difficult and embarrassing experience. By the time they had reached the inn, Nicholas was mortified with guilt. He had never considered that Thurston had not in his life ridden more than a mile on a horse and that had been on a slow, old carthorse. Thurston had made no attempt to change Nicholas' mind when he arranged for a carriage to take them the rest of their journey the following day. The relief and gratitude he felt overwhelmed him and made him uncharacteristically giddy. He drank a little more wine than he should at their simple dinner that night and talked more freely than he otherwise would, his natural shyness diluted by the alcohol.

"Where are we bound for Nicholas?" Thurston had asked him, his backside sore from the saddle and his inside warm from the wine.

Nicholas smiled in a fashion Thurston didn't recognize as fatherly.

"We are bound for Cloughridge House" he answered. "It is a house a little bigger than Moreton though not as beautiful or well built. It hath one thing in common with Moreton, however."

Nicholas finished his sentence abruptly and Thurston, intrigued, hadn't been able to stop himself from asking the question.

"What's that then?" Did it have a moat, gardens, did it also need work? Was that why he was being dragged across counties?

Nicholas answered smiling. "It also belongs to me."

Thurston was only momentarily surprised. After all, a man of Nicholas Moreton's standing might well own much property, he supposed. His mouth he could not still however.

"Why do we go to see it?"

Nicholas was quiet for a moment.

"Because Thurston, it goes to auction on the morrow and I want to see it sold to the right man."

"Who will be the right man?" Thurston asked. "Ah've no knowledge of these matters but surely if 't is an auction… shall not any man who 'as the money be the right man? And why do Ah go with'ee?"

In answer, Nicholas had clapped him on the shoulder.

"I am tired, my boy and thou I think are a little drunk. Come, a good night's rest will clear our heads and I have much to think on. Worry not, all will be revealed on the morrow, I promise thee!"

But Nicholas had not kept his promise and nothing had been revealed except more questions and mysteries yet to be solved.

Today, when he left his hiding place under the trees and went to knock on the door to Moreton House at the appointed time, then he hoped to hear the truth. He thought again of the auction as he had many times since that day two weeks before.

He and Nicholas had arrived after an hours carriage drive through beautiful country with a winding river and rolling hills. "The Bowland fells Thurston, magnificent are they not?" Thurston had nodded, wondering why any man would sell a house in such beautiful surroundings to fix a house in Appley Green. He had, by this time, decided that Nicholas was selling his house to finance the work at Moreton but when they arrived and he saw the house, he was even more perplexed.

Though it had not the faded, feminine beauty of Moreton, Cloughridge House was handsome indeed...well built, well situated and in much better condition. Yet even as he stood and looked at it, Thurston could see that it lacked the air of character and welcoming homeliness that Moreton had. It sat in a hollow and was in shade, though the morning had been bright but nonetheless it sat well in its plot and was approached by a stately, winding carriage drive. Thurston was sure it would be sold that day to the 'right' man, whoever that was.

"Well, what thinkest thou, Thurston?" Nicholas asked as they stepped out of the carriage, Thurston wincing at his saddlesoreness, worse after his night's sleep.

"Well" he replied "Ah think it is a fine 'ouse.....but not a patch on Moreton."

Nicholas laughed and put his arm around Thurston's shoulder.

"Ah lad...that is why I brought thee here, to keep me strong and firm in purpose!"

There had been many at the auction, some recognising Nicholas, others strangers. Fine gentlemen there were, escorting their ladies who no doubt were secretly imagining themselves as Mistress of the grand house. Nicholas had left him alone whilst he met with the men who managed the estate in his absence and Thurston entertained himself by looking at the prospective buyers and attempting to identify 'the right man'. Suddenly he had seen a face that he recognised in the throng... Sir William Bagshawe! What was he doing there? Did he intend to bid and take Nicholas' house from under him?

Thurston didn't know how he had known it, only that he had known for certain that Sir William Bagshawe was a dishonourable man. He had to find Nicholas and warn him. Thurston had limped hurriedly along to the meeting place they had arranged at the bottom of the grand staircase in the Great Hall.

"What is it Thurston?" Nicholas had asked, sensing his distress "What ails thee?"

He had held his shoulders and looked into his face but he was too late.

"Moreton…I did not expect to see thee here today. Good Day to thee."

Sir William Bagshawe held out his hand but as he did so, all turned at the sound of the Auctioneers' hammer, the slight of Nicholas Moreton not taking the proffered hand going unnoticed in the gathering excitement.

Nicholas had turned back to Thurston, seeing the worry on his face.

"Worry not dear boy…" Nicholas had whispered "… thou see'st before thee, the right man!"

Thurston had begun the auction in a state of utter confusion. What did Nicholas mean? Sir William the right man? Why? But as the auction progressed he had become fascinated by the process and found himself carried away by the excitement of the occasion.

It had seemed to take a very short time to get down to two men bidding against one another. One older man bidding on behalf of Sir William Bagshawe, the other a fresh faced, much younger man Thurston had seen Nicholas talking with earlier. Sir William had indeed seemed determined to buy Nicholas Moreton's house from under him. The price crept up and up, far higher than all had thought it would go as the two men attempted to outbid each other for the prize.

Sir William had sweated profusely in the summer heat, his face red with agitation, unused to not getting what he wanted. Determined to get his way, he had pushed the man who was bidding on his behalf roughly aside and shouted at the young man who was his opponent.

"I will have this house Sir! Whatever thou biddest I will outbid thee by God!" Then to Nicholas: "Name thy price Sir. I will pay it!"

Thurston would long remember the difference in the countenance of the two men that day. In sharp contrast to the man who stood, belligerent before him, Nicholas had calmly bowed, first to the assembled company then to the Auctioneer.

"Gentlemen," he said "pray continue thy business."

He had taken Thurston by the arm and led him from the house into the shaded garden and there they had waited patiently, in silence, for the outcome. Within ten minutes, Sir William had blustered out, bill of sale in hand, triumphant. He stopped by the tree under which they sat.

"I knowest not what trickery was employed here today Moreton but it failed! I am the new owner of Cloughridge House and I am sure thou did'st not will it so but ha! 'Tis mine!"

No hand was offered by either man and Sir William had walked off in the direction of his horse with the air of a man who had triumphed in a major battle.

"To the victor, the prize" Nicholas had murmured and Thurston had the distinct feeling that the victor that day had been Nicholas Moreton himself.

The rest of the puzzle he had not been able to piece together though he had thought on it till his head ached in the two weeks since that day. Nicholas had been thoughtful on the journey back and had immediately gone away to conduct 'important business'. Today would be the first time Thurston had spoken to him since their return from Cloughridge.

It was early evening, almost on the cusp of nightfall. The sun cast a beautiful pale orange glow on the garden as it slowly lost its strength. Thurston had heard tales of how the great burning orb shone its light on other places in the world while its sister the moon rested in the sky over their head and then again in turn, they would change places in the morning. Great stories he had heard in whispers of the doings of the stars and the planets and the infinity of space. He doubted not that they were only stories told to frighten children but still if truth be told, he often wondered what would happen if the great ball of fire should fall to earth. For now however, he could only marvel at the way it coloured the water as little by little its light withdrew from the deepest corners of the garden.

He had made up his mind that when the time came for him to speak to Nicholas, that he would be forthright! He would demand to know for what purpose he had been taken at painful cost to himself, miles over hill and dale. No more "Yes Sir, no Sir!" He needed an explanation. He was not a child to be denied the truth, indeed no!

"I shall ask him" he thought, silently mouthing the words. "I shall tell him…I need to know, I shall say…"

"Oh! Nicholas… Good evenin' …" Thurston looked, embarrassed, into the face of his benefactor. "…I did not see thee comin'… "

"Forgive me Thurston, I did not mean to startle thee…to whom wast thou talking?"

Nicholas looked puzzled but Thurston thought he saw that playfulness in his eyes that he had come to recognise.

Thurston flushed again. "Talkin'?" he asked.

"Aye…," said Nicholas, looking him straight in the eye "…well, not talking as such…what does Maggie call it now…Mee-mawing! Yes, mee-mawing. I do believe thou wast having an imaginary conversation with someone?"

Thurston shook his head, red-faced. "Nay, nay…" And then something happened that Thurston had very little experience of in his life. He screwed his courage up and spoke his mind.

"Well, Nicholas…to be honest…Ah was 'opin that tha would talk to me tonight. Tell me things that tha promised to tell me…Mi mind's bin turnin' o'er an' o'er …since Cloughridge y'see…Aye…well…"

He ran out of words and stood looking embarrassedly at the moat as it disappeared into the summer darkness.

Nicholas placed his hand gently on Thurston's shoulder.

"I remember, lad. I remember also our conversation when I said I would share with thee and thou wouldst share with me…as friends do Thurston?"

It was a clear question. Thurston felt a little afraid as he followed Nicholas into the house, turning and looking behind like a child, afraid he was being followed by monsters and ghosts. And of course, he had been, at some point of every day, for all of his life that he could remember.

They settled in the beautiful room overlooking the garden and just as they sat, Maggie bustled in to light the candles. Once they were lit, the garden would be plunged into darkness.

"It was here I first saw thee, Thurston...all those years ago."

Nicholas pressed a glass of wine into his hand and raised his own glass into the air.

"I raise my glass to thee and bless the day thou sought solace in my garden Thurston Hey."

Nicholas lifted his glass and as he did the candlelight shone through the crimson liquid. It reminded Thurston suddenly of a window he had seen in Church as a child and how transfixed he had been by the sun shining through the exposed sacred heart of Jesus.

Without thinking he replied. "Ah thank thee...Ah think tha saved me...Ah really do."

Nicholas was silent for a moment before replying with a tremble of emotion Thurston did not sense.

"Thurston...I think we have saved each other."

Their glasses touched, a soft tinkling sound and they drank down the wine, each feeling the warmth of their growing companionship.

"Now...," said Nicholas "...time to talk."

***

Nathaniel rose wearily from the grave that he visited daily as the sun disappeared. This was the time of day that he missed her most. He missed that easy, companionable silence they would share in the evenings. Each there when the other looked up, a shared smile, no need for talk, before heads bent again in their own pursuits. What he would not give to talk to her now...of his fear for their son and for Elspet and for the child she was carrying. He had been sorely troubled since Midsummer's Eve. Shocked though he had been and fearful for the future, it was the return of a ten year old memory that had plagued him daily since.

He thought again, as he stood by the grave, of the terrible events he and Eliza had witnessed on Easter Day 1641. Josiah had still been at home with them then and as he often did, had gone missing. Nathaniel always fretted about his son's whereabouts but that day he had fretted more than usual for there was a strange mood in the village. All the previous week, the little community had been in the grip of an uneasy religious fervour and it had grown day by day until on Easter Sunday, it bubbled over into a kind of hysteria.

He shivered as he felt again the chill of menace that had hung in the air that day and in his mind the pictures of events became intercut with the image of Elspet, held in the glow of the fire on Midsummer's Eve and for a moment, the past and the present inter-twined.

Ten years before, troublesome murmurings had begun after visits of the Vicar of Leighton Fold to their little Chapel of St. Stephen. The Reverend John Swindells had ranted and railed against a growing rumour that a priest would hear the Catholic Mass at Manor House Farm the following Sunday...Easter Day. Manor House Farm was an ancient old place tenanted for generations by the Parry family but owned by the noted recusant and local nobleman Sir Thomas Tytherton, staunchly and rebelliously Catholic who at that time, resided at Abbots Hall.

The two houses stood a mile onto the Moss, separated by a quarter of a mile of farmland and for years there had been stories of lights signalling to each other at night in the highest windows of the old houses, summoning Catholics to secret masses. It was said that there were holes big enough to hide a priest under the floors and behind chimneys, safe from the wrath of their persecutors on earth.

The Reverend John Swindells then saw himself as the leading religious light in the little Parish which encompassed Appley Green and its surrounding hamlets. A crusader of

Puritanism, he blasted popery from every pulpit at which he preached with terrifying rhetoric. He was determined to purge his Parish of Catholicism's idolatrous practices and the priests who had been reduced to peddling their services to faithful Catholic families across the land.

Father Alexander Marlowe was one of these wandering priests, seeking succour and the means to live from rich men who still practiced the Catholic faith and who were powerful enough to remain unchallenged for doing so. Conducting a mass was punishable by death but at that time, there were still small pockets of people in the communities of east Lancashire who followed the old religion. Sir Thomas Tytherton drew the faithful in secret to his safe houses of Abbots hall and Manor House Farm to take part in the ancient rituals of the religion of Rome, and Father Alexander Marlowe had been a welcome visitor for many years.

To the Reverend John Swindells, Sir Thomas was a viper in his bosom, an enemy of God himself and he was determined that he would fight until his last breath to drive the hated followers of the Pope from the boundaries of his congregation. His battlecry had echoed again from the pulpit of their little chapel on that Easter day and Nathaniel and Eliza had watched the villagers come together on the Green after the Service. Whipped into a frenzy by the Reverend's call, they began to march with terrifying purpose across the fields to Abbots Hall and Manor House Farm. He and Eliza had been unable to resist the encouragement of their neighbours and had joined the growing throng.

They would regret it all their lives. Nathaniel would never forget the sight of that weak, sick old man or the sound of his brave, steady voice rising in prayer as he was dragged from the farmhouse. He knew that he would never forgive those of his neighbours who had to be restrained from killing the old priest where he stood, without trial or justice. He had been unable to look on him, bravely attempting to stand upright as he was being dragged away to the fate that all knew awaited him. Instead Nathaniel had looked around him at the faces in the crowd, unable to recognise people he had lived among all his life, so grotesquely twisted by hatred were there features. He had seen in those moments with such clarity, the shameful seed of evil which lurks in every human being. He had led a weeping Eliza away and in their home that afternoon they had prayed together to a God they felt a little less sure of.

Sir Thomas, sickened by the incident, had sold Abbots Hall in the aftermath to Sir William Bagshawe, then a greedy, social climbing local landowner and also the generous benefactor of Reverend Swindells. Ten years on Bagshawe's wealth and influence had grown as had the terrible enmity between Bagshawe and Sir Thomas. The brave knight had spent most of the ten years since, fighting and imprisoned through this most terrible of wars, followed loyally by Nathaniel's own son.

Nathaniel looked down at his hands as he stood by the grave feeling that he had soiled them by taking money from Bagshawe these last two years. He brushed the imaginary dirt onto his coat and walked across the Churchyard to the gates of Moreton House. He would be in good time for the appointment he had made with the man he had first met on that dreadful Easter day ten years before, a man who had been his friend and ally since and who had come to his aid without question on that dreadful eve of Midsummer.

***

In Moreton House the fire was lit, the room was comforting and warm and Thurston sat enjoying the company of the man he had come to respect above all others. The wine had warmed him inside and slightly befuddled his thoughts so that he wasn't really listening to the words Nicholas was saying just enjoying the gentle tones of his voice as it rose and fell. It was like a soothing, stroking hand on his brow. Thurston was not even aware that he had closed his eyes until the talking stopped and he looked into the face of Nicholas who was staring earnestly at him. Had he heard the words he thought he had heard or had he dreamed them?

"It is true, Thurston, we are the same …thou and I."

Thurston laughed, suddenly released from the spell the wine had cast over him.

"Forgive me Nicholas...but we are not! I am a poor, ignorant, uneducated man who 'as done nothin' in 'is life when you...you are rich....you are a great man!"

Nicholas seemed excited as he responded.

"Riches...Greatness, what are they? I am rich compared to thee but poor compared to many! Why dost thou think me great? Because of deeds I have done, because of decisions I have made? How am I greater than thee Thurston?"

Thurston shook his head in disbelief not sure where the conversation was heading, unsure what Nicholas was asking of him. Uncomfortable about giving his opinion of this man who he had come to idolise, he found it easier to denegrate himself.

"Ah'm poor, un-educated an' ignorant of the world. Ah'm alone, Ah've no influence to shape no man's life not even mi own!'ow can Ah be the same as you?"

He wanted to say this is stupid, why are you talking to me in this way? Please let us talk about things I like... this house, the work I am to do. But Nicholas had warmed to his subject.

"Oh yes Thurston. I have money, I have some power, I have some influence in our little world... but all of these were given to me as they could be given to thee Thurston! And thou art not alone, my dear boy...thou hast me and I have thee!"

Thurston was silenced, believing himself now to be so drunk that he was hearing words that were not being said.

Nicholas stood and moved over to the wall opposite the fireplace on which hung a gallery of portraits.

"Come" he beckoned. Thurston stood, realising as he walked steadily that he was not drunk, that all that was being said was real. More confused than ever, he looked at the portrait to which Nicholas gestured.

"My wife...Anne," he said softly.

Thurston looked into the face of the pretty dark-haired woman. Warm, kind, nut-brown eyes, buttermilk skin, a modest strawberry blush on her cheek.

"She was the best wife any man could wish for. True loneliness is not to lose the woman thou lov'st...' tis never to have known her at all. I miss her every single day Thurston but I am never alone. Her light burned so brightly in my life even at the darkest times, I see its glow."

Suddenly Thurston understood. That was how it was with Elspet. She had lit up his life and shed that light on corners he had never seen and he knew that it would never burn out though he might live and die without her.

"I understand" he whispered. Nicholas' hand came to rest for a moment on his shoulder. Then his face darkened as he pointed to the portrait next to that of his wife and Thurston felt the sadness weighing heavily on him.

"My sons," said Sir Nicholas. Thurston looked at the boys. They were like two peas in a pod. Long, dark curling hair, bright young faces, features a strange mix of both their parents...handsome boys on the brink of adulthood and full of the promise of life to come.

"They were twelve years old when this was painted. Dost thou see the background? It was here in this room."

Thurston nodded, silently remembering a day in his past.

"I saw them once," he said.

Nicholas' face brightened. "Yes?"

"Aye... Ah did..." continued Thurston "...As Ah 'id, one afternoon, by the water. They were dressed, ready to go out. A carriage were waitin' an' they were fightin' each other wi' wooden swords, laughin'...'appy. Ah remember wonderin' worr it would be like t'ave a brother who was strong, who didn't 'ave a lame leg, somebody to fight for me and protect me from...people who would 'urt me."

Nicholas almost held his breath, afraid that if he made any sound he might stop this young man talking to him about his life for the first time.

"Tha came out Sir! What great soldiers you are my boys, you said! You were laughin...you ruffled their curls.'ow thine enemies will tremble, you said. Bring your swords to protect me on this journey! Then tha'all disappeared down the carriage drive an' Ah kept that memory, like one of these pictures..." he pointed upward "...in mi 'ead."

Thurston looked into Nicholas' eyes as he finished with the words:

"Fathers are meant to love, Fathers are meant to laugh with their son's...Ah learn't that day that it were not me who were a bad son...it were mi Father who were a bad Father."

He turned back to look at the portrait.

"Ah came back many times as ye know...but Ah never saw them no more."

He knew that beside him Nicholas was filled with emotion and he kept his eyes on the portrait to allow the older man a moment to compose himself. At length Nicholas spoke again.

"They were sixteen when they left. We were at Cloughridge then. They went away together to join the Parliamentarians. I was so enraged at their treason, I did not bid them farewell nor wish them God speed. I told them not to return until they had cleansed their treacherous hearts...all the time hoping that I was not seeing them for the last time. Within six months they were both dead...not quite as accomplished with a musket as with their wooden swords..."

Thurston looked away again as Nicholas drew his breath in as if he were about to weep. Overwhelmingly, Thurston felt the urge to give and receive physical comfort. Almost unthinkingly he turned and placed his arm about Sir Nicholas' shoulder and before he could withdraw it he found himself momentarily locked in a brief embrace...being held as a Father might hold his son, in another world, in another life.

Nicholas withdrew from the embrace and placed his hands on Thurston's shoulders, a determined look on his face.

"We are the same, thou and I Thurston Hey. We have loved and we have suffered...and through that we have learned to be better men. I am thy friend, and thou art mine and all the things I have that thou hast not...I will share with thee!"

Thurston was by now so confused and so full of emotion that he could not speak. He did not know what was happening. What did Nicholas mean? He felt lost, like the boy he had been, unsure whether to turn and try to run or to stand and take what was coming. He was afraid... afraid of life as it was, afraid of life as it might become. He wanted to shout at Nicholas: "What does all this mean? Why am I here?"

Despite the rushing blood in his head, somewhere he heard a knocking in the distance. They were still facing each other when the door opened and they both turned, arms back down by their sides to see Maggie, disapproving in the doorway.

"Master Speakman is 'ere Sir and the Reverend Kingsley. Shall I bring 'em in Sir?"

Nicholas nodded before turning to an even more confused Thurston.

"Come lad, let us sit down. We have a long night ahead and much business to do."

28.

Josiah awoke from the best sleep he had ever slept. No dreams had disturbed his rest or if they had, he could not remember them. It had been as if his mind had stopped like a clock so that time and the night had passed him by unnoticed. The light of the new day awoke in him that feeling again. He had felt it swelling inside him for days but in truth he realised he had first felt it begin to twitch into life that day on the quayside weeks before. He did not yet know what the feeling was, only that it surged within him like a tide and drove him with the force of a relentless wind.

The ship had been two days at sea through some of the roughest summer weather he had ever known. As he stood on the beach finding his land legs after a difficult crossing, he had looked over the wide Wyre estuary at the purple Bowland Fells in the distance and thanked God that he was home at last in his native county.

The beach stretched for half a mile and was filled on either side of him by hundreds of men. Some were giving orders, some waiting for orders, all playing their part in bringing some semblance of order to this army so that it may march on to its journeys end. None yet knew where that might be except that the end would be a fight to the death for some. Josiah looked at the faces of those around him, trying to read them. Some looked tired, some fearful, some confused, some sad and in some, he recognised the same feeling that coursed through his veins and which he knew shone in his own face. That feeling whose name yet eluded him.

Rachel had seen it when he had left her.

"You are different" she had said "…you wear a cloak of iron that I cannot see. I cannot reach through it to touch you."

He had laughed.

"What a foolish woman I have landed myself with! I wear no iron, you can touch me…"

He had grasped her hand and held it to his chest, her fingers splayed out over his heart. He knew he would never come back, though he had never said but when he looked down at her face, tender words came easily. He covered her cold little hand with his own.

"This is thine, Rachel. It beats with a love for you that will never fade"

A tiny, jewel-like tear balanced on her eye-lid, catching for a brief second the early morning light. As she blinked it away, it fell down to the corner of her mouth where he caught it in a kiss.

"You taste like the sea…I shall never forget you Rachel. Do you have it still?"

With her other hand she pulled from her pocket the paper on which he had written.

"And you remember what it says?"

She had nodded, her lips trembling as she spoke.

"Master Nathaniel Speakman, your Father… he lives in the village of Appley Green, opposite the Church. If ever I am in need, I must write to him and tell him I am your betrothed and he will help me."

He held her again and kissed the finger on which sparkled the little silver ring with which he had pledged himself to her. She knew it was kindness, she knew he was never coming back though she had never said. She knew too that she would never ask for help but knew how much it comforted him to tell him that she would. She had forced her closed mouth into the upward smile that she wanted him to remember and had stood waving until the ship was a grey shape in the distance.

The image of her had stayed in his mind long after the sea mist had swallowed up the island. He knew her life would be the better for having known him. He knew she could live in comfort with what he had given her… but both were completely unaware that inside her she carried the tiny seed of the child that she would raise to honour as its father, the man who had changed her life forever.

Josiah was shaken from his thoughts by the familiar shout of Captain John Featherstone. Shielding his eyes from the early morning sun, he watched his comrade approach along the beach.

"Speakman, I bid you Good-Morning! How was your crossing? In truth you look a little dazed."

Josiah smiled. "As always Captain, the voyage was an adventure. I am… heavy of heart for the loss of pleasures past. But come! I am as always looking eagerly to the challenge of the future!"

He clapped his old friend on the shoulder. "You have orders for me?"

Captain Featherstone nodded. "Indeed I do. We are to march south to join the Earl of Derby's regiment outside Preston. We will camp there this night and I will seek you out, mayhap we may talk about those pleasures past eh?"

Josiah nodded. "Aye, perhaps" he agreed, smiling. But Featherstone knew as he walked away that there was less chance of that than Cromwell surrendering. For all the years he had known Josiah Speakman, he knew nothing at all about any aspect of the man's life outside the army.

Josiah picked up his pack and prepared to walk over to chivvy his men into action. As he stood up, the full force of the wind that came off the river hit him like a cannon blast and in that second he realised with a sudden clarity of mind, what the feeling was that made him feel so invincible. Purely, simply, it was courage.

29.

The day began for Thurston in a way no day ever had in his life before. No snoozing or slug-a-bed halfdreams, no blanket pulled over his head to shut out the morning light. It was as if a window had opened in his mind and he sat up, eyes wide, thoughts as clear as if he had dipped his head in a bucket of cold water.

He took in his surroundings, the narrow bed and the beams above his head, the small, stone window overlooking his beloved gardens at Moreton. For a split second, he wondered if he had dreamed the events of the previous night. For a tiny part of that split second, the frightened boy he used to be hoped he had. But it was only a fleeting, half breath before the man he was becoming felt, with the thrill of certainty, that the events he had been a part of were real.

How confused he had been when Reverend Kingsley and Nathaniel had entered the room the night before! He could hardly take in any of what Nicholas was saying. They had been just words, words that he should be hearing someone speak through a wall, in another room. Words that by some terrible mistake were being spoken in his presence! Then suddenly he had realised that the words were actually being spoken to him!

"I have no heir Thurston" Nicholas was saying. "And if I had, well they would not be allowed to take possession of my property for long. I have been the enemy within for so many years but now my enemies have me surrounded. Dost thou hear me Thurston...dost thou understand?"

The image of Sir William Bagshawe's face as he brandished the bill of sale in Nicholas Moreton's face, danced within his head and Thurston nodded vigorously.

Nicholas patted his shoulder.

"Good lad, good lad. Thou must listen carefully now my boy."

Thurston nodded, waiting patiently, his stomach tumbling with feelings of excitement and dread. The three men had arranged themselves before him like a tableau. Nicholas sat, his eyes level with Thurston's, while beside him stood Nathaniel and behind them both, the tallest man, Reverend Kingsley. Thurston knew he would remember this moment always, certain that the words which Nicholas was about to speak would change his life.

Silence hung for what seemed minutes in the air, he felt the warmth of Nicholas's hand over his.

"...I am giving Moreton House to thee, Thurston."

Thurston did not speak and unknown to him, his face hadn't even changed. If it were not for the fact that he still breathed and sweated in the heat of the fire, all might have thought that he had expired. Nicholas had continued:

"I want thee to restore this house to its true glory Thurston and I want to turn it into a school...a Grammar School that all children in the Parish can attend with poverty no longer a barrier to education! I want it to be a place where children can learn to be better people so that all the terrible things we have lived through can never happen again! They will learn patience and humility, tolerance and humanity under the care and guidance of my old and dear friend, Reverend Kingsley."

Nicholas saw the light begin to dawn in Thurston's face as he slowly recovered from the shock and followed Nicholas' gaze to the face of the man who had come to Elspet's aid on that dreadful eve of Midsummer. Nicholas continued to speak, sensing Thurston's interest now.

"And Master Speakman, another true friend and a friend to thee also Thurston, he will help and guide thee in these efforts and in matters of business. And what shall my part be? I shall continue to live within these walls, safe and secure amongst people I respect and see a wondrous thing done in my name...oh Thurston is it not a most brilliant plan? None can ever take something that has been given as a gift to thee and one that will be used in such a way that will benefit and raise this little village to great importance!

Nicholas was almost beside himself with glee as he finished his speech.

"...and fittingly it will all be done with that fiend Bagshawe's money! It will make thee one of the most important men in the county Thurston. What say you?"

Still Thurston sat in silence, his expression blank. The three men had looked at him, expectantly, but he had not been able to speak, no matter how much he had wanted to.

"Has he lost his wits?" asked Nathaniel.

Nicholas had lifted Thurston's limp hand and squeezed it kindly, as Thurston moved his mouth attempting to speak.

"Thou art shocked I see, my boy...but pray do not let thy first words be: "I'm not worthy.""

He patted Thurston's hand.

"I know thee..." Nicholas continued "...and thou art the worthiest young man I have ever known. I would be honoured if thou wouldst accept this offer I make. Come...be a part of this adventure with us Thurston Hey!"

It was as if he had been pulled lifeless from a river, suddenly and deeply he began sucking in the air then unexpectedly, like a flood that was bursting through a dam that had held it for years, poured a rush of emotion pent up for a lifetime. Through his fears and sobs, he nodded and spluttered "Ah will... Ah will!"

They had held him, patted his shoulders, shook his hand and wept along with him and then slowly tears had turned to laughter as the plan, so long in the making, tantalisingly became reality.

This morning, sitting in the narrow bed, in the house that he loved, he knew that a new life was beginning. There was only one person he wanted to rush to and share it with...but she was also the person he wanted to see least in the world.

30.

Edwin Bagshawe found that war suited him well. The last few weeks had been so different to the boredom of the camp and the frustrations of unending preparations, discourse and changing plans. He had recently become a part of Colonel John Milburne's small company of elite soldiers since catching the attention of the fierce and battlehardened campaigner and from that moment of recognition, Edwin had found his true calling.

From his first experience of real combat, the first opportunity to put long hours of training into practice, he knew he had found a salve for all his ever-present hurts. It was as if he had been given a delicious absolution, permission to go forth and take his pain out on every man who faced him as long as he was the enemy. He was encouraged to kill and maime without guilt or fear because this was his glorious duty!

Always, even in the most confused madness of combat, he was aware of Shepherd, ever at his shoulder. Once, in the thick of fighting, he had swung his sword in Shepherd's direction meaning to take off his hated head only to find himself screaming in agony a minute later as Shepherd held his arm in an iron grip. Finally, he had been forced to drop the sword, knowing Shepherd would break his arm if he did not. It had been three days before he could lift his sword again and the hatred of the big, ugly soldier deepened. The face of every royalist he had encountered since had turned, in his blood fuelled madness, into that of Shepherd…or sometimes strangely, his Father.

It had been so long since he had seen his Father, his features had begun to blur in Edwin's mind. He only saw his face now as it had been during those terrible beatings of his childhood and hatred of him came up into his throat like burning bile at the thought of him. Plunged into the hot, ruthless forge of war, all the flawed elements of Edwin's character had fused into a fighting man who killed with relish and without mercy. For the first time in his life, Edwin was a success and he was thriving on it.

It was dusk, the very edge of nightfall, and Edwin was preparing in his makeshift tent for a mission for which Colonel Milburne had chosen him particularly. He paid less attention these days to the fine things in life which only weeks before he had craved. He had become a soldier. His closest friend and ally was his sword, a gift from his Father. It had arrived by messenger on that day in July when every other soldiers' loved ones had come to wish them well. That had been the day when all the unfulfilled craving for affection had, at long last, turned into hatred.

He took the sword now from its scabbard, holding the fearsome and beautiful weapon at arm's length in the candlelight. The hilt was wrought into a basket of steel ribbons which encased his hand and the blade stretched out glinting like molten metal as he turned it admiringly in the yellow light. Shepherd watched unseen in the open flap of the tent, saw the flashing blade reflect in the ice of Bagshawe's eyes. Not for the first time in these past weeks, Shepherd felt perplexed at the ways of God, to make a fighter out of such a man as this.

"We must go Sir…"he said breaking the spell the sword always seemed to cast over Edwin. "…the hour is at hand."

"Why must you come?" There was the child again. Shepherd was beginning to know the many facets of Edwin's character. He made no reply, just waited in the doorway, but Edwin was growing stronger… the child in him was quickly pushed away, the sword sheathed. Nothing, not even the agonies of childhood or the relentless presence of this man, would destroy the newfound sense of purpose that had come into his life.

"Come then Shepherd!" he shouted, sweeping out of the tent. "Let us go and hunt the wolves which threaten our flock!"

He laughed in Shepherd's face as he passed him, loathing flashing in his pale eyes and the big soldier knew that soon

even he would struggle to hold back the madness in this man.
The dark night he had spoken of he knew, must come soon.

31.

Here was the blackness again, here the burning in his chest and the struggle to breathe. He tasted the earth as it filled his mouth and he gasped in pain, sure his back would break. He knew he would die if he breathed in and so he kept his mouth tight closed as he stretched his leg to push with all his strength at the door that would not yield to him. Whatever was behind it could not be worse than what held him now, on the brink of oblivion and death. He pushed with the very last of his strength at the door and tumbled into blinding light. Sucking air into his lungs like a newborn, Thurston found himself awake, lying on his bed in the little cottage. He lay, breathing heavily, hating and thanking God at the same time for the release from the terror of the dream, grateful that it was only that… a dream.

He rolled onto his back, exhausted. It always came back, even when he thought it had all gone away never to return, the dream would creep up on him again in the dead of night…just when he had stopped looking behind for it. Never before however had he been so close to opening that door in the dream. Even though he knew that a worse end than waking up safe in his bed lay behind it, he needed to see…he needed to know.

As always with the coming of light, the terrifying vision ebbed away, his breathing slowly subsided and a new day beckoned although this time, even as he stripped off his shirt to wash the tears and sweat of fear away, he struggled to shake off the memory of the dream. It seemed more real these days, every time it came. He knew that one fearful night soon, he would see at last what was on the other side of the door and that he was moving ever nearer to the revelation that was locked somewhere deep in his memory.

He sat for a long time in the chair by the ashes of the fire, the sun already burning hot outside, its light beginning to flood into the little cottage. It didn't warm him, still he was cold from the aftermath of the dream and he closed his eyes against the brightness for a few minutes.

It was the twenty-third day of August 1651. Today was the day he would sign the papers that would make him the legal owner of Moreton House. Today, Nicholas Moreton would write his letter to the Magistrate to inform him and the elders of the parish that he no longer owned the building and that he had given it lawfully to Thurston Hey, prior to his death: "For the purpose of providing a place of education and pastoral care for the poor of the district." Not for the first time, Thurston was filled with emotion at the gift Nicholas was making and felt disbelief at the part he himself was to play.

Thurston had decided in his turn to make an offer to Ginny. It would mean that she and her boy would never again want for a home or the means to live the comfortable life they deserved. He no longer would need to live alone and little Isaac would have the security he needed and to grow up wanting for nothing, especially affection. Such a light now shone on him, it seemed right that those who had shown him loyalty and affection should also bathe in that light. Right that he should share the good fortune that had come into his life with those who were closest to him. He knew he would, in time, make an end to the bad dreams. One day, his battered heart would heal and allow him to speak again with Elspet and perhaps put the sadness away for ever. He vowed to try to be the man Nicholas had glimpsed the promise of these last years as he had silently watched him grow. He must overcome the old fears and memories that snarled in the shadows of his past life and move into the light of the future that beckoned.

He opened his eyes and blinked in the sunshine, allowing the prospect of a bright future to chase the ghosts of the old life back into the cracks and recesses of his mind...for the time being at least.

***

Josiah sat slumped outside the Surgeon's tent, his backside in the dirt, his head on his knees. He was dozing, exhausted partly from the strange tiredness that comes with inactivity, partly from the many broken nights sleep haunted by dreams. Strange visions plagued him in the night, forgotten by morning then suddenly remembered in flashes that caught him unaware in the daylight.

He felt a rough hand shaking his shoulder and as he struggled awake, the final scene of the dream that was playing in his head seemed absolutely real as he moved abruptly from sleep to consciousness.

"No…mother!"

The hand that was pulling him down into the grave was gone, the hand on his shoulder not his Father's but a soldier trying to wake him.

"He is awake, Sir, the man is awake!" the soldier was saying.

Josiah stood up, the horror of the dream upon him still and he remained dazed for a moment before rubbing his face roughly and entering the tent. He was used to the smell of blood and the sight of injured men but he had never lost the sense of waste that he always felt when faced with scenes like these. Five men, all of them young, were laid out before him. Two were completely covered, their trials in this world over. Two more were so badly injured that they hovered on the brink of life, mercifully carried beyond consciousness by rum and blood loss. Only one lay awake, his bare chest bleeding, his hand heavily bandaged. Josiah, his resolve weakened by the dream, fought back his emotion as the young man on the narrow cot beneath him, tried to raise his arm in salute.

"Good man," said Josiah quietly, saluting back. Sitting down by his side, he spoke to the boy: "I hear you fought bravely last night?"

The young man replied clearly, his voice strong despite his injuries.

"Aye Sir...I only got a scrape along the ribs, a musket ball through my hand..."

Josiah sensed his pride for a second before the boys' face fell.

"...I was no braver than any other Sir...just luckier...luckier than them."

He inclined his head toward his dead and injured comrades.

"I fought Sir that is all, I fought for my life...in the end, it's what we all fight for is it not Sir?"

Josiah nodded, silently understanding. It was how it was in combat, by God he knew that! These last few years, life had only meant something in those brief moments he thought he might lose it.

"You are a brave man nonetheless," he said to the young soldier. "What is your name?"

"Simon..."answered the lad ..."Simon Woodman Sir."

"Well Simon Woodman...because you are brave, you will live to see another day and because you will, these men will not be forgotten. You will live for these other brave lads."

The young man was quiet, thinking on what Josiah had said...and then he looked at him with fresh eyes, seeing a man who knew the agony of losing his friends in the same way. The sight of Josiah's face, the empathy he showed him even after all he had doubtless seen, galvanised Simon Woodman and provided him with what would be lifelong inspiration.

"Aye Sir!" he vowed "Indeed they shall not be forgotten... not while I live!"

Josiah could see the young man before him needed to sleep, to shut out the pain and horror he had been a part of these last hours.

"I will let you rest presently Simon but I am here to ask you what you saw of the enemy you fought. How many, what rank were they, anything they said? Are you strong enough to do that for me?"

The soldier nodded: "Aye Sir." After a moment of silence, he began to recollect the previous night, his voice husky and dry as he spoke.

"There were eight of them Sir. They happened upon us as we slept...quiet as mice they were. 'That's for our brave lad's' they cried. 'How do you like surprises?' I heard one say. They fell on us with knives and swords, one killing Richard Wright straightway with a blade in his throat!"

The soldier raised his hand to point at his friend, face covered with a bloody sheet. As he did so, he cried out as pain shot through his wounded arm.

"Still, lad, lie stil!" Josiah patted the boys' shoulder as he calmed again.

" I need a little more before I leave... can you remember any detail, however small, that may help me seek out these men and avenge your friend?"

Simon rallied a little at the thought of revenge and he answered quickly.

"Aye Sir, I do recall the one who slit Richard's throat. I shall remember him all my days. He had hair like a girl, soft long white hair...and the ways of a monster to kill a man so! He had no chance...he was my friend, from my village. We played together as boys we did..."

He was drifting into merciful sleep, tears on his cheeks, all bravery forgotten now. Josiah just needed one more effort from the young soldier before he could let him sleep.

"Simon," he said gently as he turned the young mans' head to face him. "Try to remember...did anyone call to this man? Did you hear a name?"

Simon nodded, exhausted. "Aye...I did...I cannot recall. Something... shaw...Bradshawe? Aye, I think Bradshawe! Kill him Sir, stick him one from me...and Richard Wright...he was my friend..."

The boy's eyes closed, unable to resist the beckoning, welcome oblivion of sleep.

"Aye, rest now soldier. I will seek him out for you...and your friend. Sleep now...rest and sleep."

Josiah stood.

"Do your best for these men," said Josiah putting a silver coin into the Surgeon's hand as he left. And so will I, he thought... so will I!

Suddenly he saw a vision of the boy Edwin Bagshawe had been, laughing in his mind, the long, white hair flying this way and that as he brandished the willow twig like a sword.

"So will I...so help me God!"

***

Ginny arrived like a whirlwind on the morning of the twenty-third of August.

"Miss Elspet! Ah'm so sorry Ah'm late!" she exclaimed, leaning on the table, arms straight, her words interspersed with ragged breaths.

"Ah've run all the way...Isaac too."

Little Isaac flopped exhausted onto the stool by the fire.

"Ah carried 'im most o't' way...but Oh Miss Elspet such news!!...ee Ah'm jiggered!"

Elspet stood, pushing Ginny to the rocking chair before she fell down.

"Whatever's up Ginny?" she asked intrigued. "What news?"

Ginny drank down the cup of cordial Elspet handed to her and sat down on the stool Isaac had vacated in favour of the garden.

Another minute passed, Elspet becoming more impatient. Thankfully, at length, Ginny recovered her breath enough to speak:

"Well... Ah cannot believe it Miss...what a tale Ah've to tell thee!"

Elspet readied herself, excited at the prospect of the entertainment to come for no-one could tell a tale like Ginny.

She began:

"This mornin' Ah went to Thurston as Ah allus do on a Thursday for 't is Thursday Ah go in an' tickle round for 'im. Ah brush up and sweep the ashes and suchlike afore Ah comes to thee Miss Elspet as tha knows..."

Elspet nodded, acknowledging the necessary introduction to the tale.

"Well…" Ginny continued "…Thurston were there, sat next to t' fire. Ah said "Thurston, worr art tha doin' 'ere?"'e laughed and said t'same thing 'e allus says "Ah live 'ere Ginny!" an' then 'Ah laughed too. But Ah could see…summat were changed in 'im Miss. 'e said "sit down Ginny"…and Ah did, which tha knows Miss, Ah don't very often."

Elspet nodded again then silence for a moment whilst Ginny awaited some kind of acknowledgement of her statement.

"Oh yes Ginny" affirmed Elspet "you are always so busy and work so hard."

Ginny accepted the compliment with a smile.

"Aye…" she continued "…well… Ah waited for 'im to speak. Thurston…or Master as Ah should call 'im 'ereafter, takes a while to summon up words unless they be a jest an' then 'e's as quick as a mouse as tha knows Miss!"

Yes, Elspet knew. She remembered fondly the endearing, playful way Thurston had had with her. Elspet suddenly became aware of Ginny's silence and she snapped her thoughts back to the present.

"Go-on Ginny, go-on!" she implored.

"Well…Ah waited an' waited while 'e kissed Isaac an' ruffled 'is 'air and suchlike as 'e does…God bless the dear, dear man…"

Suddenly Ginny's eyes filled with tears and she gave a little sob.

"Ginny!" Elspet grabbed her hand, worried now. "Is all well with Thurston? Please tell me Ginny!"

Ginny dabbed at her cheeks with her apron. Isaac came over to where she sat, concerned at his mother's tears, the way children always are.

"Oh don't worry Pet" soothed Ginny "Mammy's not un'appy. See…Ah'm laughin'!"

She smiled at the boy showing her small, yellowing teeth.

"Oh…oh Miss Elspet! What a thing 'e 'as done for us! An 'ome of me own, some comfort for me little lad. Ah'll never struggle again, our lives will be so much better! 'e 'as offered me such a gift Miss…such a wonderful gift!"

Realisation dawned at last on Elspet. Ofcourse, it was the right thing to do, Ginny was lonely...so was Thurston. He loved the boy all knew that, it made perfect sense. They could look after each other and give each other some comfort in a life that for both had been comfortless. They would be a family, Thurston, Ginny and Isaac...

Elspet as always, picked herself up and put on her brave face, knowing she must be happy for Ginny...saving her tears for when she was alone.

"Well, Ginny...I hope you will be very happy," she said, putting her arms around her "You deserve some happiness in your life."

Ginny returned Elspet's hug and began to cry again.

"Oh yes Miss Elspet. We will be so 'appy! Oh Ah can't believe it, Ah love that little cottage Ah do...it were meant for me. Ah s'll keep it spotless Ah will!"

Elspet was confused, was this the reason Ginny had accepted Thurston...for his little house? Surely she could not be so mercenary? Surely she must have some little feeling for Thurston? Elspet could not bear the thought of him sharing his life with a woman who did not love him for the man he was. For his goodness and bravery, his handsome face, his soft voice, his gentle nature and above all, despite all he had suffered, his ability to love! If anyone deserved to be really loved it was Thurston Hey. For a moment, she was afraid for him and it made her speak unguardedly.

"Ginny, you surely would not marry a man for his house? Please say you love him for the man he is? I am happy for you but please promise me you will love and respect him always, I could not bear it otherwise!"

Ginny's hands flew to her mouth.

"God forgive me! Nay, nay Miss Elspet! You have it wrong Miss!"

Elspet's heart leapt with a little glimmer of hope.

"Nay!" continued Ginny "Oh, Ah'm such a noggin! Thurston a'nt asked me t'marry im Miss. The gift Ah speak of is the cottage...Thurston 'as given me the little cottage!"

Elspet began to laugh, giddy with relief and happiness but then the meaning of what Ginny had said sunk in. Where would he go? Was he going away? Who could blame him?

"But if he has given you the cottage Ginny, where will he live?"

"Well…," said Ginny "…that's just worr Ah was goin' t' tell thee!"

***

Elspet waited in the front room at the table by the window overlooking the Green.

Ginny had left hours before leaving Elspet with literally nothing to do but sit and wait. Ostensibly she waited for her Uncle to return home from Moreton House where he had been since early morning…but, she mused, every minute of every day that dawned, she spent waiting. The child moved within her constantly, eager to be born, its little world growing too small. Elspet felt that he or she would be lusty and healthy, all that it needed was an easy passage into the world and she knew that those few inches formed the most treacherous journey it would ever make.

She had seen childbirth, seen the suffering it brought and the bliss afterwards. She feared it a little but didn't dwell on the fear. It was useless to do so for one way or another, birth was a certainty. She thought of her mother and for the first time she could remember, she needed her. She felt the stab of guilt at the thought of what her mother would say if she knew…but of course, she didn't know. Elspet had followed the example Nathaniel had set in those early days after Aunt Eliza had died and brushed all the mess under the rug. Aunt Eliza would have known what to do…her Mother wouldn't. She could hear her mother now:

"Oh, Elspet…you're with child? Oh whatever shall I do? You must help me Elspet!"

Elspet mourned Eliza Speakman as if she had been her own mother. More than she mourned her death, she mourned the fact that she had known her so briefly. Somehow Elspet knew that if she had come here years before, each would have filled a void in the other's life. Later, when the sun was going down and there was no-one about, she would walk to the Churchyard and say a prayer over her quiet grave as she often did.

She thought of Thurston, the news that Ginny had brought she could hardly believe. What did Master Nicholas mean by doing such a thing? She didn't understand at all, she had so many questions to ask her Uncle when he returned. She had said so to Ginny:

"I will ask my Uncle how this has come about. I do not understand!"

"Oh no, no Miss Elspet" Ginny was stricken. "Please tha must not! Thurston said to tell no-one, that it must be a secret until certain letters 'ave bin sent an' such! Ah s'll look faithless if Ah break 'is confidence so easy. Please Miss?"

Well of course she had had to assure poor Ginny of her silence. Oh, it was so like her Uncle to keep quiet! He could keep his own council, goodness he could! Perhaps, thought Elspet, that was why Master Nicholas trusted him so well? Well someone would have to talk to her soon or she would go mad! She had to know what Thurston's life would be. It was still there, the invisible cord. If he left her and went away for ever, she knew he would drag her lost heart behind him for all her life.

She had been looking down at her swollen belly, stroking it idly as her thoughts wandered this way and that like a toddling child when suddenly she imagined a little girl. The picture was so clear, she felt inexplicably certain in that second that her child would be a daughter and was filled with a strange sense of relief. Somehow a daughter would be so much easier to bear.

It was that time of day she loved to look out of this window. It was late afternoon, the sun long past its zenith and journeying to the point in the sky where it would set. Its gentle light shone on the trees that fringed the Green and grew behind the wall of Moreton House. As she looked over, wondering how Thurston had come to be her neighbour, she saw her

Uncle and Reverend Kingsley walk from the gates of Moreton and bid each other farewell with a firm handshake. She watched the familiar figure of her Uncle walk across the Green towards home with an unfamiliar spring in his step. He looked lighter of heart than he had for many days. Whatever had happened must be good and she determined that secret or not, he would tell her the truth and make sense of the confusing tale Ginny had told.

Elspet welcomed her Uncle in with a little more fuss than he was used to, taking his light coat, settling him down in his chair and pressing a drink into his hand.

"Is all well with thee my Dear…" asked Nathaniel "…thou seem'st…lively this evening? But no…that is good! 't is good to see thee bright of face…it is, it is!"

Nathaniel had the feeling that something was required of him but he knew not what. Why could women never just say? Always it was a guessing game! But he chuckled inwardly…he liked the game. He took Elspet's hand and in turn motioned her to sit down in the chair opposite him.

"Sit down…sit down, my dear. I have such news for thee!"

Elspet sat, waiting as patiently as she could pretend to be for the news she craved of Thurston's changed circumstances.

Nathaniel spoke: "Sir Thomas Tytherton has joined with Lord Derby at Warrington Bridge!"

Elspet was surprised.

"Oh," she said, confused, before momentarily feeling a little afraid "…the fighting…it will not come here?" Her hand instinctively flew to her stomach, worried for the child.

"Nay…nay, do not worry we shall be safe. 't is said the fighting will be in Preston…but my dear do ye not see? Where Sir Thomas is then there shall Josiah be! God willing there is a chance he may be home again soon! If they fight well and Derby is victorious, my son may yet be home for the child's birth! He may be in time for a wedding my dear!"

Elspet would never know how she kept the smile on her face through all the emotions which bubbled up inside her. Of course she wanted Josiah to return to her Uncle, it would bring him such happiness...but to be her husband? The folly of their lie had raised its head to bite her.

"Elspet... art thou not happy? Wilt thou not join me in praying for his safe return? For all I have questioned God, I shall pray that he reveals himself to me now. I go to Church tonight...Reverend Kingsley will say prayers for him. Wilt thou not come?"

Elspet shook her head vehemently.

"Please my dear..." Nathaniel continued to press her "...there shall be only us and the Reverend...none shall see" he pleaded.

"God shall see!" she snapped. Sorry to spoil her Uncle's hopeful mood she reached apologetically for his hand squeezing it gently.

"Forgive me Uncle..." she spoke quietly "...but God shall see. He shall see my shame (and my deceit, she thought) ...but I shall pray for his safe return. I shall pray here...in the house where he lived as a child and where mine shall live."

Unable to look into his face, she bent to kiss his cheek before picking up her sewing and returning to sit by the window, leaving him still and silent on his chair. He had been easily placated she reflected ...she hoped he wasn't angry with her, she couldn't bear that. She looked over to see if she could sense what he was feeling, wondering if she should speak again. From where she sat, she couldn't see the slight smile that played on his lips...she had no idea what comfort her last words had given him. Within minutes, Nathaniel was dozing, exhausted by the day, head lolling onto his chest, his snoring a gentle bubbling sound.

Elspet thankfully could cease to worry about him for the moment. All she had to worry about now was the possibility of Josiah coming home to claim his promise and the still unanswered question of Thurston's future.

Nathaniel gave a loud snore, jerking in his sleep and she rose quickly to take the drink from his hand before it should spill and spoil his Sunday best. As she took it to the table she saw Thurston walking across the Green from Moreton House, home to the cottage where they had first met. He never looked across at their house these days. He was leaving her behind, his life was carrying on and it would seem going from strength to strength without her. Perhaps it would be best if he went away? Perhaps then that leaden ache in her heart would go away too? But she knew it was hers for life if she did not have him and in a moment of madness, she ran out through the front door, down the little cobbled path and into the dusty road. She wanted to scream his name but no sound came from her and instead she just stood watching him move further away.

He continued to walk and for some unknown reason she began to move slowly, following him in silence, he totally unaware of her presence. Then suddenly, miraculously, he stopped and began to turn, until their eyes met. For a moment, she held his gaze before shame at how she looked caused her to hang her head. Then she became aware that he was walking back towards her and her heart pounded in her chest so loud, she could hardly hear his footsteps above it. He stopped, a little way from her:

"Good Evenin' Elspet…Ah 'ope tha's keepin' well?"

She looked up at him, tears welling in her eyes, forcing a smile.

"Yes," she said. "I am well…I see you are too…and I hear things go well for you."

He was silent, just looking into her face, closer than he had been for months yet so far away.

"I am glad for you Thurston…" she continued to speak, wanting to keep him there for ever "…no man in this world ever deserved good fortune more."

Still he said nothing but all the emotion he felt within was clearly reflected in his face. They stood like that for a long moment, each looking at the other, their hopes and dreams hanging in the warm air between them, shattered by secrets and lies and separate sufferings never to be shared. She wanted to tell him all. She wanted to run to him and for him to hold her and make it all alright but she knew that could never be.

After another moment he spoke quietly, breaking the spell.

"Elspet…," he said "…with all my 'eart …Ah truly wish thee well."

Then he turned and walked on. He didn't look back, not once.

***

Ginny jumped out of her skin when Thurston burst through the door a while later.

"Where's Isaac!" he demanded.

"'Thurston...'t is late. 'e's asleep at Ma's. Ah nipped out to get thi meal. What's up wi' thee?"

Something had clearly upset him, she knew the signs. Isaac had become to Thurston like a toy a child might cuddle when it was frightened or confused. Ginny never minded, she was glad that her boy had a man in his life to show him affection. She knew too that Thurston genuinely loved the boy, who couldn't? He was so beautiful and sweet natured and Ginny knew that Thurston was nurturing those traits. He was setting down a pattern for the boy, much as you would make a coat she decided. If Isaac followed Thurston's pattern, he would make a fine coat indeed! She chided herself for her fanciful notions.

"Come on...spit it out..." she urged again "...what's to do?"

He stood facing the fireplace, his hands on the shelf, his head hanging down. Patiently she waited, sitting at the battered old table, beginning to worry a little.

"Ah've just seen Elspet," he said.

Ginny sighed. She'd spent many a night in her bed at Ma Jenkins cottage trying to piece together the puzzle of this whole affair in her head. She had succeeded or so she thought. To her now it was as plain as the nose on her face what had caused this whole situation to come to pass. There had been no use telling it or talking of it, not until those involved were ready to hear it. Perhaps now was the time. She chose her words carefully, picking hesitantly round the sore to expose it with as little pain as possible.

"And what did that make thee feel like?" she asked

What a question to ask a man she thought and sure enough he was stumped.

"…Sad…? He returned questioningly. She waited:

"…'appy…to see 'er lookin' well…aye she looks grand, even…"

He gave up. Some more picking was required, she sensed.

"Did ye feel 'appy to see 'er lookin' well then? She's carryin' well…she looks 'ealthy an'…"

"No!" Thurston cut her off, almost shouting. Ginny sighed with relief, she had pushed through.

"No Ah don't feel 'appy Ginny! Ah loved 'er! 'ow can Ah be 'appy when she's big wi' another man's child?"

Ginny gave it a moment, let his anger subside. Nothing shut out words like anger.

"an' if tha could turn t' clock back Thurston? What would tha do?"

He turned towards her, laughing with the irony of the question.

"What would Ah do? What would Ah do? Ah'd ask her t'marry me like a shot! Ah should've done, before 'e came into 'er world…but Ah were too shy…Ah were different then."

She grabbed his thought and ran with it, hoping he would chase it to the conclusion she wanted him to reach.

"So it is because she carries 'is child that stops thee?"

Thurston shook his head at the question, incredulous that she need even ask it.

"Of-course it is Ginny…can ye not see that?"

She goaded him still further.

"Well, if 'e were never to come back…would it change things with thee?"

She had hardly finished her sentence before he snapped back.

"No! No Ginny! Do ye not see? She lay wi' 'im when she knew Ah loved 'er! She betrayed my love!"

He looked for all the world that he might cry but he calmed himself, resigned to his fate. He sat down on the bed in the corner, head in his hands. Several minutes passed before Ginny spoke again.

"Ah don't know why men set themselves up to be masters over women! Ah don't know one man who can open 'is eyes an'see the truth in a woman's 'eart. Ah thought with thee Thurston there might be some chance...but Ah see now th'art as blind as the rest of 'em."

He looked up at her, silent, waiting. Ginny breathed another long sigh before painting a picture for him with words she had practised.

"Elspet's child will come in September, early October time...tha knows this?"

Thurston nodded.

"Ah presume tha can do t' sum then? That means the child were conceived in January?"

He nodded again.

"So that would mean that the first time she set eyes on 'im, she let Josiah Speakman willin'ly into 'er bed?"

Thurston, a little more hesitantly now, nodded...already doubting the obvious conclusion he had previously reached. Ginny went on:

"Ah've spent every day o' t' last seven weeks wi' that young woman an' even Ah by now know 'er to be one o' t' kindest, sweetest most 'onest souls Ah've ever 'ad the pleasure to meet. Tha says tha loves 'er...an' tha can't see that?"

Thurston swallowed hard, rubbing his hands on his knees as he prepared for the realisation that was forming in his head. Ginny knew she had to make one final push.

"Thurston...that girl lay with no man by choice! She could no more do that than...an angel. If that man made a child on 'er it was not by 'er choice, do ye not see? She must've bin cruelly used Thurston!"

Ginny had not seen such rage since her feckless husband had beaten her black and blue and she had run for her life a year before. Thurston shouted, he cried, he held his head as if it might blow up. He punched the brick walls with his bare knuckles until they bled. And all the time Ginny sat, hands over her ears and eyes tight shut, telling herself that this was Thurston...he would stop. He would be calm again. When she heard the sounds of his sobbing, she uncovered her ears and went to where he sat again, on the bed. She put her arms around him and held him close while he wept like a child.

**

Josiah sat with Featherstone by the fire in their makeshift camp, huddled in the rolling Lancashire hills as evening fell. It was an uneasy camp tonight. Petty squabbles turned into fistfights, tempers rising, easily fuelled by tiredness, hunger and the need of fighting men to pump up their aggression to fight the enemy. The fact that their enemy was so close but yet unseen caused a deeper emotion to slither unbidden and unspoken in their guts, all men unwilling to recognise it as fear.

The two Captains shared their precious quart of rum given to them by their commanding officers to ease their burden of responsibility this night. Silently they savoured the warming liquor, accepting the gift as a sign that the time was near. Josiah was consciously in that state of mind he knew so well, having risen above fear. All he knew now was an absolute commitment to the mission that was now so personal to him. He was aware that John Featherstone, sitting silently by his side was gathering his own thoughts. There were not many men in this hastily assembled army whose company he would seek out tonight but John like himself was an old campaigner.

Josiah smiled at the irony of the thought...old campaigner? He was twenty-three years old. In fact in two days time, he would be twenty-four... or was it tomorrow?

"What is the date today John?"

His companion looked puzzled for a moment before hazarding a guess.

"Is it the twenty-third? No...I think it is the twenty-fourth? Aye, for sure! Tomorrow is the twenty-fourth day of August in the year of our Lord, Sixteen Hundred and Fifty one!"

I was right, thought Josiah, in two days I shall be twenty-four years old. He reached for the rum and filled their small leather beakers to the brim.

"Then I wish you a good twenty-fourth day of August, Sixteen Hundred and Fifty one Captain Featherstone!

They tapped their mugs together and drank. Their quiet laughter subsided and all fell silent but for the crackling of the fire both men becoming aware of a feeling of sadness that was settling about them. Featherstone spoke at length:

"Shall we see this day again next year think you? Do ye ever think of where we shall be... or if we shall be?"

Josiah did not want this conversation but he knew through his many years of soldiering that when men needed to talk it was best to let them talk...to save worse. He shrugged his shoulders knowing his friend would continue to talk, no response from him needed yet.

"I think of home, Josiah. I think of my wife...of how grown our daughter must be. Her youth is slipping away while I march and fight...on and on. ...I think at times I will not see them again this side of the grave. Do you ever think like that Josiah?"

But Josiah was now lost in his own thoughts, silent unspoken thoughts set running like hares by the words his friend spoke. He was watching his life like a play he had seen as a child when the mummers had come to Leighton Fold. His Father had taken him, holding his hand the three miles to the town, carrying him dozing on his back all the way home.

Silently, he slipped out of the harsh world in which he lived as he watched the scenes of his past life play out in his memory. Running with the pack in the far off days of his youth, he saw himself wielding the sticks, wishing it was his mother he was hitting or his dead sister...or even his Father who wouldn't make his wife love her son. He saw Thurston Hey's muddy, bloodied face...the brown eyes that had stared at him from the edge of his nightmares down the years. He saw Elspet's features blur into those of his mother as he remembered her when he was a child. He saw the young soldier who had died in his arms, his face changing into that of a dead child he had come across on the road and buried in a field. Tears began to dampen his cheeks as he thought of Rachel, the grey of her beautiful eyes swallowed up into the water of the North Sea and, most painful of all, he remembered the willow-fringed green of his home and imagined his Father waiting for him there.

Then finally returned the memory of being carried home on the night of the play. His mother had taken him from his exhausted Father and had carried him upstairs in her arms to lay him in his bed. He had pretended to sleep all the way knowing that if he had opened his eyes, he would have been set down to climb the stairs to bed alone. He remembered the smell of her as she stroked his hair and bent to kiss him softly on his cheek, safe in the knowledge that he would never remember her affectionate touch. But he had, all these years, though it had never been given again until he had seen her last. Involuntarily, he put his hand inside his coat and felt the letter he always kept beneath his shirt, silently repeating the words she had written…words he had read and re-read so many times these last months. Breaking the silence, he replied to his friend at last:

"My life has been a waste John…a waste of all the things that in the end matter above all others. My end will be the end of all my troubles and I hope to God, it will free those who have been troubled by me."

He looked straight ahead into the flames as he spoke. John Featherstone said nothing, just silently patted Josiah's shoulder as he nodded, drifting into rum-induced blissful sleep. Josiah covered his friend and left him to his gentle snoring knowing that merciful escape would not be his for many dark hours yet.

***

Edwin Bagshawe sat in his tent alone. It was late, all was quiet and he was preparing himself for the battle to come. All evening he had recognised the feeling that had crawled under his skin, and had struggled to control, the actions that all his life had been the inevitable outcome of it. But this was a different kind of life, different things were required of him now. Self-control…self-discipline…the suppression of that blood rush of anger which rose so quickly in him and which in his past had caused him to strike out mindlessly and with dreadful cruelty. These days he had learned to manage his feelings, to disguise the flaws in his character, to impress his Officers and so advance his career. Yet at moments like these, he knew himself. In these moments when the feeling became too powerful to fight, he felt the urge to hurt something, anything, someone, anyone… to relieve the pain that at times threatened to engulf him.

It was some weeks now since he had found a way to control the old urges, urges which he knew could never be allowed to overcome him again. He had found a way to fight one pain with another, to block out his past and control his present. He felt the need now…useless to fight it, he allowed himself the comfort of ritual. Lifting his sword, he held it aloft for a moment before sliding it slowly from its scabbard with an air of ancient ceremony.

The weapon had come to signify so much for him. As a gift from his Father, it now embodied all the bitterness and betrayal that had bestowed on him this endless, gnawing agony deep within his soul. It was a life-long ache that he knew could never be rooted out. It was with him for life and had grown as he had grown.

On the day he had received the sword, the day he had waited in vain hope that his Father would come and see at last some good in his son, he finally lost all hope of his Father ever being proud of him. He had taken the sword from the hands of the servant who had brought it and inwardly sworn to use it in any way he could to hack at and destroy those memories that haunted his life. From that day he had ceased to fear death, he began to see it as the ultimate release, the ultimate revenge on his greatest tormentor. With that had come the feeling of reckless invincibility that had seen him rise.

He had never sent a word since to his Father nor had he received any and he swallowed the bitter hurt down into his gullet. The sword had become since then, an extension of himself…hard, cruel, and deadly.

He looked at the weapon admiringly, reverently, sensing anew the power it held over him as he slowly brought it down to place the hilt between his feet. The blade stood erect held firmly by his knees, its tip pointing upwards to the apex of the tent where he now fixed his gaze. His eyes saw some other sight as he wound himself transfixed into the comforting ritual of pain. As he slowly exposed the soft white flesh of his inner forearm, he steadied his excited breathing, anticipating the moment of release. At the point he had come to recognise so well, the point when the hurt and pain inside threatened to tip the scales of his sanity, he took control over that pain and lowered his arm quickly, bringing down his flesh to kiss the cruel blade. Again and again and again he brought down his arm, gratefully embracing the relief of exchanging real, tangible pain for one he had never been able to understand or ease until now. He breathed normally again as the feeling washed soothingly over him numbing his agony for a while as his blood ran down the gleaming steel as black as ink in the firelight.

32.25th August 1651

Josiah's fears that sleep would not be his for many hours had been well founded. He had awakened with an ache in his head on the twenty-fourth day of August and spent that day until nightfall marching from the hills above the town of Preston. It had been a long and confusing march as orders had been given then rescinded, new orders given and routes re-set only to change again at a moment's notice. Men were tired and worse still, alarmed by the obvious uncertainty showed by their commanders. It had taken all Josiah's skills and experience that day to hold the little company of men in his command together and keep them firm in purpose. It was like a game of chess he had explained, though he doubted very much if any of this hastily formed army of farmer's sons and rural gentlemen had ever played the game in their lives. Nonetheless, under Josiah's careful and patient instruction, they came to understand the intricacies of their situation.

The Parliamentarian Army was so near, each army must move in a close contest to pass by the other unseen he had explained. The good Earl of Derby who led them must outwit the enemy to join with the rest of the Royalist force and so double the size of their army, while at every turn Milburne and his Parliamentarians sought them out to block their path. It was a game of skill and tactics and slowly the men came to understand the need for these intricate movements and changes of pace and direction. One by one, they passed their understanding on and the army became calmer, their trust in the Earl was renewed and orders followed without question or complaint.

After a few hours rest as the sun went down, the army had taken advantage of the cloak of darkness and begun their march toward Manchester. A long and arduous march it had been through the night, over hilly country and farmland by the light of the moon, dragging artillery and each man carrying his own weighty pack, armour and weapons. Every moment aware of the need for silence and swiftness, they relentlessly drove themselves on. As the sun came up on the anniversary of Josiah's birth, the army had rested briefly knowing that their punishing pace had put enough distance between themselves and their pursuers to risk losing a little time.

"We shall rest at Wigan...," said Featherstone, walking over to Josiah bringing a cup of water from the stream by which they had rested. "...and can you guess who is already there?"

"Sir Thomas?" ventured Josiah.

Featherstone's smile was answer enough and the two men grabbed each other's shoulders, laughing in celebration for Sir Thomas Tytherton had long been an inspiration for them both. Next to seeing his Father, seeing Sir Thomas was the thing he would have most wished for. Josiah gratefully drank the water, tapping cups with Featherstone and each winked at the other silently wishing each other good fortune.

"I am so close to my home, John. I pray to God I shall see it soon."

"Amen to that, my old friend...Amen."

After an hour, the troops had rallied again and pressed on toward the town, all the while thinking of food, a cup of ale and the sleep they so craved. Finally, by midday, they approached the buildings on the edge of Wigan and with a final flourish of vigour, the army quickened their step, eager to join the force they could see clearly now waiting to welcome them.

The sight of Sir Thomas Tytherton's noble profile raised Josiah's spirits and the courage he felt within him surged stronger than ever. With the leadership of this brave knight who he had followed through so many battles and campaigns this last seven years, surely their victory was assured! As a member of Sir Thomas' regiment, Josiah was quickly reassigned, along with Featherstone, to serve with his old leader and was greeted warmly by him.

"Speakman! Happily fate throws us together again. I could not wish for a finer Captain in my ranks Sir!"

Josiah bowed: "Nor I to serve under a nobler General My Lord. I am honoured to fight once more alongside thee!"

"Then to it, Captain! We fight to overthrow this new order. What a noble cause. God willing, victory will be ours."

The nobleman's hand fell on to his shoulder.

"Good fortune to thee, Speakman. I hope we meet on the other side of this battle to embrace once more."

"Aye Sir!" exulted Josiah, hat in hand as he watched the man whose instinctive bravery he had admired as boy and man depart, leaving behind an infectious air of confidence.

God knew where the man had been these last months, prison some said. Like himself, Josiah thought…lying low waiting for better times and new opportunities to settle old scores and set things right. No matter how they had each survived to come to this point, they were here and what would be would be!

***

Nathaniel had at long last completed the rituals of his morning. He had risen   late and had washed, shaved and dressed moving a little slower than usual, feeling the heaviness of his heart. Even the sound of Elspet humming a pretty tune could not cheer him much, wondrous though the sound was after the air of sadness she had carried through the year. He sat at his desk by the window in his bedchamber, the room where memories resided in every corner and where he felt his dear wife's presence most. It was where he most found peace. Yet today he could not shake from his suddenly weary shoulders the weight of worry for his son. Today was the anniversary of his birth here in this room, in this bed.

What a momentous day that had been. Eliza had laboured long into the night as quiet as she could be, not wanting to wake Susannah or trouble her worry worn husband. He had crept into the room as the midwife had nipped out and Eliza had chided him though he could see in her eyes how glad she was to see him. Not a word for herself, she had asked after their daughter.

"Sleeping soundly" he had whispered stroking her damp forehead.

"And how art thou my dear?" she had asked, touching his face.

"Why, worried for thee, dear heart of course! Will it be long?"

She had shaken her head and shooed him away as another pain was gathering strength.

Dawn had just broken on the twenty-fifth of August when he heard the cry that had made his heart leap in his chest. It had seemed an age before the old woman came to the door and beckoned him in. He remembered as if it was yesterday the surge of happiness as Eliza said: "We have a fine boy...come and see."

Nathaniel had wept with joy and God knew he could weep now and never stop weeping, for times past, time hopelessly lost and most of all for his boy.

"Please God...please bring him back to me!" he said aloud.

He stood for a moment, eyes closed and hands clasped fervently. Then he shut out his memories and left the room hurriedly, late now for his meeting at Moreton House.

His words and the emotion with which he had spoken them still echoed in the silence of the empty room. As he left, the first rays of the midday sun pierced the tiny window, lighting up the dust motes set dancing in the raftered ceiling by his hasty closing of the door.

***

Thurston was on his way to meet Nicholas, Nathaniel and Reverend Kingsley after spending his last night in the little cottage. He had spent the morning with Ginny as she helped him pack his few belongings and as he prepared to leave, he had pressed the iron key made by his Father's own hand, into her little palm. He felt only a little regret as he did so, grateful to the little cottage for sheltering him all his life, happy to pass it on to Ginny and little Isaac so that it may look after them.

Ginny had been overwhelmed at receiving the key as if somehow holding it in her hand made the whole thing suddenly real. She cried for the dozenth time that morning.

"Oh Thurston" she wept "if ever tha needs to come back we can go back to Ma Jenkins'. Oh Ah can't believe it, truly Ah can't."

He had patted her shoulder and put his arm round her yet again.

"Ginny Ah shan't need it! The deed is done, Ah told thee! The papers are signed...'t is all true! Ah'm the new owner of Moreton 'ouse!"

He laughed loudly then held her shoulders and looked into her tearful face.

"My life...and thine, Ginny...we turn a new page!"

Unknown to Thurston, Ginny thought: He's beginning to speak differently, he's changing somehow. She had felt inexplicably afraid of losing him.

Tears still on her cheeks, she said:

"But Thurston...shall we still see thee?"

"Ginny!" he had exclaimed exasperated "...Of-course tha shall see me! You are bringin' Isaac over tomorrow and every day after that!"

He spoke quietly then, seeing her worry.

"And just think Ginny when Isaac is old enough he shall come to the school that we shall make! Did you ever think Isaac would go to school? Every time Ah think of what this will mean for folk like us Ginny...well, Ah can scarce believe it!"

He had picked her up and swung her round in the little house and she laughed and tried to put her worries aside. It was hard to accept the prospect of a bright future when every memory or hope you ever had was tinged with fear and want and hardship. He put her down.

"Accept it" he had said "…be 'appy. Make a good future for yourself an' the lad."

They both looked up to see Isaac's face, laughing at their antics, poking from his little room in the roof. Thurston reached up and grabbed the boy, swinging him down and whirling him round too, revelling in the sound of his laughter. Setting Isaac down breathlessly on the bed, he had turned again to Ginny.

"Make 'im a good life Ginny. Let 'im not want for anythin'…'e's a lucky lad t'ave thee as a mother. Th'art a fine, good woman Ginny Green…best Ah ever knew. Me an' thee, we s'll be friends always."

She was weeping again and he had finally given up. As he walked down the lane toward the crossroads, her apron was up drying her cheeks every time he turned to wave.

What a day, what a week, what a year it had been! At every step, he recounted the events since October, at every step a pleasant memory danced in his head and he began to feel good, unbelievably good. The revelation Ginny had helped him to finally see the night before last had set off a roaring tide of turbulent emotions within him that had taken the last twenty- four hours to subside. Now finally, he realised that despite all the anger and hatred he felt for Josiah Speakman, the overwhelming emotion he felt was relief at the possibility that Elspet did not love that man he so hated…and somehow that possibility gave him hope.

He hadn't planned to walk the way he did, he just walked without thinking, his mind filled with so many things he could hardly think at all. Then he suddenly became aware as if waking from a dream, that he was at the path…the path that wound its way through the fields to the place that had wound its way round his life like a choking vine and he saw again the dream in his mind.

So often these past weeks the dream had assaulted him…broken his sleep, disturbed his daytime thoughts. Flashes of memory haunted him and hindered his progress through his new chance at life, more than his leg had done in his old one.

The truth was coming. He could feel it creeping up on him and he was powerless to stop it. The final, terrifying realisation that lay behind the unyielding door in his nightmare, eluded him still. One day soon he knew the truth would be revealed and he would remember all. He was tired of being afraid, tired of waiting. He could never dream happy dreams until it was finished but he was so desperate to grasp every opportunity that was, God knew why, being offered to him now. How could he deride Ginny for not wholeheartedly embracing the chance she had been given? How could he have failed to understand the trouble she had trusting kindness and goodness when her whole life had been devoid of these gifts? He was the same! He was letting all the wonderful precious things he was being offered be tarnished by the memory of old fears and ghosts of the past.

He looked with new eyes at the path and saw before him a choice. He could walk on down the lane to the crossroads as he did every other day...he could wait in fear for however many years while the memories receded a little. He could brush off the curling tendrils of the vine...trim it from time to time...but he would always be aware of its power to flourish anew and cover his every attempt to grow. Or, he could cut it out and destroy it at its root so that it died back slowly, powerless to invade his future again.

Since Ginny had helped him see that terrible truth about Elspet and that black hearted villain Speakman, his mind had been filled with visions of revenge. His blood had surged with thoughts and feelings he had never thought or felt in his life despite all the cruelties inflicted on him. Yet even though he had allowed the bloody visions to play out in his head...he knew they were only thoughts...human thoughts. They would never become deeds because he knew he could rise above them. For the first time he began to see in himself those qualities that Nicholas Moreton had recognised in him...forbearance, tolerance and humanity. He knew also that though it may be a long time off yet, eventually would come forgiveness. The anger would wash away and what would be left was the character of the man he had spent all his life learning to be.

Enough, he thought…enough, and then with purposeful step he turned off the road to follow the path which led to the place he had visited with Elspet on that crisp, wint'ry day months before.

***

Josiah could hardly believe his ears when the order came through to ready themselves for attack. Worn out himself, he had just watched the exhausted men he had urged on through the night, gratefully laying down their packs to rest. The cooks were preparing to cater for hundreds, the tents being unpacked and unrolled ready to erect.

"Attack…now? Are you sure that's the order?" Josiah asked, incredulous.

The Sergeant who had brought the orders nodded.

"Aye Sir, I am sure that is the order."

"Well… 't is a bloody stupid one!"

The Sergeant saluted and left to issue the order to the rest of the regiment.

"Bloody mercenaries" he muttered under his breath. "Who the hell do they think they are?"

Josiah was so furious at the order, he kicked the belongings at his feet that he had just unpacked. He was tired…he was in no frame of mind for battle or to rally men of whom so much had already been asked. Featherstone joined him.

"John! What madness is this?" His friend shook his head.

"I hear 't is the order of the Earl" Featherstone explained. "He feels the only road open to us is to attack now before we become surrounded."

Josiah spat out his anger and frustration in reply.

"But John we have the town behind us! It offers a brilliant defence! We could hold them 'till the rest of the army comes? We could trap them between our two armies? We know warfare by God and this is madness! To attack with half our men exhausted?"

Featherstone shrugged his shoulders. He had always been one to accept and follow orders unquestioningly and urged Josiah to do the same... though even he seemed unsure this time.

"What can we do Josiah? We are soldiers and bound to do as we are commanded...'t is how we live?"

"Aye!" retorted Josiah "...or die!"

Aware of the men around him, he calmed himself a little before speaking again, quietly.

"John I fear this will go badly. I have learned that no matter how well an army is trained or armed...battles are won and lost by bad decisions. This is a bad one...a bad one indeed."

The men around them were beginning to hear the spreading rumour of the order to attack.

"There is a job for us here and no mistake, John," said Josiah. "Somehow we must rally these ragtag soldiers who last week were driving the plough and all last night worked like plough horses! We must induce them to fight to the death for a cause they have ceased to care about. This is the battle we must fight first I think."

They both stood and looked at the hundreds of men before them. Some were raging against their orders, some in disbelief were searching for someone to explain, other men still slept where they had laid down their packs. Only a very few of the more resilient fighting men silently and stoically packed up their belongings and readied their muskets.

The two battlehardened Officers swallowed down their feelings of rage and disagreement, bowing to the superior will of their Commanders with the unquestioning subservience of the duty-bound soldier. It was indeed a way of life that they, and at least some of their company, had much experience of.

"Well...," said Featherstone, grasping his friend's shoulder "...Once again, we are in God's hands."

Josiah laughed mirthlessly.

"God? No John, God has long since turned his back on this war! No, today our destinies are in the hands of men deemed greater than us. Let us hope today they prove their greatness."

***

Nathaniel was shown into the Drawing room at Moreton where Nicholas and the Reverend Kingsley sat waiting for him.

"Forgive my lateness," he said, taking off his hat and handing it to Maggie who hovered at his elbow.

"'t is no matter Nathaniel" replied Nicholas, standing to shake his hand. "Thurston is not yet here. Wilt thou take a little port wine with us?"

Nathaniel accepted the small glass gratefully and sat down at the table on which were laid all the papers relating to the ownership and transfer of Moreton House and its lands. He knew today he had no stomach for business, he couldn't stop the flutterings in his chest and the feeling of sadness flowing in his veins so fast it threatened to drown his heart. Reverend Kingsley saw the look in his eyes and laid his hand on Nathaniel's shoulder.

"Art thou well Nathaniel…thou seem'st troubled?"

Nicholas turned to look at them both, then back toward Maggie who still hovered, twisting her apron by the door.

"Maggie what is it?"

She walked back, slowly and painfully to where they sat.

"Oh Sir's…forgive me, but the knife sharpener just called afore…'e's come from Wigan way Sir."

Nathaniel stood up again suddenly, knowing that the pedlars who came to the village regularly throughout the year plying their trades of knife sharpening or woodturning or lacemaking were also the deliverers of important news. Their information networks criss-crossed the country as they met fellow pedlars from all corners of England and beyond.

"What news?" Nathaniel asked. "'ad he news of the fightin'?"

Maggie nodded. "Aye Sir…'e said Lord Derby's men were on their way to Wigan town and Sir Thomas 'ad been waitin' for 'im there Sir."

"And what of Milburne's army?" Nathaniel was desperate for news now, however bad it may be. "Where be their enemy? Did 'e say?"

The old woman nodded again, her apron twisted round her hands.

"Aye Sir…they be on their tail 'e said, marchin' from Preston. 't is sure the two will meet in the next few days 'e said."

Nathaniel sat back down heavily in his chair, the wind knocked out of him. Nicholas walked over to Maggie, who was fretting now.

"Oh Sir…did Ah do right? Ah could not just sit on t'news Sir could Ah? It wouldn't be right would it?"

Nicholas quietly reassured her that she had been right to let them know and when she left the room, he returned to sit with Nathaniel and Kingsley at the table.

It was a strange secret that all who knew Nathaniel kept, all who stood friend to him were aware of what his son did. Yet, because of the danger, none ever spoke of it or let him know they knew. Nicholas was only too well aware of the pain his friend had suffered all these years, imagining the dangerous life his son lived and the constant fear he suffered knowing that his son's hold on life was so tenuous. They must talk of it now.

"Thou think'st thy son is there?" asked Nicholas.

Nathaniel nodded, unable to speak.

Samson Kingsley clasped his hands together and bent his head onto them.

"Oh merciful God…," he said, his deep voice reverberating in the large room. "…lay thy guiding hand on the shoulder of our dear friend's son, Josiah, who fights for his cause in thy name. Keep him safe dear God. Let him pass through his enemies uninjured. Show him thy mercy and light his way through the darkness of battle. We pray in thy son,

Jesus Christ's name, dear God…let him come safely through his trials."

The three men responded loudly together: "Amen!"

***

Thurston was standing at the spot where seven years before he had been beaten to within an inch of his life. He waited for the memories to come, for the pictures to flash in his head and the remembered sounds to assault his ears. He waited, here now at the scene of all his nightmares, for the first time ready to fight them. Nothing happened, his mind was blank. With what cruel irony did this thing taunt him? Ever in the rare times when he'd been happy, whenever he had been free of the memory for a precious few moments, it would suddenly come to him! Always ready to pull him down, always eager to crush his confidence and bring him to his knees with stomach-churning fear! So ready was he to face it now, to punch it and kick it and send it running from his life that the frustration he felt became unbearable and pounded in his head like a pain.

"Come on!" he wanted to shout. "Come on! Ah'm ready for thee now…where art tha, come-on!"

Silence… nothing but the birds singing and the low summer hum of insects. His sigh was a long groan and he looked up as a startled bird flew from the tree above him, scattering faded leaves about his head. He looked up at the Oak tree…God, how was it still standing? He remembered it being here in this place all his life, strong and proud…but it stood now blighted, strangled by ivy that had grown up and around it's trunk, covering it's bark and choking the life out of it. Only a dozen pale green leaves hung from it like tattered ribbons, its branches broken and dying, sticking out into the summer sky like helpless arms begging for nourishment. He looked with new eyes at the tree and saw a living thing stifled by the ruthless, cloying bonds that held it in torment.

"'t is me!" thought Thurston "'t is just like me!"

The long pent up feelings of injustice and anger suddenly burst in his chest and without thinking, he lurched at the ivy like it was an enemy he had been waiting to encounter all his life, attacking frantically the thick growth of leaves at the base of the tree where it pushed up from the earth. The dust of hundreds of dead, burrowing insects and ancient spider's webs coated his hair and filled his mouth and still he wrestled with the ivy. It raked the skin of his hands and cut into his flesh where it had intertwined with brambles that had crept across the ground to join in the assault on the old tree and the blood mingled with the dirt on his hands.

In a few moments the bark beneath was revealed, soft and vulnerable, home to thousands of ants and insects who fed on its frailty. Thurston couldn't remember being so angry about anything before in his life. He pulled and battled with the ivy as if it were a hated old adversary until he had to stop, breathless and exhausted in the summer heat. Then as he stood panting the memories came, like a hot wind from a suddenly opened furnace, they blasted him when he was most unprepared for their power...

He could see them all now, running around him shrieking, their heads covered in cloth bags with holes for eyes. One, two, three, four, five different fabrics...it was the only way he could count how many had turned out for sport on that day. It had been a year that summer since the last attack. He had thought it was over...but here they were again, taller, stronger, their voices deeper. They had brought their weapons...the willow sticks of old, but thicker, short sticks too...one in each of their hands. He burned now with the embarrassment at the memory of warm liquid running down his leg ,his bladder involuntarily emptying as the leader of the gang had walked slowly toward him, swirling the willow stick, all happening again now before his eyes. He saw again the blue of the leader's eyes, like the pale sky of winter, strangely out of place on that bright warm day in May. He had run or tried to but he hadn't got far. As he fell by the edge of the field at the base of this tree where the dry grass met the peat moss, they had caught him, their sticks beating down on his back in cruel rhythm as they each swung their weapons high.

He felt again so real, the agonising sting of the willow and wondered how a tree so beautiful could inflict such pain. He had fought of course though he always wondered why. He knew that if he had just lain there and taken it they would have had little sport...but no matter how he tried he could never stop himself fighting. His arms had flailed like a windmill, his uncut nails grabbing at the cloths and he remembered now the face that had been revealed to him...a dark face with a soft boy's beard and thick black eyebrows from one of which flowed bright red blood.

The memory of the pain and the terror of the screams ebbed away and in his newly opened mind's eye, Thurston watched now the bleeding boy. He watched him lift his hand and grab the arm of the leader as he brought down his stick. Thurston saw, as if it was happening before him at that moment, his tormentor raise his other hand and hit the bleeding boy so hard that his lip split like a fallen berry. He saw the wounded mouth open and the word "stop!" formed in silence. And then, as he recalled the relief of the coming blackness washing over him, the memory of the boy sitting head in his hands beneath the tree. Looking up at the scene before him he had begun shaking his head from side to side, the bloody gash of his mouth open and crying "No!" over and over again.

Thurston again remembered so clearly the taste of earth filling his mouth and with it the recollection of a welcome sensation of floating into blackness. As he had begun to sink into unconsciousness, his newly reclaimed memory recalled looking across to the dark boy who sat, his face smeared with blood and tears, as powerless as he was.

As suddenly as they had assailed him, the memories were gone. He was back, beneath the tree, on a peaceful summer day on which he was happy to find himself alive...on the twenty-fifth day of August, in the twenty-fourth year of his life.

***

Half an hour later, Maggie opened the door of Moreton House.

"Oh my life!" she exclaimed "What 'as 'appened to thee?! Sir! Sir!" she shouted, running to fetch her master as fast as her aching legs would allow.

"Sir...'t is master Thurston...'e 'as bin attacked!"

Nicholas, Nathaniel and Samson Kingsley had been waiting for Thurston this last hour and all three ran to the door but Thurston was already walking into the hall as the door banged shut behind him.

"My boy," exclaimed Nicholas. "What has happened to thee? Where hast thou been?"

Suddenly Thurston was aware of how he must look, realising now the reason why the few people he had passed had looked so puzzled at the sight of him. He looked down at his hands and his shirt, bloody and dirty. His mind had thought of nothing else on the way to Moreton except the memory of the dark boy, sitting on the ground...unable to help him but sitting apart from the terror being inflicted on a helpless victim. He had remembered as he had walked as of old to the house that was his place of sanctuary, those last moments of the attack. He had remembered a final, terrible pain surge through his body and he had looked across to where the dark boy had been sitting, stretching out his arm for the help that somehow he knew the boy wished he could give him. But the place where the young Josiah Speakman had sat was empty.

Thurston looked at Nicholas Moreton's anguished face as he waited for an answer.

"Ah think..." murmured Thurston, so quietly they could hardly hear "...Ah think Ah need to tell thee where Ah've bin for a long, long time."

* * *

Elspet hardly knew what to do with herself. She had been in turmoil these last few days but that had been nothing compared to the panic she had woken up with this morning...

and now that trouble had paled into insignificance when she heard the news of Thurston that her Uncle had brought home!

For the last three days she had struggled with the possibility that her child would be a boy. She had so willed it to be a daughter that she had come to believe it was and the belief had made the whole situation somehow more bearable. It was only Ginny's innocent comment a few days earlier that had sent her off into a spiral of worry that had finally become fear when she had awakened from a dream that morning with the image of those ice-blue eyes embedded in her head.

"Be careful not to set too much store on 'avin a girl" poor, ignorant Ginny had said. "Anyway it'll not matter when you set eyes on it worr it is…long as it's a baby wi' an 'ead, two arms and legs! Tha'll love it…Ah promise…when tha looks into them little eyes…"

She hadn't finished when Elspet had suddenly felt sick and the sickness had grown over the last few days into a fretting she couldn't control. She hadn't thought on that terrible night for weeks now having packed it all away neatly in an imaginary box and buried it along with the green gown now rotting away in the earth. It was what she'd always been taught…what cannot be cured must be endured. And she had endured all…alone and in silence and that was how it must continue to be. She would endure it and never speak of it but please God she prayed, let this child be a daughter and let me not have to see those eyes every day of my life!

And now Nathaniel had brought home this news to worry her more! She could hardly sit still for worry for Thurston. Nathaniel had no answers for her questions only saying that Thurston had arrived late, looking as though he had been attacked and business was over for the day. That was all he knew, he insisted, and finally he had put his finger to her lips to silence her questions. Concerned for Thurston though he was, Nathaniel was beside himself for worry over Josiah. It was clear now that his son was probably preparing to fight not ten miles away and Elspet felt his pain. She remembered her Aunt's words: "When a woman has a child it is as if some part of her leaves her body forever and never will she get it back."

Was it like that for Nathaniel? He certainly looked as if some part of him was somewhere else at that moment. Would it be like that for her? She bent to kiss her Uncle's forehead and left him in peace or as near to peace as he could get.

She went out into the little kitchen garden, feeling helpless and with nowhere else to go or no one with whom to share her spiralling fears, she began to pace up and down driven by worry and frustration. It was mid-afternoon by the time she stopped and feeling suddenly exhausted, went indoors to rest. She climbed wearily up the stairs to her narrow bed feeling an overwhelming desire to lie down and sleep...just for a few minutes, she thought...just a few minutes.

***

Nicholas had taken Thurston into the garden and they sat together quietly in Thurston's favourite spot, by the moat. They sat in silence, Nicholas waiting for the place to work its magic on Thurston. He knew that whatever the lad would have to say had been shut up inside him for a long time, and so he was patient knowing that the words would come if he waited. And at length they did.

"Ah came to this place to 'ide..." Thurston spoke at last with quiet, cracked speech. "...to 'ide from them when they were after me...or after they 'ad found me and beaten me...an' Ah'd got away."

He looked up at the face of his benefactor, anxious to see his reaction to what he was saying and Nicholas was struck once more by the face of this young man...this fine, open face. Thurston's head bent again.

"Ah were safe 'ere...always safe. 't is 'ow Ah feel with you Sir."

Nicholas nodded but did not speak, waiting for the trickle of words to grow stronger and bring forth the secrets that must be shared if this young man of whom he was so fond was ever to leave his past behind. Patience was needed now, all words must be Thurston's and he gave him the time to find them. Slowly, hesitantly, Thurston began to recount all the events that had brought him to this day. He told of how from being a child, he had been afraid to walk alone, always looking behind, alert to every cracking twig or crow's squawk. He couldn't remember the first time it had happened but he had been young, five or six. It was how he had begun to be tied to the little cottage.

Thurston told of how his Father would send him home alone from his work on the moss and reflected for the first time in his life that somehow he had always known that his Father had not wanted to be seen out in broad daylight with his crippled son. To Thurston that long walk home had seemed like being sent across a treacherous sea filled with terrifying monsters. He would beg to be allowed to wait for his Father, promise to carry any load as long as he was not sent home alone but his Father would lose his temper and send him on his way, crying. Even as young as he had been, he had sensed his Father's deepening dislike of his child and knew a cruel loneliness because of it.

The monsters were only out there half a dozen times in all the years he had walked home alone but the fear of them being there, wherever he went, became his constant companion. He had never asked them why because he knew why…it was his leg and he was different…slow and quiet, easy prey. He could not run or call for friends or brothers to help. He was too ashamed to tell his Father who would have seen him as a cowardly cripple. Too afraid to tell his mother lest she boxed the boys ears and got him, and herself, into more trouble. He would explain his injuries away…a fall, a fight, and as he got older he would hide them.

As he told his story to Nicholas, he realised that the beatings had only happened perhaps ten times in all over the years…but so much a part of his life had fear become it had swallowed up his youth. Then Thurston told of the final beating as he had just seen it in his new found memory. He told of the revelation he had had months before, that Josiah Speakman, the black-hearted villain who had kicked and beaten him as a child, was the same man who had taken the only bright light that had ever burned in his life in his love of

Elspet Sydall and smothered that too. The realisation that he had used her in the worst way and destroyed her life as much as he had destroyed Thuston's own, by cruel abuse, tortured him now as much as any of those beatings! Finally Thurston related the scene at the end of that last terrifying day as he slipped into longed for oblivion. The scene that his shackled and blindfolded memory had just that afternoon revealed to him...that the boy Speakman had fought for him? Had wept for him? He didn't understand why...he didn't understand any of it.

Thurston had run out of words, lost still in the confusion of those long forgotten recollections and the way they were causing him to question what he thought he knew. He did not speak of the knowledge that he had, that the remnants of the story were still hidden... somewhere in a deep dark place in his head that one day soon would open. He knew that he must prepare himself for that...knew it would take all his new found courage. He put his head in his hands, wondering what the old man would make of all this. Would he think him weak...a coward? It was how he felt at that moment...as vulnerable and exposed as the boy he had been.

Nicholas had been silent, listening to the story, his face betraying nothing but absolute attention to every word Thurston had spoken and still he sat... saying nothing. Thurston's courage began to ebb away, how stupid he had been to think himself courageous? Unable to defend himself, less able to defend and protect the woman he loved...too cowardly to fight for her even now! Just as he was beginning to allow his old feelings of inadequacy and uselessness to get the better of him, Thurston felt the welcome weight of Nicholas' hand on his shoulder and that comforting feeling enveloped him.

The old man's voice was soft and quietly defiant, his words warming Thurston's heart as the August sun warmed his skin.

"And still, my dear Thurston, through all thy trials...through all thou hast witnessed of man's inhumanity...still thou art a true and honest man! And thou art brave Thurston...braver than any I ever knew in my life. I am proud to know thee...I wish I had been a Father to thee instead of the one thou had. I wish I could have fought for thee when thou suffered those fearful cruelties...!"

Nicholas breathed in deeply and placed his arm about Thurston's shoulder and Thurston felt the strength of this man's affection as he held him tightly, willing him to believe in himself.

"...but Thurston I am here now! And I will make up for all thou hast suffered in the years I have left. I will be as a Father to thee and thou wilt be as a son to me and we will bring each other comfort. Shall we promise this? Eh lad? Shall we promise this...?"

For the second time, Thurston found himself in the embrace of the man he wished had been his Father and the words he spoke to affirm the promise were lost in the sobs that wracked his body. Tears blinded the eyes of Nicholas Moreton as he held the young man tight to his chest in the way he wished he could hold again, the sons he had lost.

***

Over a thousand men began the march away from the town of Wigan straight into the path of the oncoming Parliamentarian army on that fateful day of the twenty-fifth of August. Lord Derby and his royalist force of three hundred led from the front, many of those marching with him the manxmen whom Josiah had lived amongst these last months. Forming the rear-guard was the force commanded by Sir Thomas Tytherton and Josiah took his place twenty yards behind the old campaigner.

The infantry, musketeers and dragoons marched ten abreast leading from the front and behind and between them marched the pike-men. Josiah with the other cavalry rode alongside them, flanking the foot soldiers, all in close proximity filling the lane along which they advanced. From his vantage point astride his tall black mare, Josiah watched the army snake ahead along the lane. Through the lattice work of raised pikestaffs, he scanned the empty road ahead, his face shadowed by the dark mood that bubbled in his chest.

It was two in the afternoon, the sun was hot and there had hardly even been time to fill up the leather water bottles which each soldier carried. Inside his armour, Josiah's upper body sweated in the heat and the sun reflecting on hundreds of helmets as the army moved along the lane, gave the illusion of molten metal running into a mould. Josiah looked up toward the hills where they had spent the previous night and thought briefly of blue sky and empty hillsides but he pushed the thought from his mind. There were only two things to think of now... fulfilling his mission and living through this day. He struggled to rid himself of the mood that had descended on him when the order to march came through. He couldn't shake off a sense of unease and impending catastrophe. He knew he must overcome it before the fighting began, knowing also that he must drive the men surrounding him forward with confident self-assurance.

Looking ahead, again he saw the Earl round the bend ahead, slowly disappearing from sight. He knew the scouts in front would sound the alarm at the first sight of the enemy. Then every man's step would quicken like his heartbeat and the blood would rush through his veins like hot oil. There was no conversation as each man wrestled silently with his own demons of heat and thirst, fatigue and fear. Those among them who had fought before knew that the fear would be extinguished as soon as the fighting began, to be replaced by an energy that nothing but mortal combat could bring about. It would come out of their mouths like a roar and propel them forth with the strength of five men. But for now the only sound was hundreds of tramping feet and the clang of metal on metal as each man jostled for space in the narrow lane.

For a moment, Josiah cast his eye about him at the faces of those who marched below. Did each man have his own reason for this? Why did they fight? Did they truly believe this cause was worth fighting and dying for? Did it matter who ruled the land? Would it make a difference to him or any of the men who faced the end of their lives today? Life was now, this moment and all of his life before had led him to this place. He looked up to the hills again feeling his black mood ebbing away. It had to make a difference! He saw Sir Thomas at the head of the rear guard rounding the bend now, his army snaking after him. It seemed an age before Josiah caught sight of him again when all of the army halted on the straight lane, for the first time sighting the enemy arranged and waiting, only two hundred yards between the two forces. All could see that the enemy's army was smaller than their own but Josiah and every other experienced soldier knew that Parliamentarian reinforcements were close and that Derby's forces had no other choice but to be the aggressors today with speed and numbers their only strength. They must despatch the opposing force quickly before help arrived. The tactics Lord Derby would employ this day were the bravest Josiah had ever witnessed. Was it bravery or madness? History would make the judgement, he mused. Just as he had formed the thought in his mind, he saw Sir Thomas raise his hand to him from his position in front. Though he could not see his face, Josiah knew there would be a flash of fire in those eyes!

Suddenly, he realised that Sir Thomas, the Earl, all those who made decisions on their behalf that day, were in the same frame of mind that he was. All or nothing! What would be would be! Whatever it took to win they would throw at this battle this day! He began to feel the thought infect his body, feel the surge of the chemical that had yet to be known as adrenalin, pump through his veins. He welcomed the growing feeling that he was invincible, recognising it as the familiar friend of the fighting man. It grabbed hold of him and shook the trepidation from his body and he sat his horse with a backbone of steel, holding the growing force inside of him, ready to unleash it at the second the signal to charge was sounded.

***

In the army opposite, Edwin Bagshawe sat astride his horse and watched the enemy force approach. They marched as if in a parade he thought, amused. It was almost as if they were all preparing to act out some great entertainment for some unseen, largely disinterested audience. In all his weeks of fighting, this was the first time he had seen a force this large, his own army clearly outnumbered. He felt no fear, just a detached curiosity. He felt nothing at all until he thought on the information that had come his way by letter from one in his old life who he held power over still, the answer to a question he had asked. It had confirmed the likelihood of one being in the enemy ranks who had betrayed him years before and for Edwin the possibility of added sport added a further frisson of excitement to the afternoon's proceedings.

He had always struggled with his feelings of betrayal and in fighting with a sword, he had found a wonderful way of vanquishing them at last. The feelings had begun to form even before he was old enough to know what they were. As a child, he had so often been got ready in his best clothes and presented to a Father who hardly noticed he was there, by a mother who had promised him that his Father would be proud of his fine boy. But always he had been dismissed and sent to a lonely room by his Father whilst his mother urged him to go, get out...suddenly angry...betrayal. It was only as he'd grown into a man that he realised what his Father did to his mother behind those hastily shut doors. She should have fought! She should have been braver! She should have taken him with her when she made her escape! She had promised to love him always...betrayal.

His Father, his nemesis, the one person left in his life who should have nurtured him, instead had neglected and despised every aspect of him, showing his disdain and disinterest at every opportunity...betrayal. Down the years the feeling had grown, twisting his mind and squeezing all feeling out of his heart as he became a man.

Then as an adolescent, had come the final betrayal...that of the one who had been his friend. He had left him too...driven away by fear of him and his cruelty when he should have stayed. He should have helped him to be better. He should have been his friend always. Betrayal!

Edwin hoped as he began to relish the fight to come that the boy who had been his friend would be in the army who faced him this day. He knew the rumours of Josiah Speakman's flight to join the fighting all those years ago...knew he had been in the service of the King and knew he fought for the royalist cause still. He had seen the fear in Nathaniel Speakman's eyes as he squirmed when questioned about his son on the night he had violated Josiah's young cousin. Nathaniel, he knew, would never betray his son, no matter what was threatened. He hated Josiah for having a Fathers love, he hated Nathaniel for being a better Father than his own. He hated everyone...it was why he had raped Elspet...somebody had to pay for his pain with their own. That was the only way he had been able to survive the hurt...and today, if he could seek him out, he would make Speakman pay too.

Josiah and his army waited as if standing on a cliff edge, waiting and ready to throw themselves into the void. The only sounds around them were the nervous snorting of horses, drawing of swords and priming of muskets. No man spoke but an imperceptible movement began and a slow ripple of activity flashed through the ranks as energy pulsed through the army.

"Jesu!" sounded the cry ahead and it was passed on from one Officer to another as the mass of men began to move as one. The cry came to Josiah and he turned to search out the face of his comrade Featherstone, twenty yards behind. They shared the look they had shared so often before, the look that held so many unspoken words. His horse began to move without urging, sensing the irresistible momentum that was building.

"Jesu!" cried Josiah in his turn, his horse beginning to trot alongside the hundreds of men who were now moving by his side, an unstoppable force, all repeating the battle-cry: "Jesu!"

The moment had come, the royalists were attacking. Edwin heard the trumpet charge and saw the mass of men moving toward them. Quickly he tied the white cloth about his arm which would identify him as a Parliamentarian in the chaos of battle, feeling as he did so that longed for sense of belonging wash over him again. He drew his sword and let out a loud roar, his pale eyes flashing as his horse lurched forward to meet the inescapable, oncoming roaring tide of men.

***

Ginny was just finishing the meal that she and Isaac would eat that evening. She had had a good cry after Thurston had left that morning and things were always better after a good cry...that was Ginny's theory and she had put it to the test many times in her young life. As she had busied herself in the cottage that afternoon placing her meagre belongings and beginning to make the place her own, she felt a new feeling begin to gnaw at her that she couldn't quite put her finger on. If someone had asked her a few months ago what would she wish for if she could have anything, she would have answered without hesitation: A home of her own, food on the table, warmth and security for herself and little Isaac. Now she had all those things, yet frustratingly some unresolved need for something else frayed the edges of her happiness. She shook it away and, her work done, settled on a chair by the back door watching her boy play in the sunshine.

There was nothing to be seen from the back of the cottage for miles, nothing but the wide blue sky framing the moss and flat land stretching out into the distance. The field behind the cottage waved with acres of yellow, ripening wheat, dotted only with sporadic, isolated clumps of trees standing like wooden islands in a rippling, golden sea. She loved this place and it was hers now. This must have happened to her for a reason...nothing happens without a reason... another theory of Ginny's. Short on learning, short on nurturing, she had a wealth of life experience despite her young age and she had never been short on thinking.

"Piggy bed...mama, piggy... bed." Isaac pointed to his rolled up blanket which lay in a bed of straw he had made in the long empty pigsty.

"Oh yes!" exclaimed Ginny, pretending along with the child "Ah see that piggy there! What's'e sayin' that little piggy?"

They both laughed as they each made 'piggy' noises.

Thurston, inspired by Ginny's "mitherin'", had finally fixed the old, neglected pigsty, preparing it for the new occupant she felt it should have. She remembered her words:

"If tha want's to 'elp thi neighbours tha mun ger a pig!"

All her life she had accepted charity from her neighbours, had relied on it, never even knowing it was charity. It was just how it was. Those in the community who had the means would raise and fatten a pig and at killing time, all would benefit. Such a feast the little community would have!

Thurston had remembered as she told her stories, watching a pig being chased through the town having escaped, he could still hear it screaming and had shuddered at the memory. She hadn't understood, after all she didn't see the parallels he silently drew with his own young life. In that moment though she had realised that Thurston had never known real hunger not even during the worst of the war when there was famine and poor starving strangers had wandered into the village searching for food. How clearly she remembered the pain of hunger...a real physical pain that nothing but sustenance could ease. She never wanted her son to know that terrible pain and the hunger that had been always a part of her life and that of her brothers and sisters. It was why she had wanted the pig. Suddenly she knew what the feeling was that gnawed at her. It was the unshakable bond with her family and those of her siblings who lived in want still. She would bring the younger two to live with her she decided! She must share her good fortune lest she get too used to it. She resolved to get Thurston's permission when she next saw him not quite believing yet that it was her house now, hers to offer shelter to whomever she chose.

She was sorting out in her head how to make her thought become reality when there came a loud knocking at the door. That knocking meant trouble, she sensed it, through her long experience of trouble coming knocking. Billy, the boy from Moreton House, stood at the door.

"What's to do? Is it Thurston?" she asked, worriedly.

"Nay Mrs," said the boy. "'t is Mistress Elspet. Th'art to come quick...she's reet poorly, Master Speakman asks for thee."

Ginny was already taking off her apron as she beckoned the lad inside.

"Come in lad an' get thee a drink...then get off. Ah'll see to the child then get straight to the lady."

The boy drank the proffered cup of freshly made raspberry cordial gratefully before returning to the Speakman's house with Ginny's message.

"Come on Isaac, bring that little piggy. Th'art goin' to see Ma Jenkins...see what treat she 'as for thee today eh?"

The boy rushed in, cuddling the rolled up blanket, dirty from the garden. He waited by the door excitedly knowing that Ma Jenkins table would be heavy with summer fruits. Ginny grabbed the key from the fireplace where Thurston had left it earlier and locked the door hastily behind her. Running over to Ma Jenkins cottage, she left Isaac in her care and ran on to Appley Green, fretting over Elspet and the child that was coming into the world too soon.

***

Thurston and Nicholas' separate days were both turning out to be days of discovery.

For Thurston the day had started well with the handing over of his home to Ginny and the feeling of pleasure it had given him. It had taken an unexpected turn when he had chosen the path through the fields and it had taken a fight with a tree to reveal long hidden answers but yet more unanswered questions. And now, as he sat in Nicholas' and Reverend Kingsley's company, moments after Nathaniel had been summoned home by Becca Thomas...now came the realisation that he loved Elspet despite all. He wanted to rush to her side no matter whose child she was going to bear. He realised now that he did not care if she never loved him, loving her would be enough…and so much easier to bear than life without her.

"Ah must go to 'er …" he begged Nicholas "…Ah must!"

Nicholas was firm. Though it hurt him to deny Thurston anything after what they had shared in the garden a few hours before, he used every bit of the power he knew he had over the young man to keep him from Elspet's door.

"'t is no place for thee, my boy. Bide thy time…wait. Childbirth is a time for waiting, for women and men. All will be well and if thou art needed, Nathaniel will surely send for thee."

There then followed one of the longest hours of Thurston's life. There was no talk just silence as both men buried their heads in books, Nicholas occasionally looking up to give Thurston a comforting look. Just when Thurston thought he would go mad if he didn't get out, just as he stood to go into the garden beneath the willow tree, there was a knock at the door. It was quickly answered by Maggie who shuffled in closely followed by Nathaniel. Thurston was at his side in a moment.

"'ow does she do? Will she live?"

Nathaniel grasped Thurston's hand, smiling.

"Worry not lad!" he said. The child is not coming…she is well. It seems she has not slept all night and has become over-wrought…pacing about all afternoon…probably with concern over Josiah. She sleeps now and Ginny will stay with her this night. It is a sign from God I think, Reverend!"

Nathaniel left Thurston and walked over to grasp the hand of Samson Kingsley who stood by the window.

"I feel it is meant to be" Nathaniel continued. "The child waits for its Father and my son will come home…I feel he will come home!"

Desolate though Thurston was and frustrated by his words, he could not help but feel sorry for Nathaniel. He was so desperate to get his son back, so eager to believe that the child Elspet carried was conceived in love. Blinded by the desire that all be true and all turn out well, that he had failed to uncover, as Thurston himself had, the terrible wrong done to a young and innocent girl. The guilt he felt at ever thinking badly of her overcame Thurston again and he sat down heavily on the nearest chair, devastated by it.

Nicholas watched the scene in silence. His old friend, clutching at any straw he could find that might bring his son back and secure his future. Thurston twisted by the truth he felt he had uncovered about Josiah and though it destroyed Nathaniel, wishing with all his heart that his son would not return. He knew of course how Thurston burned with the burden of what he thought was unrequited love for Nathaniel's niece but her clear avoidance of Thurston indicated something…Deep down Nicholas felt that there was still a part of this story that had yet to be uncovered. For now though, he feared that fate was set to play cruelly with the hearts of people who he truly loved for a while longer.

Suddenly Nicholas felt incredibly tired, weariness such as he had never felt in his life washed over him like a wave. What had indeed been a long and eventful afternoon was drawing to a close and more than anything he wanted to be alone…just for an hour or two. The memory of his own son's loss, fresh again in the face of Nathaniel's suffering, weighed heavily on his heart. The talk he had had with Thurston too had troubled him greatly. Although he was absolutely certain that he had made the right choice in putting his trust in this young man and regretted none of his decisions or actions, he had been shocked at the story the lad had recounted. He had been so sure that all his trouble and suffering could be laid at the door of William Hey…but the truth was more disturbing. What was the truth in the involvement of Speakman's son…and of others still unknown? His heart went out to Thurston all over again as he was filled with admiration at the way he bore his suffering with such forbearance and good nature. He would make it all up to him in the future God willing but for now he needed to rest, overwhelmingly he needed to rest.

All three men were surprised when Nicholas announced that he was leaving their company.

"Friends," he said quietly "I am tired, I need to rest awhile. Please stay as long as you wish...my house is thine. I fear all the excitement this day hath proved too much for me!"

Thurston was at his side in a moment to help him to his feet.

"Nicholas...art alright? Shall Ah see thee up the stairs?"

"Nay Thurston, worry not" Nicholas replied. "I am tired that is all."

He looked over to Samson Kingsley who had come to stand beside Thurston. As the two men's eyes met, Kingsley saw the silent plea in Nicholas' eyes...look after him awhile, they said. Kingsley understood.

"Aye Sir" Kingsley agreed "It has indeed been a taxing day. Such great doings we are caught up in eh? Thurston, might I trouble thee for thy arm to see me home? The good news about Nathaniel's niece seems a good place to end our afternoon."

Thurston was torn between staying with his benefactor and assessing he was well or observing the request of the Vicar to aid him home. Nicholas rescued him.

"Of course Thurston, thou must go with the Reverend. I need no help to climb my own stairs and I shall be asleep as soon as my head touches the pillow!"

He patted Thurston's shoulder. "Worry not Thurston" he added kindly "We shall meet for dinner...and by then a few passing hours will have put all in perspective, I assure thee."

Nicholas shook Kingsley's hand before turning to Nathaniel who now stood and respectfully bowed.

"Thou ...and thy son, old friend, I shall keep in my thoughts. Whatever thou need'st...come to me."

Nathaniel bowed again, hand on heart. "I thank thee Nicholas...rest well. Thy wits and strength are sorely needed now... by all of us."

Nicholas nodded and smiled before leaving the room, moving a little slower than usual, they all thought.

33.

Josiah struggled from a momentary disorientation, dizzy and sick, unsure of where he was, his head throbbing with an agonising pain that shut out reality. It was only as the pain ebbed away that he began to remember. It was the noise that had brought him out of his semi-conscious state, a relentless loud clamour of rhythmic musket fire, a percussion of clanging, discordant sounds of metal on metal and the chilling chorus of the shrieks and cries of men fighting and dying.

The first moments of battle had been as all others he had known, the ride, the first encounter, the effort of wielding his poleaxe with one hand and trying to control the terrified and powerful animal he rode with the other. The noise and feel of metal on metal, metal on bone, metal sucked from flesh, its gory job done. Kill or be killed, on and on, an unstoppable, unquenchable thirst…a spreading plague of incurable madness. He had counted his kills as he always did in those first moments and he had counted to ten by the time he looked over to see Featherstone poleaxed by a cavalry man not ten yards from him.

Josiah had known from the way his friend fell from his horse that his war was over.

"No!" he cried "No you bastard, no!!!"

The emotion that had charged through him at that moment made all else disappear as he turned his horse in pursuit of his friend's killer, fighting to cross the melee of fighting between, all the while shouting to draw the enemy to him.

"Come. Come on, son of a whore! Come and fight me!!"

Featherstone's horse was screaming, its nostrils flaring in terror as it tried to find a way out of the mayhem it found itself in without the guidance of its rider. It was confused by the dead weight of Featherstone whose foot was still caught in the stirrup. Wildly the animal darted this way and that, dragging Featherstone's lifeless body across the ground until in a fatal attempt to jump out of the press of men that held it captive, it was brutally halted by the parliamentarian pikes. The horse's chest was pierced deeply by the cruel shafts, its heart torn in two and its blood poured onto the men who crawled beneath it for defence as the animal struggled through its last moments.

All the while Josiah had battled, enraged beyond reason by the killing of his friend, struggling in vain to turn his horse against an unstoppable tide of men caught up in hand to hand combat. He had been desperate to give chase to the cavalry man who had taken his friend's life so viciously when his back was turned.

"Coward, bloody coward!" he cried, frustrated. It was no use, he would not get through. He looked about him, assessing the situation mechanically as he had been trained to do. This was the part of the battle when, to those who fought in it, everything seemed to have descended into chaos. Ranks were broken as men fought for their lives in whatever way they could and such was the bloodlust, no identifying shouts of 'Jesu!' or pieces of cloth tied about the arm, could guarantee that in the madness, a man could not mistakenly kill another from his own side.

From his vantage point astride his tall horse and from his long experience, Josiah could see that the battle was not going as well for them as he would have liked. Colonel Milburne had cleverly lined the hedgerows with musketeers and dragoons who hid unseen until Derby had committed his army to charge and dozens had been picked off ruthlessly by musket fire. The royalist force had not recovered from that fatal early blow and every man would need to fight like ten men if they were to save the day now. By the time Josiah had turned his attention back to the cavalryman who had killed his friend, the man had gone and Josiah tried to block out the picture of his friends' body trampled into the ground by hundreds of men and horses. He would look for him later and bury him if he himself lived through this carnage, he thought. Just as Josiah gave up the fight to turn his horse and looked about him for his next opponent, he spotted the cavalryman yards behind him, fighting with another royalist rider.

"I need not worry..." thought Josiah "...he will find me or I will find him" He committed the man's helmet and colours to memory and added the taking of his life to another he had vowed to take that day. The thought of finding Bagshawe spurred Josiah on and he had soon fallen into savage fighting again.

There were so many men and horses in the narrow confines of the lane that the fighting had pushed through the hedgerows into the fields and wooded copses beyond. The air was thick with the smell and fog of cordite and the fighting continued heavily as the afternoon wore on. Josiah was unable to see the bigger picture of the battle through the smoke of musket fire and now the cannon blasts coming from the Parliamentarian army but he suspected with a heavy heart that the enemy had gained the advantage. He had been in battle before when the order had come to retreat and he prayed for it now knowing there was nothing to be gained from continuing to fight except the needless death of his comrades. But he knew also that Cromwell would have ordered no quarter and that nothing but a complete and total routing of the royalist cause would do now. It was only a matter of time before his own army would take matters into their own hands and turn and run to save themselves. Then he would be taken captive or shot and all would be lost. At that moment he decided that he must accomplish his mission to find and kill Edwin Bagshawe...all else would have to be abandoned now. For the last seven years he had given all to the royalist cause and this war and now it was time to fight for his own cause. Surely God would forgive his selfishness now in the face of all the trials he had undertaken in His name? Well...if God did not then he would be damned...and in that moment Josiah cared not.

With a new vitality, he had set himself to the task of finding Edwin Bagshawe in the chaos about him. It was a task that would have seemed impossible to most but to Josiah it was his destiny...he would find him or die in the attempt. Every man who faced him from that moment was quickly despatched and then suddenly, just as fatigue and a feeling of hopelessness was beginning to overtake him he saw, just yards ahead, the man who had killed his friend, miraculously still on his horse as he himself was, still hunting down royalist cavaliers. Josiah felt a momentary twinge of guilt as he realised he had forgotten the death of his friend, that moment seeming like days ago now. As he remembered Featherstone talking that night in the camp about the family he dreaded he would never see again, Josiah's anger reignited and he set himself to kill this man now and avenge his friend.

The helmet the rider wore shielded his eyes and covered his nose but there was some stirring of recognition in the split second that the two faced each other.

"I knew you would come looking for me...!" cried Josiah"...as I have been looking for you!"

Even in the noise and madness of battle, the voice that replied was unmistakable, reaching through the years, obliterating time.

"So, Josiah Speakman...the hunter becomes the hunted."

As the truth dawned on Josiah in that brief moment that his friend's killer and the hated boy from his youth were one and the same, it was as if the years fell away and he was once again in the power of his nemesis. He never noticed the dragoon concealed in the hedge beside him until the deafening sound of a musket shot at close range rang out and the sudden searing shaft of pain rendered Josiah unable to control his horse. The animal bolted, blindly running and jumping the hawthorn hedge and Josiah was thrown into the air, landing heavily on the parched earth before rolling and rolling to God knew where. It was only when he stopped and tried to sit that he saw the blood seeping from the gunshot wound in his chest and only for a moment did he instinctively try to draw his sword before falling backward again onto the ground as blackness swallowed him.

***

Thurston limped along beside Reverend Kingsley unsure who was supporting who, feeling mentally exhausted by the events of the day. He thought of Isaac and the way the boy screamed when he was swung round and round, up high and down low and, though without the thrill the child experienced, he felt the same disorientation from the extreme emotional ride he had been through this day. He felt like someone had taken his heart and bounced it like a ball.

Reverend Kingsley noticed his silence.

"It hath been a heavy day Thurston, hath it not?"

Thurston forced a smile, unwilling to offend this man he hardly knew but strangely knew he could trust. Not for the first time, Thurston wondered what Samson Kingsley's place was in the events that had turned, it would seem, all their lives in an unexpected direction. In Thurston's new and growing interest in events beyond his own life, he questioned why this man had been brought to this place by Nicholas' enemy? Why this man who preached a faith that was in such clear opposition to the (albeit hidden) religious beliefs of Nicholas and to a lesser extent he suspected, Nathaniel, would befriend them? He was sure that the three of them had been previously acquainted, could sense that the plan with which they had presented Thurston had been long in the making, but how...? How had it all come about?

They had reached the door of the Vicarage.

"Wilt thou come in and take some refreshment with me Thurston?"

Suddenly Thurston felt the need for answers. If there was a plan and he was a part of it then he wanted to be a full part... no more secrets or surprises. No more truths kept from him as if he were a child.

"Aye Sir...Ah thank thee, Ah will." He screwed up his courage on the doorstep, keen to set the seeds of the discussion before he stepped over the threshold.

"Ah would ask thee some questions Reverend...there are things Ah would like to know...things Ah should know."

Reverend Kingsley nodded and on his face Thurston thought he saw a look of...pride?

"Well, come in my boy...," said the Reverend "...and we will see how the conversation goes."

***

An hour later Ginny was picking up Nathaniel's plate from the table in the front room. He had eaten a good meal and washed it down with more than one cup of wine. Clearly exhausted, he had fallen asleep as Elspet had told her he would and was now snoring gently in his chair by the empty hearth. She moved quietly, eager not to disturb him or Elspet sleeping upstairs. Poor Elspet, she just needed rest, her nerves were so frayed. Ginny would keep her in bed for a day or two, make sure she was alright. She would stay tonight but would need to get Isaac tomorrow. He would be fretting without her, they had not been apart before, bless him. Just as she was wondering what to do, she looked through the window to see Thurston walking slowly from the Vicarage. She stood for a minute watching him, sensing he had something on his mind. You could always tell how Thurston was feeling by the way he walked and he looked ...weighed down, world weary, she thought. She gently put the plates down, thinking she would nip out and catch him before he went back into the gates of Moreton. It would cheer him to know Elspet was well.

Thurston never reached Moreton House however instead he crossed the cart road to the Church and sat on the wall.

Well, now what is he up to? Ginny thought.

Thurston sat looking up at the church, at its pristine, newly re-built tower and the new glass in the East window sparkling in the sun. He wished he could say he truly believed in a kind and just God who looked down on him...but secretly he suspected that God was far too busy to bother Himself with Thurston Hey's insignificant life.

He thought on the story that Reverend Kingsley had just related to him and he wondered if God, if indeed He was an all-seeing being, just chose to ignore some things...and why? Thurston preferred to believe that, if He was up there, He hadn't seen what had happened to himself as a child…or to the man Reverend Kingsley had talked about. It was easier to think that God had just been busy doing something else…not that He had seen it and simply turned away to more important things.

Samson Kingsley had told Thurston of his own childhood. How he had been baptised Samuel but had grown so tall and strong, he had been nicknamed 'Samson' after the biblical character. He had told of how his Father had died when he was five years old and how his mother's brother, a priest, had stood guardian to him. Until he was fourteen years, old his Uncle had replaced the Father he had lost, been kind to him… had loved him and inspired him to love God. In Samson's fourteenth year his Mother had been married again, to a protestant gentleman. Young Samson had not been allowed to see his Uncle, the Catholic priest for many years, but he had been allowed to study theology and had eventually been ordained as a Minister of the Protestant faith. He had told Thurston how he had met his Uncle again when he was twenty-five years old and many times in secret over the twenty years that followed. The last time Samson had seen him was ten years ago when Samson had been ministering to a parish in Cheshire and had made the journey to visit his beloved Uncle at a house near Appley Cross. He had known for many years that intolerance of the Catholic faith had forced his Uncle to eke out a living by travelling the country saying mass and ministering to powerful, Catholic families. Samson had seen his Uncle, Alexander Marlowe, dragged from Abbots Hall to his death that day and had met Nathaniel and Eliza Speakman also fleeing in shock and horror from the scene. All distressed, Eliza hysterical, they had run into Nicholas Moreton on his way to try and avert what he feared was going to happen only to find out too late from his neighbours that the old man was already taken away. All four of them had returned to the Speakman's house that afternoon and had sat, curtains drawn against the horror that had spread like a wildfire through their little community, singeing beyond repair the very fabric their lives were made of. The acquaintance which had sparked that day in the fires of religious intolerance, had grown into friendship over the ensuing years as together they witnessed society sorely bruised by the horror of Civil War. They had watched as the spreading plague caused Englishman to kill Englishman while belief systems were cruelly overturned, old loyalties ruthlessly crushed and families torn apart.

Now the alliance that had formed in grief and disbelief had grown into something that would heal and repair their broken society and ensure that the seeds of peace and tolerance could be nurtured, blossom and re-seed for generations to come. Out of the ashes of the past, their new school would come and bring hope for the future.

Thurston felt the last heat of the afternoon sun on his back and the warmth of realisation flooded through him. Perhaps God had been watching all this time? Perhaps all these dreadful things that he, Eliza, Kingsley and Nicholas had suffered had happened for this very purpose...to drive this venture which they all stood on the edge of now? He longed to believe it...he longed to believe. He bent his head and prayed silently, with a little more conviction than he had ever had.

"God...if th'art watchin'...listenin'...Ah've asked nothin' of thee but Ah ask thee now...if it is right God...let me make a..."

"Thurston?" His silent prayer was interrupted as Ginny sat on the wall beside him. "Art t'alright?"

He nodded, happy to see her, leaving his unfinished prayer to float away, the favour he had been about to ask of God left unasked.

"Aye...," he said "...'ow is Elspet?"

Ginny laid her hand on his arm.

"She's alright...just tired...an'she 'as been worried of late."

He nodded again. "Aye...Ah know she 'as been worried over..." he struggled to form the words for a moment "...Nathaniel's son."

Ginny punched him, not altogether gently, on the shoulder.

"Ah don't know Thurston, th'art such a noggin!"

He looked hurt.

"Why would she fret for 'im?" So sure was Ginny of Josiah Speakman's guilt, Thurston could feel her loathing for the man as she spoke.

"Oh Thurston t'is thee she frets over! Master Nathaniel come 'ome at dinner...tellin' tales of thee fightin' an' all upset! She could not sit nor eat or do owt but walk about in th'ot sun all afternoon...waitin' for news of thee!"

She shook her head in disbelief at his stupidity, searching his face for a sign that the truth had dawned on him. When it did, his expression was not what she had expected.

She herself became suddenly thoughtful, aware that she had failed to ask an important question:

"Who did tha fight with Thurston?"

He looked at her, knowing he could never even begin to explain what had happened earlier that day.

"A tree...," he said. Then before a perplexed Ginny could comment, he grabbed her hand.

"Ginny! What if 'e should come back an' wed 'er? Ah'd be lost for ever!"

A patch of pretty blue cornflowers grew by the wall near his feet and impulsively he stooped to pick them. He no longer wore frayed shirts so he plucked out two strands of his strong dark hair and wound them round the posy.

"Ah left 'er flowers once...an' Ah never saw 'er after...Give 'er these Ginny will you? She will know the meanin'."

Ginny nodded, taking the flowers and comfortingly patted his hand, sorry now that she had scolded him. She rose to leave and then turned back.

"Oh Ah nearly forgot why Ah come to find you. Will ye get Isaac from Ma Jenkins for me in't mornin' an' bring 'im to me at Master Speakman's? Ah'm frettin' for 'im. We sh'll stop 'ere tomorrow an' Ah'll tek 'im 'ome tomorrow night."

Thurston smiled at her "Course Ah will, tha knows Ah'd do anythin' for thee...even though that does shout at me..."

She punched him playfully again as she turned to walk away.

"'t is only because Ah'm lookin' after thee…," she said gently "…somebody 'as to!"

A few steps further on she turned to shout to him again:

"Oh and please'can ye go to t'cottage and make sure that back doors shut proper…Ah don't think Isaac shut it an' Ah don't want t'mice gerrin in!"

He nodded and waved, knowing how she hated mice just as he hated pigs. He watched her go over to the house where Elspet lay, wondering what she would think when Ginny gave her the flowers. Suddenly overcome with an overwhelming tiredness after the emotional turmoil of the day he felt a craving for the peace and seclusion of the old willow tree drooping over the moat in his beloved sanctuary. Picking himself up, he stretched and left the Church to walk slowly back to Moreton House…home.

***

Josiah awoke from the blackness not knowing how long he had been in it and it was some minutes before he took in the scene around him, his vision blurred, his head hammering still. The noise of the battle seemed further away somehow and as his vision cleared, he saw trees about him and realised he was lying at the bottom of a sloping field in a wooded copse. His first thought as his mind began to find its bearings once again was to stand and fight but as he moved his good arm to push himself up onto his elbow, he felt the muzzle of a pistol at his temple and heard a deep voice behind him:

"Be still or die."

Josiah did not trust his body to move with its usual speed and skill. Were he not feeling so sick and disorientated he would have grabbed the barrel of the pistol, drawn his sword and sliced off the arm that held it before his enemy had realised what was happening. He imagined doing it but knew his body had suffered enough damage to render the act impossible. Instead he tried to turn his head to eye the man who had spoken.

"Shoot the bastard! What are you waiting for?" Another voice, the one he recognised so well, coming from his left.

Josiah couldn't turn his head to where the voice had come from. He felt as if something were moving deep inside it, making every movement seem as if he were fighting against a powerful tide. He looked up slowly, terrified of the pain he knew was waiting to burst within his brain if he moved too quickly and he saw the face of the man who held the pistol. A big and bearded man, tall, wide and strongly muscled. Josiah could no more have overpowered him than a newborn could...he was trapped.

"What are you waiting for Shephered? Kill him and get me free God damn you!"

Josiah turned his eyes as far to the left as he could and saw a horse lying still on the ground, clearly dead. Slowly he pushed against the tide and moved his head to take in the rest of the scene. Edwin Bagshawe lay not ten feet away, his body trapped by his dead mount in such a way that only his left arm and upper torso were free.

"For God's sake, my leg is crushed. Shoot him and free me!" The childish shriek he so remembered.

"No!" Josiah found his voice at last. "Soldier I beg you, shoot me if you will but let me put a musket ball in this man before I die...I know he is on your side and I am the enemy but this man...this man is a devil!"

Josiah gasped at the effort of speaking, suddenly finding it hard to breathe, his ribs cracked by the musket ball grinding painfully together as he moved. He tested his injury, breathing as deeply as he could until he felt another stab of pain. Well, this injury won't kill me, he thought. Feeling stronger at the knowledge he continued:

"This man does not deserve to live. He has committed foul deeds...he has ruined the life of a boy...and a girl I knew. Please...please soldier. I will run myself through before you if I can take his life first! I beg you ...I made a vow!"

As the blood rushed through his veins in helpless anger, his head began to throb with a pain so unbearable he could not think. Still again, as the pain subsided, he reached instinctively for his pistol, nothing to lose now.

"Is this what you're lookin' for Sir?"

The pistol in Shepherd's hand was Josiah's and despite the fact that he knew his time had come, he smiled at the irony. He tried one last time.

"I beg you...let me go to my rest knowing that I have fulfilled my vow. It is all I have lived for...please?"

Shepherd slowly shook his head, saying nothing.

"Speakman!" the hated voice again. "How touched I am that you have thought on me all these years! And here I was, thinking that you had turned your back on me! None turns their back on me and lives, Speakman. Kill him Shepherd...what are you waiting for?"

Josiah knew then that he would die here, that Bagshawe would live saved by his man and God knew what would happen to his Father, to Elspet...to Thurston. He tried once more...unashamed to beg now.

"Please...soldier...I am happy to die but I beg you let me take this evil man with me."

Again Shepherd, regretfully it seemed, shook his head.

"Forgive me Sir...you are a brave man indeed...but I too made a vow."

Helpless beneath his dead horse, Edwin Bagshawe felt a long forgotten emotion stirring somewhere in his memory. He couldn't put his finger on what it was but it made him feel...braver? Worth something...grateful that someone put him before all else? Whatever it was, it was fleeting.

"Shepherd...faithful Shepherd...I am amazed at your loyalty...truly amazed. Now finish him you smelly bastard and free me! Do it now... I order you!"

Josiah closed his eyes and waited for the pistol shot. After a moment he looked up at the sudden sound of Bagshawe's screaming and shouting. Shepherd ignored him, impervious to the noise as he spoke, the pistol pointing at Bagshawe's head.

"This is for William Watkin...fourteen years old, who died at your hands. God bless his soul...and God damn yours!"

The shot hit Bagshawe in the middle of the forehead and he fell back stone dead. Josiah, shocked, closed his eyes again, waiting for his turn in silence, praying that his own death would be as swift. At least Bagshawe was dead...at least he could go to his own end knowing that. But no shot came, no pain. Slowly Josiah opened his eyes.

"Come on royalist," said Shepherd, sliding his strong arm under his shoulder: "We roundheads have won this battle and they will be hunting all of you down now. Take off your shirt!"

Josiah stood feebly, weakened by his injury, the realisation of what had just happened and the shock that his life had been saved by the man before him, now stripping off his own shirt and tunic.

"Quick!" urged Shepherd, his voice shaking Josiah out of what seemed to him a dream. The tide of pain rose again in his head as he began to move, stripping off the clothing that identified him as a royalist, taking his mother's letter in his hand as he threw down his own shirt. Shepherd walked over to Bagshawe's body reaching between it and the horse's carcass to pull out the dead mans pistol.

"You will need this...and this...," he said, as he handed Josiah the cap that Bagshawe had worn beneath his helmet. "...cover up that cavalier hair."

Shepherd still held both mens' pistols in his big hand.

Josiah looked the man square in the face, without trace of fear.

"You will let me escape ...Why?"

"Do not ask why...just go...there is nothing but death for you here...no wait!"

The soldier walked over to him as Josiah put on his shirt and quickly he examined the wound under his arm. Tearing up Josiah's own shirt, Shepherd wrapped it around his ribs.

"No hearts blood...and your wind is sound. You will live to fight another day...hah...if your lot have another day...royalist!"

Josiah smiled at the man's good natured joke, the shared moment strangely odd in the midst of the death and destruction wreaked all about them.

"Wear this."

Shepherd tied the white piece of cloth that would identify his enemy as a parliamentarian around Josiah's arm.

"Now get away from this place and keep going…don't go back…believe me, all is lost."

Josiah nodded slightly, painfully. He had made his decision to leave the fight when he went off to find Bagshawe and his friend's killer who against all odds, had proved to be one and the same man. He had not pulled the trigger but the deed was done. His war was over.

"Why?" he asked again, needing to know.

The big man looked down at him and picked up his hand, shaking it firmly.

"Because he was a bad man and would always be a bad man. This land will need good men when this war is over…and you I think are one of those. Go now, through the woods and away. God speed to you…"

He gave Josiah Edwin's pistol, slapped him on the back and turned away, running swiftly back up the field towards the lane.

Josiah knew that if he went back he would die…and he knew that he had been saved for a purpose. Something had happened to him…deep inside his head, he could feel it sapping his strength. He looked briefly into the dead face of his old enemy…and friend in his misguided, lonely youth. Edwin's pale blue eyes were wide open, looking up to heaven, mirroring the paling sky. Then slowly Josiah put one foot in front of the other, again and again and somehow found the strength to walk away from that place. He carried on walking, away from the lost battle, the lost war, free at last of the burden he had carried for so long. He walked without stopping all through the night…all the while thinking only of home…only of home.

34.

Summer's end

The little blue cornflowers were the first thing Elspet saw when she awoke the next morning, and the sight of them tantalisingly tugged at her heart strings. It was so, so long since she had felt that inexplicable surge of happiness at the start of a day...it seemed a lifetime ago. The message was clear...he loved her still, even after all. But the warm, sweet, long forgotten feeling ebbed away rapidly as the reality of her situation cruelly ordered her thoughts, crushing the fragile bud of happiness like a careless heel. Even if Thurston still loved her, how could she marry him now? What if Josiah came back? What would Nathaniel think? How could she take his 'grandchild' away from him? Why would he ask her anyway? Why would he marry a woman who he thought had got with child by his enemy? Thurston was kind but he was no fool...to have the world think him a cuckold? She could never, ever tell him the truth...the secret had been a part of her for so long it had wound itself round her heart like a creeping thorn...so deeply rooted it would never be pulled out. It had lasted a few, fleeting seconds but that feeling of happiness had shone a brief light on the desolate world her heart had become.

Slowly, sadly, her vision readjusted and she saw once again the same dark and unclear future she had woken up with the day before. But when she closed her eyes again against the new day as she often did, the little blue flowers danced and bounced in the blackness behind her eyes…as if they were determined to seed the message of hope in her mind.

**

Thurston awoke to the new day early and his first thoughts were of Elspet. Why on Earth had he sent the flowers? What had she thought when she saw them? Was he a fool to think of forgiving her? What was the truth? He thought back to his unfinished prayer of the day before…if you think it is right, God, let me make a life with Elspet. Now he knew the attraction of religion. It was God's will…if He thought that Thurston should make a life with Elspet…He would find a way. Although he closed his eyes tightly and finished that prayer with tightly clasped hands as his mother had taught him in his youth, the prayer was half-hearted.

He felt like a drowning man, clutching at faith to save him from drowning in the misery that threatened to engulf him every time he thought of life without her… or worse still, watching her live out her life with another. He swallowed down the pain as he had every morning since January and, well practised now at pushing all thoughts of her to the periphery of his mind, he turned his thoughts to Nicholas.

He had stayed in the garden at Moreton long after leaving Ginny last evening and had sat by the moat until dusk. He had turned over and over the events of the day in his head…wondering what the next day would bring and the day after that. Reflecting and marvelling still on the changes that had turned his life on its head. It was only when his stomach had begun to rumble that he had looked across to the house and saw lights burning in Nicholas 'chamber upstairs and darkness in the downstairs room where he spent every evening. Was he still in bed? Was he ill? Suddenly dreading the prospect of his life without his beloved benefactor, he had rushed into the house and met Maggie coming down the grand staircase.

"Maggie. Is the Master unwell?" he had asked.

The old woman had patted his arm soothingly, touched by his concern and love for the master...almost as strong as hers, she had to admit.

"'e's just very tired Master Thurston. Snorin' 'is 'ead off 'e was just then when Ah went in. 'e wants no dinner...just to sleep 'e said."

Eeh this lad, thought Maggie, unbeknown to Thurston...can't 'elp but love 'im.

She had clasped Thurston's hand and held it between her own rough, work-worn palms, stroking it kindly.

This is my family, he had thought as her warmth flowed through him.

"Master said to tell thee 'e'd meet thee for breakfast...'e said not to worry. Come on...come an' 'ave some dinner wi' me in t'kitchen eh?

He had sat with Maggie until the candles were almost burnt out and then he had followed her slowly up the stairs, their way lit by the last remnants of the candle and despite his many worries, he had slept peacefully.

As he struggled awake this morning he suddenly remembered his promise to Ginny to collect Isaac from Ma Jenkin's cottage. If he got off now he would be back in time for breakfast with Nicholas. Practising his praying again in another attempt at kindling the faith that sustained and comforted so many others, he silently asked that Nicholas would remain well and with him for many years to come.

It was a beautiful morning and Thurston felt his spirits rising as he walked. The early sun slanted through the trees as he crossed the Churchyard and was already hot enough to warm the back of his neck as he walked down to the crossroads. He thought again of Nicholas and the things he had said to him only yesterday when he had heard Thurston's story. It had felt so right to share his inner struggles with someone, especially with Nicholas Moreton who had treated him with such warmth and kindness these last months. It seemed as if he had known the man all his life and he felt again the growing closeness in their relationship.

He remembered Nicholas' words about honesty all those weeks before and the talk of sharing confidences with each other and he couldn't believe how it felt to have shared that burden with another human being after all this time. His Mother's words played again in his head as he remembered her saying so often that a trouble shared is a trouble halved. So many things she had said he heard these days as if he hadn't recognised her wisdom in his youth and it was only resonating with him now. If only he could break through that final barrier and push through that which stood between past and future. Bit by bit, the seemingly immoveable wall that had imprisoned him for so long was coming down...he could already see the tantalising prospect of life beyond...life without fears. The next time he dreamed of that door and he was in no doubt that the nightmare would come again...next time he would push at that door until it opened.

He passed Ma Jenkins cottage and as the front door was still firmly shut against the day, he carried on to the little cottage and his coming battle with the mice if, as Ginny feared, the door had been left open. In a few days the first of the wheat would be cut and at this hour the lanes would be filled by men with their scythes hoping for a day's work in the fields but for now the wheat was left to ripen a while longer and all was quiet in the lanes around the little cottage. The wheatfield was flat calm as Thurston walked on the narrow path that fringed it, round to the back of his old home. No ripple disturbed the golden sea on this windless morning and there was an eerie silence as Thurston turned his back on the field. Passing the pigsty he approached the back door and saw that it was indeed open. As he drew nearer he felt the hair on the back of his neck inexplicably rise and a frisson of fear passed through him briefly, almost unrecognised. As he slowly pushed open the door, for some reason he could not fathom, his heart was hammering.

He knew that the man who lay on the bed was Josiah Speakman long before he saw his face. His first instinct was to run...not because he was afraid of the man but because he was afraid to look on another's suffering...and he knew that there was suffering here. He could smell the blood as he walked round the bottom of the bed and as he looked into his enemy's grey face he could see that the hand of death was already upon him. I must go and fetch Nathaniel, thought Thurston, shock driving his mind mechanically and he turned quickly to leave by the door through which he had entered.

"Wait..." Thurston stopped. The voice was weak, but firm and in a moment Thurston stood over him again.

"Water..."

Thurston grabbed the jug that stood on the table and held it for Speakman as he drank thirstily. As he finished and fell backwards exhausted on to the pillows, he groaned with the sound of a wounded animal and Thurston knew the man was in great pain. It was a few moments before the dreadful, agonising throbbing passed and Josiah could speak again.

"Thurston Hey...do not leave...I have walked...the last miles I shall ever walk on this earth...to speak to thee."

Josiah closed his eyes, allowing his breathing to regulate...the pain in his head was almost bearable if he was still and breathed slowly.

"Sit...," he said "...I cannot raise my eyes...to look at thee....And I must look at thee."

Thurston could hardly believe what was happening here. He should run for Nathaniel, not sit here talking to a dying man and one, God forgive him, that he had no wish to talk to at all.

"It...it is thy Father tha needs now," he said haltingly. "Let me fetch 'im."

Thurston needed to get out, he needed to breathe the air...he didn't want to be here.

"I beg thee sit...please!" The pain was clearly on the injured man again and Thurston, trapped by the compassion in his character, drew over a stool to sit by the bedside. As he waited for Speakman's pain to subside, he looked at the man's face, eyes closed, struggling to pull himself through his agony...to say what? He owed this man nothing but his hatred for what he had done to him...and to Elspet but he waited patiently, wondering what he was going to hear and for some reason, fearing it. At length Speakman opened his eyes.

"I am weak," he said, his voice almost a whisper. "I know I have not…much time…I need to talk to you…and when I am finished…I ask that you fetch…my Father."

Thurston nodded, knowing there was nothing he could do but make the required promise.

Josiah sighed deeply.

"Forgive me for the part I played…in the sufferings of…your youth…It was my own sufferings…that led me to do…those terrible things…Please forgive me?"

Thurston spoke without hesitation. "I forgive you," he said, suddenly knowing it was time. Josiah's face brightened a little at his words and he rested for a moment, his face grey.

Thurston recognised the enormous effort Josiah Speakman was making to speak every word and again he wondered why this man who was so clearly dying, was choosing to waste his last words on him? Speakman continued:

"It was I…who ran for your Mother…that day…and on that day I left…my own family…to escape from the one…who had ruled me for many years…I was free…and you too…you were free?"

Thurston nodded, that day indeed had marked the end of his beatings.

"Tha came 'ere?" Thurston asked. "Tha fetched mi Mother?"

"Yes" Josiah answered. "I will never…forget what she said to me….she said…"by comin' ere tha's saved thi self."

Thurston bent his head as he tried to remember and sure enough the memory came.

"She carried me back 'ere…," he said "…on 'er own…to this bed."

He recalled only flashes of the memory, the strongest recollection being the comfort of her strong arms.

"She must… have loved thee well Thurston…"

He nodded, tears in his eyes. "Aye …she must."

Josiah's eyes closed again and remained closed for so long Thurston wondered if those had been his last words. Should he go now and fetch Nathaniel? Just as he prepared to rise, Josiah's eyes were open again.

"He is dead now Thurston. He cannot hurt us any more...not me, not you...not Elspet..."

Thurston flinched at the sound of her name spoken by this man.

"Elspet?" he said "What of Elspet?" Then realising what Josiah Speakman had said thought to himself: Who...who is dead?

"Who is dead?" Thurston gave voice to the question that echoed in his head. "Who is dead?"

Josiah was struggling to speak now but he answered very slowly.

"Bagshawe...the devil...is dead...shot between the eyes...Blue eyes ...like the sky...looking....up into ...the sky."

Josiah was seeing again the scene he had left ...it seemed so long ago. Thurston too remembered blue eyes, the colour of winter, strangely out of place on a warm day in May.

He shivered as the pieces of the puzzle began to slot together in his head. He did not know why he dreaded the answer but he asked the question anyway.

"Elspet? What of Elspet?"

Josiah, his strength failing rapidly now, realised that Thurston was in ignorance of many things. These were revelations that would change Thurston's life...this was why he had walked ten miles through the night. The reason he had pushed through the dreadful agony that threatened to burst his head like the over ripe marrows he had fired at in his training as a young soldier. The reason he had resisted the overwhelming urge on that long walk through the darkness to fall down into the hedgerows and sleep his life away. He had pushed on to ensure that two good and wronged people had the chance to make the most of their brief time on this earth. It was what would bring him the salvation of being able to die with a clear conscience.

Thurston pressed him. "Don't thee die now...what of Elspet? She carries your child. Do you know that? What of Eslpet?"

Josiah answered, stronger now.

"Thurston...Elspet does not...carry my child...she...is not bound to me...in any way save that...I sought only to help her...in any way I could...if she did not wed you."

Wed me...wed me? None of what Speakman was saying made any sense. Was this it? Was this the madness that had afflicted his Mother at her end?

But there was firmness and conviction in Josiah's voice as he continued and Thurston knew a truth was coming...but he was not ready, he knew he was not ready.

"The child is Bagshawe's...do ye not see...what he did to thee...he did to Elspet...do ye not see Thurston?"

Thurston stood up by the bed, his mind completely blank, empty of all thoughts of past present or future. In his head he was standing in the middle of the wheat field and all about him was desolate and dead and he was alone, as he had always been. Then realisation hit him with such force that he let out a roar at the pain of the blow. The door finally opened and he saw for the first time what had been hidden in his memory...the pain and shame of it so terrible that the power of his mind had locked it away. He felt again the weight of the body on him, tasted the dirt in his mouth, felt again the final agonising pain deep in his gut. He burned with the suddenly revealed knowledge of the final, degrading act that his broken and bleeding body had been subjected to and he retched emptily, again and again, onto the floor beside Josiah Speakman who lay dying in his Mother's bed.

"He is dead...," said Josiah weakly as a stillness descended on Thurston "...he cannot hurt you...ever again...please ...please fetch my Father now."

Thurston pulled himself back with an enormous effort of will from the terrible precipice of despair on the edge of which he stood. Still reeling with the shock of what he had seen through the opened door in his memory, he sat down heavily again beside the dying man. He knew he had to push away the terrible rush of recollection, this was not the time. Now was the time to do what he could for the dying man before him who he now realised had pushed through dreadful horrors of his own to come here and free Thurston Hey from the bonds that had held him down for so long. After a moment, Thurston found his strength again...and his voice.

"Ah thank thee...," he said, grasping Josiah's hand "...Ah thank thee."

"Make her happy..."Josiah whispered now, deed done, strength failing "...and in whatever way you can...please aid my Father."

Thurston nodded vigorously, silently acquiescing to his request, not trusting himself to speak anymore. Josiah held on to Thurston's hand and with the other he searched within the clothing covering his chest.

"My letter..." he murmured "...my mother's letter."

Thurston pulled out the folded paper from beneath Josiah's bloodied shirt and watched his face visibly change as it was put into his hand. He began to look as if a peace was descending on him...a peace long in coming.

Thurston covered him and left him, clutching his letter, breathing softly, his eyes closed. As he left through the back door, he prayed again to his elusive God that Josiah would still be alive when he brought Nathaniel back.

Josiah Speakman lay quietly, alone again in the empty room. The face of his Mother was so clear in his mind he could see every line and wrinkle plainly, just as he had seen her in the candlelight that last time. In his head, he recounted every word of the letter she had sent, read so often he knew its contents by heart. As he gave himself up at last to sleep, her face changed into the one he had known as a little boy and he remembered the smell and the feel of her arms as she had carried him up the stairs, a lifetime ago.

***

Thurston, as Josiah had done the night before, just put one foot in front of the other and walked. All thought of Isaac forgotten, he passed Ma Jenkins cottage and walked on, looking at the ground. He could not stop. If he stopped he would have to think...and if he thought, he would go mad. Past...present... future. All the things he had heard and seen echoed in his head and they all fitted perfectly now into place to show him the full picture. The sight he had seen through the open door was so much worse than anything he could have imagined. How had he forgotten it? It was all so vivid and terrible now...how had it been locked so securely in his head all this time? And Elspet, his poor Elspet. Oh God ... she had been used so cruelly too, humiliated and violated. He felt sick at what she had suffered and how bravely she had borne it in such isolation...deserted by him. She couldn't simply 'forget' what had happened as he had, she had conceived a child. Oh God, how had she borne it? How he hated himself at that moment for abandoning her so cruelly! He should have known her better...known her like Ginny. He felt her pain, so much worse than his own and unknown to Thurston at that moment...that was the very thing that would save his sanity now.

He had reached Nathaniel's door and he took a moment to pull his thoughts to the present. He must be strong now, as she had been strong. He must take what action he could now to support those to whom he owed so much. It was time for him to rise above his own trouble and help those who had pulled him out of his old life. After breathing deeply for a few seconds, he knocked on the door. At length, Ginny answered.

"Where's Isaac? Then seeing Thurston's white face she panicked.

"Is 'e alright...where is 'e?!"

Thurston held her shoulders and put his finger to his lips. She felt a new purpose in him as he spoke in a whisper.

"Isaac is well Ginny, he is at Ma Jenkins still...but a bad thing 'as 'appened...Ah must take Nathaniel to the cottage...Josiah is there... 'e is dyin'."

Ginny's hands flew to her mouth. Thurston continued purposefully:

"Bring Nathaniel down 'ere to me...do not tell Elspet. When Ah return Ah will fetch Isaac."

She nodded, apron up to her mouth.

Just then Nathaniel appeared on the stairs, and from the murmured conversation and the look on both their faces, he knew something was wrong.

"What is it..." he asked "...Nicholas?"

Thurston shook his head.

"Tha must come with me now Nathaniel," he said.

Thurston and Nathaniel took the shortest route through the fields...there were no memories lying in wait for Thurston now, they were vanquished...as was his enemy. He began to realise what Josiah Speakman had done for him, by coming to reveal to him truth of his past, Thurston's life could begin. His shackles had been unchained and he could throw them away forever. Behind him on the narrow path, he could hear Nathaniel struggling to breathe, partly because of the speed at which they walked, and partly suspected Thurston, from the emotion that he was struggling to keep in. Nathaniel hadn't spoken a word since Thurston had given him the news, as sensitively as he could. He had simply set off at a pace, knowing that time was of the essence now. Thurston too had said little, knowing there was little he could say. He couldn't tell Nathaniel that his son had lain in an empty house waiting for Thurston Hey, to tell him that he had killed Sir William Bagshaw's son for the part he had played in the rape of Elspet...and himself. The shock of the truth hit him again and he stumbled a little. Nathaniel stopped behind him, thinking that Thurston was waiting for him.

"Lad...," he said, his breathing ragged, "Go on ahead...do what thou cans't for 'im. I shall be there as fast as I can...tell 'im I come."

Thurston nodded and grasped Nathaniel's hand for a brief moment before running on with his hopping gait, past the undulating ground where he had suffered his own agony and past the tree that he had fought with only yesterday. Josiah's words had freed him from torment, even the reality of what had been done to him that day could not dim the gratitude he felt that it was over. The truth was less terrifying than the fear of the truth.

"God...let 'im be alive to see 'is Father," he prayed.

But Thurston's prayer had gone unheard. As he entered the little cottage through the back door, he could see that Josiah was dead and that he had not been granted a peaceful death. His body was twisted so that his head was hanging over the side of the bed and his face looked as though death had come upon him in a terrible spasm that had caused him to grimace in pain. His eyes were bloodshot, the eyeballs rolled back in his skull and a trickle of blood ran from his nose and mixed with vomit on his cheek. The letter he had been clutching so closely to him was on the floor and Thurston hoped, with all his heart, that Josiah had been already dead when he dropped it.

A sudden sob came up into Thurston's throat catching him by surprise, noisy in the quiet of the cottage. He put his hand over his own mouth to still the tears he knew would come if he let them. Now was not the time for weeping. Now he must make Josiah Speakman ready to be seen by the Father who loved him. Nathaniel must see his son sleeping, gone peacefully to his rest. It was all he could do for Josiah now...and for Nathaniel. With every ounce of effort he could find within him, Thurston pulled at the tall, hard-muscled body again and again until Josiah lay straight in the bed. He closed his eyes and washed the vomit and blood from his face before forming his lips into a peaceful line. Gently he pulled the blanket up to Josiah's shoulders, covering the bloody shirt, and finally he laid his uninjured arm over the blanket, his hand covering the letter which was placed next to his heart.

Thurston stood back, gratified. For the entire world, Josiah looked as if he had slipped from peaceful slumber to eternal rest without pain or fear.

Nathaniel's face appeared at the back door and as he looked at him Thurston could see that Nathaniel had not for a moment expected to see his son alive.

"Is 'e gone?" he asked quietly.

Thurston nodded.

Nathaniel seemed to age visibly in that short, slow walk over to the bed, his countenance surprisingly calm until he looked into the face of his son. At the sight of him, finally facing the reality of the fear he had he had lived with for so long, his hands flew to his mouth to stifle the sobs that rose unbidden from deep within his chest...but they would not be quieted. All the emotions that he had held inside him for such a long time....worry, fear, dread, regret, guilt and love...most of all love, burst out in a loud, discordant, uncontrollable wail, which broke unbidden into a long sentence of single words.

"My...boy...My poor...boy...Oh ...God...my poor...son."

And then he cried as Thurston had never in his life seen a man cry. His sobs were so pitiful, tears ran down Thurston's own face as he watched Nathaniel go through a pain that seemed more terrible than any he had ever known existed...his own paling beside it.

Suddenly Nathaniel stumbled, as if all the strength had drained out of him and Thurston quickly pulled the chair from the fireside to the bedside and eased him gently into it. Nathaniel was quiet then, head in his hands, he wept almost silently, his shoulders shaking.

Thurston felt the need for air and he walked out into the garden leaving Nathaniel to mourn his son in private. Once outside, he closed his eyes and breathed deeply for a few moments, calming the emotions that raced within him. As he opened his eyes again the brightness of the sun blinded him for a split second but then as he looked about him... at the little rows of vegetables and flowers that Ginny had planted, at the yellow wheatfield beyond and up at the birds soaring above him freely in the blue summer sky...he began to see the promise of all he had wished for waiting for him in the future. Nothing stood between him and Elspet now. "Make her happy..." Josiah had said. He felt suddenly, overwhemingly lucky to be alive.

"I will keep my word to you Josiah Speakman..." Thurston whispered the words with an intensity far deeper than any prayer he would ever make and they rose up into the still, summer air. "...Her life shall be as dear to me as my own!"

**

Isaac trailed the blanket that the day before had been his piggy behind him as he wandered aimlessly about Ma Jenkins cottage like a little lost soul.

"Well tha'll save me sweepin' up that's for sure!" said the old woman.

Isaac looked up at her, big eyes swimming with tears as he prepared to cry for the dozenth time that morning. He wanted his mama, her kind face, her morning hugs and kisses. Ma Jenkins frightened him a little when she said things in a loud voice that he didn't understand. He didn't know she always shouted because Pa Jenkins was deaf. She bent down to chuck him under the chin just at the moment he could hold the cries in no longer. His wailing was pitiful.

"Well Ah've lost mi touch an' no mistake!" she said to herself as she tried to bend down far enough to cuddle him.

"Shush...thi mammy'll be 'ere soon."

"What's up wi' 'im? What's tha done to t'child?"

Ma rounded on Pa Jenkins as he came in to see what the commotion was about.

"Ah've done nowt!" she cried. " 'e wants 'is mam t'little love...'e doesn't want me...an' 'e doesn't want thee either so sling thi 'ook!"

Isaac cried louder at the raised voices. He had witnessed ma and Pa's verbal sparring before...his mother had laughed at it, realising they didn't mean what they said. It was just the way they had always been. Just as Ma was about to risk her back in an attempt to pick Isaac up, there was a knock at he door and Thurston walked in.

"Oh thank the Lord!" Ma cried.

Isaac's tears were forgotten as Thurston lifted him in his arms and soothed him, tickling him under his chin.

"It's alright lad...what's up wi'thee? Come on, buck up...Ah'll tek thee to thi Mam eh?"

"Eeh Thurston...t'lad thinks world o' thee!" said Ma Jenkins, amazed at the sudden change in the boy.

"Aye...well...'e's a grand little lad i'nt 'e?"

As Thurston looked into the boy's innocent eyes, he was suddenly and inexplicably hit by the realisation of how momentous were the events he had been a part of that morning. Ma Jenkins saw the change on Thurston's face and was at his side in a moment, laying her hand gently on his arm.

"Why lad...what ail's thee? Is it Master Speakman's niece...is she badly?"

The idea formed in his head at that moment and he saw clearly what he needed to do. He had almost crumbled into the emotional collapse that threatened to engulf him at every unguarded moment but once again he pulled his courage back with an enormous effort. Impulsively he grabbed the old woman's hand.

"Ma...Pa...Ah need your 'elp," he said.

Half an hour later Thurston left the Jenkins' cottage carrying Isaac on his back, walking towards the crossroads. Just before he reached the the Grapes Inn, he cut down a ginnel to his left and stopped at the last door of a long line of dilapidated stone cottages. At his knock, Arthur White opened the door only a narrow chink at first then at the sight of Thurston he threw it wide, like the smile on his face.

"Why, Thurston lad! What brings thee 'ere? What can Ah do for thee? Come in lad, come in."

Thurston shook the proffered hand and seemed to Arthur to look about him furtively as if afraid of being seen.

"Aye" Thurston replied, lifting Isaac down "Ah will Arthur...Ah've a favour to ask thee."

Arthur pulled him gently in. "For thee lad...Ah'll do owt!"

Before closing the door behind them, Arthur popped his head into the ginnel for a quick look round also though he had no idea what or who he was looking for.

Ginny was so happy to see Isaac when Thurston eventually dropped him off at the Speakman's house. When she'd finally finished covering his face with kisses while he wriggled and squirmed, she set him down and he ran off toward the kitchen at the end of the hall.

"'pet…'pet!" cried the boy, looking for Elspet.

"'ast told 'er?" whispered Thurston.

Ginny shook her head and just then Elspet appeared at the kitchen door, bending to kiss Isaac and ruffle his hair before he headed off happily into the garden. She stood slowly, hand on the small of her back and looked at Thurston. Silently he looked back at her just as he had that day when she had followed him up the lane before he knew the reason behind her hiding away. So many unspoken thoughts still hung in the air between them…but it was different now. Now Josiah Speakman lay dead in the little cottage… Edwin Bagshawe was lying dead in a field somewhere with a bullet between those fearful eyes…and the rest of their lives were a yet unwritten story.

She sensed a change in him and they looked deep into each other's eyes, each unable to tear their gaze away.

"Thurston?" Ginny at last broke the silence, and he quickly came back to reality. Dreams must be put away for a while yet.

"Aye….aye…can we sit down…," he said quietly "…Ah've some grave news to tell thi both."

Some time later as midday approached, Thurston left the Vicarage with Reverend Kingsley after paying his last call of the morning. When they reached the gates of Moreton, they shook hands and went their separate ways…the Reverend to the little cottage to comfort Nathaniel…Thurston to meet Nicholas at last, much too late now for the breakfast he had promised to share with him. He walked up the carriage drive, shady and cool away from the hot afternoon sun and for the first time that morning allowed the guilty feeling of hope to flood into his chest. Hope because at last the prospect of happiness was so tantalisingly near…guilt because that hope had only been made possible by the young death of one who deserved a second chance at life.

Reverend Kingsley had tried to put all in perspective. He had said, predicatably, that it was "God's will" and Thurston had inwardly scoffed...it was all too convenient. What kind of God played these games with the hearts of good men and women? He felt that he would ask these questions for all his life to come...and he didn't want to. He wanted faith, he wanted absolute faith. He had yet to learn that faith was not cheaply bought. The Reverend had cautioned against waiting. It would be a shame, he said, to let the child be born with the stigma of illegitimacy. God knew he would be happy to take on ten children to have his Elspet but more than this he knew that this child, because of its beginnings, needed to be brought up in love. Love he knew he could give it... but to ask for her hand at such a time? And would she accept him? His stomach churned and his head ached with the uncertainty of it all. He needed to speak to Nicholas...more than the willow tree and the peaceful spot by the moat. More than that physical place that had offered him solace and comfort in the sufferings of his past...that place had now been replaced by the kindness and affection of Nicholas Moreton. He needed to talk to him now more than anyone in the world. Involuntarily he began to run to the house, eager to see him and seek his advice on the most important decision he would ever make.

He was so relieved to see his benefactor looking his old self again after his clearly much needed rest. They greeted each other warmly and sat in the comfortable chairs by the windows. Thurston had thought that Nicholas would be full of questions, eager to know what he had missed the previous day but somehow he seemed to recognise that Thurston needed a few moments of quiet.

"Take a moment Thurston," he said. "I can see thou art looking tired. Breathe for a minute or two...and calm thyself."

Thurston sank gratefully back into the chair, amazed as always by the perception of the man before him. He needed a few minutes peace, God knew he did. The cool breeze from the open casement cooled his sweating brow and as he relaxed he became aware of how his leg ached, tired from walking miles that morning, backwards and forwards. He felt too for the first time since waking, hunger and thirst though his stomach still churned so much he doubted that he could keep anything down. Then, as he adjusted to the brief respite, the full force of his delayed reaction to the emotional events of the morning hit him in an overwhelming surge that made him gasp and weep suddenly and noisily. Thurston was as shocked at the emotional outburst as Nicholas...he hadn't seen it coming at all.

"My boy! What is it? What has happened? Is it Elspet?"

Thurston could not speak and Nicholas recognised the symptoms of shock. He poured a glass of wine and pressed the goblet into Thurston's hand.

Drink this lad...drink!"

Thurston took the wine in his shaking hand and drank it down. Thankfully, within a few moments, he was calm again and breathing normally, the emotional onslaught over as quickly as it had begun.

"Forgive me," Thurston whispered.

"Nothing to forgive, lad...there's nothing to forgive." Nicholas patted Thurston's shoulder, gently, comfortingly, until he felt the young man could speak again.

"I think ...if thou canst...thou must talk to me now, my boy? Whatever has troubled thee so deeply...I think I need to hear of it."

Thurston nodded, and after gathering his thoughts for another moment, he slowly, haltingly related to Nicholas all the events of that morning. His discovery of Josiah, his running to fetch Nathaniel, Josiah dying before his Father could see him and finally, all the arrangements he had put into place since leaving Nathaniel in the little cottage and coming here to Moreton. The full story of why Josiah had come to the little cottage and all the secrets involving Elspet, he kept to himself for the moment...why he didn't quite know. As he finished the telling of all the events, Thurston asked Nicholas what he thought...whether he approved of all he had done.

Nicholas was silent for a moment, seeming to find it difficult to speak. At last he did.

"What do I think? What do I think? Why, my dear boy, I am so proud and touched by thee. To do all thou hast done…to take on the weight of this burden after witnessing what thou hast witnessed this day! To think so little of thyself and the suffering thou hast endured at this man's hands…to put all that aside to comfort him in his hour of need. To grant him the forgiveness he asked of thee and so aid him to peaceful rest…and then after all, to deal so lovingly with his Father in his terrible bereavement. Well, Thurston Hey… thou art the best friend to have in any crisis…and long may'st thou be mine. That is what I think!"

He patted Thurston over and over again on his shoulder as if to physically reinforce the depth of feeling he had and the sincerity of the words he had spoken. Silent then for a few moments, at length he spoke again:

"So…," he said "…to clarify…"

Thurston knew from experience of talking with this man that these words always preceded any conversation when Nicholas felt there were things that had still to be fully explained. He knew he was not strong enough for the kind of mental tussling Nicholas was wont to pursue and he awaited the questions nervously.

"So… Kingsley is with Nathaniel now…at thy cottage? And he will stay with him until evening?"

Thurston nodded.

"And then…Mistress Jenkins shall go and make ready the poor lad's body for burial…and after nightfall her husband shall bring the body to his Father's house on his cart and pretend he is moving thy belongings?"

Thurston nodded again.

"And shalt thou be with Nathaniel then?"

"Aye…" replied Thurston. "…Ah must be…Pa Jenkins will need 'elp."

Nicholas nodded.

"And Josiah…his body shall rest this night in Nathaniel's house?

Thurston nodded again, explaining:

"Aye Sir…when Ah left Nathaniel t'was all 'e could say. "Ah want 'im 'ome" 'e said "Ah just want 'im 'ome"…an' Ah promised Ah would see to it Sir."

"Quite right" agreed Nicholas "…quite right…it is right. And then he will be buried at dawn?"

Thurston nodded again, and clarified:

"Arthur White and young Billy from thy kitchen…they shall dig the grave and remove the soil and stones carefully so none shall see it 'as bin disturbed when tis filled in again. An' the Reverend…'e will say the words 'e must over the grave. It must 'appen so Sir…'e must be laid to rest wi' 'is Mother …'e deserves that.'e deserves to be 'onoured after…"

Thurston could not finish the sentence. His mood had changed, almost imperceptibly…and in those few seconds, he knew that he would need to keep the revelations Josiah had made, locked within his own heart for ever. None could ever know that Josiah had killed Edwin Bagshawe…that would bode ill for Nathaniel. None could ever know why he had killed him…who would it serve? Nathaniel looked forward to the birth of the child he thought had been fathered by his son…and if Sir William found out that his own son had fathered the child…well…he was cruel enough to make a claim on it. And what of the great crime committed against Elspet and himself? These secrets he decided, kept for so long, need never be told. Thanks to Josiah, justice had been done…the only purpose served to talk of it now was the easing of their hearts…his and Elspet's…sometime in the future, if ever. Not even Nicholas could be told these things…he saw that now.

Nicholas looked deep into Thurston's eyes as the young man hesitated, deep in thought and he knew that something had at last fallen into place for the lad. That missing piece of the puzzle that frustrated all Thurston's thinking and belief in himself, had come to light at last and bridged the gaping hole in his path to the future.

Thurston waited for Nicholas to speak, hoping he would not ask a question that he could not answer. Nicholas waited for his moment before asking the question that he hoped would encourage Thurston to reach for and grasp the happiness that had eluded him and that now was so achievable.

"So... what will be thy future Thurston Hey? What about what thou deserv'st? Art thou going to ask the woman thou lov'st...the woman who is now free, to be thy wife? And before thou asketh what I think...I think thou must marry her Thurston...and with all speed!"

35.

As the sun rose on the twenty-seventh day of August 1651, Josiah Speakman was committed to rest with his mother and sister for eternity in the quiet churchyard of St. Stephen. All Thurston's thoughtfully laid plans had enabled Nathaniel's wishes to be carried out and although he was still deep in shock and exhausted by his emotional night's vigil with the body of his son, he had expressed his gratitude emotionally at the graveside that morning.

There had been no time to make a coffin to bury him in, all knew that speed and secrecy were of the essence now to ensure that Josiah was buried with the proper recognition of the bravery with which he had lived and died. All present knew that he was a soldier in a vanquished army, a fighter for a lost cause…there were some who would call him traitor but all those who stood at the graveside that morning held Josiah Speakman in high esteem for reasons of their own. Once Josiah's body was gently lowered into the grave wrapped in a linen winding sheet, his Mother's letter safely in his hand, the Reverend gave his short service of prayer and blessed all who mourned for this young life so sadly lost. Then, one by one, the few mourners expressed their condolences to Nathaniel and left the Churchyard, aware of the gathering light.

Thurston hovered by the grave for a moment, somehow feeling that he should stay yet unsure whether his company was wanted.

Elspet watched him, knowing what he was feeling, absolutely and completely unable to deny her feelings any longer. She looked at his bowed head for a long time…testing the chord…and then he raised his eyes to look at her as she knew he would.

"Uncle" she laid her hand gently on Nathaniel's arm. "I will go back, you stay a little while. Thurston...please will you see him home?"

Thurston nodded silently as did Nathaniel. He watched her go, tip-toeing guiltily over the gravestone path lest she should disturb those at rest in the ground beneath, stepping lightly over the dewdamp grass...he watched her till she reached the house and closed the door. Why had she left him with Nathaniel? Thurston looked over to Arthur White, hunched over his shovel, waiting, pointing upwards to the lightening sky. Thurston understood his meaning. They needed to fill in the grave before any in the little community stirred. He touched Nathaniel gently on his arm.

"We must go Nathaniel...it grows light."

Nathaniel nodded "Aye...of-course we must." He turned to Arthur and Billy:

"I am ever in thy debt for this great favour thou do'est me."

Both bent their heads: "God speed him to his place in heaven Master Speakman," said Arthur.

Nathaniel took hold of Thurston's arm, weakened by the events of the last day and night.

"See me home lad."

Slowly, with Nathaniel turning from time to time to look back at the grave, they both left the Churchyard. When they reached the bridge, Nathaniel suddenly stopped.

"Thurston...," he said "... what is to be done about Elspet think you? What would Josiah have wanted? Did he say anything to thee on the subject?"

Thurston stood still, breathing deeply, still confined by his uncertainty despite all the advice he had been given. Would Nathaniel agree with it? Was he worthy of her? Would she want him? Despite all his fears he knew he had to try...or he would never know. He screwed up all his courage and recalled the words Nathaniel's son had spoken in his last moments.

"Josiah...before Ah left 'im to fetch thee...'e said: "Make Elspet 'appy...an' if tha can... be an 'elp to my Father." That's what 'e said."

Nathaniel nodded slowly, fighting back the tears that threatened to engulf him constantly. When he felt calm enough to speak, he grasped Thurston's arm tightly.

"Many months ago, my son bid me make 'im a promise...and Ah did. Ah promised to try and look out for thee Thurston...My son and thee...there was somethin' hidden between thee that I think would be eased by our closeness now."

Nathaniel was silent for a moment before speaking the words that would bring the prospect of Thurston's happiness tantalisingly close.

"Ah can think of no better man to take my son's place and to be a Father to my grandchild. Ah think Elspet would be a very happy woman if she were married to thee. If thou need'st my blessin' tha has it. Ah only ask that tha wait a respectful time...Ah know that cannot be long...and Ah ask that the child knows me as it's Grandfather...and though Ah know tha'rt not short of a place to live...well... th'art welcome to make thi home with me."

Thurston was lost for words, overwhelmed by what Nathaniel had said.

"Aye...well..."murmured Nathaniel "...of course tha must think on it." Threading his arm through Thurston's, he continued to walk slowly in the direction of the house.

"Come-on lad...let's go 'ome."

36.

Harvest

As the first crops were gathered in gratefully from the fields surrounding the two villages, a feeling of hope for the ending of bad times stirred in the heart of the little community. The fields were picked clean by men thirsty for work and the sheaves were neatly stacked while the mill wheel turned daily and the granaries were filled higher than they had been for the last few years.

During the month of September, the long war finally came to an end and all the unfinished business and untold stories were gathered up and neatly stored like the gleanings from the wheat field...clearing the ground to sow the seeds that would grow, all hoped, a peaceful future.

The battle following which Josiah died had been the pen-ultimate battle of eight long years of Civil War. Only one more was fought, days after in the town of Worcester and the romantic tale of the young Charles evading his captors by hiding in an oak tree before escaping defeated to France was spreading across the nation. Loyal Lord Derby had fled from Wigan Lane and though badly injured, had joined his master, the would-be King at Worcester, only to be captured. He would be sent for trial and eventual execution to the town of Bolton, the scene of the massacre Josiah had witnessed as a young soldier.

Locally, the tale was told from one to another, of how brave Sir Thomas had been seen among the last standing in Wigan Lane fighting all comers to the death, dying the hero he had always aspired to live. And on the twentieth day of

September, early in the morning, Thurston and Elspet were quietly married in the Church of St. Stephen.

He had asked her on the day they had sat with Nicholas, Nathaniel, Ginny and Isaac in the drawing room at Moreton. The day they had chosen to absent themselves from an occasion which all in the Parish had been obliged to attend…the burial of Edwin Bagshawe. Sir William put on a fine show on the death of the son he had treated so brutally and neglected so cruelly in life. A fine monument had been made ready to house the body and honour the memory of his only son…killed fighting in battle…as much a hero as Sir Thomas Tytherton. So the story was told. The truth of it all was buried with Josiah and all others on that day would make up their own mind regarding the mettle of the man who was laid to rest in that cold, stone mausoleum.

As Thurston had stood by the windows looking out to the garden, he had glanced over to where she sat, on the fringes of their little company. She was quiet, head down, subsumed perhaps in her own thoughts and secrets about Bagshawe…as he was. As he looked at her he thought: If she looks at me now…if she feels my love and I see love in her eyes when she looks up at me…then I will take her from this room and into the garden and I will ask her. He had looked at her then and drank her in, in a way he had not been able to do for so long. He drank in the beautiful black hair and the way it escaped no matter how she tried to tame it with ribbon or cap. The curve of her cheek and the blush upon it and …like a glorious light in the darkness…the little smile she gave to Isaac who sat on the floor at her feet. Then, wonder of wonders, she had looked up at him and in that moment all else had disappeared. There was just the feeling that danced in the distance between them, the need and promise of everything they could be to each other. True to his word. he had taken her from the room and they had sat in the garden beneath the willow tree by the moat as they had on that cold day in November when he had first been drawn into her spell in the green gloom. This time he did not pull away as their lips were drawn magnetically to each other...he simply took her face in his hands and drew her to him.

A week after their wedding, Elspet had awakened in the darkness with a feeling she couldn't quite describe as pain...just a little discomfort. By the time breakfast was over she was standing by the kitchen window, pain like a squeezing circle of iron gripping her tightly around her hips. She hadn't known she had cried out but Thurston had been at her side in a moment. When it was over and she could speak again, they both looked at each other and spoke the same words: "Send for Ginny?"

Thurston hadn't been able to stand it...despite all he had been through over the years he knew that this was the worst day of his life. What if she died? What if he should lose her now? What if, after all, Bagshawe would take her from him in the end? They had spoken only briefly about him and Thurston had kept his own secret from her...now was not the time...sometime in the future perhaps, he would tell her. As the evening wore on and he convinced himself that the sounds above him surely meant that she was dying, he had run upstairs and burst into the room where she was confined with Ginny and Becca Thomas. He had been distraught as they had ushered him out and the sight of her crouching on the bed like a frightened wounded animal would stay with him always.

"Just go out!" said Ginny. "Go to Moreton...she'll be alright...Ah promise thee. Ah'll not let owt 'appen to 'er...go."

And he had had no choice but to leave and go and wait it out in the place and with the man who had been a salve for all his hurts. Nathaniel joined them as darkness fell:

"Ah cannot stand it either...," he said helplessly as Maggie ushered him in.

The three men sat in silence, each caught up in their own thoughts. Both Nicholas and Nathaniel, each unknown to the other, were caught up in their own memories of the landmark events of birth and death and all the turbulent tides of happiness and sadness that turn between. Thurston's head was reeling at the knowledge that all the events of the last month, monumental though they had been, now paled into insignificance at the momentous event that was taking place now. His whole world was in that little bedchamber in Nathaniel's house, there was nothing now without her. None of them knew that this was a night they would remember for years to come, a night they would look back on and see as a new beginning...a time in their lives when the whole world was born anew.

Nicholas and Nathaniel were sleeping noisily in their respective armchairs by the time the knock came at the door in the early hours and Ginny entered with an exhausted Maggie shuffling behind. Thurston had only to look at her face to see that all was well and without waiting for any details or knowing whether the child was a boy or a girl, he shot out of the house like lead from a musket.

Ginny laughed and turned to the two older men: " 't is a little lass Masters...pretty as a picture, and she takes after thy colourin' Master Speakman...proper fair she is!"

Thurston burst into the Speakman's house and took the stairs two at a time until he came to the door of the room where she lay. He calmed himself for a moment before entering, delighted to see her sat up looking tired but happy, the little bundle cradled in her arms.

"I have a girl," she said proudly.

He walked over slowly and kissed her on the top of her head, so grateful to see her come though her ordeal looking so well.

"Thank God...thank God tha'rt alright...'ow Ah love thee!"

She leaned into his embrace and as she did he saw the child for the first time. She was a beautiful little thing with damp golden curls and a face shaped like a little pink and white heart.

Nathaniel came in then, peeping sheepishly round the door. Thurston went to him and putting his arm round his shoulder, brought him to the bedside.

"Well...what does tha think Nathaniel? Is she not the prettiest child tha ever saw?"

As Nathaniel took the baby in his arms, she opened her dark blue eyes and looked straight at him…and he was to be completely her slave from that moment.

"She is that…" he whispered "…she is that. What shall 'er name be?"

Elspet waited a moment before answering, bringing her emotion under control. She had not even told Thurston of the name she had decided upon…it had only come to her the night of Josiah's death and she had known that it was right.

"I will name her Joannah."

Nathaniel was moved beyond words by Elspet's thoughtful joining of the names of his two dear children. He could do nothing about the silent tears that coursed down his cheeks as he kissed the baby's head over and over.Though it was so hard to finally accept that his dear Eliza and the family they had made together were gone, his heart lightened as he realised that here in his arms lay cradled all his hope for the future.

37.

All Hallows Eve Autumn 1651

In the hamlet of Appley Cross, a year from the night that Elspet let on the doorstep, a candle burns in the window of the little cottage on the edge of the moss. No fear of any creature, living or dead, pervades this house or worries its inhabitants this night. The fire burns brightly in the neat little home and a colourful rag rug covers the stone floor in front of the hearth where children have played and discarded wooden toys still lie where they were left.

Up the ladder in the tiny attic room, Ginny tells the three rapt children a tale she makes up as she goes. It is a story of three little hedgehogs that sneak out from their winter sleep to play in the snow. She tells them how their mother wakes up to find her little ones gone and searches until she finds them, asleep in the cold. Carrying them home one by one, the mother lays them gently down and covers them with leaves until spring. As the story ends Ginny pretends to be the mother hedgehog and snuffles each one of their laughing faces before tucking the three little bodies up to their chins in Thurston's old bed. She stays for an extra moment stroking her own dear little boy's cheek before leaving them all contented in a clean bed with full bellies, nodding off to sleep.

Downstairs she picks up the toys and then sits in the rocking chair watching the pictures in the fire and counting her many blessings.

Outside the parish lantern lights the dark, deserted lanes which weave their way past sleeping houses and silvery fields to the village of Appley Green. A lonely light burns in the upstairs bedroom of the Speakman's house and inside Elspet hovers over the cradle, settling her little daughter who has had her fill of milk and will sleep for a few hours now. She moves across to the window and looks out at the moon above recalling as she always does, that night, so long ago it seems now when she so longed to go to Thurston and bring him comfort. She looks across at her husband sitting in their bed, watching her, a contented smile on his face. Happy just to look at her and when she climbs exhausted into their bed, happy just to hold her close, only that, as he has done every night since their wedding.

Nothing more has he asked, none of those…what had Eliza called them? She remembers…those times between husband and wife that thaw all frosts. There is only one little piece of ice left in her now and she knows Thurston could melt that…if only she can overcome her fear. Suddenly the words Aunt Eliza had spoken surface from beneath the trouble and trauma that have cluttered up her mind for so long. She hears her voice so clearly: "face it, fight it…and fix it!"

It is time she thinks, time to claim my happiness. Thurston sees the way she looks at him…feels a change come over her. She goes to him and kneels on the bed.

"Do you know what today is?" she asks. He teases her and pulls a puzzled face.

"It is a year today" she whispers. "A year…since we met!"

He shakes his head, his face blank. "Nay" he replies. He lifts up her hand and kisses it as her face falls with disappointment and she smiles with him as she sees he teases her again.

"We met on the first day of November" he whispers, curling a tendril of her hair round his finger. "It was just a little after sunrise when Ah opened my door and saw thee there. And now Ah can do anytime what Ah wanted to do from that very first minute."

He kneels before her, takes her face in his hands and presses his soft, beautiful mouth to hers for a moment. The love shines in his eyes as he ends his kiss, still holding her face, marvelling at the way her green eyes reflect the candlelight. Elspet takes his hands and places them on the bare skin of her chest, his palms just below her collar bones, his fingers in the soft, lustrous black hair that curls into the nape of her neck. He looks at her, the question in his eyes.

"I am ready," she says. "I want to be a wife to you...I am not afraid anymore."

And they kiss again, the only guidance needed is the passion they share and the deep love they will have for each other for the rest of their lives to come.

38.

Summer 2013

If you stand at the black and white house built by Nathaniel Speakman as handsome as ever in the village of Appley Green, you will see the same pretty view across the willow fringed village green to the church beyond.

Cross the now busy road and take the path to the right which skirts the brook and leads to the old lychgate at the back of the Churchyard. Go through the gate and as you tip-toe over the ancient gravestone path, you may recognise the names on old weathered headstones standing by the wall...one in particular...but unless it is wreathed in flowers on the annual school founders day, you will probably pass it by unnoticed.

As you walk on, you will see on your left, taking pride of place in the Churchyard, a neglected, once grand monument. The inscription on it, composed by Sir William Bagshawe to his son's memory is unreadable now, long since obliterated by weather, age and the relentless clambering of ivy.

Beautiful, silvered oak doors will beckon you in to the ancient Church and you will be enchanted by the uneven floor worn by the feet of generations of worshippers. Let your fingers linger on the dark, old wood of pews waxed and polished by loving hands over centuries and as you reach the top of the aisle gasp at the light which pours onto the altar.

Look up to its source and admire the East window, beautiful in its simplicity and as you lower your eyes take a moment to read the plain white marble tablet to the left, a little above the level of your head. As pristine now as the day it was first raised, the words on it are as clear as when they were inscribed over three hundred years ago:

"Sacred to the memory of Thurston Hey 1627-1701

Generous friend and benefactor of this Parish and co-founder

Of the Moreton Hey School which adjoins this site.

This tablet was raised to commemorate his life and in gratitude

for his tireless support for the poor and unheard in this community.

He was a devoted and beloved husband, affectionate Father to his

six children and was held in the most high esteem by all who knew him

He lived an honourable life and was a memorable man."

THE END